Dr C H Hanumantha Rao is a Professor at the Institute of Economic Growth, Delhi. He was awarded the Ph.D. degree by the University of Delhi in 1962.

He was a post Doctoral Fellow at the University of Chicago during the academic year 1966-67. During 1973-74. Prof. Rao served as a Director of the Food Corporation of India.

Prof. Rao had an opportunity to discuss some of the issues raised in this study at the Rice Policy Conference (May 1971) held at the International Rice Research Institute, Los Banos, Laguna, Philippines; at the conference held by the International Economic Association (August-September 1972), Bad Godesberg, West Germany, and at the International Conference on the Socio-Economic Consequences of Introducing HYV in Bangladesh (April 1975) held at the Bangladesh Academy of Rural Development, Comilla.

Prof. Rao's other publications are: *Agricultural Production Functions, Costs and Returns in India,* and *Taxation of Agricultural Land in Andhra Pradesh.*

STUDIES IN ECONOMIC GROWTH
No. 17
General Editor : A. M. Khusro

Technological Change and Distribution of Gains in Indian Agriculture

Institute of Economic Growth

Institute of Economic Growth
STUDIES IN ECONOMIC GROWTH

1. *The Role of Small Enterprises in Indian Economic Development* by P. N. Dhar and H. F. Lydall
2. *Indian Tax Structure and Economic Development* by G. S. Sahota
3. *Agricultural Labour in India* by V. K. R. V. Rao
4. *Foreign Aid and India's Economic Development* by V. K. R. V. Rao and Dharm Narain
5. *Agricultural Production Functions, Costs and Returns in India* by C. H. Hanumantha Rao
6. *Resource Allocation in the Cotton Textile Industry* by Dharma Kumar, S. P. Nag, and L. S. Venkataramanan
7. *India's Industrialisation and Mineral Exports* by V. P. Chopra
8. *Taxation of Agricultural Land in Andhra Pradesh* by C. H. Hanumantha Rao
9. *Some Aspects of Cooperative Farming in India* by S. K. Goyal
10. *Demand for Energy in North-West India* by P. N. Dhar and D. U. Sastry
11. *Some Aspects of the Structure of Indian Agricultural Economy 1947-48 to 1961-62* by P. V. John
12. *Wages and Productivity in Selected Indian Industries* by J. N. Sinha and P. K. Sawhney
13. *Inventories in Indian Manufacturing* by K. Krishnamurty and D. U. Sastry
14. *Buffer Stocks and Storage of Major Foodgrains in India* by A. M. Khusro
15. *Bangladesh Economy: Problems and Prospects* edited by V.K.R.V. Rao
16. *The Economics of Land Reform and Farm Size in India* by A. M. Khusro

Institute of Economic Growth

Technological Change and Distribution of Gains in Indian Agriculture

C H Hanumantha Rao

First published 1975 by

THE MACMILLAN COMPANY OF INDIA LIMITED

Delhi Bombay Calcutta Madras

Associated companies throughout the world

SBN : 33390 098 7

Published by S G Wasani for
The Macmillan Company of India Limited
and printed at Mayur Press,
B 99, G T Karnal Road,
Industrial Area, Delhi 110033

To
My Wife

Foreword

As part of its research programme, the Institute of Economic Growth has been bringing out a series of monographs entitled *Studies in Economic Growth* setting out some of the results of the research work of its staff and scholars. These monographs mainly concentrate on some of the major problems concerning the economic growth of India.

This book contains an analysis of the economics of technological change in Indian agriculture in the recent period. According to the author, technological changes explain only about 27 to 40 per cent of agricultural growth achieved after the mid-sixties, and that, despite these gains, the growth of agricultural output slowed down in 1960's when compared to 1950's. The author attributes this slow growth to the deficiency of public investment in agricultural infrastructure, especially in irrigation. Agricultural policy has been directed to solving the problems of shortage of foodgrains and rising prices mainly through technological changes and the concentration of resources, e.g., fertilisers in the developed irrigated pockets and large farms who have a better resource position.

According to the author, the steep rise in the prices of agricultural commodities has been responsible for capital-intensive or socially high-cost agricultural growth through private investment. This is because the cost of biological sources of energy (e.g., human and bullock labour) rises relative to mechanical sources under such circumstances despite, and in fact owing to, the growth of population. Also, the supply of labour among the high-growth pockets has been lagging behind the demand for farm labour despite some immigration of labour. It should not be surprising, therefore, that tractorisation in these areas has been associated with an increase in output and employment. However, as the author suggests, the right question to ask is whether output and employment and social benefit-cost ratio would not have been greater for a similar investment in alternative techniques such as irrigation and the spread of high yielding seeds and fertilisers among the small-farms as well as the lagging regions.

The study reveals that technological changes *as such* have contributed to widening the disparities in income between different regions, between small and large farms, and between landowners on the one hand and landless labourers and tenants, on the other. In absolute terms, however, the gains from technological change have been shared by all sections. This is indicated by the rise in real wages and employment and in incomes of small farmers in regions experiencing technological change. However, sale of land by large landowners and subdivision of their holdings have had an opposite tendency of lowering their incomes from agriculture. Owing to the shortfalls in output resulting from the slow growth of public irrigation—which has a greater potential for reducing the regional disparities as well as fluctuations in output over time—the uncertainties of supplies have increased in the food deficit regions resulting in unrest and tensions, particularly in urban areas.

The author thinks that the prospects for agricultural growth through technological change are limited and uncertain in the short-run. According to him, the largest prospect for increasing output and employment with certainty in the next two to three decades (with wider application of known technology such as high-yielding seeds and fertilisers) and for improving the distribution of income—horizontal as well as vertical—lies with public investment in irrigation projects including the exploitation of ground water. He feels, however, that this course is least attractive for the elite because it has a sizeable demand on public resources for investment that cuts into elitist consumption and has smaller immediate political gains.

The author throws light on several aspects of technological change and income distribution in a labour-abundant agriculture and on the nature of agricultural strategy and policies followed in India. The policy conclusions implied in this work are interesting. The Institute hopes that the findings of this study will stimulate a fruitful discussion on the nature of agricultural policies to be followed in India for meeting the needs of economic development with social justice.

Institute of Economic Growth
Delhi

A M KHUSRO
Director

Preface

This work is an attempt to understand the process of agricultural growth in India in the recent period which is characterised by technological changes such as the use of High Yielding Varieties of seeds and tractorisation, etc. The first part gives an assessment of the magnitude of these technological changes as well as of the factors accounting for such changes. It also contains an analysis of costs and returns—private as well as social—associated with the use of modern inputs. An attempt is made in the second part to know how the gains from technological changes have been distributed between different regions as well as between different classes of farm people within the regions experiencing change. The socio-political factors and agricultural policies (e.g., land reform, credit, taxation and price policies) underlying this experience are discussed in the third part where an attempt is also made to assess the prospects, as well as to bring out the expected trends, with regard to technological change, agricultural growth and distribution of income.

This study draws upon several sources for the data including, particularly, the Census and the Farm Management Studies. Directorate of Economics and Statistics, Ministry of Food and Agriculture, have generously extended the necessary help and cooperation in getting most of the data for this study. The study covers the country as a whole, although, with regard to many aspects, the focus has inevitably been on areas experiencing a high rate of technological advance such as Punjab and Deltaic Andhra Pradesh. Ever since this study was undertaken in early 1970, the subject of 'Technological Change and Income Distribution in Indian Agriculture' has been explored by several scholars in India and abroad and considerable amount of literature has appeared. I have benefited very much from their findings and have taken into account, to the extent necessary, the work done in this field.

Some of the work on farm mechanisation was done while

x *Preface*

I served as a consultant to the Planning Commission during 1971-72. I am indebted to Sukhamoy Chakravarty, Member, Planning Commission, for the help and encouragement and to G A Sastry and R C Chanda for their help in processing the data from the Programme Evaluation Organisation of the Planning Commission. I also benefited from discussions at the meetings of the Working Group on Farm Mechanisation set up by the National Commission on Agriculture.

As indicated in the text, certain portions of this work were presented at the *Rice Policy Conference* held at the International Rice Research Institute, Los Banos, Philippines, in May 1971; at the International Economic Association Conference on *Place of Agriculture in the Development of Developing Countries* held at Bad Godesberg, West Germany, in August-September 1972; at a joint Seminar convened by the Indian Statistical Institute (Planning Unit), Delhi, and the National Commission on Agriculture; and at a staff seminar in the Institute of Economic Growth. I have greatly benefited from the discussions at these seminars.

I am indebted to Dharm Narain, T N Srinivasan, V K R V Rao, Suren Navlakha, Raj Krishna, S N Mishra, Ashish Bose, T W Schultz, Shigeru Ishikawa, RM Sundrum, KL Krishna, Paul Duane, Asok Mitra, Amartya Sen, J N Sinha and Pranab Bardhan who read different portions of this work at various stages and helped me with their criticisms and suggestions.

I have received very able assistance from G Doraswamy for a major part of this study. Ashok Kumar joined during this period and provided competent statistical assistance. Later, Krishna Gopal did considerable amount of statistical work till the close of this study. I am grateful to them for the fruitful collaboration and assistance. I would also like to thank Shyam Sharma who did a painstaking job of typing out the manuscript carefully through several stages.

Institute of Economic Growth　　　　　　C H HANUMANTHA RAO
Delhi

Contents

Part II: Distribution of Gains

Appendices

Part I

Magnitude, Pattern and Efficiency

CHAPTER 1

Technological Change and Agricultural Growth in India

Objective

We are concerned, in this book, with technological change defined as the use of new or modern inputs such as fertilisers, High Yielding Varieties of seeds, tractors, pump-sets, threshers and harvest combines.[1] 'Technique' refers to the actual mix of input factors—whether traditional or modern or both—which is a function of both technology and the relative prices of input factors. Thus, technological changes may lead to changes in techniques but some of the changes in techniques may be entirely due to the changes in the relative prices of inputs.

The magnitude of technological change can be assessed either by estimating the increase in output attributable to modern inputs, or by measuring the growth in the use of modern inputs themselves. The former is beset with several problems—the non-availability of the relevant information as well as the difficulties of estimation. The latter course is more manageable, although it would provide only a

---

[1] T.W. Schultz has argued for the need to reduce 'technological change' to the concrete or identifiable new factors of production—material as well as non-material—which exhaust the increase in output unexplained by traditional factors. See his *Transformation of Traditional Agriculture*, Yale University Press, 1964, pp. 130-44. Robert M. Solow follows essentially the same approach in his paper, 'Technical Progress, Capital Formation and Economic Growth' (*American Economic Review*, 52, May 1962) when he assumes that 'new technology can be introduced into the production process *only* through gross investment in new plant and equipment'.

It has not been possible in our study to deal with education and skills among farm people except insofar as the differences in income and wealth across regions and farms reflect also the differences in farmers' educational levels.

TABLE 1.1: GROWTH RATES OF CROPPED AREA, OUTPUT AND PRODUCTIVITY PER CROPPED ACRE

	Cropped Area			Output			Productivity per Cropped Acre		
	1949-50 to 1959-60	1960-61 to 1970-71	1949-50 to 1970-71	1949-50 to 1959-60	1960-61 to 1970-71	1949-50 to 1970-71	1949-50 to 1959-60	1960-61 to 1970-71	1949-50 to 1970-71
	(1)	(2)	(3)	(4)	(5)	(6)	(7)	(8)	(9)
Rice	1.1	0.8	1.1	3.2	1.6*	2.6	2.2	0.8	1.5
Jowar	1.2	-0.1	0.7	2.8	0.0*	1.6	1.6	0.1	0.9
Bajra	2.0	1.5	1.1	2.6	5.9	3.0	0.7	4.4	2.0
Maize	3.0	3.3	2.8	4.3	4.7	4.0	1.3	1.4	1.1
Ragi	0.9	-0.2	0.3	4.5	-0.1	1.4	3.6	0.0	0.9
Small Millets	0.7	-0.1	-0.5	0.7	-1.1	-0.7	0.0	-0.9	-0.3
Wheat	3.7	2.8	2.4	4.5	7.7	5.0	0.9	4.7	2.4
Barley	0.6	-1.4	-0.9	0.7	0.4	0.0	0.1	1.8	0.9
Gram	3.6	-2.5	-0.1	5.8	-1.6	0.7	2.1	1.0	0.8
Pulses	3.0	-1.1	0.7	3.1	-0.9	0.4	0.1	0.2	-0.2
Groundnut	4.7	0.7	2.9	4.7	1.0	2.8	0.1	0.2	-0.1
Oilseeds	2.7	0.4	2.0	3.4	1.6	2.4	0.7	1.2	0.6
Cotton	4.1	-0.3	1.3	4.9	-0.2	2.9	0.8	0.1	1.6
Jute	2.7	-1.2	1.5	2.7	-1.2	1.7	-0.1	-0.1	0.2
Fibres	4.0	-0.3	1.4	4.6	-0.7	2.5	0.6	-0.4	1.2
Sugarcane	2.9	0.8	2.6	4.0	1.8	3.6	1.0	0.9	1.0
Foodgrains	2.1	0.6	1.0	3.3	2.5*	2.7	1.4	2.0	1.6
Non-foodgrains	3.0	0.3	1.7	3.4	1.4	2.8	0.4	1.0	1.0
All Commodities	2.1	0.6	1.2	3.3	2.1*	2.7	1.3	1.6	1.5

*Following are the rates of growth when the values for 1965-66 and 1966-67 are excluded:

Rice	1.8
Jowar	0.0
Foodgrains	2.8
All Commodities	2.3

rough approximation to the magnitude of technological change. We shall use both the procedures in this chapter.

GROWTH OF AGRICULTURAL OUTPUT

Despite the technological changes characterised mainly by the use of High Yielding Varieties of seeds in the case of wheat, bajra, rice, maize and jowar after the mid-sixties, the growth rate of the output of foodgrains and of agricultural commodities, as a whole, has decelerated during the decade ending 1970-71 as compared to the previous decade. Table 1.1 gives growth rates of agricultural output, area and productivity per cropped (harvested) acre.[2] The output of foodgrains grew at the rate of 2.5 per cent per annum during the decade 1960-61 to 1970-71, as against 3.3 per cent in the previous decade, 1949-50 to 1959-60, and 2.7 per cent over the whole period from 1949-50 to 1970-71.[3] The annual growth rate in the output of agricultural commodities, as a whole, declined from 3.3 per cent to 2.1 per cent between these two decades.[4] However, in

[2]These growth rates have been obtained by fitting the equation

$Y=ab^t$ (where Y=Output or Area or Yield; a=constant; $b=1+(r/100)$ where r=growth rate; and t=time) to the relevant series of index numbers published by the Directorate of Economics and Statistics, Ministry of Food and Agriculture. These index numbers are comparable over time, as adjustments have been made for changes in coverage and methods of estimation.

[3]However, as shown later, growth of foodgrains output between the two peak years, i.e., between 1964-65 and 1970-71 (the Green Revolution period) was higher than between the peaks in the preceding period. For an analysis of the performance of major cereals in the Green Revolution period in comparison to the pre-Green Revolution period, see V.K.R.V. Rao, 'New Challenges before Indian Agriculture', Dr. Panse Memorial Lecture, 27th Annual Conference of the Indian Society of Agricultural Statistics, 25-28 April 1974, New Delhi, *Journal of the Indian Society of Agricultural Statistics*. Vol. 26, June 1974.

[4]Commenting on Ashok Mitra's article 'Bumper Harvest Has Created Some Dangerous Illusions', *The Statesman*, 14, 15 October 1968), B.S.Minhas and T.N. Srinivasan argued ('Food Production Trends and Buffer Stock Policy' *The Statesman,* 14 November 1968) that the two 'unusual' drought years, 1965-66 and 1966-67, should be excluded while fitting the trend. However, as T.N. Srinivasan has shown in a subsequent paper ('The Green Revolution or the Wheat Revolution?', in *Agricultural Development in Developing Countries—Comparative Experience*, The Indian Society of Agricultual Economics, Papers and Proceedings of International Seminar held at New Delhi, 25-28 October 1971), the trend rate of growth of all agricultural commodities falls from 3.2 per cent per annum during the period 1949-50 to 1964-65, to 2.9 per cent per annum for the period from 1949-50

the case of wheat and bajra, there has been a marked acceleration in the growth rate owing to the adoption of new technology. But in the case of all other crops except maize, there has been a marked deceleration in the growth rate.

During the decade 1949-50 to 1959-60, the cropped area grew at the rate of 2.1 per cent per annum. If all the other inputs were to increase such that productivity per cropped acre remained constant, output would have grown at the same rate as cropped area. Since the actual growth rate of agricultural output in this decade was 3.3 per cent per annum, about one-third of the increase in output (1.2 per cent) could be attributed to the increase in productivity per cropped acre. The growth rate of cropped area declined significantly to 0.6 per cent per annum during the decade 1960-61 to 1970-71. Since the output of agricultural commodities grew at the rate of 2.1 per cent per annum during this period, increase in productivity per cropped acre accounted for about 70 per cent of output growth (1.5 per cent). However, there was no marked acceleration in the growth rate of productivity per cropped acre.

The crops showing a high rate of growth in productivity and output, e.g., wheat, bajra and maize, account also for a high growth rate in area. It is true that higher profitability associated with the application of yield-raising technology may have induced the farmers to allocate more area to these profitable crops at the expense of others. But yield-increasing inputs and practices such as irrigation and high-yielding cum short-duration varieties contribute at the same time to the expansion of the total cropped area through multiple cropping. Therefore, slow growth of perennial irrigation could well be responsible for the slow growth in productivity per cropped acre as well as for the sharp deceleration in the growth rate of cropped area.

CONTRIBUTION OF CAPITAL AND KNOWLEDGE

Our primary interest in the components of agricultural growth is to assess the contribution of technological change to the growth of output. We have identified technological change as the use of new (modern) factors of production. However, for a developing economy

to 1969-70 even when the two 'unusual' years are excluded. As indicated in Table 1.1 the growth rates of output do not seem to change significantly for the decade 1960-61 to 1970-71 when these two observations are excluded.

like India, the extension of some of the the 'known' inputs, such as irrigation, water and fertilisers, is associated with significant changes in the attitudes and skills of farmers and in the institutions affecting the supply of such inputs. It would, therefore, be of some interest to know the contribution of the factors other than land and labour, e.g., capital and knowledge, to the growth of output. Capital and knowledge would thus include the extension of the hitherto known inputs such as irrigation and fertilisers as well as the use of entirely new factors such as High Yielding Varieties of seeds with the associated package of inputs.

Between 1960-61 and 1970-71, agricultural output (all commodities) increased at the rate of 2.1 per cent per annum while cropped area increased by only about 0.6 per cent per annum (see Table 1.1). Although population has been growing at the rate of about 2.2 per cent per annum, the actual growth of employment in agriculture is unlikely to have exceeded 2 per cent per annum. Assuming the production coefficient for land to be 0.3 (i.e., a 1 per cent rise in land input would increase output by 0.3 per cent), other factors remaining constant, the growth of cropped area would yield an output growth of 0.18 per cent (0.3×0.6) per annum, i.e., only about 8.6 per cent of the growth achieved in this period. If we take a similar output response with respect to the labour input,[5] the contribution of labour amounts to 0.6 per cent (0.3×2.0) or about 28.6 per cent of output growth. Thus the growth of capital and knowledge together accounted for the remaining 63 per cent of the growth in output.

The experience in the districts where the Intensive Agricultural District Programme (IADP) has been in progress, confirms that capital and knowledge have become major factors in agricultural growth. Between 1961-62 and 1967-68, output of foodgrains in the IADP districts rose by 12.4 per cent or by about 2.1 per cent per annum, whereas the area under foodgrains increased by only about 0.33 per cent per annum.[6] The actual employment of labour (man-days) seems to have increased by 2.5 per cent per annum[7]—

[5]We have made these assumptions regarding output elasticities on the basis of the available studies on production functions.

[6]Ministry of Food and Agriculture, Government of India, *Modernising Indian Agriculture, Report of the Intensive Agricultural District Programme (1960-68)*, Vol.I, p.100.

[7]Ibid., p. 114

which should not be surprising, since the new techniques applied in these areas are, by and large, labour-absorbing. Since, on an average, about 60 per cent of the cultivated area in the IADP areas is irrigated,the production coefficient with respect to land input is likely to be 0.4 instead of 0.3 assumed for the country as a whole. In the case of labour input, however, the output response is likely to be lower, i.e., around 0.25.[8] On this basis, cropped area accounts for only about 6 per cent of the output growth, and labour for 30 per cent. Therefore, as much as 64 per cent of the growth in the output of foodgrains in the IADP areas can be attributed to the growth of capital and knowledge. The latter's contribution must have increased further, as a result of technological change in the period following 1967-68. The contribution of capital and knowledge to the growth of output would thus be much higher in the IADP areas when compared to the average for the country as a whole.

CONTRIBUTION OF THE GREEN REVOLUTION

In principle, the contribution of technological change or the Green Revolution to the growth of output should be obtained through the production function analysis, where all the traditional as well as the technologically new factors are identified and indroduced explicitly as input variables. Such an analysis is ruled out at present owing to the non-availability of the relevant data as well as to the problems of estimation. We have, therefore, to adopt a modest course that can provide a meaningful, even though rough, estimate of the contribution of the Green Revolution. If we could form an idea as to the growth of output that would have occurred in the absence of the Green Revolution, the difference between the observed growth and the hypothetical growth would give a rough measure of the contribution of the Green Revolution.

Since the Green Revolution has affected mainly the cereals, the analysis is confined to the foodgrains sector only. The Green Revolution technology is identified as the use of High Yielding Varie-

---

[8]The production elasticity with respect to land input is generally found to be higher among the irrigated holdings as compared to unirrigated holdings. The production elasticity with respect to labour input, on the other hand, is generally higher among the unirrigated tracts when compared to irrigated areas. See C.H. Hanumantha Rao, *Agricultural Production Functions, Costs and Returns in India*, Asia Publishing House, 1965.

ties of seeds together with the associated package of inputs, e.g., water, fertilisers, pesticides and improved implements. That is, some of these inputs including fertilisers which were known before the onset of the Green Revolution, would have been used at a certain rate in its absence. It would be reasonable to regard 1964-65 as the base year because High Yielding Varieties of seeds in the case of wheat, rice, and bajra were introduced in Indian agriculture, in a big way, in the period beginning from 1965-66. If the years of peak output can be considered to be the best in terms of weather, a comparison of output between successive peaks would give an idea of the output growth adjusted for weather and when the potential created is, by and large, realised. However, this procedure suffers from an important limitation in that all the peak years may not be alike in respect of weather.

Table 1.2 gives figures of the foodgrains output in the peak years in the fifties and sixties. From a comparison of the four pre-Green Revolution peak years, i.e., 1953-54, 1958-59, 1961-62 and 1964—65, it appears that the output of foodgrains would have grown by about 2 —2.5 per cent per annum in the absence of the Green Revolution. There are reasons to believe that even without the Green Revolution, the growth rate would have been maintained at

TABLE 1.2: Foodgrains Output (million tons) in Peak Years

Peak Years	Gap (Years)	Rice	Kharif Cereals	Wheat	Total Foodgrains
	(1)	(2)	(3)	(4)	(5)
1953-54	—	29.8	50.0	8.1	72.2
1958-59	5	32.0	52.8	10.0	78.7
1961-62	3	35.8	55.7	12.1	82.7
1964-65	3	39.0	62.2	12.3	89.4
1967-68	3	37.6	62.9	16.5	95.1
1970-71	3	42.5	70.1	23.5	107.8
ANNUAL PER CENT DIFFERENCE OVER THE PRECEDING PEAK:					
1958-59	5	1.5	1.1	4.7	1.8
1961-62	3	4.0	1.8	7.0	1.7
1964-65	3	3.0	3.9	0.6	2.7
1967-68	3	−1.2	0.4	11.4	2.1
1970-71	3	4.3	3.8	14.1	4.5
Between 1964-65 and 1970-71	6	1.5	2.1	15.2	3.4
Between 1961-62 and 1970-71	9	—	—	10.5	—

about 2—2.5 percent per annum. The growth of population at about 2.2 per cent per annum has been exerting an upward pressure on the prices of agricultural commodities. This would have provided incentives to the farmers for expanding output and would have induced the Government to invest in irrigation, fertilisers, etc. On the supply side, the growth of population results in increased labour input in the agricultural sector which induces multiple cropping and the use of more labour-intensive and yield-increasing techniques, especially by the small family farms. These factors may explain why, even before the onset of the Green Revolution, deceleration in the growth of cropped area was accompanied by a rise in the growth rate of productivity per acre.

It would be desirable to measure the contribution of the Green Revolution in terms of its contribution to output and not in terms of its contribution to the increase in productivity per cropped (harvested) acre alone. This is because, although the major impact of the Green Revolution has been a breakthrough in the productivity per cropped acre for the crops concerned, it has also contributed to an increase in the total cropped area through (induced) investments in irrigation and the use of short-duration varieties, etc. Between 1964-65—the base year—and 1970-71, the output of foodgrains increased at a rate of about 3.4 per cent per annum (see Table 1.2). If it is assumed that the output would have grown at 2 per cent per annum without the Green Revolution, then the contribution of the Green Revolution comes to 1.4 (3.4—2.0) per cent per annum or about 41 per cent of the output growth. This amounts to about 7.5 million tons of foodgrains out of an increase of about 18.4 million tons between 1964-65 and 1970-71. Alternatively, if it is assumed that the output would have grown at 2.5 per cent per annum, then the contribution of the Green Revolution amounts to about 26.5 per cent of the output growth or about 4.9 million tons. It seems reasonable to conclude that the contribution of technological change to the growth of foodgrain output may be somewhere between 27 to 40 per cent or between 5 to 7 million tons. This constitutes between 5 to 6.5 per cent of the total foodgrains output in 1970-71.

It should be noted, however, that the impact of technological change has been much greater than is indicated by the contribution in terms of the increase in output. Insofar as the traditional methods are replaced extensively by the new methods, the cost-reducing effects of the new technology would be significant. In the case of wheat, for instance, new varieties have replaced old varieties to a considerable extent so that the bulk of the wheat output is now produced with an altogether new technology.

In the case of rice and *kharif* cereals in general, the Green Revolution does not appear to have contributed to their growth to any significant extent. In the case of wheat, however, if it is assumed on the basis of its peak-to-peak performance before 1964-65, that its output would have grown at about 5 per cent per annum without the use of new technology, the contribution of the Green Revolution seems to be around 7.5 million tons or about two-thirds of the output growth (10.2 per cent) between 1964-65 and 1970-71. It appears from the data in Table 1.2 that 1964-65 was not as good a peak year as 1961-62 for wheat. This is evident from the fact that the annual per cent difference was the lowest (0.6) between 1961-62 and 1964-65. Therefore, if 1961-62 is regarded as the base year in the case of wheat, the contribution of the Green Revolution comes to about 6 million tons or about 54.3 per cent of output growth (5.5 per cent). This constitutes the gross contribution of the Green Revolution to wheat, a part of which may have been achieved at the expense of other foodgrains. Wheat would, nevertheless, predominate in the net contribution of the Green Revolution to the growth of foodgrain output.

USE OF MODERN INPUTS

In view of the scarcity of land relative to labour in Indian agriculture, one should expect the land-augmenting inputs to spread at a relatively faster rate than the labour-substituting inputs. Recent experience in India shows that the use of modern inputs like high yielding seeds and fertilisers, which are essentially land-augmenting, has been spreading at a relatively faster rate than the use of pumpsets and tractors which perform the tasks hitherto performed by bullock and human labour.

Within a period of four years from 1967-68 to 1971-72, the proportion of area under High Yielding Varieties of seeds to the area under foodgrains trebled from about 5 per cent to 15 per cent (see Table 1.3). Over a period of seven years from 1964-65 to 1971-72, the consumption of fertilisers per cropped hectare quadrupled[9] from

[9]The total consumption of fertilisers rose from 0.65 million tons to 2.62 million tons. See Fertiliser Association of India, *Fertiliser Statistics, 1971-72*.

TABLE 1.3: Area Planted to High Yielding Varieties (HYV) in India

(Figures in thousand hectares)

| | 1967-68 | | 1971-72 | |
	Area Under HYV	Percentage of HYV to Total Area	Area under HYV	Percentage of HYV to Total Area
	(1)	(2)	(3)	(4)
1. Wheat	2942	19.6	7489	39.1
2. Rice	1785	4.9	7215	19.3
3. Jowar	603	3.3	913	5.4
4. Bajra	419	3.3	1832	15.6
5. Maize	287	5.1	489	8.7
6. Total	6036	5.0*	17938	14.7*

*Percentage of total area under HYV to total area under foodgrains.
Source: Directorate of Economics and Statistics, Ministry of Food and Agriculture.

about 4 kg to 16 kg. The number of tractors may have nearly doubled from 54,000 in 1966 to about 0.1 million in 1971-72.[10] The number of tractors has increased from 54,000 in 1966 to 80,000 in 1968-69, i.e., by about 50 per cent.[11] The number of diesel and electric pump-sets, on the other hand, doubled over the corresponding period from about 886 thousand to 1775 thousand.[12] Thus, mechanisation of lift irrigation has progressed at a faster rate than that of ploughing or of transportation. In terms of horse power, pump-sets are estimated to have provided 5 times as much energy as tractors did, in 1971.[13]

If it is assumed that one tractor (of average H.P.) would be sufficient to plough 25 cropped hectares, about 2 million hectares out of the total cropped area of about 160 million hectares or about 1.25 per cent of crop land in India in 1968-69 could have been ploughed by tractors. If large farms (over 20 hectares) are assumed to hold 5 per cent of the total operated area[14] and if all the tractors are

[10]This estimate may be on the high side as it relates to the year 1973-74. See Government of India, *Fourth Five Year Plan*, p. 135.

[11]Government of India, *Quinquennial Livestock Census in India, 1966;* and *Fourth Five Year Plan*, p. 135.

[12]*Fourth Five Year Plan*, p. 249.

[13]P.S. Majumdar, 'Farm Mechanisation in India', (mimeo) submitted to the National Commission on Agriculture, 1972.

[14]According to the 17th Round of the National Sample Survey, such holdings accounted for about 11.6 per cent of operated area in 1961-62.

assumed to be owned and used by them, then it would appear that about one-fourth of the area held by large farms is ploughed by tractors. Thus, over 98 per cent of the energy requirement for the ploughing of fields as well as for the transportation of the produce must have been met by the traditional biological sources, namely, bullock and human labour. In Punjab, which accounts for the highest rate of tractorisation in India, the number of tractors was 10,646 in 1966 for the cropped area of about 5 million hectares, indicating that about 5 per cent of the cropped area could have been served by tractors. If we assume a doubling of the rate of tractorisation in Punjab by 1971-72, it would appear that as much as 90 per cent of the crop land in Punjab is still dependent upon the traditional biological source of energy for ploughing.

The use of mechanical threshers is widespread in the wheat belt. About 0.3 millions of power threshers were used in India in 1971, concentrated largely in Punjab, Haryana and western Uttar Pradesh, with a capacity to serve 3 million hectares[15] or about 17 per cent of the total wheat area (17.5 million hectares) in India in 1971-72. There were about 400 harvest combines[16] and assuming that one combine can harvest and thresh wheat grown on 200 hectares,[17] these combines could have served the requirements of about 0.5 per cent of area under wheat in 1971-72.

SUMMARY

Despite technological changes, the growth rate in the output of foodgrains and of agricultural commodities, as a whole, decelerated during the decade ending 1970-71, compared to the previous decade. Foodgrain output, however, shows an upward trend in the post-Green Revolution period. Increase in productivity per cropped acre accounted for 70 per cent of the output growth during the decade 1961-71 as against one-third during the previous decade. Slow growth of perennial irrigation may have been responsible for the slow growth in productivity per cropped acre, as well as for a sharp deceleration in the growth rate of cropped area during 1961-71.

Traditional factors like land and labour have ceased to be the predominant sources of growth in Indian agriculture. The growth

[15]Majumdar, op. cit.
[16]Ibid.
[17]For details see Table 2 in Chapter 6.

of capital and knowledge together accounted for as much as 63 per cent of the growth in output during 1961-71. The contribution of technological change to the growth of foodgrain output may be between 27 to 40 per cent or between 5 to 7 million tons. In the case of wheat, the contribution of the Green Revolution seems to range between one-half to two-thirds of the increase in output.

The use of land-augmenting inputs, such as high yielding seeds and fertilisers, has been spreading at a faster rate than pump-sets and tractors. The mechanisation of lift irrigation progressed at a faster rate than that of ploughing or of transportation. About 1.25 per cent of crop land in India in 1968-69 and about 10 per cent of crop land in Punjab in 1971-72 may have been ploughed by tractors. Tractor-ploughing may account for about one-fourth of operated area held by large farms in the country. Mechanical threshers and harvest combines could have met about 17 per cent and 0.5 per cent of the requirements of wheat area, respectively, in 1971-72.

CHAPTER 2

Technological Change and Fluctuations in Output

HYPOTHESIS

The relative importance of *rabi* cultivation in Indian agriculture has been rising in the recent period. This is due, partly, to the rise in the cropping intensity or multiple cropping under traditional techniques following the increasing demand for agricultural commodities. More recently, the introduction of High Yielding Varieties has raised further, the importance of *rabi* cultivation because wheat is a *rabi* crop and even the output response of rice and other crops to the modern inputs and profitability is greater in the *rabi* season owing to favourable weather. Moreover, the use of short-duration (high yielding) varieties as well as pump-sets and tractors enables the farmers to grow two or even three crops in a year on the same land.

All these factors have contributed to even out the output stream between monsoon and the post-monsoon seasons of the year. A more even distribution of output over the seasons, during the year, can be expected to reduce the seasonal fluctuations in the prices of agricultural commodities and reduce the costs of distribution associated with carrying over stocks from one season to another. However, the regional distribution of such benefits would vary, depending on the availability of (assured) irrigation facilities.

Whereas the technological change can be expected to even out the output and employment stream over different seasons in any normal year, the same does not appear to be necessarily true as regards the annual variations in output.

It is difficult to conceive of a neutral relationship between agricultural growth and the amplitude of weather-induced (annual) fluctuations in yields. Nor should there be any unique relationship between the two. Yield variability may depend on the pattern of investment or the methods by which growth is brought about. For instance, irrigation water from perennial sources (e.g., major river valley projects and tube-wells) may counteract the vagaries of weather and if increases in agricultural yields are brought about mainly through investments in such inputs, then the growth may be associated with a decline in the amplitude of fluctuations. The use of pesticides may also reduce fluctuations in the output. Irrigation through tanks or ponds and rain-fed wells, on the other hand, may accentuate the fluctuations by increasing the dependence on weather. While these sources cannot provide an adequate cushion in the event of failure of rains, they may, nevertheless, push up yields in a year of good rainfall by making possible the storage of water. Thus, the growth in productivity per acre through an increase in the proportion of area irrigated by tanks and rain-fed wells may have built-in tendency to increase yield-instability.[1]

Inputs like fertilisers and improved seeds, if used under conditions of assured irrigation, may promote growth with stability, but, if used under conditions of uncertain rainfall or in areas irrigated by tanks and wells, may increase the range of fluctuations in output with growth. Owing to the complementarity between these inputs and water, the output may be pushed up significantly in a year of good rainfall, while, in the event of failure of rains, they are unlikely to provide a significant cushion, thus, widening the gap in yield between the good and bad years.[2]

If the production and growth policy is ineffective in reducing the fluctuations in output and if, in fact, it accentuates fluctuations, then, the costs of stabilising consumption through procurement,

[1]Since the coefficient of variation is used as a measure of instability, the above argument implies that *both* the mean and the standard deviation of yields are increased (by tank irrigation as compared to no irrigation) but the latter is raised proportionately more than the former.

[2]For an earlier exposition of this hypothesis, and for the evidence regarding the relative impact of assured and uncertain sources of irrigation on the amplitude of fluctuations in yield, see C.H. Hanumantha Rao, 'Fluctuations in Agricultural Growth: An Analysis of Unstable Increase in Productivity', *Economic and Political Weekly*, Annual Number, January 1968. S.R. Sen also suggests that the increasing use of fertilisers could be one of the factors responsible for the increasing yield instability. See his 'Growth and Instability in Indian Agriculture', *Journal of the Indian Society of Agricultural Statistics*, June 1967.

storage and distribution of foodgrains would assume much greater importance.

Seasonal Distribution of Output

Table 2.1 shows that the proportion of area allocated to *rabi* cereals increased from about 16 per cent of the total area under cereals in the triennium 1949-52 to about 19 per cent in the triennium 1968-71. Because of the steeper increase in the yield per acre of *rabi* cereals, the increase in the share of *rabi* cereals in the output has been more pronounced, especially between 1958-61 and 1968-71. The share of *rabi* cereals in the total cereal output increased from about 20 per cent to 26 per cent, as against the increase in the share of area from about 18 to 19 per cent over the corresponding period.[3]

Annual Fluctuations in Output

In regard to the annual fluctuations in output, experience

TABLE 2.1: Relative Share of Rabi Cereals in Area and Output

	1949-52	1958-61	1968-71
	(1)	(2)	(3)
Total Cereals			
Area (100,000 hectares)	785.0	911.0	1007.3
Output (100,000 tons)	442.7	660.7	892.0
Yield (Per hectare; kg)	563.3	724.3	885.7
Rabi Cereals			
Area (100,000 hectares)	128.0	162.3	195.3
Output (100,000 tons)	86.7	131.7	233.3
Yield (Per hectare; kg)	677.3	809.3	1193.3
Percentage of Rabi to Total			
Area	16.3	17.8	19.4
Output	19.7	20.0	26.2

Source: Directorate of Economics and Statistics, Ministry of Food and Agriculture.

[3]In 1971-72, the consumption of fertilisers in the *rabi* season amounted to

seems to warrant two conclusions. First, there has been a decline in annual fluctuations in the output of wheat owing to the concentration of modern inputs in Punjab and Haryana which account for the highest percentages of sown area under assured irrigation. To this extent, therefore, technological changes have contributed to increasing stability in the output of foodgrains. Second, fluctuations in the output of all foodgrains and agricultural commodities, as a whole, in the country seem to have increased in the recent period owing to the combined impact of technological as well as non-technological factors. There has been some use of modern inputs like fertilisers in the rain-fed areas and in areas served with unstable sources of irrigation such as tanks and wells, which are dependent on rainfall.[4] The non-technological factors include the rising importance of yield per acre which fluctuates more than area (see Table 2.2) in growth, and the increase in   yield

TABLE 2.2: COEFFICIENTS OF VARIATION IN AREA, OUTPUT AND PRODUCTIVITY (ALL INDIA)

	Area		Output		Productivity per Acre	
	1949-50 to 1959-60	1960-61 to 1970-71	1949-50 to 1959-60	1960-61 to 1970-71	1949-50 to 1959-60	1960-61 to 1970-71
	(1)	(2)	(3)	(4)	(5)	(6)
Wheat	5.56	6.67 (2.3)	7.21	14.92 (6.1)	6.09	9.20 (4.4)
Bajra	7.15	2.75	13.90	18.51	10.41	16.73
Foodgrains	2.40	1.98	6.28	8.98	4.35	7.37
Non-foodgrains	3.36	2.38	3.95	5.22	3.87	4.88
All Commodities	1.63	1.62	3.97	7.51	2.85	6.08

Note: The figures in brackets indicate coefficients of variation for the period 1965-66 to 1971-72.

Source: For data on Area, Output and Productivity per Acre : Directorate of Economics and Statistics, Ministry of Agriculture, *Estimates of Area and Production of Principal Crops in India.*

as much as 58 per cent of the total consumption during the year. See, Fertiliser Association of India, *Fertiliser Statistics of India, 1971-72.*

   [4]For instance, even a state like Gujarat where the proportion of area irrigated is very small (mainly through uncertain sources such as tanks and wells), has shown significant increase in productivity per acre indicating that the application of modern inputs like fertilisers was spread into uncertain areas also. See, C.H. Hanumantha Rao, 'Fluctuations in Agricultural Growth: An Analysis of Unstable Increase in Productivity', op. cit.

instability itself owing possibly to the addition of marginal lands which are more vulnerable to the vagaries of monsoon.[5]

Table 2.2 gives a measure of fluctuations in the area, output and the productivity per acre. Fluctuations are measured by the coefficient of variation. Since the coefficient of variation would be different for series showing differing trend movements, it is necessary to make corrections for such trend movements. This is done by measuring the deviations for each year from the estimated trend value for the year concerned instead of from the mean value. The overall mean for the period is then used for computing the coefficient of variation.[6] However, even this method would not be satisfactory if there are significant changes in the trend itself, within the period under consideration. Therefore, in the case of wheat, which has experienced a sharp break in its trend since 1965-66 when High Yielding Varieties were first introduced, the coefficients of variation have been computed separately for the period 1965-66 to 1971-72 (given in brackets in Table 2.2).

Fluctuations in productivity per acre are greater than in area. Fluctuations in area seem to have declined during the decade 1960-61 to 1970-71 in comparison to the previous decade. Fluctuations in productivity per acre, on the other hand, increased significantly between these two decades. The rise in fluctuations in the output over this period is, therefore, understandable because area has been a declining component while productivity per acre has been a rising component of growth. Figure 2.1 shows the upward movement of foodgrains output in the country to be relatively smooth since 1965-66. However, since there was a sharp decline in the output and productivity per acre of foodgrains in 1965-66 and 1966-67 followed by a recovery in 1967-68, it may not be appropriate to treat 1965-66 as the base and the period after 1967-68 is too short to warrant inferences on the changes in fluctuations. It would, therefore, seem reasonable to conclude that the fluctuations in the output of foodgrains, as a whole, have increased in the decade 1961-71 when compared to the previous decade.[7]

[5]Sen, 'Growth and Instability in Indian Agriculture', op. cit.

[6]A similar method was used by Shephered for estimating the fluctuations in corn production in the United States. See Shephered, Geoffrey S.,*Agricultural Price and Income Policy*, The Iowa State College, Ames, Iowa, 1947, p. 102.

[7]S.R. Sen observes that during the 15 years from 1951-52 to 1965-66, which witnessed unprecedented rate of growth of agricultural output in India, 'a most disturbing fact was that the instability tended to increase with the rate of

In regard to wheat, however, the dip in the yield per hectare in 1965-66 was not sharp, whether for the country, as a whole, or for Punjab-Haryana and Uttar Pradesh (see Figure 2.2) which account for about 60 per cent of the wheat output in the country. Therefore, even if we take the pre-Green Revolution peak year, i.e., 1964-65 as the base, the curve of rising yield for the country appears smoother in the later period as compared to the previous period (i.e., from 1949-50 to 1964-65). The curve is much smoother for Punjab. In Uttar Pradesh, however, it appears from Fig. 2.2 that, unlike in Punjab and Haryana, breakthrough in wheat yield has not been associated with a decline in fluctuations. The reason seems to be that, unlike in Punjab, sugarcane competes with wheat for irrigation to a considerable extent in Uttar Pradesh, so that irrigated wheat is comparatively less important.[8]

Bajra is next to wheat in respect of the growth of productivity per acre between 1960-61 and 1970-71 (Table 1.1, Chapter 1). The rise in its yield is not characterised by a decline in the amplitude of fluctuations (see Fig. 2.3), because it is essentially an unirrigated crop grown largely in the western dry region.[9] A similar position holds when the performance in Gujarat is examined (see Fig 2.3) where the new variety has made a significant impact, and where only about 2.9 per cent of area under this crop was irrigated.[10]

Since wheat accounts for the bulk of the output growth attributable to technological change, it appears that technological changes *as such* have, on balance, contributed to reducing fluctuations in foodgrains output, so that the observed increase in fluctuations in the output of foodgrains may be attributed to non-technological factors.

Summary

Technological changes, insofar as they have raised the impor-

growth'. See, his 'Growth and Instability in Indian Agriculture', op. cit.

[8]As much as 83 per cent of wheat area was irrigated in Punjab in 1969-70 as against 63 per cent in Uttar Pradesh. See Ministry of Agriculture, *Indian Agriculture in Brief*, 12th ed.

[9]Only about 4.2 per cent of area under bajra in the country was irrigated in 1969-70. See *Indian Agriculture in Brief*, op. cit.

[10]Ibid.

tance of *rabi* cultivation, have contributed to even out the output stream over the year. However, the annual fluctuations in the output of foodgrains in the country seem to have increased during the decade 1961-71 when compared to the previous decade. Apart from the non-technological factors such as the increasing significance of yield as a component of growth, the addition of marginal lands and the incidence of two drought years of unusual intensity (i.e., 1965-66 and 1966-67), the increasing use of modern inputs like fertilisers under conditions of unstable irrigation could be an important factor responsible for this increase in fluctuations. The performance of bajra provides an example of persistence in the amplitude of fluctuations in yield, when the crop experiencing technological change is largely unirrigated. In the case of wheat, however, there seems to be a decline in fluctuations due to the concentration of modern inputs in Punjab, Haryana and Uttar Pradesh which account for the largest percentage of cultivated area under assured irrigation and contribute about 60 per cent of wheat output in the country.

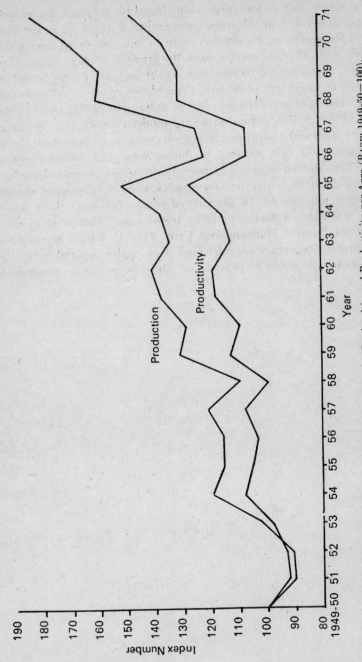

Fig 2.1. All India Index Numbers of Foodgrains Production and Productivity per Acre (BASE: 1949-50=100).
Source: Directorate of Economics and Statistics, Ministry of Agriculture, *Estimates of Area and Production of Principal Crops in India.*

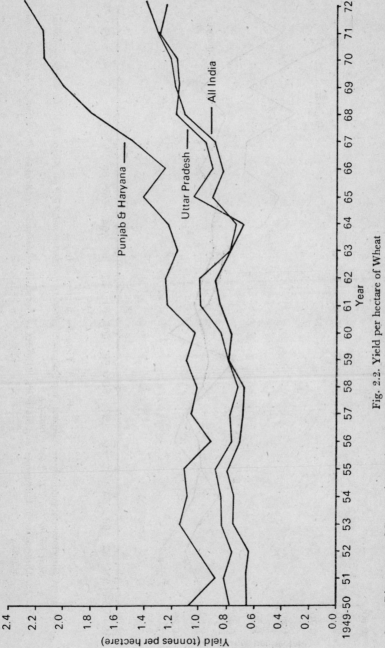

Fig. 2.2. Yield per hectare of Wheat

Source: Directorate of Economics and Statistics, Ministry of Agriculture, *Estimates of Area and Production of Principal Crops in India.*

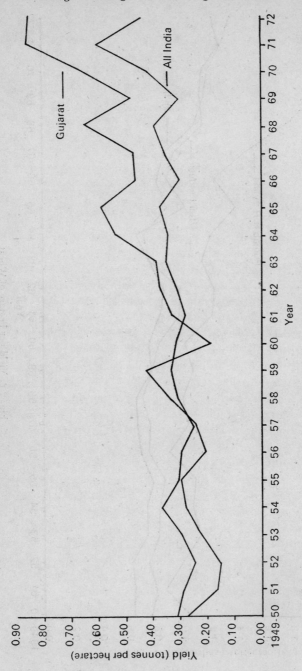

Fig. 2.3. Yield per hectare of Bajra.

Sources: (1) Directorate of Agriculture, Gujarat State, *Statistics of Area, Production and Yield per Acre of Principal Crops in Gujarat State for the period 1949-60 to 1963-64.*

(2) Directorate of Economics and Statistics, Ministry of Agriculture, *Estimates of Area and Production of Principal Crops in India.*

CHAPTER 3

Factors Affecting Farm Mechanisation

HYPOTHESIS

Farmers, whether in the developed or developing economies, mechanise farm operations when the biological sources of energy, e.g., human and animal labour, become costlier than the mechanical sources. There is a secular tendency everywhere, for the biological sources to become costlier than the mechanical sources. This is due, in part, to the labour-saving bias of technological change as well as the increasing ease with which capital can be substituted for labour (rise in the elasticity of substitution) in agriculture and partly to the rise in the cost of human and animal labour relative to that of machines and fuel.

Technical progress and industrial development contribute, in general, to increasing the ease with which capital can be substituted for labour and also to reduce the cost of machines and fuel. On the other hand, economic development and the growth of per capita income raise the cost of biological sources of energy, by increasing the demand for labour in the non-agricultural sector.[1] Also, in view of high income elasticities of demand for milk and meat, especially in the developing countries, it becomes more profitable to allocate the feed resources for augmenting the supply of such animal products than for maintaining draft animals. The increase in the incomes of farmers raises their investable surplus as

---

[1] In the United States, for instance, while the price index of farm machinery doubled between 1940 (153) and 1956 (330), the cost of labour to farmers quadrupled (the index rising from 129 to 536). See Earl O. Heady, 'Extent and Conditions of Agritural Mechanisation in the United States' in J.L. Meij (ed.), *Mechanisation in Agriculture*, North-Holland Publishing Company, Amsterdam, 1960.

well as their credit-worthiness for the purchase of machines. Further, with the rise in the income of farmers, the desire to lessen the drudgery and hard work asserts itself. Farm mechanisation can give them more leisure time, apart from rendering work more agreeable.[2] It may even raise the participation rate among those who could afford to abstain from drudgerous manual work. Indeed, the prospect of saving on labour cost, through the greater participation of family labour, may induce farm mechanisation in situations where the participation rate among (large) farmers is quite low under traditional non-mechanised techniques of farming.

The context in which farm mechanisation is taking place in India is different from that in the developed countries. Population has been growing at a significant rate resulting in an increase in the supply of labour for the agricultural sector. The growth in per capita income has been negligible, particularly after the mid-sixties when the rate of farm mechanisation seems to have accelerated. The puzzle then is: How does the cost of biological sources of energy increase relative to that of the mechanical sources when unemployment and underemployment is growing in the economy and when growth in per capita income is negligible?

Neo-classical tradition in economic theory may be helpful for understanding this situation insofar as farm mechanisation represents the response of the demand for capital to the changes in relative factor prices, or the ratio of factor prices to the price of output.[3] But it is not quite as helpful in illuminating: Why do the

[2]Heady (ibid.), found that the marginal value produtivity of annual machine expenses ($0.93) was less than the annual input ($1.00). On the other hand, crop services, including fertilisers, return ($1.08) more than the annual input ($1.00). Thus, 'Farmers have invested in some machinery...to lessen the drudgery and hard work...the expenditure is justified in the utility and satisfaction provided for the operator and his family'.

A. J. Rayner and Keith Cowling show that, whereas the dominant explanatory variable in the demand for tractors in the UK has been the real price of tractors relative to agricultural wages, the dominant variable in the US appears to have been the price of tractors relative to crop prices. Since family labour is more important in the US than in the UK (where labour cost itself is more important), the authors attribute the US demand for tractors to the leisure preference of family labour as a result of the increase in income. See their 'Demand for Farm Tractors in the United States and the UK', *American Journal of Agricultural Economics*, Vol. 50, Number 4, November 1968.

[3]Dale W. Jorgenson, 'Capital Theory and Investment Behaviour', *American Economic Review*, May 1963.

relative factor prices move against biological sources of energy despite the growth in the supply of labour? Indeed, the phenomenon itself defies neo-classical reasoning. Ricardo's work is perhaps more relevant for answering this question:

> With every increase of capital and population, food will generally rise, on account of its being more difficult to produce. The consequence of a rise of food will be a rise of wages, and every rise of wages will have a tendency to determine the saved capital in a greater proportion than before to the employment of machinery.[4]

Population explosion increases the supply of labour as well as generates an increasing demand for foodgrains and agricultural commodities. If one considers exclusively the increasing supply of labour as a result of population growth, one is confronted with the above puzzle, because it then appears reasonable to believe that when the labour force increases, other things remaining equal, wages should come down and consequently it should become more profitable to adopt labour-intensive techniques of production in preference to capital-intensive or mechanised techniques. But, if one focuses on the implications of the rising demand for agricultural commodities as a result of population growth, one finds clues to resolving this puzzle.

As the prices of foodgrains rise, consequent on the growth of population, the money value of wages paid in kind (which are substantial in Indian agriculture) automatically rises. Even cash wages may not lag behind prices very much, because they are already at subsistence level and so a significant fall in real wages would be strongly resisted. These factors are hidden from view if one focuses only on the supply of labour in terms of growth in numbers. Labour in the sense of effective energy or efficiency units cannot be abundant when food is in short supply and the cost of labour can rise despite, and indeed owing to, the growth of population.

Apart from the rise in money wages and in the price of bullocks, the cost on human and bullock labour may have increased on two other counts. In the first place, the rise in prices of agricultural commodities might have induced the extension of cultivation

[4]David Ricardo, *On the Principles of Political Economy and Taxation*, Vol. I, Edited by Piero Sraffa with the collaboration of M.H. Dobb, Cambridge University Press, 1966, p. 395.

to the less productive or marginal land, requiring harder and more labour per unit of output. Second, the possible decline in per capita consumption by labourers, especially in the sixties, owing to the higher dependency ratio in the face of stickiness or decline of real wages, might have reduced their efficiency.

Owing to the prevailing unequal distribution of land, the cost of draft power per acre is higher among the large farms than would be the case if land were more equally distributed. This is because, unlike for a small farmer, who contributes own labour on the farm, labour forms a paid-out cost for a large farmer. The real cost of draft power for large farms is higher still, owing to managerial and supervisory costs which may increase steeply with the increase in the size of holding under labour-intensive techniques. Moreover, with the expansion of output, the uncertainty in regard to the availability of required labour for crucial operations such as ploughing raises the anticipated or *ex ante* costs for the large farmers. Small farmers, of say 5 or 10 acres, owing to the availability of sufficient labour from their own families, can keep to the time schedule by making up the time lost because of adverse weather when it delays ploughing. The large farmers, on the other hand, may need tractors for ensuring timeliness of operations and to insure against the uncertainties of hired labour. Therefore, in the context of expanding agricultural output, large farmers may find mechanical sources less costly, especially because the participation of family labour may rise with mechanisation which may further reduce their labour costs.

FARM CREDIT AND TRACTORISATION

It may be argued that farm machinery has been made artificially cheap through the liberal import policy and through the extension of institutional credit for the purchase of tractors on unduly liberal terms. It may also be argued that the rich farmers in the prosperous pockets, owing to the lack of alternative sources of investment, have a tendency to over-invest in farm machinery—such as tractors, which have now become status symbols for them.

The data on loans advanced by the cooperative land mortgage banks to farmers for the purchase of tractors (up to the end of 1966) reveal that only about 10 per cent of the then existing stock of private tractors could have been purchased from such loans.[5] The

[5]C.H.Hanumantha Rao, 'Farm Mechanisation in a Labour-Abundant

rates of interest charged were around 9 per cent in most cases, which are not lower than the rates charged on similar long-term loans by the institutional agencies for non-agricultural purposes. This does not imply, however, that the availability of institutional credit at 9 per cent interest rate did not constitute an incentive for tractorisation. Nevertheless, the above evidence does suggest that such an incentive has not been a major factor so far, and that the investment in tractors seems to be profitable even in the absence of an easy availability of credit. It is true that tractors were exempted until recently from import duty, but, considering the high black market prices for tractors, it would appear that the demand for them may not be affected by the recent levy of an import duty of 30 per cent, in addition to the excise duty of 10 per cent, which together bring market prices of tractors more in line with the social valuation of foreign exchange and capital, in general.

One can not rule out some misallocation of resources by the farmers, in view of the large remittances from outside (into Punjab), limited opportunities for investment in the non-farm sector and their shyness to step up bank deposits. But in view of the prevailing high interest rates in the rural capital market and the opportunities for investment opened up by the new technology in the agricultural sector, it is very unlikely that savings would be invested in farm machinery unless the rate of return is reasonably high.

CHANGES IN PRODUCT AND FACTOR PRICES

PRICES OF AGRICULTURAL COMMODITIES

Population pressure in India has been one of the chief factors accounting for the steep rise in prices of agricultural commodities, despite the technical progress that has taken place or is still under way in agriculture. In the course of less than a decade since 1961-62, prices of agricultural commodities—especially of foodgrains—doubled (see Table 3.1). The prices of textiles and manufactures, on the other hand, rose by not more than 70 per cent over the corresponding period. Thus, the prices of foodgrains relative to those of textiles and manufactures rose significantly reaching their peak by 1967-68. The relative prices showed a gradual decline in the subsequent period, when the Green Revolution resulted in a steady increase in agricultural

Economy', *Economic and Political Weekly*, Annual Number, February 1972.

TABLE 3.1: Price Indices of Agricultural Commodities and Manufactures in India (1961-62=100)

Year	Price Indices				Relative Price Indices		
	Foodgrains	Agricultural Commodities	Textiles	Manufactures (Total)	Foodgrains Relative to Textiles	Foodgrains Relative to Manufactures	Agricultural Commodities Relative to Manufactures
	(1)	(2)	(3)	(4)	(5)	(6)	(7)
1962-63	105.4	102.3	102.0	102.6	103.3	102.7	99.7
1963-64	115.2	108.4	104.0	104.8	110.7	109.9	103.4
1964-65	145.5	130.9	110.0	109.0	132.2	133.4	120.0
1965-66	154.3	141.7	122.8	118.1	125.6	130.6	119.9
1966-67	182.9	166.6	123.2	127.5	148.4	143.4	130.6
1967-68	288.4	188.2	123.1	131.1	185.5	174.2	143.5
1968-69	201.0	179.4	135.2	134.4	148.6	149.5	133.4
1969-70	208.2	194.8	140.7	143.5	147.9	145.0	135.7
1970-71	206.8	201.0	160.3	154.9	129.0	133.5	129.7
1971-72	214.9	199.6	170.7	167.1	125.8	128.6	119.4

Sources: R.B.I. Bulletin, January 1970, p. 160.
R.B.I. Bulletin, September 1972, p. 1671.

TABLE 3.2: GROWTH OF AGRICULTURAL RESOURCES IN INDIA (1951-1969)

| | 1951-52 | 1961-62 | 1968-69 | Per cent Change Between: | | |
				1951-62	1961-69	1951-69
	(1)	(2)	(3)	(4)	(5)	(6)
1. Population (Million)	361.0	439.1	523.8*	21.6	19.3	45.1
2. Per Capita Income (in Rupees) at 1948-49 prices	250.3	294.3	322.8	17.5	9.7	29.0
3. Net Sown Area (thousand hectares)	119,400	135,352	137,512	13.4	1.6	15.2
4. Gross Sown Area (thousand hectares)	133,234	156,099	159,623	17.2	2.3	19.8
5. Net Irrigated Area (thousand hectares)	21,049	24,885	29,065	18.2	16.7	37.9
6. Gross Irrigated Area (thousand hectares)	23,180	28,461	35,432	22.8	24.5	52.9
7. Net Irrigated Area through Government Canals (thousand hectares)	7,490	9,338	10,857	24.8	16.7	45.0
8. Net Irrigated Area through Wells (thousand hectares)	6,517	7,352	10,734	12.8	46.0	64.7
9. Total Consumption of Fertilizers (metric tons) (N, P_2O_5&K_2O)	—	406,899	1,674,648	—	311.5	—

Sources: 1. *Fertiliser Statistics*, 1961-62, 1969-70 and 1971-72.
2. Planning Commission, *Basic statistics Relating to the Indian Economy*, 1968.
3. Directorate of Economics and Statistics, *Indian Agriculture in Brief* (11th ed.).
4. Department of Economic Affairs, Ministry of Finance, *Indian Economic Statistics*.
* Population for 1969 has been estimated by applying the growth rate of 2.229.

output. However, despite these technological changes, the relative price indices of foodgrains varied between 126 to 129 in 1971-72.

The persistence of higher relative prices over a long period suggests that the cost of production of agricultural commodities at the margin relative to that of manufactures may have risen during this period despite the softening impact of the technological changes. Indeed, the rising cost may have provided incentives for technological changes, in the absence of which the relative prices of agricultural commodities would have been higher still.

This is also suggested by the slow growth of major agricultural resources relative to the demand for agricultural commodities (as indicated by the growth of population and per capita income) over the plan period. Table 3.2 shows that the growth of net sown area and net irrigated area lagged very much behind the growth of population, indicating a significant decline in agricultural resources in per capita terms. It is important to note that the growth of area irrigated through government canals was much slower than that from wells (which are, predominantly, a private source) during 1961-69 when the prices of agricultural commodities recorded a sharp rise. Evidence available from the Farm Management Studies conducted in different parts of the country shows that the unit cost or the percentage of output absorbed as cost is significantly lower for crops served with public sources of irrigation such as canals when compared to those served with private sources and unirrigated crops. Again, it was during this period that there was a significant breakthrough in the use of fertilisers, representing an increase of about 300 per cent. On the other hand, during the first decade of planning, i.e., between 1951-52 and 1961-62, the sown area as well as the irrigated area registered a significant increase, the growth rate of irrigation from government canals being twice as high as from wells. This was responsible for keeping the prices of agricultural commodities at a reasonably low level during this period.[6]

[6]In the Central Plain of Thailand, the irrigated area increased at the rate of 4.5 per cent, the harvested area at 2.7 per cent and the yield per harvested acre at 3 per cent per annum between 1958-59 and 1966-67. This, in conjunction with the price policy, was responsible for the low price of rice, little use of fertilisers and slow pace of technological change. In Central Luzon of the Philippines, on the other hand, the expansion of traditional resources was slow and prices rose thus providing incentives for technological change and capital-intensive commercial farming by large farms. A rapid increase in the yield per acre of rice was associated with a decline in the area planted with rice. See

TABLE 3.3: CHANGES IN AGRICULTURAL WAGE RATE

	Agricultural Operation	Wage Rate (Rs) per Day 1961-62	Wage (Rate Rs) per Day 1969-70	Per Cent Change
	(1)	(2)	(3)	(4)
Punjab	Plougher	2.81	6.34	125.6
Kerala	Field Labourer	2.10	4.67	122.4
Bihar	Plougher	1.33	2.70	103.0
Uttar Pradesh	Plougher	1.31	2.61	99.2
Maharashtra	Field Labourer	1.48	2.85	92.6
Tamilnadu	Plougher	1.43	2.65	85.3
Orissa	Field Labourer	1.26	2.15 (1968-69)	70.6
West Bengal	Field Labourer	1.85	3.17 (1967-68)	71.4
Andhra Pradesh	Field Labourer	1.46	2.46	68.5
Assam	Field Labourer	2.29	3.80	65.9
Madhya Pradesh	Plougher	1.32	2.11	59.8
Gujarat	Field Labourer	1.97	2.94	49.2
Karnataka	Field Labourer	1.64	2.35	43.3

Note: The wage rates are the simple averages of wages at different centres in each state.

Sources: (1) For column (2) Ministry of Food and Agriculture. 'Agricultural Wages in India, 1961-62'.

(2) For column (3) Unpublished data from the Ministry of Food and Agriculture, Directorate of Economics and Statistics.

RELATIVE PRICES OF TRADITIONAL AND MODERN INPUTS

Despite the weaker bargaining power of agricultural labour, the money wages of plougher/field labour rose by not less than 50 per cent during this period (see Table 3.3). In about half the number of states, money wages rose roughly in proportion to the rise in prices of agricultural commodities.

However, while considering the cost of biological sources of energy one needs to give greater weight to animal than to human labour. Agricultural tractor, for instance, displaces human and animal labour for ploughing, threshing, and transportation. About 19 bullock-days are needed for ploughing and threshing of (irrigated)

Shigeru Ishikawa, *Agricultural Development Strategies in Asia: Case Studies of Philippines and Thailand*, Asian Development Bank, 1970.

wheat on an acre in Punjab.[7] Since one human labour-day is needed for every two bullock-days, the requirement of human labour-
days comes to 9.5. On the basis of the cost per bullock-day (Rs.
5.80) and the average wage rate (Rs.6.39) in 1968-69,[8] the total
bullock and human labour cost for such operations amounts to Rs.
171, of which bullock labour accounts for as much as 64 per cent.

The prices of bullocks in Punjab during 1961-69 rose roughly
in proportion to the prices of agricultural commodities (see Table
3.4).[9] This is what one should expect, because fodder crops compete
with other crops for the same agricultural resources, so that the
maintenance of bullocks means, to a large extent, the sacrifice of
crops grown for human consumption. Such a competition between
the animal and the human population for land and other agricultural resources can be expected in the context of population growth
and rising food prices.

Whereas the money wages and bullock prices rose faster than
did prices of agricultural commodities in many regions where the

TABLE 3.4: Bullock Prices in Punjab (for class 1 bullock)

Year	Price (Rs.)	Index (1961=100)
1961	515.0	100.0
1962	650.0	113.0
1963	750.0	130.4
1964	850.0	147.8
1965	875.0	152.2
1966	875.0	152.2
1967	900.0	156.5
1968	1135.0	197.4
1969	1135.0	235.7

Source: Government of Punjab, *Statistical Abstract for Punjab, 1969*, p. 628.

[7]Ministry of Food and Agriculture, 'Studies in the Economics of Farm
Management in the Punjab', Combined Report, 1954-55 to 1956-57, issued
by the Directorate of Economics and Statistics, 1963, Table 5.11.

[8]Ministry of Food and Agriculture, 'Studies in the Economics of Farm
Management in Ferozepur (Punjab), 1968-69', by A.S. Kahlon and others,
Punjab Agricultural University, Ludhiana, (mimeo), pp. 12, 62.

[9]A similar relationship between the prices of bullocks and of agricultural commodities was found in the three markets of Andhra Pradesh during
1935-50. See C.H. Hanumantha Rao, *Taxation of Agricultural Land in Andhra
Pradesh*, Asia Publishing House, 1966, p. 118.

rate of mechanisation has also been rapid, the prices of tractors and tractor-fuel seem to have risen by not more than 50 per cent between 1961 and 1968—compared to a 100 per cent rise in the prices of agricultural commodities over this period. The prices of tractors, e.g., Eicher (27 HP) and TAFE (35 HP), rose by only about 47 per cent between 1961 and 1968 as against a rise of over 124 per cent in foodgrains prices (see Table 3.5). Even after the mid-sixties, i.e., after the commencement of the bulk of indigenous production of tractors, tractor prices lagged very much behind the prices of foodgrains.[10] Between 1961 and 1971, the price of high speed diesel oil increased between 48 to 49 per cent in the major markets, e.g., Bombay, Madras and Calcutta.[11]

REGIONAL VARIATION IN THE RATE OF MECHANISATION

POCKETS OF HIGH AGRICULTURAL GROWTH AND
MECHANISATION

The rise in prices of agricultural commodities in the wake of population pressure and the deficiency of public investment in agriculture has caused a shift in the distribution of agricultural income in favour of certain agriculturally better-endowed regions (in terms of physical resources and entrepreneurial ability) as well as of the large farmers, for whom it has become profitable to invest in the expansion of agricultural output. The emergence of such pockets of rapid agricultural growth has been very much in evidence in the recent period in the northern wheat belt of west Uttar Pradesh, Punjab and Haryana, and in the deltaic rice belts of Tamilnadu and Andhra Pradesh.

In Punjab, for instance, the index of foodgrains output rose

[10]A number of studies on mechanisation in countries of East Asia have brought out similar facts. These are contained in Herman Southworth (ed.), *Farm Mechanisation in East Asia*, Agricultural Development Council, New York. Jin Hwan Park shows that in South Korea, the nominal price index (1965=100) of wages rose to 285.5 in 1970 and that of power tillers to 133.4. Sung Ho Kim shows that in Japan while the price of a power tiller increased only by 40 per cent during 1955-69, the average farm wage rate rose by 312 per cent. According to Weng Chieh Lai, in Taiwan the price of a power tiller remained more or less constant between 1960 and 1971 while the wage rate rose by 75 per cent.

[11]Petroleum Information Service, *Indian Petroleum Handbook*, 1969, p. 277; and *Oil Statistics : A Petroleum Quarterly*, April-June 1971, p. 13.

TABLE 3.5: SELLING PRICES OF INDIGENOUS AGRICULTURAL TRACTORS

Name of the Company	Type of Tractor (1)	Year of Commencement of Production (2)	Price at the Commencement of Production (Rs.) (3)	Prices Fixed in the Middle of 1968 (Rs.) (4)	Prices Fixed in Early 1971 (Rs.) (5)
Eicher	27 HP	1960	11,900	17,480	19,460
(a) Tractor price index			100	146.9	163.5
(b) Foodgrains price index			100	224.2	204.3
Escorts	27 HP	1966	13,100	13,840	—
(a) Tractor price index			100	105.7	—
(b) Foodgrains price index			100	148.0	—
Escorts	37 HP	1966	15,400	17,910	19,930
(a) Tractor price index			100	116.3	129.4
(b) Foodgrains price index			100	148.0	134.9
Hindustan	50 HP	1964	17,500	22,350	24,900
(a) Tractor price index			100	127.7	142.3
(b) Foodgrains price index			100	198.3	180.7
Hindustan	35 HP	1965	12,500	15,710	17,470
(a) Tractor price index			100	125.7	139.8
(b) Foodgrains price index			100	158.1	144.1
International	35 HP	1965	16,380	19,570	22,890
(a) Tractor price index			100	119.5	130.7
(b) Foodgrains price index			100	158.1	144.1
TAFE	35 HP	1962	14,450	21,140	—
(a) Tractor price index			100	146.3	—
(b) Foodgrains price index			100	228.4	—

Sources: (1) Government of India, *Report on the Fixation of Prices of Agricultural Tractors*, Government of India Publications, Delhi, 1970.
(2) The Planning Commission, New Delhi.

from 104 in 1961-62 to 198 in 1968-69, and the index of output of all agricultural commodities rose from 103 to 180 over the same period.[12] If we omit the figure for 1965-66 as being abnormal, the annual compound rate of growth of all agricultural commodities in Punjab, for the seven year period, works out to 8.7 per cent. Part of this growth has been achieved through extension of cropped area, in which case the demand for draft power and farm labour would have risen, in the absence of tractorisation, at about the same rate as the extension of area. It has been estimated that, with a one per cent increase in yield per acre—as a result of better irrigation, adoption of improved varieties, etc.,—the requirement of human labour rises, in general, by about 0.75 per cent.[13] On this basis, the demand for farm labour in Punjab would have risen by at least 6.5 per cent (0.75×8.7) per annum in the absence of mechanisation. This is far above the possible rate of growth of the labour force in Punjab and may explain why the money wage rates as well as the prices of bullocks in Punjab rose at higher rate than the prices of agricultural commodities (see Tables 3.1, 3.3 and 3.4), despite the migration of casual labour from Rajasthan and eastern Uttar Pradesh for various farm operations, particularly harvesting. Labour cost can be expected to rise despite such migration owing, among other things, to the economic and psychic costs of migration which raise the supply price of labour. Also, insofar as the skills among the migrant labour are not suited to the local needs, the cost of such labour (per efficiency unit) could be higher when compared to that of local labour.

EXPLANATORY FACTORS

It has been argued before that, whereas in a developed economy the incentives for farm mechanisation emanate from rapid industrialisation and growth of per capita income resulting in the shortage of labour for the farm sector, in a developing economy like India, the incentive for farm mechanisation is provided by the rise in the prices of agricultural commodities as a result of rapid growth of population and the failure of public investment in inputs like irrigation to match the growing demand for agricultural

[12] Government of Punjab, *Statistical Abstract of Punjab*, 1969.
[13] See Part II, Ch. 9. This estimate is based on the Farm Management data pertaining to Ferozepur (Punjab) for 1968-69.

commodities. The cost of biological sources of energy rises in such a situation, due to the rise in the prices of foodgrains as well as to the demand for labour outstripping the supply, in pockets of high agricultural growth. One should thus expect a high rate of mechanisation to be associated with higher per capita agricultural incomes. In view of this, one should expect the relationship between the rate of mechanisation on the one hand, and wage rates, leisure preference and the demand for animal products, etc., on the other, to be in the same direction as in a developed economy.

Table 3.6 gives the relevant data for 265 districts of India,

TABLE 3.6: Variables Associated with Tractorisation in India

	Number of Tractors per 10,000 Agricultural Workers in the District				
	Below 3	3 to 7	7 to 13	13 to 25	25 and Above
	(1)	(2)	(3)	(4)	(5)
Number of districts	164 (61.9)	58 (21.9)	20 (7.5)	8 (3.0)	15 (5.7)
Number of tractors in 1966	9650 (20.2)	10940 (22.9)	7125 (14.9)	3526 (7.4)	16483 (34.6)
Annual crop output (Rs) (Average of 1959-60, 60-61 and 1961-62) per capita of Agricultural population (1961)	182.52	217.8	211.1	244.1	357.5
Daily wage rate (Rs), 1965-66 (Plougher/field labourer)	1.93	2.06	2.09	2.50	3.56
Per cent of area held by large farmers (above 30 acres), 1961	24.3	30.1	31.7	43.8	34.6
Cropped area in acres (average of 1964-65, 1965-66 and 1966-67) per 100 agricultural population (1961)	125.5	153.9	161.6	222.1	205.4
Percentage of net area irrigated to net area sown (average of 1964-65, 1965-66 and 1966-67)	16.1	18.0	19.7	22.3	48.5
Cropping intensity: per cent of gross cropped area to net sown area (average of 1964-65, 1965-66 and 1966-67)	113.9	111.9	109.8	116.2	127.0
Participation rate, 1961: (a) Males	94.1	93.8	94.6	93.4	91.3
(b) Females	53.6	50.0	48.6	27.4	18.7
Number of buffaloes (in milk) in 1966 per 10,000 rural population (1961)	257	375	597	572	790

Note: The figures in brackets give the percentage distribution of districts and tractors according to the rate of tractorisation.

Sources and Method:

1. Number of tractors and buffaloes (in milk) are obtained from the Livestock Census, 1966, Directorate of Economics and Statistics, Ministry of Food and Agriculture.
2. Crop output is obtained by multiplying the average cropped area of 1959-60, 1960-61 and 1961-62 by the estimates of per acre crop output taken from 'Pattern of Land Concentration (1961 Census) and Elasticity of per Acre Composite Productivity', by P.S. Sharma in *Agricultural Situation in India*, August 1965.
3. The agricultural population is arrived at by assuming that the proportion of agricultural workers to agricultural population is the same as the proportion of rural workers to rural population. Participation rate has been worked out by dividing the rural workers, male/female, in the age-group 15-59 by the rural population, male/female, in that age-group.
4. Data on population and workers are taken from Part II-A, General Population Tables and Part II-B (i) General Economic Tables, Census of India, 1961.
5. Percentages of area held by large farmers (above 30 acres) in 1961, district-wise, are borrowed from P.S. Sharma's unpublished work.
6. Data on gross sown area, net sown area and net irrigated area are from Season and Crop Reports and Land Utilisation Statistics of different states, and are obtained from the Directorate of Economics and Statistics, Ministry of Food and Agriculture.
7. Wage rates are taken from *Agricultural Wages in India*, 1965-66.

grouped according to the rate of tractorisation—the latter being defined as the number of tractors per 10,000 agricultural workers in the district. About 15 or 5.7 per cent of the total number of districts accounted for over one-third of the total number of tractors in 1966; 43 or only about 16 per cent of districts accounted for as many as 57 per cent of the total number of tractors.[14] That tractorisation may have been induced by the greater requirements of draft power, is indicated by the fact that the cropped (harvested) area per 100 people engaged in agriculture, percentage of area irrigated, and

[14]Regional concentration is greater in the case of diesel and electric pump-sets as their use is dependent on the availability of ground water. Electric pump-sets are more concentrated regionally than the diesel pump-sets, as the use of the former is dependent on the availability of ground water as well as power. According to the Livestock Census of 1966, the number of districts (arranged in the descending order of the number of machines in the district) accounting for one-fourth, one-half and three-fourth the number of machines in the country in each case, is as follows:

	Tractors	Diesel Pump-sets	Electric Pump-sets
25%	9	8	3
50%	33	21	9
75%	85	52	35

cropping intensity (ratio of harvested to operated area) increase with
the increase in the rate of tractorisation. It is possible, however, that
part of the rise in cropping intensity itself may be the result of tractorisation. Per capita agricultural income is significantly higher in
areas where the rate of tractorisation is high.[15]

It may be noted that for arriving at the cropped area per 100
people in agriculture as well as per capita agricultural income, the
denominator used is the agricultural population and not agricultural workers. Insofar as the number of agricultural workers
would be lower where the rate of tractorisation is high, one should
anyway expect a positive correlation between the rate of tractorisation, on the one hand, and cropped area as well as agricultural
income per worker, on the other. To this extent, therefore, the
measures adopted are free from spurious correlation.

As can be expected, the participation rate among females is
markedly lower in high income pockets indicating a higher work load
on the male labour force.[16] The higher wage rates for plougher/
field labourer in high income pockets could thus be the result of increased demand for labour as well as of the reduced participation
of female labour. The number of buffaloes (in milk) per 10,000
people in the rural areas is markedly higher in regions of high income
and high rate of tractorisation, indicating greater demand for milk
in high income pockets as well as the probable rise in cost of draft power owing to greater allocation of feed to milch animals. The positive

[15]In Thailand, the Central Region in which the rate of mechanisation is
highest accounted for the highest household income in 1963, whereas the lowest
household income related to North East where the rate of mechanisation is also
the lowest. In 1965, out of 9.5 million *rais* irrigated by state irrigation projects,
as many as 8.3 million *rais* were in the Central Region. The average size of holding was also higher in the Central Region. See I. Inukai, 'Farm Mechanisation,
Output and Labour Input: A Case Study in Thailand', *International Labour Review*, Vol. 101, Number 5, May 1970.

[16]A similar result is obtained by Martin H. Billings and Arjun Singh in
an inter-regional analysis for Punjab. See their 'Mechanisation and the Wheat
Revolution: Effects on Female Labour in Punjab', *Economic and Political Weekly*,
Review of Agriculture, 26 December 1970.

The participation rate of female labour has generally been found to be
more sensitive to the increase in affluence than the male participation rate. For
instance, in Taiwan, whereas male participation rate declined from 89 per cent
to 71 per cent between 1940 and 1956, the female participation rate which was
as low as 48 per cent declined even more sharply to 20 per cent. See Anthony
Y. C. Koo 'Agrarian Reform, Production and Employment in Taiwan', *International Labour Review*, Vol. 104, Number 1-2, July-August 1971.

association between per capita agricultural income and rate of tractorisation is also suggestive of the impact of greater investable surplus
on mechanisation in these areas. The above inferences are reinforced
by the fact that in areas with a high rate of tractorisation, the proportion of area held by large farms (above 30 acres) is somewhat
higher. Regression analysis based on these data reveals per capita
income to be more important than wage rate in explaining the inter-
district differences in the rate of tractorisation (see Appendix A).

SUMMARY

Contrary to the usual expectation, farm mechanisation currently underway in Indian Agriculture represents, in a sense, the response
of the prevailing economic system to the population explosion. Among
other factors, the failure of the Government to step up investments in
the expansion of agricultural resources such as irrigation and land
reclamation to meet the requirements of a growing population, accentuates the shortage of agricultural commodities and, thus, provides
an impetus to farm mechanisation via the rise in the product and
(traditional) factor prices.

The rise in the prices of agricultural commodities has led to
a rise in the money value of the wages of agricultural labour as well
as to a rise in the cost of bullock labour. This has resulted in traditional biological sources of energy becoming more costly in relation
to mechanical sources. Thus, despite the increasing supply of labour,
it has become profitable for the large wage-based farms to adopt
mechanised techniques.

The developed or better-endowed regions and the large farmers have taken a lead in this process of technological change.
Higher per capita income implies a greater demand for energy to
cope with the increased scale of operations. On the supply side,
higher income is associated with higher wage owing to the withdrawal of labour from manual work. Also, animal power may become
costly owing to the diversion of feed resources for milch animals. The
capacity to invest and bear risk in the high income areas may also
be working as important contributory factors for mechanisation. A
high rate of growth among these limited pockets accentuates the rise
in the cost of biological sources of energy thus making the use of
mechanical inputs more attractive. Thus, per capita income seems
to be the most important factor affecting farm mechanisation. This

cross-sectional finding is consistent with the response of farm mechanisation to the changes in the relative product and factor prices: a rise in the relative prices of agricultural commodities raises the farmers' real income, apart from causing a rise in money wages relative to the prices of modern inputs.

CHAPTER 4

Factors Affecting the Use of Biological-Chemical Techniques

HYPOTHESIS

The use of biological-chemical (BC) techniques such as High Yielding Varieties of seeds (HYV), fertilisers and insecticides can be traced to the same factors as those affecting farm mechanisation. Such innovations are land-saving as well as labour-saving and represent the increasing ease with which capital can be substituted for land as well as labour. So far, the land-augmenting character of these techniques has attracted much attention, but recently some studies have emphasised their labour-saving character.[1] Where new seeds and fertilisers double output per acre, half the existing land resources would be sufficient to produce the same level of output. For the same reason, the draft power needed to produce the same level of output would be substantially reduced, though not proportionately to land. Draft power needed for operations such as ploughing bear roughly a proportionate relationship to the land area so that their requirement would be reduced in proportion to the saving on land. The labour input per acre required for inter-culturing, harvesting, transportation, etc., may increase with the increase in the yield per acre but less than proportionately to the rise in yield.

Thus, in countries where land is abundant and labour is scarce such as the United States, the major economic incentive for the adoption of BC techniques might have been their labour-saving

[1]For the substantial evidence on how some of the so-called land-substituting techniques are labour-substituting as well and vice versa, see Yujiro Hayami and V.W. Ruttan, 'Factor Prices and Technical Change in Agricultural Development: The United States and Japan, 1880-1960', *Journal of Political Economy*, Vol. 78, Number 5, September-October 1970.

character. Even in some of the labour-abundant economies, such as in India, the managerial diseconomies seem to be a major constraint for the large farmers who are found to cultivate land less intensively than the small farmers by employing substantially less labour input per acre. It is highly probable, therefore, that the labour-saving character of new seeds and fertilisers is an important factor favouring their adoption among large farms in such economies. In the case of small farmers, however, the land-augmenting character of these innovations would be the major factor favouring their adoption.

Insofar as the labour-saving character of BC innovations provides an economic incentive for their adoption, the factors inducing farm mechanisation would, in general, be favourable to the adoption of BC innovations also. For example, a rise in wages relative to the price of fertilisers may induce the wage-based or capitalist farms to grow crops which are less labour-intensive and to use more fertilisers for raising yield per acre. Another feature, common to both mechanical and BC techniques, is the increased investment requirement. Investable and risk-bearing capacity is a necessary condition for the adoption of both the categories of techniques. However, in the case of BC techniques, capital invested is not lumpy and partakes the character of current inputs so that the adoption of such techniques can be expected to be more widespread among farmers.

REGIONAL VARIATION IN THE USE OF FERTILISERS

We shall examine the above hypothesis by analysing the inter-district variation in the consumption of fertilisers per acre in 1964-65. We have classified the 265 districts of India for which the necessary data are available into eight groups according to the level of nitrogen used per acre. The data on some of the relevant variables for these groups of districts are presented in Table 4.1.

The use of nitrogen per worker rises steeply as the use of nitrogen per acre increases. As is evident, the net area sown per hundred agricultural workers does not show any systematic variation with the amount of fertilisers used per acre. The rise in the consumption of fertilisers per acre is associated with a steep increase in the percentage of the sown area irrigated and with a decline in the level of rainfall. This is what is to be expected because the

TABLE 4.1: Factors Associated With the Use of Fertilisers in India

Nitrogen (Mtc. tons) per 1000 Acres 1964-65	No. of Districts	Use of Nitrogen (Mtc. tons) per Agricultural Worker 1964-65	Net Area Sown (acres) per 100 Agricultural Workers 1966.	Percentage of Net Area Irrigated to Net Area Sown (average of 1964-65, 1965-66 and 1966-67)	Normal Annual Rainfall (mm)	Daily Wage Rate (Rs) 1965-66 Plougher/ Field Labour	Annual Crop Income (Rs) (average of 1959-60, 1960-61 and 1961-62) Per capita of Agricultural Population (1961)	Tractors per 1000 Acres Net area Sown, 1966	Percentage of Urban Population 1961	Percentage of Literates Among the Agricultural Population in the Age Group 15-59 in 1961
		(1)	(2)	(3)	(4)	(5)	(6)	(7)	(8)	(9)
0.0—0.5	80	0.0005	296	6.2	1023	1.96	179.5	0.07	10.7	16.5
0.5—1.0	50	0.0017	253	16.5	1071	1.99	165.5	0.09	12.7	20.9
1.0—2.0	46	0.0036	252	21.7	1077	1.92	193.3	0.12	15.1	24.0
2.0—3.0	39	0.0052	269	21.0	903	2.13	196.2	0.16	17.8	22.8
3.0—4.0	14	0.0076	235	30.7	950	2.14	232.4	0.15	18.1	31.0
4.0—5.0	13	0.0099	253	28.6	808	2.09	246.8	0.36	20.3	27.0
5.0—6.0	11	0.0129	323	38.2	753	2.57	283.9	0.49	20.3	24.8
6.0 and above	12	0.0197	256	46.3	939	2.24	354.0	0.60	21.0	32.4
Overall	265	0.0043	268	18.8	990	2.04	200.1	0.15	15.1	22.6

Note: The sources of data and methods used are the same as for Table 6 in Chapter 3. Data on nitrogen (metric ton nutrients) are obtained from the Ministry of Food and Agriculture.

availability of controlled irrigation raises the profitability of investment in fertilisers. But these data also imply that labour input per
acre does not rise despite the increase in the percentage of the area
irrigated and with the rise in fertiliser consumption per acre. There
is, thus, an indication that land-augmenting inputs such as fertilisers
may have served, to a certain extent, as substitutes for labour. It
is significant to note in this connection that the wage rates are
generally higher in districts where the level of fertiliser-use is
higher.[2]

The increase in the consumption of fertilisers is associated
with a significant increase in per capita income. Although the rise
in per capita income itself could be the result of the increasing
fertiliser-use, the inference that fertiliser consumption may have been
induced by the rise in the per capita income and investable surplus
seems reasonable in this case because the proportion of area irrigated, which can be regarded as a rough index of the income level,
is higher in the areas where fertiliser-use per acre is higher and
also because the figures of per capita income relate to the period
1959-61 whereas the data on fertiliser consumption relate to 1964-65.
This inference is strengthened by the positive association between
the rate of tractorisation and the rate of fertiliser-use. Literacy does
not seem to be significantly related to the use of fertilisers whereas
urbanisation does show such a relationship. Nearness to the market,
access to know-how and the general awareness associated with urbanisation seem to be more important than literacy *as such*.

FARM SIZE AND THE USE OF BC INPUTS

Although High Yielding Varieties (HYV) and fertilisers are
size-neutral in the sense that they are perfectly divisible and can be
used irrespective of the size of the farm, they are not resource-
neutral. Since the large farms have a better command over resources—own as well as borrowed—and since their risk-bearing capacity
would be greater than that of the small farmers, one should expect
the adoption of BC techniques to be more extensive among the large
farms. The availability of land is not a constraint among the large

---

[2]Between 1961 and 1971, the prices of fertilisers rose by not more than
47 per cent indicating a steep decline in its cost relative to the prices of output and
wages. For the relevant data on the prices of fertilisers, see Fertiliser Association
of India, *Fertiliser Statistics, 1971-72*, pp. 259-61.

farms, as they very often fail to use even their irrigated land as intensively as the small farmers owing to the higher labour and managerial cost. Since the expansion of output through multiple cropping requires more labour input per unit of output than through the increase in yield per cropped acre from HYV, it appears that the labour-saving character of BC inputs provides a major incentive for their adoption among the large farms.

Some of the recent farm management data relating to the areas where the Green Revolution has made an impact such as Punjab and Andhra Pradesh support the above propositions. Tables 4.2 and 4.3 show that in Ferozepur (Punjab) and West Godavari (Andhra Pradesh), cropping intensity (i.e., the harvested area as a ratio to the size of holding) of cultivated holding as well as of irrigated holding declines with the increase in the size of holding. Although the percentage of area irrigated is higher among the small farms in Punjab and 100 per cent in West Godavari, which should enable them to allocate a larger proportion of holding to HYV as compared to the large farms, the percentage of the area actually allocated to the High Yielding Varieties seems to be somewhat higher among the large farms, and fertiliser input per acre increases with the rise in the size of holding. The input of labour (hired plus family) per acre declines with the increase in the size of holding so that the ratio of the fertiliser input to labour input rises steeply with the increase in the size of holding. Thus, large farms opt for high capital-intensity by using mechanical equipment like tractors and pump-sets as well as chemical-biological inputs. The small farms have an advantage over the large ones in regard to the traditional labour-intensive irrigated farming whereas the Green Revolution, based on capital-intensive modern inputs, seems to be favouring the large farms, owing to their better resource position as well as greater risk-bearing capacity.

ENVIRONMENTAL FACTORS AND THE USE OF BC INPUTS

Investment in modern inputs like fertilisers can be expected to be greater under conditions of high profitability and relative certainty of yields. Although there can be a trade-off between the level of profit and the degree of yield-certainty, the profitability of modern inputs is generally higher when irrigation is assured and controlled so that the certainty of yield would also be greater in such a situation. Weather-wise, *kharif* season (June-October) is characterised by

TABLE 4.2: INTENSITY OF INPUT-USE ACCORDING TO THE SIZE OF OPERATIONAL HOLDING IN FEROZEPUR (PUNJAR) 1969-70

Operational Holding: Size Group (acres)	Average Size (acres) of Operational Holding	Percentage of Operated Area Irrigated	Percentage of Cropped (harvested) Area to Operated Area	Percentage of Gross Irrigated Area to Net Irrigated Area	Percentage of Cropped (harvested) Area under High Yielding Varieties	Expenses (Rs.) on Labour per Cropped (harvested) Acre	Expenses (Rs.) on Fertilisers per Cropped (harvested) Acre	Output (Rs.) per Cropped (harvested) Acre
	(1)	(2)	(3)	(4)	(5)	(6)	(7)	(8)
5—10	7.6 (13)	93.7	143.6	148.4	28.4	205.9 (16.5)	18.2	540.4
10—20	15.2 (46)	93.2	141.3	147.0	37.6	159.4 (38.6)	27.8	557.5
20—30	24.5 (31)	89.9	135.1	140.1	31.8	156.6 (49.9)	33.0	643.5
30—50	39.2 (42)	89.8	135.8	142.4	42.0	146.9 (58.6)	35.4	593.9
50—75	60.4 (10)	80.8	112.3	116.3	19.0	119.4 (70.5)	18.7	550.9
75—100	86.0 (6)	96.4	119.7	116.8	46.2	119.5 (81.5)	71.5	871.3
100 & above	129.5 (2)	62.8	105.6	118.1	26.0	98.7 (89.6)	43.5	748.3
Overall	30.6 (150)	88.5	130.1	135.6	36.3	143.9 (55.9)	35.6	626.1

Note: Figures in brackets under column (1) give the number of holdings in each size-group. Expenses on labour in column (6) include the imputed value of family labour. The figures in brackets under this column give the percentage of hired labour to total labour input.

Source: Directorate of Economics and Statistics, Ministry of Food and Agriculture, *Studies in Economics of Farm Management,* Ferozepur (Punjab), 1969-70.

TABLE 4.3: INTENSITY OF INPUT-USE ACCORDING TO THE SIZE OF OPERATIONAL HOLDING IN THE DELTAIC WEST GODAVARI (ANDHRA PRADESH), 1969-70

Operational Holding: Size Group (acres)	Average Size (acres) of Operational Holding*	Percentage of Cropped (harvested) Area to Operated Area	Percent of Cropped Area Under Paddy to Total Cropped Area				Expenses (Rs.) on Labour per Acre (year)	Expenses (Rs.) on Fertilisers per Acre (year)	Output (Rs.) per acre (year)
			Kharif		Rabi				
			Local	HYV	Local	HYV			
	(1)	(2)	(3)	(4)	(5)	(6)	(7)	(8)	(9)
Up to 2.49	1.1 (44)	191.6	89.9	3.2	65.6	6.2	480.0 (46.2)	113.5	1383.6
2.50— 4.99	3.2 (36)	192.8	92.7	—	40.8	37.9	432.2 (67.4)	155.7	1418.3
5.00— 7.49	5.8 (38)	172.1	93.0	1.7	48.7	30.5	319.6 (76.8)	150.2	1078.4
7.50— 9.99	8.1 (24)	177.8	81.9	5.6	33.2	40.8	405.5 (80.4)	178.6	1425.0
10.00—14.99	12.0 (16)	166.6	90.5	6.2	15.8	57.9	325.0 (80.6)	155.2	1188.6
15.00—19.99	16.2 (7)	182.8	99.1	—	22.1	44.2	268.4 (90.8)	174.6	1263.1
20.00—29.99	23.6 (10)	180.5	83.1	10.2	17.0	38.4	292.8 (92.2)	166.7	1362.1
30.00 & above	37.1 (5)	172.7	91.9	4.7	37.4	54.0	299.4 (89.7)	164.5	1584.4
Overall	7.2 (180)	177.2	89.3	4.7	31.6	41.8	336.6 (80.8)	161.5	1326.6

Note: Figures in brackets under column(1) give the number of holdings in each size-group. Expenses on labour in column (7) include the imputed value of family labour. The figures in brackets under this column give the percentage of hired labour to total labour input.

Source: Waheeduddin Khan and R.N. Tripathy, *Intensive Agriculture and Modern Inputs—Prospects of Small Farmers: A Study in West Godavari District,* National Institute of Community Development, Hyderabad, 1972, pp. 13, 40, 47, 64, 67 and 76.
*Irrigated area constitutes almost 100 per cent of holding among all the groups.

greater uncertainty than the *rabi* season (November-March). Apart from the uncertainty of rainfall and the frequent flooding and water-logging, the incidence of pests and diseases is greater in the *kharif* season which is also characterised by cloudiness. Where irrigation is available—especially from private wells—water management would be more controlled for the *rabi* season which is endowed with abundant sunshine. In view of these factors, the incentive to invest in fertilisers would be greater in the *rabi* than in the *kharif* season.[3] Even in 1959-60, i.e., much before the High Yielding Varieties came to be used in India, the expenditure on fertilisers per acre was several times greater for the *rabi* paddy as compared to the *kharif* paddy.[4] This tendency persisted in 1969-70 when the High Yielding Varieties for paddy were used.[5] These environmental factors explain why the proportion of harvested area allocated to HYV paddy is much greater in *rabi* than in *kharif* (see Table 4.3).[6]

THE 'COMPLEMENTARITY' BETWEEN TRACTORS AND HIGH YIELDING VARIETIES

There is no technical complementarity between the use of tractors and High Yielding Varieties because each of them can be used independently of the other and there is no evidence to suggest that the combined productivity of these inputs is higher when used simultaneously, than the sum of their individual productivities when used separately. However, among the large farms, costs (per acre) of hired labour are higher than for the small family farms and the costs of management and supervision (per acre) would also be higher. Therefore, the large farms may find it more costly to ensure timeliness of ploughing operations with the biological sources of

[3]V.K.R.V. Rao noted the rising significance of *rabi* cultivation in Indian agriculture owing to its profitability as well as the relative certainty of yields, in his *Convocation Address to the University of Agricultural Sciences*, Bangalore, in November 1967.

[4]C.H. Hanumantha Rao, *Taxation of Agricultural Land in Andhra Pradesh,* Asia Publishing House, 1966, p. 51.

[5]Waheeduddin Khan and R.N. Tripathy, *Intensive Agriculture and Modern Inputs—Prospects of Small Farmers: A Study in West Godavari District*, National Institute of Community Development, Hyderabad, 1972, pp. 107-11.

[6]This is also borne out by a detailed study for several important paddy states made by P.K. Mukherjee and B. Lockwood. See, their, 'High Yielding Varieties Programme in India : Assessment' paper presented at the 28th International Congress of Orientalists, Canberra, 6-12 January 1971.

energy, especially when they plan to allocate larger area to the High Yielding Varieties. The use of tractors may enable them to allocate more area economically to the High Yielding Varieties. Beyond a point, therefore, a 'complementarity', in this sense, may emerge between the mechanical and BC techniques among the large farms.

This aspect is examined below, on the basis of some of the recent data collected by the Programme Evaluation Organization (PEO) of the Planning Commission,[7] as well as the Farm Management data for Ferozepur (Punjab). From the PEO data, it is possible to classify the farmers into two groups: those resorting to tractor-ploughing and those not using tractor services at all. The Ferozepur data, on the other hand, could be classified according to whether one owns a tractor or not. In the case of the PEO data, we have selected two states, namely, Punjab and Haryana from the north, and two states namely, Andhra Pradesh and Tamilnadu from the south. These states have been selected because in these areas the percentage of cultivators adopting tractor-ploughing is appreciably high.[8]

In Andhra Pradesh, tractor-using farmers allocated a much larger proportion of the total harvested area (20 per cent as against 6 per cent among the bullock farms) to HYV rice, whereas a reverse position obtained in Tamilnadu (33 per cent as against 46 per cent among the bullock farms). It is important to note that it was possible to allocate as much as 46 per cent of the gross cropped (harvested) area to HYV rice in Tamilnadu without the use of tractors. Tractor farms accounted for a much larger proportion of the total harvested area under HYV wheat (44 per cent in Punjab and 30 per cent in Haryana) than the bullock farms both in Punjab and Haryana. However, non-tractor (bullock) farms were able to allocate as much as 38 per cent of the cropped area to HYV wheat in Punjab and about 16 per cent in Haryana.

It does not follow, however, that the entire difference between the bullock and tractor farms in regard to the allocation of area to HYV should be attributable to tractorisation *per se*. Since the

[7]These data have been collected for their project 'Study of Financing of Capital and Current Inputs by Farmers adopting High Yielding Varieties (HYV) 1969-70' (unpublished).

[8]G. A. Sastry and P. K. Mukherjee, 'Tractor Farming and Employment of Hired Labour: A Case Study in HYVP Areas', in *Problems of Farm Mechanisation*, Seminar Series IX, The Indian Society of Agricultural Economics, 1972.

capacity to invest in fertilisers could be an important factor influencing the area under HYV and since the tractor farms can be expected to have a better resource position than the bullock farms owing, among other factors, to their larger holding size, tractor-use *per se* may account for part of the difference, with respect to the area under HYV, between tractor and bullock farms. Multiple regression analysis based on the PEO data indicates that apart from tractorisation, farm size and the proportion of area irrigated have a positive effect on the proportion of gross cropped area allocated to HYV (see Appendix B).

Since the investable capacity of farmers is an important factor influencing the rate of adoption of innovations, it would be difficult to disentangle this factor from the complementarity between modern inputs which, as discussed above, is expected to obtain among the large farms having a better command over resources. As is clear from Table 4.4 based on the Farm Management data for Ferozepur (Punjab), tractor-owning farms, in general, invest more (per acre) in tube-wells and threshers as compared to non-tractor farms. The investment in tube-wells per acre is about 50 per cent higher among the tractor farms and that in threshers is about 4 times as high as among non-tractor farms. The percentage of holding allocated to HYV is about 50 per cent among the tractor farms as against about 27 per cent among the non-tractor farms. However, the percentage of holding allocated to HYV among the largest non-tractor group is as high as 50 per cent. But such farmers may be hiring tractor services from tractor owners, the information on which is not available. The use of fertiliser per acre among tractor farms is twice as high as among non-tractor farms.

From the available data, it is not possible to determine the exact sequence of investments in different inputs. However, the hypothesis of 'complementarity' cannot be rejected whatever the sequence of investment: a decision to invest in a pump-set this year may involve the decision to invest in a tractor next year owing to the better ability to grow HYV and to the greater needs of managing intensive agriculture. Conversely, a decision to invest in a tractor now may facilitate an investment in pump-set subsequently owing to greater managerial ability.

SUMMARY

The factors inducing the adoption of BC innovations seem

TABLE 4.4: RATE OF ADOPTION OF MECHANICAL AND BC TECHNIQUES IN FEROZEPUR (PUNJAB) 1969-70

Operational Holding: Size Group (acres)	Expenses (Rs) on Tube-well (per acre)		Percentage of Farms Owning Threshers		Percentage of Cropped (harvested) Area Planted to HYV		Expenses (Rs) on Fertilisers per Harvested Acre	
	Non-tractor Farms	Tractor Farms	Non-tractor Farms	Tractor Farms	Non-tractor Farms	Tractor Farms	Non-tractor Farms	Tractor Farms
	(1)	(2)	(3)	(4)	(5)	(6)	(7)	(8)
10— 20	31.7	31.0	15.9	50.0	36.6	61.2	28.1	20.0
20— 30	14.2	61.8	14.8	50.0	27.7	52.0	30.2	46.9
30— 50	18.2	49.2	21.7	84.2	22.7	59.2	20.8	48.5
50— 75	5.2	8.4	28.6	33.3	10.4	36.7	13.9	28.8
75—100	28.1	14.8	—	60.0	49.7	45.7	81.0	70.2
Overall	20.2	30.9	16.5	65.7	26.8	49.9	25.3	50.4

Source: Directorate of Economics and Statistics, Ministry of Food and Agriculture, *Studies in Economics of Farm Management,* Ferozepur (Punjab), 1969-70.

to be broadly the same as those favouring farm mechanisation. The incentive to save on labour cost by the large farmers, especially in the high-wage areas and when the output prices and wages rise relative to the price of fertilisers, seems to be important in explaining the rapid adoption of BC techniques. This is supported by the fact that there is considerable scope among the large farms for a more intensive utilisation of the available land and water through multiple-cropping by applying more labour inputs. The investment in fertilisers and HYV is much greater in the *rabi* season, because of higher profitability as well as the relative yield certainty in this season.

Different types of mechanical and BC inputs are generally used together. This is because the factors affecting the adoption of these inputs are broadly the same. Also, there seems to be a 'complementarity' in the large farms, between the different mechanical inputs such as tractors and pump-sets as well as between mechanical inputs and HYV, in the sense that the use of tractors and pump-sets among large farms facilitates the expansion of output through the allocation of larger area to HYV. This 'complementarity' notwithstanding, non-tractor farms are able to allocate a substantial proportion of the cropped area to HYV.

CHAPTER 5

Investment in Farm Tractors in Punjab: Private versus Social Costs and Benefits*

OBJECTIVE AND SCOPE

Except in the case of a few large mechanised farms run by the Government, the decisions in regard to the bulk of investment in farm tractors in India are made by the farmers themselves. Presumably, therefore, the private benefits from such investments exceed the private costs. However, there could be a divergence between the private and the social benefits from these investments. An attempt is made in this chapter to evaluate, from the social point of view, the private investment decision in regard to the farm tractors by using the data pertaining to Ferozepur (Punjab) farms in the year 1968-69.

The comparison is, as it has to be, between the existing or *known* techniques. At present, these are bullock and tractor technologies. One may consider some other technique, which is intermediate, to be more appropriate to the Indian conditions but until such a technique becomes feasible and comes into shape, one has to limit oneself to the economic evaluation of the known techniques. Although the range of alternative techniques of doing the *same job*, e.g., ploughing and transportation, may be narrow, the range of alternatives for producing the same output may be wide. For instance, the cropping intensity and the yield per acre can be increased, either by using the tractor, or, by increasing the area under irrigation, or, by applying more fertilisers to the existing irrigated area,

*The author has benefited from the discussions on an earlier version of this chapter at the Institute of Economic Growth, Delhi, where he is working, and at the joint seminar convened by the Indian Statistical Institute, Planning Unit, Delhi, and the National Commission on Agriculture.

or, by simply redistributing the land from the large to the small farmers. However, among the farms under study, the percentage of area under irrigation as well as the levels of fertiliser-use are quite high. As such, given the prevailing structure of landownership, there may be some complementary relationship between the tractor on the one hand and irrigation, fertilisers and High Yielding Varieties on the other, in the sense that further expansion of output through the intensification of the latter inputs may not be profitable without the use of tractors for coping with the seasonal shortages of labour and for ensuring timeliness of operations.

The range of alternatives to tractorisation for increasing the output would, however, be wider from the social point of view if one looks beyond the irrigated and high-growth pockets, where tractorisation is being resorted to. For instance, public investments in irrigation in the hitherto dry regions could be an important source of output growth. This increase in the output could reduce the incentives for tractorisation in the former irrigated areas through its impact on the output prices. Indeed, as argued in Chapter 3, the high rate of tractorisation noticed, recently, in certain regions, may be attributable mainly to the steep rise in the prices of agricultural commodities which itself is traceable to the inadequate public investment in irrigation during the sixties. The present chapter is confined to the analysis of private versus social benefits and costs of tractor-use in the irrigated and high-growth pockets such as Ferozepur (Punjab).

In this exercise, we have taken into account mainly the direct benefits and costs of tractor-use. Indirect effects of tractorisation such as changes in employment and the consequential change in income distribution are also accounted for, to the extent that (shadow) pricing of labour below the market wage takes care of these objectives. This is because the results of a social benefit-cost analysis, which assigns a very low (shadow) price for labour, will be biased in favour of labour-intensive techniques. However, the changes in income distribution, in general, and in consumption and saving, etc., are left out in this analysis. It may be argued, that certain important indirect effects of tractorisation, such as changes in income distribution ought to be taken into account while calculating the benefit-cost ratio. For instance, any adverse change in the income distribution such as the increase in the share of the large farms and the developed regions should be regarded as a social cost and should be quantitatively accounted for. Similarly, the possible increase in conspicuous consumption by the rural rich should also be accounted for as a social cost. As against this, it can be argued that the increase in the share of the developed regions and the large farms would lead to a rise in the marketed surplus of foodgrains which can, in principle, be used through appropriate policy instruments, for creating non-farm employment through labour-intensive schemes, such as rural works and thus ensure optimum capital-intensity for the economy, as a whole. It can be argued further that the tendency for conspicuous consumption can be arrested by taxing the rural rich or by channelling additional incomes into productive investments in the farm as well as non-farm sectors. These arguments apart, there are intractable problems of quantifying such indirect benefits and costs. We, therefore, believe that whereas questions such as the above are relevant and judgements on them should influence the policy decisions, such value judgements cannot, and need not, be translated into quantitative magnitudes for the purposes of cost-benefit calculations of the type attempted in this chapter.

HYPOTHESIS

The large farmers have better access to capital resources on favourable terms, whereas the small farmers are short of capital resources and face very high interest rates. With regard to labour input, on the other hand, the small farmers are better placed, owing to the larger availability of family labour. The real cost of such labour may be much lower than the wage rate.

Since technological advances have, in general, a labour-saving bias in the sense that they tend to raise the capital-labour ratio, a reduction in costs would be proportionately greater for the large farmers, for whom capital is cheaper than labour. This is particularly so in the case of mechanical innovations which are characterised by a greater labour-saving bias. From the social point of view, however, the relative (social) prices of factors should favour less capital-intensive techniques in India, so that cost-reduction and profitability, in respect of labour-saving techniques, would be (proportionately) lower, than for the large private farms. Certain technological advances, especially of the mechanical type, which are essentially labour-saving in character, may not be profitable at all for the small farmers owing to the availability of cheap family labour.[1]

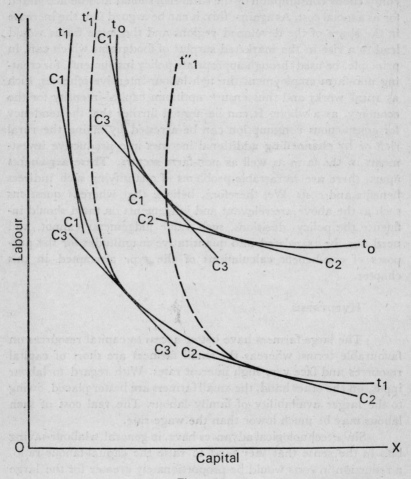

Figure 5.1

[1]Figure 5.1 illustrates how certain technological changes, whether of the mechanical or BC type, may bypass the small farmers and how even when the innovations can be adopted profitably by them, the cost reduction and profitability would be proportionately lower than for the large farmers. It also illustrates the lower social profitability, when compared to the private profitability for large farms. With technological changes, the isoquant is shown to shift from $t_0 t_0$ to $t_1 t_1$ between two periods indicating cost-saving for the same level of output. Isoquant $t_1 t_1$ represents a labour-saving bias, as a unit of capital substitutes for more units of labour than in the case of isoquant $t_0 t_0$. Given the relative prices of labour and capital for the small farmers represented by the isocost line $C_1 C_1$ it would

DATA AND METHOD

In this study, private (social) profitability of tractorisation is inferred from the ratio of change in the private (social) benefits to the change in private (social) costs, with the introduction of a tractor on a hitherto bullock-operated farm. If the amount of the output produced remains unchanged with tractorisation, then the change in benefits would consist of bullock and labour costs saved. If tractorisation enables an increase in the output (e.g., through changes in cropping intensity and yield per acre) which could not have been attained with the bullock technology at the relevant margin, then the changes in benefit would include the net output added apart from the bullock and labour costs saved.

We have taken the benefits of tractorisation to consist of the net output added and costs saved on human and bullock labour, as a result of the introduction of a tractor. Data on the inputs of bullock and human labour per acre relates to the 3-year period between 1954-55 and 1956-57 when the use of tractor power was negligible.[2]

be profitable for them to adopt the innovation unless the isoquant is represented by $t_1 t'_1$. For the large farmers, on the other hand, it would be profitable to use more capital and less labour as indicated by the points at which the isocost lines $C_2 C_2$ are tangent to the isoquants $t_0 t_0$ and $t_1 t_1$. However, from the social point of view, labour would be cheaper and capital costlier than for the large farms, though not to the same extent as for the small farms. This is indicated by the isocost line $C_3 C_3$. The reduction in cost (increase in profit) from the social point of view, as indicated by the distance between the parallel isocost lines, is proportionately lower than for the large farms. It is, however, possible that, from the social point of view, it may not be profitable at all to adopt certain innovations. This is indicated by the isoquant $t_1 t''_1$. Cost reduction and profitability would be the lowest (in proportionate terms) for the small farms, if they are not indeed by passed by the new technology.

[2]According to the Farm Management Report for Ferozepur, 18 bullock days were used per acre for crop production (excluding transport) during the 3-year period 1954-55 to 1956-57 (see the Combined Report p. 68). Since according to this Report (p. 35), the bullock days spent for transportation among large farms constitute about 20 per cent of total bullock days, the above figure has to be raised by 25 per cent for arriving at the total number of bullock days. About 25 per cent of total bullock days on account of threshing have to be deducted from this figure for arriving at the bullock days displaced by the tractor when productivity per acre is assumed to be constant. The number of human labour days displaced by the tractor has been worked out on the same basis as above by applying 2:1 ratio between bullock and human labour days. According to the latest Farm Management Reports for this district, the net cost of a bullock day was Rs. 5.80 in 1968-69 and the wage rate per day (plougher) in 1969-70 was Rs.6.34.

Since the agricultural output, as a whole, has nearly doubled during the corresponding period, due to the increase in cropped area as well as yield per acre, the present requirement of bullock and human labour inputs, for a farm, cannot be assumed to be the same as before. The requirements of these inputs increase, with the increase in output but less than proportionately. We have assumed two alternative magnitudes, i.e., 25 per cent and 50 per cent, with regard to the increase in the requirement for such inputs.

The costs consist of direct investment cost of a tractor and the additional annual operational costs. We have chosen an imported tractor, namely, International B 276 (U.K.), for our analysis. From the available information it appears that this tractor can be fully utilised on a 50-acre farm. We have done this exercise for a 50-acre farm as well as for a small farm of 10 acres assuming that tractor services would be available on a hire basis to the small farms. Thus, the capital and operational costs of tractor-use on a 10-acre farm are assumed to be one-fifth of those on a 50-acre farm. We have assumed a life of 10 years, for these tractors.

The flow of annual benefits and costs is assumed to be constant, for the entire 10 year period, although, in practice the annual increments in output can be expected to rise over a period of 3 to 5 years after the tractor is introduced and then taper off over the remaining period. However, the figure we have used on the output added is the average for the sample farms which differ with respect to the period of tractor-use. Since tractorisation is a relatively recent phenomenon, the farms in the initial stages of tractorisation are likely to predominate the sample, in which case our estimate of the added output would be on the lower side. Besides, the figure of the output added has been obtained by comparing the predominantly tractor-using farms with the predominantly bullock-operated farms of similar size and irrigation levels. That is, the tractor farms still use some bullock power and the bullock farms hire-in tractor services, to some extent. Such a comparison would underestimate the additions to the output as a result of tractorisation.

The tractor farms, in the sample studied, are found to save only about 50 per cent of bullock costs incurred on the bullock farms. It is possible that the displacement of bullocks would be lower in the initial stages of tractorisation, owing partly to the uncertainties of tractor-use such as a high probability of mechanical failures, the non-availability of spare parts and inadequate servicing facilities, etc., and partly to the time lags involved, in disposing of the bullocks, especially because they are a source of farm-yard manure. Since, the bullock costs incurred, at present, would be wholly saved when the adjustment is complete, we have assumed that the bullocks are displaced completely when a tractor is introduced. This means the entire cost incurred on the bullocks and bullock-associated human labour are assumed to be saved, when the tractor is introduced and that the tractor is used for all the operations performed by the bullocks except threshing. The bullock costs are taken net of the value of the farm-yard manure. This procedure takes into account the benefit (farm-yard manure) foregone, when the bullocks are displaced.

The annual net benefits are obtained by deducting the added annual costs on items, such as tractor repairs, tractor fuel, tractor driving, fertilisers, human labour and interest on working capital. The cost data for Ferozepur suggest that the labour costs among the large tractor farms constitute about 10 per cent of the gross output; fertilisers about 5 per cent and interest on working capital, another 5 per cent. We have, therefore, deducted 20 per cent of the gross output added on account of tractor-use, as added costs on the above items. To these net returns or benefits is added the scrap value of the tractor at the end of its life. The benefit-cost ratio B/C is computed as follows:

$$\left(\sum_{n=1}^{10} R \frac{1}{(1+r)^n} + \frac{S}{(1+r)^{10}} \right) \Big/ C$$

where R is the net return in the year n, S is the scrap value of the tractor after 10 years, r is the discount rate and C is the investment cost of the tractor. The rate of return on the investment in tractors is arrived at as the discount rate at the cut-off point, i.e., when the benefit-cost ratio is unity. The scrap value is taken to be Rs. 5,000.

PRICES

The individual farmer will be guided by the market prices of the output and the input, while making investment decisions. However, these prices need not necessarily serve as guidelines from the social point of view. A country is free to import agricultural commodities at the ruling international prices or to sell its agricultural surpluses in the international market and augment its foreign exchange. Therefore, the prices of the output and the inputs adjusted for the scarcity value of foreign exchange would be the appropriate prices to use for the benefit-cost analysis from the social point of view. It is immaterial, to this procedure, whether the prevailing international prices themselves are distorted, or, constitute true equilibrium prices. For a single country, the ruling international prices would be relevant, so long as foreign exchange is scarce. The shadow rate of exchange generally considered appropriate for India is Rs. 10 to a dollar, about 33 per cent higher than the official rate. We have taken this shadow rate of exchange, as the basis for the present exercise. In principle, one should arrive at the shadow price of foreign exchange through a programming model. However, the data problems are too immense, to permit a meaningful exercise for India at this stage.

The agricultural tractor is used for operations, such as, ploughing and transportation, which are common to all the crops grown. Therefore, while making a comparison between the domestic and the international prices, one should use the weighted prices of this commodity basket. Since our study relates to Ferozepur (Punjab), we have taken the product-mix pertaining to the sample farms as the basis for arriving at the weighted prices. The average domestic and international prices of these major commodities for the quinquennium 1966 to 1970 are given in Table 5.1. Although, the domestic price of wheat was higher by about 92 per cent, when compared to its international price, the weighted domestic price of four major commodities, e.g., wheat, cotton, rice and maize was higher by only about 36 per cent.[3] Thus, if we adjust the weighted international price for the scarcity value of foreign exchange, i.e., if we raise it by 33 per cent, then it would approximate to the ruling domestic prices of the output. In view of this, we consider the domestic prices of the output to be all right for the purposes of the present analysis. It is clear, however, that if the shadow rate of exchange used by us is considered unduly low, then our estimate of the benefit from tractor-use would be on the low side.

[3]Swadesh R. Bose and Edwin H. Clark II, in their analysis of the benefits of tractorisation in Pakistan, took into account the price of wheat alone, which was 100 per cent higher when compared to its international price. See their 'Some Basic Considerations on Agricultural Mechanisation in West Pakistan', *The Pakistan Development Review*, Vol IX, Autumn 1969, Number 3.

TABLE 5.1: Prices of Certain Agricultural Commodities in the Domestic and the International Markets

(U.S. cents per kilogram)

Crop	Weight	Domestic Price		International Price		% Difference between the International and the Domestic Price
		Name of the Market	Average Price (1966 to 1970)	Name of the Market	Average Price (1966 to 1970)	
(1)	(2)	(3)	(4)	(5)	(6)	(7)
Wheat	52.4	Moga	11.9	U.S.A. f.o.b. Gulf Ports	6.2	+92.0
Cotton	18.3	Bombay	58.2	U.S.A. (wholesale)	50.8	+14.6
Rice	23.3	Sambalpur	13.1	Bangkok (wholesale)	9.1	+44.0
Maize	6.0	Bahraich	9.9	Mexico City (wholesale)	7.5	+32.0
Weighted Average	100.00		20.5		15.1	+35.8

Note: The c.i.f. prices would be higher than the international prices quoted, so that the difference between the domestic and international prices would be lower than that stated in the table.

Sources: F.A.O. Production Year Book, 1970.

F.A.O. Monthly Bulletin of Agricultural Economics and Statistics.

We assume that the ratio of domestic prices to international prices will not show an upward trend over the next decade. For one thing, technical progress currently underway, in respect of the production of several foodgrains, e.g., wheat, rice, bajra and maize, is likely to make an appreciable impact in India, which may lead to a decline in their prices relative to other commodities. Second, as the economy advances, the non-food crops, in respect of which the difference between the domestic and the international price is relatively narrow, will progressively increase their weight in the commodity basket. Our analysis assumes, further, that the present price levels will continue over the next decade. In all probability, however, the prices will rise. But if the costs of the current inputs and the prices of tractors rise at the same rate as output prices, then the benefit-cost ratio would remain unchanged. On the other hand, if the costs lag behind output prices, as is very likely, then our benefit-cost ratio would understate the true value.

About 25 per cent of the bullock costs consist of maintenance expenses on human labour.[4] We have valued this component of bullock costs and other labour costs saved, as well as the added labour input at three alternative shadow prices of labour—25 per cent, 50 per cent and 75 per cent of its market cost. This procedure involves the assumption that the social opportunity cost of labour is neither so low as zero, nor as high as the market wage but is somewhere between the two. As for the remaining cost of the bullocks, consisting of their purchase and feed cost, we believe that their market value would be an appropriate measure of the social cost. This is because the prices of bullocks have been rising roughly in proportion to the prices of the agricultural commodities (Chapter 3). This is what one should expect, because, as mentioned earlier, crops and bullock feed compete for the same agricultural resources, such as land, water, labour, etc., and the maintenance of bullocks means, to a large extent, the sacrifice of crops grown for human consumption.[5]

Tractor fuel (high-speed diesel oil) is the major component of the annual added costs. The domestic market price of diesel oil (Rs. 742 per kilo litre) was about 214 per cent higher than its import price (Rs. 239 per kilo litre), the difference being attributable to the excise duty.[6] We have used the domestic market price for computing the private cost and have taken the social cost to be 50 per cent higher than the import price, as it takes into account the scarcity value of foreign exchange. In regard to fertilisers, the domestic market price can be regarded as reflecting the social cost as well, because the domestic price (Rs. 924 per ton) after import and

[4]A.S. Kahlon, S.S. Miglani and S.K. Mehta, *Studies in the Economics of Farm Management, Ferozepur District (Punjab)*, 1968-69, Directorate of Economics and Statistics, Ministry of Agriculture, p.62.

[5]An estimate of the social cost per bullock per annum in Pakistan (Rs. 550) does not reveal it to be very much different from the private cost Rs. 485). See Swadesh R. Bose and Edwin H. Clark II, 'The Cost of Draft Animal Power in West Pakistan', *The Pakistan Development Review*, Vol. X, Number 2, Summer 1970.

[6]See (i) Petroleum Information Service, *The Indian Petroleum Hand Book*, 1967-68 p. 176; and (ii) Petroleum Information Service, *A Petroleum Quarterly*, April-June 1971, p. 13.

the excise duties was about 49 per cent higher, compared to its import price (Rs. 620 per ton).[7]

The market cost of labour is taken to be the relevant cost for the large farm of 50 acres. Among the small farms of below 10 acres, family labour is used essentially for operations involving the use of bullocks, such as, ploughing, threshing and carting and a good part of the labour needed for operations such as weeding and harvesting has to be hired. For the latter operations, therefore, labour input of the small farms is valued on the basis of the relevant market wage. With regard to the family labour associated with the upkeep and the use of bullocks, the own cost is taken to be zero. However, as the level of income rises, some of these 'small' farmers may prefer to withdraw from hard manual work by hiring labour. As mentioned earlier, we have taken three alternative values, i.e., 25 per cent, 50 per cent and 75 per cent of market cost of labour for computing the social cost. The market wage, as well as the net cost of bullock labour per day, relate to the year 1968-69. Since these rates relate to the period when tractorisation made considerable headway, which must have had some downward impact on these rates, the true *ex ante* rates faced by the farmers could be higher. To this extent, therefore, the private costs saved on bullock and human labour are underestimated.

The prices of the imported tractors are now higher than those of the indigenous tractors, because of a 30 per cent customs duty on the c.i.f. plus 10 per cent excise duty on the landed cost. The import content of the indigenous tractors is subject to the same import duty, apart from a 10 per cent excise duty on the tractors. With these levies, the market price of the imported tractor—International B 276 (U.K.)—comes to around Rs. 25,270 (see Table 1 in Appendix C) which is about 25 per cent higher than the price of an indigenous tractor, say, Escorts 37 (about Rs. 20,000; see Chapter 3). We have taken the domestic market price of this imported tractor (which includes the customs and excise duties) plus the value of the complementary equipment as the investment cost from the private as well as from the social point of view.[8] This procedure is

[7]See (i) Fertiliser Association of India, *Fertiliser Statistics*, 1969-70, p. 184; and (ii) Government of India, *Monthly Statistics of Foreign Trade of India*, Vol. II-Imports, March 1970, p. 135.

[8]As Amartya Sen points out in his comments on an earlier version of this chapter (see, his *Employment, Technology and Development*, Oxford, London, 1975),

in line with the shadow rate of exchange adopted for the purpose of this exercise.

We have used two alternative rates of discount, i.e., 9 per cent and 12 per cent for arriving at the present value of the future stream of annual net benefits—private as well as social. As much as 88 per cent of the amount advanced to the farmers as tractor loans, by the institutional sources, was at 9 to 12 per cent interest rate in Ferozepur in 1968-69.[9] However, as mentioned in Chapter 3, such loans may account for only a small fraction of the purchase value of the tractors. The rates of interest at which the large farmers borrow in the free market seem to be around 12 per cent,[10] which can be taken to reflect the scarcity of capital. The very high rates of interest at which the small farmers borrow, usually for consumption, contain, apart from a monopoly element, a high risk premium as well as the cost of administration, which cannot be regarded as a social cost, especially when it is possible to provide tractor services by public agencies on a hire basis.

RESULTS

The additional net returns from the crop output, as a result of tractor-use, constitute 40 to 45 per cent of the added benefits in the case of large farms and over 70 per cent in the case of small farms (see Table 2 in Appendix C).[11] Tractor fuel constitutes the most important element in the added costs, whether from the private or from the social point of view. The divergence between the private and social returns derives from the difference in the valuation

if the appropriate social rate of discount is taken to be below the social contribution of investment, the shadow price of investment must be taken to be higher. But it is extremely difficult to find an 'appropriate' social rate of discount in an objective manner (see UNIDO, *Guidelines for Project Evaluation*, 1972, Ch. 13, Sec., 13.6-13.8) and to assess the reinvestment benefits in the absence of dynamic savings functions for the different sections of the project beneficiaries. However, the above omission may not be serious if the investment decision in regard to farm tractors is guided by the relative social benefit-cost ratios of alternative projects, e.g., irrigation, fertilisers, etc.

[9]Kahlon, Miglani and Mehta, op. cit., p. 70.

[10]C.H. Hanumantha Rao, 'Farm Size and Credit Policy', *Economic and Political Weekly*, Review of Agriculture, 26 December 1970.

[11]For the estimate regarding the contribution of tractor-use to the output see Part II, Ch. 9.

of the tractor fuel and human labour, the social costs on them being lower than the private costs (Tables 2 and 3 in Appendix C). However, whereas the lower social cost of labour reduces the social benefits of tractor-use, the lower social cost of tractor fuel has the effect of raising the net social benefits, so that the divergence between the private and social net benefits does not turn out to be significant, over a wide range of the shadow price of labour.

Thus, as can be expected, the social benefit-cost ratios are not significantly different from the private benefit-cost ratios (see Tables 5.2 and 5.3). The private benefit-cost ratio among the large farms exceeds unity at 12 per cent discount rate, even when the net output added as a result of tractor-use is ignored and bullock and human labour costs saved, alone, are considered. Of course, the benefit-cost ratios are higher still for those large farmers who drive the tractors themselves and save the cost on drivers. Since the market rate of interest at which the large farmers borrow could be around 12 per cent, the observed result indicates the remunerativeness of private investment in tractors.[12] In the case of the small farmers, using family labour, however, the comparable benefit-cost ratios are less than unity which suggests that tractor-use may not prove to be profitable to them. Even if tractorisation is assumed not to lead to an increase in the output (through an increase in the cropping intensity or the yield per acre) and if bullock and human labour costs saved constitute the only benefit from tractorisation, the investment in tractors will be profitable on the large farms from the social point of view.[13] The results suggest further that when the output added is taken into account, the (internal) rate of return or the discount rate at the cut-off point for the large farms would range between 30 to 38 per cent and the social rate of return would range between 25 to 36 per cent (see Tables 5.2 and 5.3).

[12]It is interesting to note, however, that the benefit-cost ratios would be significantly lower than unity for the large farms when the inputs of human and bullock labour are held at the level obtaining in 1954-57 and only the rise in their cost is taken into account.

[13]Swadesh R. Bose and Edwin H. Clark II, who in their analysis of the benefits of tractorisation in Pakistan assumed that tractorisation will not lead to an increase in the output either through cropping intensity or the yield per acre, came out with the conclusion that investment in tractors may be privately beneficial but not so from the social point of view. See, their, 'Some Basic Considerations on Agricultural Mechanisation in West Pakistan', op. cit.

TABLE 5.2: Investment in Farm Tractors: Private Benefit-Cost
Ratios and Rates of Return

Labour Coefficient:		Small Farm (10 acres)		Large Farm (50 acres)	
		25%	50%	25%	50%
		(1)	(2)	(3)	(4)
Net Return	Discount Rate	(a) Benefit-Cost Ratios			
A	9%	0.22	0.40	1.17 (1.31)	1.54 (1.69)
A	12%	0.18	0.34	1.02 (1.15)	1.35 (1.48)
B	9%	1.13	1.31	2.08 (2.23)	2.46 (2.60)
B	12%	0.98	1.14	1.83 (1.95)	2.15 (2.28)
		(b) Rates of Return			
A		Below 1%	Below 1%	12.50% (15.25%)	19.75% (22.25%)
B		11.50%	15.25%	29.50% (31.75%)	35.75% (38.00%)

Note: Benefit-Cost ratios in brackets exclude the wages of tractor driver. Net return A excludes the net output added as a result of tractor-use.

TABLE 5.3: Investment in Farm Tractors: Social Benefit-Cost Ratios and Rates of Return

(*Large farm of 50 acres*)

Labour Coefficient:		25%			50%		
Shadow Price of Labour (ratio to market wage):		.25	.50	.75	.25	.50	.75
Net Return	Discount Rate	(1)	(2)	(3)	(4)	(5)	(6)
		(a) Benefit-Cost Ratios					
A	9%	0.81	1.01	1.21	1.03	1.29	1.54
A	12%	0.70	0.88	1.06	0.90	1.12	1.35
B	9%	1.80	1.98	2.15	2.03	2.25	2.48
B	12%	1.58	1.73	1.89	1.78	1.98	2.17
		(b) Rates of Return					
A		4.75%	9.25%	13.50%	9.75%	14.75%	19.50%
B		24.50%	27.50%	30.50%	28.50%	32.25%	36.25%

TABLE 5.4: INVESTMENT IN FARM TRACTORS: SOCIAL BENEFIT-COST RATIOS
(with a five-fold increase in fuel cost)

Value in rupees per farm (large farm of 50 acres)

Labour Coefficient:		25%			50%	
Shadow Price of Labour (ratio to market wage)	0.25	0.50	0-75	0.25	0.50	0.75
Net Returns Discount Rate	(1)	(2)	(3)	(4)	(5)	(6)
A 9%	—	—	0.23	—	0.30	0.55
A 12%	—	—	0.19	—	0.26	0.48
B 9%	0.82	1.00	1.17	1.05	1.27	1.49
B 12%	0.71	0.87	1.02	0.92	1.11	1.30

The above exercise is based on the fuel prices prevailing before the recent rise of about five times in the international price of crude. However, so far, the domestic price of diesel has not been raised significantly, not even in proportion to the recent rise in the prices of agricultural commodities. Therefore, the private benefit-cost ratios with regard to the investment in tractors might now be even higher than those given in Table 5.2. However, when the five-fold rise in the international price of fuel is taken into account, the social benefit-cost ratios are reduced drastically to less than unity in most cases, and are very much lower than the private benefit-cost ratios (see Table 5.4).

SUMMARY

The incentive for tractorisation among the large farms arises owing to the increasing requirements of bullock and human labour with the rise in the scale of operations as well as to the rise in wages and the cost of bullocks. Investment in tractors is not profitable for the small farms using family labour. It would appear from this that if the large farms are split into small family farms, the demand for tractors may decline significantly. Thus, the private as well as the social profitability of tractor-use obtaining until recently, derives largely from the existing structure of land holdings. The private and the social profitability of investment in tractors did not diverge much, until recently. However, with the recent rise of about five times in the international price of the crude, investment in farm tractors appears to be socially unprofitable.

CHAPTER 6

Relative Costs of Traditional and Mechanical Methods of Harvesting and Threshing Wheat

OBJECTIVE

Traditionally, wheat is harvested by human labour and threshed with the use of bullocks as well as human labour. Mechanical threshing has become quite common, recently, in Punjab, Haryana and parts of Uttar Pradesh but harvesting is still done by human labour. The use of combine harvesters, which replace human and bullock labour for harvesting as well as threshing, is also spreading gradually. In this chapter, we shall compare the costs under three alternative techniques: (a) harvesting and threshing with human and bullock labour; (b) harvesting with human labour and threshing by mechanical thresher; and (c) harvesting as well as threshing by mechanical methods, i.e., by using harvest combines.

DATA AND METHOD

We are using the data contained in the Farm Management Studies relating to Punjab, for estimating the costs under traditional methods of harvesting and threshing. The data on the mechanical threshers were collected by us in the course of a visit to certain farms in the Meerut district (Uttar Pradesh). In the case of mechanised harvesting and threshing, we have used as an illustration the data pertaining to the E-512 (GDR) harvest combine run on custom-service basis by the Punjab Agro-Industries Corporation.

The costs of human and bullock labour for harvesting and threshing and winnowing have been worked out for large farms (above 25 acres) as well as for small farms (10 acres). Also, an estimate of the social cost on these items has been made by assuming three alternative measures regarding the social cost of human labour—75 per cent, 50 per cent and 25 per cent of the market (wage) cost. However, the last measure seems reasonable because a good part of the harvest labour in Punjab consists of seasonal migrants from the low-income pockets such as east Uttar Pradesh and Rajasthan, where the marginal productivity of such labour can be expected to be very low. Moreover, when harvest combines are introduced, there would be large-scale displacement of local labour too, which may have very few opportunities for alternative employment during the season.

For valuing human labour, we have used the wage rate for the harvesting operation prevailing in the year 1968-69 (Rs. 7.43), which represents a rise of 187 per cent over that in 1960-61.[1] For the small farmers we have taken the cost of family labour (used for harvesting and threshing) to be the same as that of hired labour. The small farmers can find employment at the going wage rates during these busy seasons (in the initial stages of mechanisation), so that when faced with an opportunity to hire the services of a combine harvester, they may value their own labour at par with hired labour. However, in this process of individual decision-making, they may collectively drive down the wage rate, in course of time, when these operations are mechanised on a large-scale. About one-third of the bullock costs among the small farms consists of the cost on the labour for the upkeep of bullocks. We have assumed the cost of such labour for the small farms to be 25 per cent of the market cost because family labour is used for this purpose during the slack period of the year also.

According to Farm Management Studies, the net cost per working day of a bullock increased from Rs. 1.80 in Ferozepur during 1954-55 to 1956-57 (see the Combined Report, p. 38) to Rs. 5.80 in 1968-69 (see the Report for the year 1968-69, p. 63). We have taken the social cost of bullock labour to be the same as the private cost except that the labour cost for their upkeep is valued at 25 per cent of the market cost. As explained in the previous chapter, the market cost of bullocks consisting of their purchase price and the feed cost would be an appropriate measure of the social cost.

The average yield per acre of Mexican wheat (irrigated) in

[1]Government of Punjab, *Statistical Abstract of Punjab*, 1969, p. 300.

TABLE 6.1: Cost of Mechanical Threshing for Wheat

(Rs. per acre)

	1. *Big Thresher* (Service Centre)
1. Capital Cost	Rs. 5,000
2. Working days in a year	45
3. Working hours per day	12
4. Number of quintals threshed per hour	6
5. Power (units) consumed per quintal	5
6. Service charges per quintal	5
Annual Costs:	
1. Depreciation	1,000 (20 per cent)
2. Repairs	1,000
3. Power	3,240 (Rs. 0.20 per unit)
4. Wages	750 (2 persons at the rate of Rs. 250 per month)
Total cost	5,990
Cost per quintal	1.85
Cost per Acre	22.20
	2. *Small Thresher* (Farm-owned)
1. Capital Cost	Rs. 1,200
2. Number of quintals threshed per hour	1
3. Power (units) consumed per quintal	5
Annual Costs:	
1. Depreciation	300 (25 per cent)
2. Power	100
Total Cost	400
Cost per quintal	4
Cost per Acre	48

the years 1967-68 and 1968-69 was about 100 per cent higher, when compared to the yield per acre of *desi* wheat (irrigated) in the period 1954-55 to 1956-57.[2] It has been found that when the yield per acre increases, the requirements of human labour increase but less than proportionately to the increase in the yield. As in the previous chapter, we have assumed two alternative magnitudes, i.e., 0.50 and 0.25 regarding the labour coefficient or the per cent increase in the hu-

[2]The yield increased from 5.5 quintals to 12 quintals per acre. See the Combined Report for 1954-55 to 1956-57, p. 79, and the Report for 1968-69, p. 13.

man and the bullock labour input associated with a one per cent increase in the yield per acre.

Table 6.1 gives the cost of mechanical threshing per acre, separately for the big thresher run on a custom-service basis and for the small thresher owned by the farmer. There are considerable economies of scale in mechanical threshing, the cost per acre in the case of a big thresher being less than half (Rs. 22) of that for a small thresher (Rs. 48). However, the service charge per acre in the case of big thresher is Rs. 60 (Rs. 5 per quintal), yielding a substantial profit. Since these benefits are not accruing to the farmers at present, we are taking the private cost of mechanical threshing to be equivalant to the service charge, i.e., Rs. 60 per acre. The social cost of mechanical threshing may not be higher than this service charge, as it is already more than twice the actual cost.

TABLE 6.2: Cost per acre (rs.) of a Harvest-Combine: E-512 (GDR)
(Average for 1970, 1971 and 1972)

1. *Capital Cost*	1,71,600	
(a) c.i.f. value	1,20,000	
(b) Import and excise duty	51,000	
2. Working days in a year	31.30	
3. Working hours per day	11.10	
4. Number of acres harvested per day	16.10	
5. Operational Cost (Fuel and operating charges)	10.50	(8.3)
6. Other variable costs	17.00	(13.5)
7. Depreciation (20%)	67.02	(53.2)
8. Interest (8.75%)	14.96	(11.9)
9. Insurance and taxes	4.73	(3.7)
10. Overhead charges	11.82	(9.4)
11. *Total Costs*	126.03	(100.0)
12. Rental Charge	100.00	

Note: The figures in brackets give the percentage of each item to total costs.
Sources: (a) Baldev Singh, 'A Note on the Cost of Tractor-Use and Combine Harvester-Use' (mimeo).
(b) The Planning Commission, Government of India.

The rental charge for a combine harvester was about Rs. 100 per acre in the year 1970-71. As against this, the cost per acre for the services of a harvest combine comes to about Rs. 126 (Table 6.2). This includes the import duty of 30 per cent and an excise duty of 10 per cent imposed recently. The fixed cost of a harvest combine constitutes over 75 per cent of its total cost. With the levy of the import and excise duties as above, the capital cost of a combine can be expected to be roughly the same from the private as well as the social point of view, if we assume the shadow price of foreign exchange to be about 40 per cent higher than the ruling exchange rate. Although, as discussed in the previous chapter, the social cost of fuel can be expected to be lower than the private cost owing to a very high excise duty (around 200 per cent) on the diesel oil, a correction on this account is unlikely to alter, significantly, the divergence between the private and social costs because the fuel cost constitutes less than 10 per cent of the total costs.

Results

Table 6.3, which gives the cost of harvesting, threshing and winnowing from three alternative techniques shows that over 70 per cent of the cost under the traditional method consists of labour input, so that the harvest combine—which displaces labour on a large scale—turns out to be the costliest from the social point of view. This conclusion would be reinforced if the recent rise in the international price of fuel is taken into account. The private cost of traditional methods ranges from Rs. 150 to Rs. 185 per acre. From the private point of view, mechanical threshing or even the use of combine harvester—the cost on which ranges from Rs. 106 to Rs. 126 per acre—would thus be less costly than the traditional methods. This would be so even if the rental charge of the combine harvester is raised to cover the actual cost, i.e., Rs. 126 per acre. Thus, the profitability of the mechanical methods, from the private point of view, derives from the predominance of labour costs for these operations, which itself derives, in part, from the high wage rates. Manual harvesting combined with mechanical threshing turns out to be the cheapest from the private as well as social point of view.

The above calculations do not take into account the uncertainties faced by the farmers regarding the timely availability of hired labour. Nor do they take into account the risk of damage to the harvested crop from rain, etc. It is, thus, possible that the *ex ante* costs of traditional methods are much higher, which may explain why the large farmers prefer to go in for harvest combines despite

TABLE 6.3: Cost per acre (rs.) of Harvesting, Threshing and Winnowing for Mexican Wheat in Punjab with the Traditional and Mechanised Techniques

	Private Costs		Social Costs		
	Above 25 Acres	10 Acres	Shadow Price of Labour (proportion to market cost)		
			75%	50%	25%
	(1)	(2)	(3)	(4)	(5)
Labour Coefficient =0.5					
1. *Traditional Method*					
Human labour					
(a) Harvesting	55.7	55.7	42.0	28.0	14.0
(b) Threshing and winnowing	78.0	78.0	58.3	38.9	19.4
Bullock labour (threshing)	52.2	47.0	47.0	47.0	47.0
Total	185.9	180.7	147.3	113.9	80.4
2. *Manual Harvesting-cum-Mechanical Threshing*	115.7	115.7	102.0	88.0	74.0
3. *Harvest Combine*	126.0	126.0	126.0	126.0	126.0
Labour Coefficient =0.25					
1. *Traditional Method*					
Human labour					
(a) Harvesting	46.7	46.7	35.0	23.3	11.7
(b) Threshing and winnowing	64.8	64.8	48.6	32.4	16.2
Bullock labour (threshing)	43.5	39.2	39.2	39.2	39.2
Total	155.0	150.7	122.8	94.9	67.1
2. *Manual Harvesting-cum-Mechanical Threshing*	106.7	106.7	95.0	83.3	71.7
3. *Harvest Combine*	126.0	126.0	126.0	126.0	126.0

the relative cheapness of manual harvesting-cum-mechanical thre-shing and despite the fact that the risk of damage to the harvested crop is considerably reduced when the mechanical thresher is used.

Mechanical methods of harvesting and threshing may turn out to be cheaper even for those farmers who have to maintain bullocks for ploughing and transportation, because even when the bullock costs are ignored, the traditional method works out to be costlier than the mechanical methods when the labour coefficient is 0.5. However, the decision to maintain or replace the bullocks is made not for each operation, in isolation, but by weighing the costs of alternative techniques for all the operations together.

SUMMARY

The use of a harvest combine turns out to be the costliest from the social point of view because of its labour-displacing potential, as the labour input accounts for over 70 per cent of the cost under the traditional method. From the private point of view, however, the use of a harvest combine is cheaper than the traditional method of harvesting and threshing. Manual harvesting combined with mechanical threshing is the cheapest from the private as well as social point of view.

CHAPTER 7

Changes in Costs and Returns with the Use of High Yielding Seeds

OBJECTIVE

This chapter examines the changes in the costs and the returns with the use of High Yielding Varieties (HYV) of seeds together with the package of practices, e.g., water, fertilisers, insecticides, etc. First, the changes in profitability and in the cost structure arising purely from the adoption of HYV, in place of local practices will be analysed. Second, the changes in the costs and returns since the mid-fifties will be examined. These changes are the combined result of the use of HYV, farm mechanisation and the changes in the prices of inputs and the output. Cost-reduction among the large farms when compared to all the farms as a group and the changes in the respective factor-proportions will be examined next. Finally, an attempt will be made to explain the slow rate of adoption of HYV in the case of rice when compared to wheat. The analysis of costs and returns is based on the Farm Management data relating to Ferozepur district (Punjab).

HYPOTHESIS

The High Yielding Varieties, typically, increase profit per unit of the output, i.e., they lead to a reduction in the unit costs of production including the rental value of land and the value of family labour. The demand for output and the supply of factors of production remaining unchanged, the factor demand would be altered in such a way that the unit costs (proportion of costs to output) are saved on land, fixed capital as well as labour, though not to the same proportionate extent in each case. The unit cost on fertilisers seems to rise generally, in the first instance.

Where the output per acre can be increased significantly, say doubled, with the adoption of land-augmenting technology such as HYV, land ceases to be a critical or a limiting factor to the same extent as before. Where land is already irrigated, the requirements of fixed capital such as bullocks or machinery per acre may increase only marginally. Whereas the requirement of human labour per acre may increase, especially for interculturing and harvesting, this rise would be less than proportionate to the increase in the output per acre. The greatest (proportionate) cost-saving should, therefore, be on land followed by fixed capital and labour. With farm mechanisation, however, saving on the labour costs could be greater than on land and fixed capital.

Since the HYV technology is much less labour-saving than farm mechanisation, the small farmers may find it profitable to adopt it.[1] Cost reduction for them may, however, be proportionately less than that for the large farmers, even when the capital-labour ratio resulting from the adoption of the new technique is lower, which may explain the slow rate of adoption of the BC techniques by the small farmers.

Similarly, regions, where labour is abundant and capital is scarce and costly, may lag behind in the adoption of innovations even of the BC type. The inter-crop differences in the adoption of innovations, such as between wheat and rice may, in part, be the result of such inter-regional differences in factor-endowments where there is regional specialisation in the production of crops. Within the same region, however, the inter-crop differences in the adoption of innovations should be explainable in terms of the relative shifts in the production functions as well as the factor-saving biases of the respective technologies. In a labour-abundant region, for example, a shift in the production function with a labour-use bias would make the technical advance more readily and widely acceptable than when the shift in the production function is biased towards the use of capital.

[1]Keith Griffin in his analysis (see his, *The Green Revolution: An Economic Analysis*, United Nations Research Institute for Social Development, Geneva, 1972) suggests that the Green Revolution technology may not be profitable at all to the small farmers because of their poor access to capital resources. However, the fact that small farmers are found to use HYV and fertilisers to some extent suggests that they are not entirely bypassed by the Green Revolution. Nevertheless, in Griffin's words the new technology may be 'landlord biased' insofar as the small farmers are unable to adopt it to the same proportionate extent as the large farmers.

TABLE 7.1: Unit Cost and Profit under Different Farm Technologies in Ferozepur (Punjab)

	1968-69 & 1969-70 Desi Wheat	Mexican Wheat	1969-70 Paddy (Local)	Paddy (IR-8)	Farm Business as a whole			
					All Farms		Large Farms (above 50 acres)	
					1954-55, 1955-56 & 1956-57	1968-69 & 1969-70	1954-55, 1955-56 & 1956-57	1968-69 & 1969-70
	(1)	(2)	(3)	(4)	(5)	(6)	(7)	(8)
Rupees per Acre								
Gross output	494	774	543	901	151.3	748	143	803
Total input	488	656	482	617	150.6	685	127	602
Current inputs (excluding land and fixed capital)	177	272	202	300	52.0	281	46	230
Profit	6	118	61	284	0.7	64	16	201
Unit Costs and Profit (Percentage to Gross Output)								
1. Land	35.5	27.8	29.6	17.0	34.8	29.4	34.5	29.5
2. Labour	23.7	20.8	27.2	20.6	26.9	24.7	24.8	15.1
3. Capital	39.6	36.2	31.9	30.8	37.8	37.4	29.5	30.4
(a) Fixed capital	27.5	21.8	21.9	18.1	30.1	24.6	22.1	16.9
(b) Fertilisers and manures	5.1	8.6	7.7	10.3	2.2	6.6	2.7	7.4
(c) Other working capital	7.0	5.8	2.3	2.4	5.5	6.2	4.7	6.1
4. Profit	1.2	15.2	11.3	31.6	0.5	8.5	11.2	25.0
5. Percentage of current inputs to total input	36.3	41.4	41.9	48.6	34.5	41.1	36.2	38.2

Sources: (1) Directorate of Economics and Statistics, Government of India, *Studies in Economics of Farm Management, Punjab, 1954-55 to 1956-57*.

(2) A.S. Khalon, S.S. Miglani and S.K. Mehta, *Studies in Economics of Farm Management, Ferozepur District (Punjab), 1968-69 and 1969-70*, Directorate of Economics and Statistics, Government of India.

HYV versus Local Varieties

Columns 1 to 4 of Table 7.1 give the unit costs and profit for the local and HYV practices in the case of wheat and rice.[2] There is a significant reduction in unit costs and a rise in the share of profit. HYV technology turns out to be cost-saving on all the three factors—land, labour and capital (fixed and variable)—though the greatest cost-saving is on land followed by labour. However, there is a significant reduction in the unit cost on fixed capital and a significant rise in the unit cost on fertilisers.[3] The greater decline in the labour costs compared to the capital costs indicates a rise in the overall capital-labour ratio, despite a decline in the ratio of fixed capital to labour. This rise in the capital-labour ratio is attributable essentially to the rise in the input of fertilisers.

Changes since the Mid-Fifties

Figures in columns 5 and 6 of Table 7.1 indicate the changes in unit costs and profit for the farm business, as a whole, between the mid-fifties and the recent period. These changes are the combined result of the use of HYV, farm mechanisation and the possible changes in the relative prices of the output and the inputs. The reduction in unit cost and increase in the profit for the farm business, as a whole, over this period, is less than that arising from the adoption of HYV *per se*. This is to be expected because technological changes like farm mechanisation were not as important in this period as HYV which, however, relate to a single, though major, crop in the farm economy, as a whole. The cost-saving on land is more than on labour, the saving on the capital cost being negligible. Again, the cost reduction in the case of fixed capital is significant, and is proportionately greater than that on labour. Thus, the rise in the capital-labour ratio over this period is due essentially to the rising importance of work-

[2]The Farm Management Reports for Punjab—pertaining to the mid-fifties as well as the late sixties—contain a detailed description of the methodology followed for estimating the costs of production.

[3]The marginal (and average) products of fertilisers are much higher in the case of old (local) wheat when compared to HYV because of the restricted use of fertilisers per acre for the former, as they are susceptible to lodging under high fertiliser applications. See Surjit S. Sidhu, 'Economics of Technical Change in Wheat Production in the Indian Punjab', *American Journal of Agricultural Economics*, Vol. 56, No. 2. May 1974.

ing capital. Farm mechanisation does not appear to have become a significant factor in raising the capital-labour ratio for the farm sector, as a whole.

LARGE VERSUS SMALL FARMS

In the case of the large farms (above 50 acres), there is a sharp decline in the unit cost on labour over this period and this reduction is proportionately greater than that on land and fixed capital (see columns 7 and 8 of Table 7.1). This may be attributed to mechanisation of large farms. Interestingly, however, even when the costs on labour and fixed capital (which includes farm machinery) are combined, the proportionate reduction in the unit costs on them is greater than on land. Also, this reduction is proportionately greater than the reduction in similar costs among farms, as a whole: the combined cost (labour and fixed capital) declined from 47 per cent of the output to 32 per cent in the case of the large farms as against 57 per cent to 49 per cent for farms, as a whole. This is understandable in view of our finding in Chapters 5 and 6 that farm mechanisation enables the large farms to effect significant cost reductions. The rise in the capital-labour ratio is greater among the large farms when compared to farms as a whole. Also, the reduction in total unit costs and the increase in profit is proportionately greater for them than for farms as a whole.

WHEAT VERSUS RICE

TECHNOLOGICAL FACTOR

The slow rate of adoption of HYV rice, relative to HYV wheat, is attributable to the environmental-technological factors as well as to the behaviour of the product prices.[4] We have seen above that the land-augmenting character of HYV is the main source of cost-reduction and an increase in profit: HYV contribute to a more intensive utilisation of the existing resources such as land, fixed capital and labour. It is now a well-established fact that HYV

[4]Some of the arguments in this section are adopted from the paper, 'Rice: Policies and Problems', by Dharm Narain prepared in collaboration with the author for the *Rice Policy Conference*, 9-14 May 1971, held at the International Rice Research Institute, Los Banos, Laguna, Philippines.

perform better in the *rabi* season (November-March) owing to environmental factors.[5] In view of greater consumer preference for the traditional rice varieties, if a price discount of 20 per cent is applied to the HYV rice, the latter ceases to be profitable when compared to the local varieties in the *kharif* season (June-October).[6] As such, wheat being a *rabi* crop scores over rice because the land-augmenting potential of HYV rice cannot be realised for the bulk of the resources now committed to rice production in the *kharif* season.

Thus, unlike wheat, the decision in the case of rice concerns not so much the allocation of the existing crop area and other inputs to new varieties as the expansion of resources including the planted area for the *rabi* crop itself. This requires additional investment in irrigation and draft power, apart from extra expenditure on current inputs, such as labour. The existing studies on the output response are concerned mainly with the profitability of HYV as compared to the local varieties, assuming that the basic resources such as land, water and draft power, etc., are given. However, what is relevant in the case of rice is not merely the relative profitability of allocating the given resources to HYV but also the rate of return on additional investment for expanding the *rabi* cultivation itself.

The rate of return on additional investment in irrigation and draft power does not seem to be as attractive in the case of rice as for wheat. Among cereals, the requirements of water per unit of output seem to be the lowest for wheat and highest for rice.[7] The return on investment in water, e.g., tubewells could, thus, be higher in the case of wheat. This may be an important factor responsible for the recent tubewell boom in certain wheat areas.

The predominance of *kharif* rice may persist for a long time in India. This is because rice, like many other foodgrains, is grown

[5]For an important contribution in this field see Randolph Barker and Mahar Mangahas, 'Environmental and Other Factors Influencing the Performance of New High Yielding Varieties of Wheat and Rice in Asia', *Policies, Planning and Management for Agricultural Development : Papers and Reports of the Fourteenth International Conference of Agricultural Economists* (Minsk, U.S.S.R. August-September 1970), Institute of Agrarian Affairs for International Association of Agricultural Economists, Oxford, 1971.

[6]Robert W. Herdt, 'Profitability of High Yielding Wheat and Rice', *Economic and Political Weekly*, Review of Agriculture, 27 December 1969.

[7]N.G. Dastane, 'New Concepts in Irrigation: Necessary Changes for New Strategy', *Economic and Political Weekly*, Review of Agriculture, 29 March 1969.

TABLE 7.2: AREA PLANTED TO PADDY IN THE WEST GODAVARI DISTRICT
(lakh acres)

	1968-69	1969-70	1970-71	1971-72
	(1)	(2)	(3)	(4)
Area under:				
Paddy in *kharif*	5.9	6.3	6.8	6.2
Total *kharif*	6.5	8.6	7.5	6.8
Paddy in *rabi*	1.9	2.7	2.7	2.1
Total *rabi*	2.6	2.8	3.8	3.1
Kharif paddy as a per cent of total *kharif* acreage	92.1	73.3	89.9	91.0
Rabi paddy as a per cent of total rabi acreage	72.9	96.4	72.4	67.9

Source : IADP Project Office, West Godavari District, *Plan of Action, 1972-73.*

by the farmers largely for self-consumption. Also, local rice is relatively more profitable than the competing crops in the *kharif* season. This accounts for the low sensitivity of the rice area to the changes in the relative prices of crops.[8] Thus, the HYV rice grown in the *rabi* season would be a supplementary crop for meeting the residual demand for rice. As such, the fortunes of the *kharif* crop would very much determine the allocation of resources to the HYV in the *rabi* season. For instance, a substantial output of the *kharif* rice because of either good weather or, the pre-*kharif* higher prices, can reduce the incentives for the allocation of resources to the HYV in the *rabi* season. This is borne out by the fact that in the West Godavari, the percentage of the *rabi* area allocated to rice is lower whenever the percentage of the *kharif* area allocated to rice is higher and vice versa (see Table 7.2).

From the technological angle, therefore, a major breakthrough in the rice output seems possible only if HYV capable of withstanding the vagaries of monsoon are evolved.[9] Alternatively, short-duration varieties for the monsoon season even if low-

[8]Dharm Narain, *Impact of Price Movement on Areas Under Selected Crops in India, 1900-1939*, Cambridge University Press, 1965, p. 109.

[9]W. David Hopper and Wayne H. Freeman take an optimistic view about such a possibility. See their, 'From Unsteady Infancy to Vigorous Adolescence: Rice Development', *Economic and Political Weekly*, Review of Agriculture, 29 March 1969.

yielding, can be helpful if the land released thus, can be used to grow two non-monsoon HYV crops in a year.

PRICE FACTOR

Although the technological gap in the case of the HYV rice is a major explanatory factor for the slow rate of its adoption, the price factor appears by no means unimportant because the use of fertilisers is concentrated among the irrigated pockets and the actual doses applied in such limited pockets may be fairly high, so that further application of fertilisers could be very much sensitive to the product-factor price relationship.

Table 7.3 shows that the index of the farm harvest prices of wheat in Punjab, with 1961-62 as base (=100), rose to 184.6 in 1970-71, whereas that of rice lagged behind in Andhra Pradesh (153.9) as well as Tamilnadu (165.3) over the corresponding period. The farm harvest prices of wheat in Punjab rose during this decade at the rate of 7.9 per cent per annum as against 5.2 per cent and 5.9 per cent in the case of rice in Andhra Pradesh and Tamilnadu respectively.[10] This favourable price situation in the case of wheat, despite a breakthrough in output, is attributable to (a) a favourable demand; (b) a domestic supply gap as evidenced by the sizeable imports prior to the breakthrough in the wheat output; and (c) the influence of the producers' interests on the price policy.

A relatively favourable demand for wheat is indicated by the fact that the expenditure elasticity, in the case of this cereal, is significantly higher than that for rice. The expenditure elasticities for wheat are estimated to be 1.48 and 0.68 for the rural and the urban areas, respectively, as against the corresponding elasticities of 0.54 and 0.13 in the case of rice.[11] The annual import of rice was well below 1 million tons during the 1960s whereas that of wheat was substantial before the mid-sixties and reached the highest figure of 7.8 million tons in 1966—the year when HYV wheat was introduced.[12] The import of wheat declined gradually in the subsequent

---

[10]The rate of rise has been obtained by fitting the equation $Y = ab^t$.

[11]N.S. Iyengar and L.R. Jain, 'Projection of Consumption, Rural/Urban, India: 1970-71 and 1975-76', *Economic and Political Weekly*, Review of Management, 29 November 1969.

[12]Directorate of Economics and Statistics, Ministry of Food and Agriculture, *Bulletin on Food Statistics*, Twenty-second issue, p. 96.

periods and was around 2 million tons in 1971. Thus, a good part of the domestic output of wheat in the late sixties replaced imports. This together with a significant build-up of buffer stocks contributed to the maintenance of the wheat prices at a higher level.

There is some evidence to suggest that the interests of the producers may have outweighed those of the consumers in the prosperous wheat areas in determining the procurement effort as well as the procurement prices. On the other hand, in the 'surplus' states in rice, there are chronic deficit pockets, so that the interests of the consumers seem to have predominated over those of the producers. The zonal restrictions on the movement of grain have been imposed from time to time with a view to facilitate public procurement. As a consequence, the prices within zones from where the movement of grain is restricted seem to have lagged behind the price prevailing elsewhere in the country. This lag is more pronounced in the case of rice in Andhra Pradesh and Tamilnadu, when compared to wheat in Punjab: The index of wholesale prices of wheat for the country, as a whole, with 1961-62 as the base (=100) rose to 209 in 1970-71 as against 184.6 in the case of the farm harvest prices of wheat in Punjab. Over the corresponding period, whereas the wholesale price index of rice in the country rose to 201, that of the farm harvest price rose to 153.9 in Andhra Pradesh and 165.3 in Tamilnadu (see Table 7.3).[13]

The procurement prices fixed by the state governments indicate that in the case of wheat in Punjab, the procurement price approximated to the free market (farm harvest) price during the recent period of the breakthrough in the wheat output (see Table 7.4), when the unit cost of production declined significantly. In the case of rice in Andhra Pradesh, on the other hand, the procurement price was significantly lower than the free market (harvest) price during this period.

[13]In terms of the growth rate, the wholesale harvest price lag in the case of wheat is 2.3 per cent (10.2−7.9) per annum, whereas in the case of rice, the lag amounts to 3.5 per cent (8.7−5.2) in Andhra Pradesh and 2.8 per cent (8.7−5.9) in Tamilnadu.

Despite this 'unfavourable' price situation, the agricultural performance in Tamilnadu has been better than in many other rice-growing states. This may be attributable to non-price factors, such as rural electrification, the credit institutions and the administrative efficiency in the implementation of the developmental programmes, etc.

TABLE 7.3: FARM HARVEST AND WHOLESALE PRICES OF WHEAT AND RICE

Year	Farm Harvest Prices						Wholesale Price Index: All India (Base: 1961-62=100)	
	Rice				Wheat			
	Andhra Pradesh		Tamilnadu		Punjab		Rice	Wheat
	Price in Rupees per Quintal	Index: Base 1961-62 =100	Price in Rupees per Quintal	Index: Base 1961-62 =100	Price in Rupees per Quintal	Index: Base 1961-62 =100		
	(1)	(2)	(3)	(4)	(5)	(6)	(7)	(8)
1960-61	58.1	93.7	54.1	94.9	40.7	97.8	102.8	98.9
1961-62	62.0	100.0	57.0	100.0	41.6	100.0	100.0	100.0
1962-63	60.2	97.1	52.1	91.6	42.3	101.7	105.0	98.0
1963-64	64.0	103.2	63.7	111.8	50.1	120.5	118.0	106.0
1964-65	64.0	103.0	65.5	115.0	56.9	136.7	127.0	138.0
1965-66	79.0	126.9	71.0	124.6	66.6	160.1	137.0	149.0
1966-67	87.4	140.9	77.9	136.8	80.5	193.3	169.0	178.0
1967-68	68.0	109.8	73.8*	129.5	78.9	189.5	200.0	214.0
1968-69	98.4	158.8	73.7	129.4	69.3	166.4	196.0	204.0
1969-70	83.3	134.3	96.3	168.9	77.0	185.0	196.0	215.0
1970-71	95.4	153.9	94.2	165.3	76.8	184.6	201.0	209.0

*Controlled Price.

Sources: For Wholesale Price Index Numbers: 1. *Reserve Bank of India Bulletin*, January 1970.

2. *Reserve Bank of India Bulletin*, September 1972.

For Rice (Andhra Pradesh):

1. *Statistical Abstract of Andhra Pradesh* (from 1962-63 to 1970-71).

2. *Agricultural Situation in India* (from 1960-61 to 1961-62).

For Wheat (Punjab) and Rice (Tamilnadu):

1. *Agricultural Situation in India*, August 1971.

2. *Season and Crop Report of Punjab*, 1965 (for 1960-61, 1961-62 and 1962-63).

For Farm Harvest Prices:

TABLE 7.4: PROCUREMENT AND FREE MARKET (HARVEST) PRICES
(Rs. per quintal)

Year	Rice (Andhra Pradesh)		Wheat (Punjab)	
	Free Market Price	Procurement Price (Akkulu)	Free Market Price	Procurement Price (Mexican)
	(1)	(2)	(3)	(4)
1967-68	68.0	72.7	78.9	74.5
1968-69	98.4	72.7	69.3	76.0
1969-70	83.3	72.7	77.0	76.0
1970-71	95.4	80.3	76.8	76.0
Average	86.3	74.6	75.5	75.6

Sources: 1. Government of India, Ministry of Food and Agriculture, *Reports of the Agricultural Prices Commission*: For Procurement Prices.
2. Table (7.3): For Farm Harvest (free market) Prices.

HYV typically raise the importance of the working capital towards the payment for the current inputs, such as fertilisers and labour. According to the figures in Table 7.1, the costs on the current inputs like fertilisers, labour, etc., constitute 41 per cent of the total costs for HYV wheat as against 36 per cent for the local wheat; in the case of HYV rice, such costs constitute 48.6 per cent of the total input as against 41.9 per cent for the local variety. Between the mid-fifties and the post-Green Revolution period, the current inputs increased from 34.5 per cent of the total costs to 41 per cent for the farm business as a whole. The increase appears much less in the case of the large farms, i.e., from 36.2 per cent to 38.2 per cent. However, in the case of the small family farms, a good part of the labour input partakes the character of a fixed input, which cannot be readily varied in response to the changes in prices. It is, therefore, probable that the variable current (cash) inputs are relatively more important in the case of the large farms. It is clear, however, that the current inputs are relatively more important in the case of rice, when compared to wheat and that their importance in the case of rice increases considerably more with the introduction of HYV.

The application of current cash inputs would be particularly sensitive to the changes in the product-factor price relationships.[14]

[14]For a thoughtful presentation of this problem see Michel CEPEDE, 'The Green Revolution and Employment', *International Labour Review*, Vol. 105, No.1, January 1972. CEPEDE expects an increase in the proportion of working capital (current cash inputs on fertilisers and labour, etc.) to output with the adoption of Green Revolution technology. However, as pointed out above, such an increase is improbable in the case of labour input.

As such, with the adoption of HYV, the price certainty assumes a greater importance for increasing the output and employment, especially for the large farms, as these have to hire labour. This would be more so in the case of rice. But rice seems to be unfavourably placed in this respect on two counts. In the first place, the price of rice is more sensitive to the changes in its output than in the case of wheat: the price flexibility coefficient, i.e., per cent change in the price as a result of a one per cent change in the output, is found to be as high as —1.10 in the case of rice, whereas it is —0.47 for wheat.[15] This is a consequence of the lower price elasticity of demand for rice as compared to wheat. In view of the greater sensitivity of the prices to output, the price incentive for the rice producers would be lower than for the wheat producers when the output expands. Also, the rice farmers would face greater price uncertainty.

Second, there is evidence to suggest that the response functions with respect to fertilisers for HYV wheat are steeper than for rice.[16] As such, a given change in the factor-product price ratio or a given price discount for uncertainty would lead to a greater change in the input and output in the case of rice than in the case

[15]R. Thamarajakshi, 'Determinants of Rice Prices', *Agricultural Situation in India*, March 1970; and 'The Determinants of Wheat Prices', *Agricultural Situation in India*, May 1970.

[16]Following are some of the response functions for HYV wheat and rice which indicate a steeper response curves for wheat than for rice:

1. Wheat (Sanora-64) : $Y=2068.20+49.07\ N-0.18\ N^2$
2. Rice (IR-8)   : $Y=5870.12+16.90\ N-0.05\ N^2$
3. Wheat (Sanora-64) : $Y=2232.00+33.78\ N-0.10\ N^2$
4. Rice (IR-8)   : $Y=3768.00+29.27\ N-0.06\ N^2$

Where Y=Output ; and N=Fertilisers

Equation 1 is based on the data obtained from the fertiliser experiments conducted at the U.P. Agricultural University, Pantnagar, for three years, 1965-67. Equation 2 is based on the experimental data at the same university for the year 1967-68. Equations 3 and 4 are based on the data of the All India Co-ordinated Rice Improvement Project representing the experiments conducted under irrigated conditions at several locations. *Sources*: (1) Equation 1: I.J.Singh and K.C. Sharma, *Production Functions and Economic Optima in Fertiliser use for some Dwarf and Tall Varieties of Wheat*, U.P. Agricultural University, Pantnagar, 1969. (2) Equation 2: I.J.Singh, T.K. Chaudhury and Dinkar Rao, 'Response of Some High Yielding Paddy Varieties to Nitrogen: An Economic Analysis', *The Indian Journal of Agricultural Economics*, Conference Number, October-December 1968. (3) Equations 3 and 4: Randolph Barker and Mahar Mangahas, op. cit.

of wheat.[17] Both these factors, namely, the relatively inelastic demand and elastic supply[18] in the case of rice suggest the greater impact of the price factor on its growth.

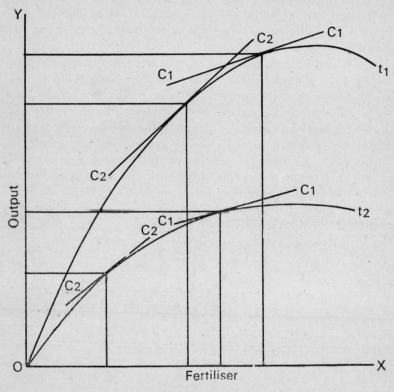

Figure 7.1

SUMMARY

HYV technology is cost-saving on land, labour and capital.

[17]In Figure 7.1 the total product curve t_1 is steeper than the total product curve t_2. Assuming that these curves relate to two different varieties of the same crop, and assuming further that the prices of these varieties are the same, the factor-product price ratios are represented by parallel lines $C_1\,C_1$ and $C_2\,C_2$. A change from $C_1\,C_1$ to $C_2\,C_2$ would lead to a greater reduction in input and output in the case of t_2 when compared to t_1.

[18]This response of yield to the changes in the fertiliser-output price ratio should be distinguished from the low acreage response for rice mentioned earlier.

The greatest cost-saving is on land followed by labour. However, the unit cost on fertiliser increases significantly leading to a rise in the overall capital-labour ratio.

In the case of the large farms, there has been a sharp decline in the unit cost on labour owing to mechanisation. The reduction in the total unit costs and increase in the profit is greater for them than for the farms, as a whole.

Wheat being a *rabi* crop scores over rice because the land-augmenting potential of HYV rice cannot be realised for the bulk of the resources now committed to rice production in the *kharif* season. The price of wheat has been rising at a faster rate than that of rice because of a favourable demand, the existence of a domestic supply gap reflected in the sizeable imports and the greater influence of the producer interests on the fixation of the procurement prices. Apart from the less favourable demand, the output response to fertiliser input is less steep in the case of HYV rice, as compared to HYV wheat. These factors result in greater price uncertainty as well as greater sensitivity of the output to given changes in the fertiliser-output price ratio, in the case of rice.

Part II

Distribution of Gains

CHAPTER 8

Regional Distribution of Gains

OBJECTIVE AND SCOPE

We shall examine in this chapter the inter-state variations in the distribution of (a) agricultural credit from cooperatives which constitute a predominant institutional source and whose importance in the overall supply of credit has been rising rapidly; (b) public and private irrigation; (c) fertilisers; and (d) the output of certain important foodgrains experiencing technological change namely, wheat, bajra, rice and maize, as well as foodgrains as a whole. The comparison is made between the pre-Green Revolution period and 1970-71—the latest post-Green Revolution year for which the relevant data are available.

In quite a few cases, the states constitute highly heterogeneous economic regions so that the inter-state variations in gains may not reflect the pattern of regional distribution within each state. It would be useful, therefore, if the analysis of regional variation in the distribution of gains could be conducted for each state by treating the district as a unit of observation, because a district is usually far more homogeneous than a state. Since such disaggregated data are not available for certain important components of input and output, especially for the post-Green Revolution period, our analysis had to be confined to inter-state variations only.

Despite these limitations, a study of inter-state variations in gains is of considerable significance for a large country like India, as the reduction in inter-state disparities in development is an accepted social objective. The state being a political unit, and agriculture being a state subject under the Indian Constitution, state governments play an important role in the acquisition and the allocation of resources for agriculture in the Federation, thus influencing, in an important way, the regional disparities in economic development. Besides, the inter-relationships between certain factors revealed by an analysis of inter-state disparities can be expected to hold good even at a more disaggregated level. Moreover, barring a few states which are highly heterogeneous, it is possible to classify the states broadly into two sub-types of agrarian social structure, one consisting of the former *zamindari* areas in eastern India and another consisting of the former *ryotwari* areas such as Punjab, Tamilnadu, etc. A comparative study of these two sub-structures is necessary because the former is not conducive to speedy growth, as it was characterised by the statutory type of landlordism in property structure and the dominance of the parasitic upper castes whereas the 'low caste' peasant proprietors who are thrifty, industrious and enterprising, constitute a dominant stratum in the latter.[1]

Hypothesis

An increase in regional disparities in the wake of technological change has been a common feature of agricultural growth in many parts of the world.[2] These disparities derive, partly, from the character of the technological change and, partly, from the regional differences in factor endowments, physical and institutional infrastructure, and entrepreneurship.

Innovations embodied in new or modern inputs have in general been capital-intensive, particularly because the developing countries have had to borrow wholly, or adapt with minor variations, technological changes suited to the factor endowments of the developed countries. Such innovations are likely to be adopted more readily by the prosperous or better-endowed regions. Besides, certain technological changes, such as High Yielding Varieties, are crop-bound and benefits from such innovations accrue mainly to the regions having comparative advantage in the production of crops concerned. The persistence of regional differences in factor earnings, despite inter-regional trade, may be attributed to the extreme

[1]P.C. Joshi, 'Agrarian Social Structure and Social Change', *Sankhya: The Indian Journal of Statistics*, Series B, Vol. 31, Parts 3 and 4, 1969.

[2]T.W. Schultz, *The Economic Organization of Agriculture*, McGraw-Hill, 1953, pp. 146-51; and K. N. Raj, 'Some Questions Concerning Growth, Transformation and Planning of Agriculture in the Developing Countries', *Agricultural Development in Developing Countries*: *Comparative Experience*, Indian Society of Agricultural Economics, Bombay, 1972.

disparities in factor endowments.[3] The prevailing regional differences in factor endowments, physical and institutional infrastructure and entrepreneurship are usually the outcome of the complex process of socio-economic development over a very long period.[4] These disparities cannot, therefore, be corrected in the short- run despite some inter-regional migration of labour and capital. There is, thus, an element of inevitability with regard to the increase in regional disparities in income in the initial phases of modernisation, although there would be considerable scope for reducing, if not eliminating altogether, these disparities in course of time through public policy.

DISTRIBUTION OF INSTITUTIONAL CREDIT

Table 8.1 gives figures of short-term loans in rupees per hectare and per capita advanced by the Primary Agricultural Credit Societies in 1960-61 and 1970-71. Short-term loans are far more important in quantitative terms than medium-term loans. In 1970-71, short-term loans advanced in the country amounted to 5,193 million rupees as against about 585 million rupees advanced as medium-term loans.[5] Some of the former *ryotwari* areas, for example, Tamil-

[3] P.A. Samuelson, 'International Trade and the Equalisation of Factor Prices', *The Economic Journal*, June 1948. This qualification introduced by Samuelson would gain strength if factor endowments are defined to include cultural factors such as those relating to entrepreneurial ability and human motivation for growth, etc. However, Gunnar Myrdal observes that trade theory—which asserts the tendency towards the equalisation of factor prices—has never been designed to explain the facts of growing economic inequalities as between regions. He tries to explain such inequalities in terms of 'Backwash Effects' of economic growth under *laissez-faire*, characterised by the migration of capital, labour and skills from the backward to the developed regions. See, his *Economic Theory and Underdeveloped Regions*, Duckworth, 1957, Chapters 3 and 11. A detailed examination of the Indian experience in the light of Myrdal's hypothesis would be rewarding.

[4] Joshi, op.cit. Punjab, for instance, belongs climatically to the arid and semi-arid zone but is endowed with human motivation and attitudes favourable for rapid economic growth. However, these qualities would have remained fruitless without massive public investments made in irrigation in this region between 1860 and 1947: Punjab alone accounted for nearly one-third and Punjab and United Provinces together accounted for half the total investments made in irrigation in India during this period. See, M. J. K. Thavaraj, 'Regional Imbalances and Public Investments in India, 1860-1947' (paper presented at the seminar on 'Regional Imbalances: Problems and Policies', Indian Institute of Public Administration, March 1972), *Social Scientist*, India, November 1972.

[5] Reserve Bank of India, *Statistical Statements Relating to the Cooperative Movement in India, 1970-71*, pp. 101-2.

TABLE 8.1: Short-term Loan in Rupees Per Hectare and per Capita (rural population) Advanced by Primary Agricultural Credit Societies

State	Per Hectare		Per Capita		Percentage Distribution of Total Amount Advanced		Net Output per Worker 1960-61 (in Rs.)	Agricultural Loans by Commercial Banks per Hectare	Percentage Distribution of Advances to Agriculture by Public Sector Banks as on 30 March 1973
	1960-61	1970-71	1960-61	1970-71	1960-61	1970-71			
	(1)	(2)	(3)	(4)	(5)	(6)	(7)	(8)	(9)
Andhra Pradesh	15.1	20.3	6.0	7.6	9.8	5.1	365	20.0	9.5
Bihar	1.2	10.4	0.3	2.3	0.7	2.2	302	3.6	2.3
Gujarat	23.1	81.8	14.8	43.4	12.4	16.1	578	29.6	10.0
Kerala	12.7	90.1	2.1	14.7	1.7	5.1	1159	33.2	3.4
Madhya Pradesh	8.5	22.6	5.6	13.2	8.4	8.9	360	3.7	2.9
Maharashtra	20.1	48.7	13.4	27.3	20.7	18.2	467	21.6	18.1
Karnataka	11.9	32.1	6.9	15.6	6.9	6.7	476	20.7	9.3
Orissa	2.4	9.3	0.9	3.9	0.8	1.5	488	1.0	0.4
Punjab & Haryana**	10.2	65.0	6.1	36.5	5.4	13.1	861	15.3	10.6
Rajasthan	3.9	10.9	3.3	7.3	3.0	3.0	343	5.4	2.7
Tamilnadu	25.9	59.6	7.7	14.9	10.4	8.2	530	32.7	12.7
Uttar Pradesh	14.2	21.1	4.8	6.4	16.9	9.3	479	7.6	13.1
West Bengal	5.0	7.7	1.2	1.6	1.7	1.0	824	11.2	3.4
Others	—	—	—	—	1.2	1.6	—	—	1.6
Total	63.4	75.3	76.4	84.4	100.0	100.0	—	—	100.0 (4289)*
Coefficient of Variation	—	—	—	—	—	—	—	—	—

* Million rupees   ** Including Chandigarh

Sources: (1) For data on loans advanced: Reserve Bank of India, *Statistical Statements relating to the Co-operative Movement in India, 1960-61 & 1970-71.*

(2) Net output figures are taken from *Agricultural Income by States*, Occasional Paper 7, by National Council of Applied Economic Research.

(3) For column 8: Tara Shukla, 'Regional Analysis of Institutional Finance for Agriculture', *Indian Journal of Agricultural Economics*, Conference Number, October-December, 1971.

(4) For column 9: *Reserve Bank of India Bulletin*, April 1974, pp.655-6.

nadu, Gujarat and Maharashtra, accounted for significantly larger amounts advanced both in per hectare and per capita terms in 1960-61 when compared to other states. These states maintained their predominant position accounting for about 43 per cent of total credit in both the periods, and for about 41 per cent of total advances from public sector banks in 1973 (see column 9 of Table 8.1). Punjab, Haryana, Kerala and Karnataka recorded sharp increases in the supply of institutional credit, their share in total credit rising from about 14 per cent in 1960-61 to about 25 per cent in 1970-71 (their share in the credit advanced by the public sector banks comes to 23 per cent). Eastern states, for example, Bihar, Orissa and West Bengal (former *zamindari* areas) which accounted for low levels of institutional credit in 1960-61 continue to lag behind the other states in respect of the supply of institutional credit. In 1960-61, they accounted for only about 3.2 per cent of total advances from credit societies and their share improved marginally to 4.7 per cent in 1970-71. These states accounted for only about 6 per cent of credit advanced by public sector banks.

The inter-state variation in the amount of short-term loan advanced increased between 1960-61 and 1970-71 in respect of per hectare as well as per capita loans, the variability in the latter being higher than that in the former in both the years. The correlation between net output per agricultural worker on the one hand and the amount of short-term loan per hectare as well as per capita (rural population) on the other, was not significant in 1960-61 (the correlation coefficients being 0.09 and −0.12 respectively). By 1970-71, however, the correlation of per hectare and per capita loans with net output per agricultural worker (as of 1960-61) improved (to 0.63 and 0.26 respectively), suggesting that cooperative credit tended to flow into the high income and 'credit worthy' regions which can be expected to account for larger funds from their own sources. Credit from the commercial banks revealed the same pattern, as there is high correlation ($r = 0.84$) between loans advanced per hectare by the cooperatives and commercial banks.[6]

[6]Rank Correlations (inter-state) between the average value of assets per household in a state on the one hand, and agricultural finance (aggregate) and finance from commercial banks on the other, were found to be 0.65 (significant at 1 per cent level) and 0.59 (significant at 5 per cent level) respectively. See, Tara Shukla, 'Regional Analysis of Institutional Finance for Agriculture', *Indian Journal of Agricultural Economics*, Conference Number, October-December 1971.

GROWTH OF IRRIGATION

For the country as a whole, the proportion of net sown area under irrigation increased from 18.3 per cent in 1961-62 to 21.8 per cent in 1969-70. That is, the annual addition to irrigation was below 0.5 per cent of the net sown area. The growth of irrigation from canals, which are predominantly a public source, was much slower over this period. It increased from 7.7 per cent of the net sown area to 8.8 per cent. On the other hand, irrigation from wells, which are predominantly private, increased at a faster rate, i.e., from 5.4 per cent of the net sown area to 8.0 per cent.

As Table 8.2 shows, the inter-state disparities (measured by the coefficient of variation) in the percentage of the net sown area irrigated (from all sources) are lower than that from individual sources indicating a significant compensatory influence of these individual sources.[7] The inter-state variability of irrigation from wells increased significantly during this period whereas that from canals declined so that the variability in total irrigation (from all sources) remained the same. In per capita terms, however, the variation in total irrigation (from all sources) showed an increase.

In states like Gujarat, Maharashtra, Madhya Pradesh and Karnataka where the percentage of the net sown area irrigated (from all sources) was significantly below the national average in 1961-62, the rate of increase was much higher than the national average. In Andhra Pradesh, Bihar, Tamilnadu and West Bengal where the percentage of area irrigated was above the national average, the rate of increase was smaller than the national average. However, Punjab, Haryana and Uttar Pradesh which were significantly above the national average in respect of irrigation, recorded much higher increases than the national average.[8] This is mainly due to the steep increase in irrigation from private wells in these states.

DISTRIBUTION OF FERTILISERS

Consumption of fertilisers per hectare in the southern rice

[7]The correlation coefficient (r) between the percentage of area irrigated by canals and wells, though positive (0.15 and 0.27 in 1961-62 and 1969-70 respectively), is not significantly different from zero at 10 per cent level.

[8]These states which accounted for as much as 45 per cent of irrigated area from wells in the country in 1961-62, improved their share in well irrigation to 52 per cent in 1969-70.

TABLE 8.2: PERCENTAGE OF NET SOWN AREA IRRIGATED: SOURCE-WISE

State	Canals			Wells			Total: All Sources		
	1961-62	1969-70	Per cent Change in Area	1961-62	1969-70	Per cent Change in Area	1961-62	1969-70	Per cent Change in Area
	(1)	(2)	(3)	(4)	(5)	(6)	(7)	(8)	(9)
Andhra Pradesh	11.2	12.9	17.6	3.6	4.4	24.8	26.8	27.7	5.3
Bihar	6.7	9.7	45.2	3.9	5.8	50.0	23.6	27.2	17.3
Gujarat	1.1	2.0	86.3	6.2	9.6	55.3	7.9	12.0	53.3
Kerala	7.6	9.4	39.6	0.1	0.2	147.0	17.0	19.5	29.2
Madhya Pradesh	2.8	3.6	46.6	2.0	2.8	57.8	5.8	7.8	51.6
Maharashtra	1.3	1.7	29.1	3.4	4.5	34.4	6.0	7.8	32.3
Karnataka	2.6	3.9	50.8	1.5	2.5	68.8	9.0	11.2	24.4
Orissa	3.9	3.9	4.4	0.7	0.7	5.2	16.8	16.9	5.1
Punjab and Haryana	29.2	29.8	2.7	13.0	25.9	100.3	42.6	56.0	32.2
Rajasthan	4.2	5.8	29.6	7.1	8.3	11.2	13.3	15.7	12.9
Tamilnadu	15.4	14.9	-2.0	9.9	11.4	16.3	41.6	41.3	0.2
Uttar Pradesh	11.0	13.9	27.3	13.4	21.7	63.7	28.1	39.0	40.4
West Bengal	14.2	16.9	21.0	0.3	0.3	1.4	24.6	26.5	9.4
Others	24.3	13.5	-19.5	1.4	2.1	114.5	30.2	26.1	24.9
All-India	7.7	8.8	18.2	5.4	8.0	51.7	18.3	21.8	22.5
Coefficient of variation in percentage of area irrigated	88.1	77.0	—	88.9	102.8	—	59.1	59.1	—
Coefficient of variation in per capita (rural population) area irrigated	107.6	95.6	—	91.4	104.6	—	62.4	68.5	—

Note: Population (rural) figures for 1971 are used for arriving at per capita area irrigated in 1969-70.

Sources: (1) Directorate of Economics and Statistics, Ministry of Food and Agriculture, Government of India, *Indian Agricultural Statistics, 1962-63*, Vol. I.

(2) Directorate of Economics and Statistics, Ministry of Food and Agriculture, Government of India, *Indian Agriculture in Brief.*

growing states, e.g., Andhra Pradesh, Tamilnadu and Kerala was signficantly higher than the all-India average in the pre-Green Revolution period, i.e., in 1964-65. Their per hectare consumption continued to be higher than the all-India average in 1971-72, that for Tamilnadu still being the highest in the country (see Table 8.3). But the rate of increase in these states was lower than the average for the country. Many states which were below the national average in respect of per hectare consumption, for example, Bihar, Orissa, Rajasthan and Uttar Pradesh, recorded growth higher than the national average. Consequently, the inter-state disparity in the level of fertiliser-use per hectare declined, as is indicated by the reduction in the coefficient of variation. However, there was a significant increase

TABLE 8.3: CONSUMPTION OF FERTILISERS $(N+P_2O_5+K_2O)$: STATE-WISE

State	Per Hectare in kgs.		Per cent Charge	Per cent Distribution	
	1964-65	1971-72		1964-65	1971-72
	(1)	(2)	(3)	(4)	(5)
Andhra Pradesh	8.2	22.6	174.2	14.8	11.3
Bihar	2.1	9.8	361.8	3.2	4.1
Gujarat	4.7	17.9	283.5	6.7	7.0
Kerala	10.1	22.3	119.8	3.5	2.5
Madhya Pradesh	1.7	5.8	245.2	4.5	4.5
Maharashtra	4.4	12.4	184.9	11.8	9.2
Karnataka	4.7	15.5	226.6	7.2	6.4
Orissa	1.4	6.0	319.0	1.5	1.9
Punjab and Haryana	6.3	35.6	466.3	9.0	14.2
Rajasthan	0.7	5.0	601.4	1.5	2.7
Tamilnadu	15.4	48.3	214.0	15.5	13.2
Uttar Pradesh	2.5	20.9	725.7	7.9	18.3
West Bengal	5.9	13.5	130.2	5.5	3.6
Others				7.4	1.1
All-India	4.5	16.0	257.7	100.0 (711)	100.0 (2621)
Coefficient of variation in per hectare consumption	75.5	66.1			
Coefficient of variation in per capita (rural) consumption	61.7	70.7			

Note: Figures in brackets represent total consumption of fertilisers in thousand metric tons.

Source: The Fertiliser Association of India, *Fertiliser Statistics, 1964-65* and *1971-72.*

in variation as regards the use of fertilisers in per capita terms. Punjab, Haryana and Uttar Pradesh which improved their share in irrigation through investment in wells were the only states which improved their share in the consumption of fertilisers substantially from about 17 per cent of all-India consumption in 1964-65 to 32 per cent in 1971-72.

DISTRIBUTION OF GAINS IN OUTPUT

We shall examine first the regional gains in the output of crops in respect of which High Yielding Varieties have made some impact, for example, wheat, rice, bajra and maize. Table 8.4 gives coefficients of variation in area, output and productivity per acre for these four crops between 1964-65—a peak year prior to the Green Revolution—and the latest peak year, i.e., 1970-71. Since, weather-wise, both 1964-65 and 1970-71 were normal years, a comparison between these two years may yield a dependable picture as to the distribution of gains in output.

TABLE 8.4: COEFFICIENTS OF VARIATION (INTER-STATE) IN AREA, OUTPUT AND PRODUTIVITY (PER ACRE) OF MAJOR FOODGRAINS

Crops	Area		Output		Productivity	
	1964-65	*1970-71*	*1964-65*	*1970-71*	*1964-65*	*1970-71*
	(1)	(2)	(3)	(4)	(5)	(6)
Rice	71.2	70.1	67.1	62.6	23.4	28.5
Wheat	126.1	128.0	143.3	143.0	53.6	66.5
Bajra	139.8	136.6	107.0	123.8	61.3	41.9
Maize	110.2	110.5	103.7	104.9	37.6	55.1

Source: (For data on Area, Production and Productivity), Directorate of Economics and Statistics, Ministry of Food and Agriculture, Government of India, *Estimates of Area and Production of Principal Crops in India, 1964-65, and 1971-72.*

The coefficient of variation (inter-state) with regard to production was the lowest in the case of rice and highest for wheat in both the years. The inter-state variation in productivity per acre increased in the case of rice, wheat and maize. Despite this, it is significant that variability in output remained the same in the case of wheat and showed some decline in respect of rice. This can be attributed to the compensatory movements in area, as output is a function of both area and yield. In the case of bajra, however, a significant decline in variability in respect of productivity has been associated with a significant increase in variability of its output. On the whole, it would appear that the Green Revolution has led to an increase in variability in respect of productivity per acre of major crops but not to an increase in variability as regards their output owing to the compensatory movements in area.

The changes in the variability of output in respect of individual crops affected by the Green Revolution do not give a picture of inter-state variability with regard to the output of crops as a whole. For one thing, since the inter-state variability in respect of wheat and bajra is much higher than for other crops, a breakthrough in their output could lead to an increase in the variability of output of crops as a whole, even if there is some decline in variability in respect of these individual crops experiencing a breakthrough. Second, there may be some compensatory movements among the

TABLE 8.5: OUTPUT OF TOTAL FOODGRAINS

State	Percentages to All India		Per Capita Output in kgs.*		Per cent Change
	1964-65	1970-71	1964-65	1970-71	
	(1)	(2)	(3)	(4)	(5)
Andhra Pradesh	8.3	6.4	188.7	158.3	—16.1
Bihar	8.4	7.5	148.7	144.5	— 2.8
Gujarat	3.2	4.1	128.0	165.0	28.9
Kerala	1.3	1.2	62.3	60.6	— 2.7
Madhya Pradesh	11.5	10.0	290.0	259.2	—10.6
Maharashtra	7.6	5.2	156.4	110.9	—29.1
Karnataka	5.4	5.5	188.2	203.5	8.1
Orissa	5.5	4.8	258.5	234.7	—9.2
Punjab, Haryana and Chandigarh	7.5	10.9	304.6	493.0	61.9
Rajasthan	5.9	8.2	241.5	342.0	41.6
Tamilnadu	6.4	6.5	155.0	170.5	10.0
Uttar Pradesh	17.1	18.1	189.9	220.5	16.1
West Bengal	7.0	6.9	164.4	167.4	1.8
Others	4.9	4.7			
All-India	100.0 (89.4)**	100.0 (107.8)**	186.6	196.7	5.4
Coefficient of variation	50.5	53.6	34.2	50.3	

*Total population (of each state) is used for arriving at per capita output.
**Million tons.
Source: Directorate of Economics and Statistics, Ministry of Food and Agriculture, Government of India, *Bulletin on Food Statistics.*

crops, in the sense that a rise in the output of certain crops could be at the expense of certain other crops so that the variability in the total output could decline despite an increase in variability in the case of individual crops. It is, therefore, necessary to examine the inter-state variability in the output of foodgrains as a whole between 1964-65 and 1970-71 in order to know the net impact of the Green Revolution on the regional distribution of gains in the foodgrains sector.[9]

Table 8.5 shows that inter-state variation in the output of foodgrains as a whole increased somewhat during the period, the coefficients of variation being 50.5 and 53.6. Punjab, Haryana and Rajasthan improved their share significantly in the foodgrain output of the country, whereas Andhra Pradesh and Maharashtra experienced a significant decline in their share. However, a better measure of the distribution of gains is the change in the inter-state variation in the output of foodgrains in per capita terms. The co-efficient of variation (inter-state)in the output of foodgrains per head (of total population) increased significantly from 34.2 in 1964-65 to 50.3 in 1970-71.[10] Several states where per capita foodgrain out-put in 1964-65 was either below or slightly above the all-India aver-age, for example, Andhra Pradesh, Bihar, Kerala, Tamilnadu, Maha-rashtra and West Bengal, recorded either a decline or much slower rate of rise in 1970-71. Although Orissa and Madhya Pradesh with per capita foodgrain output above the national average in 1964-65 showed some decline, states like Punjab, Haryana, Rajasthan and Uttar Pradesh with per capita output significantly above the national average in 1964-65, registered sharp increases in per capita output in 1970-71. This experience suggests that the expecta-tion regarding the growth of output through the widespread use of

[9]Owing to the non-availability of some of the relevant data, the analysis cannot be extended to agricultural commodities as a whole.

[10]V.S. Vyas in his study 'Regional Imbalances in Foodgrain Production in the Last Decade: Some Preliminary Results', (*Economic and Political Weekly*, Review of Agriculture, 29 December 1973) finds that the coefficient of variation in the production of foodgrains per hectare in the triennium 1969-71 was not signi-ficantly different from that in the triennium 1959-61. However, the coefficient of variation in per capita terms (computed by us on the basis of the figures of per capita production of foodgrains given in his study) shows a significant increase from 34.3 in 1959-61 to 49.0 in 1969-71. When Punjab and Haryana are exclud-ed, the coefficient of variation shows a slight decline from 32.0 to 30.0 indicating that the observed increase in regional variation is on account of the technological breakthrough in the output of foodgrains in these two states.

new inputs either in the favourable rainfall areas or in areas served with assured irrigation in the initial period[11] is not likely to material-ise because, crop-specificity of new technology, investable surplus, growth of controlled irrigation such as from wells, and the nature of institutional framework, etc., are important factors in growth.

The coefficients of variation (inter-state) in per capita inputs and output before and after the Green Revolution given in Tables 8.1 to 8.5 are reproduced below:

Credit	76.4	84.4
Irrigation (canals)	107.6	95.6
Irrigation (wells)	91.4	104.6
Fertilisers	61.7	70.7
Foodgrains	34.2	50.3

Among the inputs, well-irrigation and fertilisers show the lar-gest increase in inter-state variability. This may be explained by the importance of private investment in these cases as well as the crop-specificity of HYV technology. The relatively smaller increase in variability in the case of institutional credit and the significant de-cline in variability with regard to public (canal) irrigation is under-standable in view of the greater influence of public policy in such cases. It is significant that the inter-state variability in per capita output of foodgrains increased at a much higher rate than the variability in inputs. This may be explained mainly by the steep increase in the productivity of investment in areas experiencing technolgical change.

MIGRATION OF LABOUR

Both the 1961 and 1971 Censuses reveal rural to rural migra-tion to be the most important in India for females as well as males.[12]

[11]On the basis of this expectation, B. Sen predicted that some of the hitherto lagging states might become leading states in respect of agricultural growth and that there may not be any marked increase in inter-state inequalities in respect of agricultural income. See his 'Regional Dispersion of Agricultural Income: Implications of the New Technology', *Economic and Political Weekly*, Review of Agriculture, 27 December 1969.

[12]A. Chatterjee, 'Some Aspects of Internal Migration and Urbanization in India', *Population in India's Development, 1947-2000*, edited by Ashish Bose, P.B. Desai, Asok Mitra and J.N. Sharma, Indian Association for Study of Popu-lation, Vikas Publishing House, 1974.

In the absence of such migration, regional disparities in per capita output as well as differences in wages could have been greater,[13] because in the case of unskilled male labour,[14] a large majority of migrants might be moving from low income areas to the prosperous regions[15] and capital and skills might be moving from developed to the low income regions. It is possible, however, that part of the rise in per capita agricultural output in Punjab and Haryana is attributable to out-migration induced by the prosperity resulting from technological change in these regions: Punjab and Haryana are much above other states in respect of the proportion of outmigrants to the total population. This proportion rose steeply from 6.5 per cent in 1961 to 9.4 per cent in 1972.[16]

Since enumeration under the Census is confined to a few weeks, it does not capture fully the number of seasonal inmigrants within a year. To this extent, therefore, the estimates of per capita agricultural output presented above give an exaggerated picture of regional disparities, especially because Punjab absorbs a large number of labourers from eastern Uttar Pradesh and Rajasthan for seasonal operations such as harvesting when wage rates are high.[17]

SUMMARY

Inter-state disparities in regard to the supply of institutional credit per hectare and the percentage of net sown area irrigated

[13]Using the data for Punjab and Haryana pertaining to the late sixties, S.V. Sethuraman estimates that every 10 per cent increase in potential labour force is likely to result in a reduction of 4 to 7 per cent in the agricultural wage rate. See his 'Mechanization, Real Wage, and Technological Change in Indian Agriculture', paper presented at the *International Association of Agricultural Economists Conference*, Sao Paulo, Brazil, 20-30 August 1973.

[14]Migration on account of marriage constitutes a major component among female migrants.

[15]According to S.S. Johl, labour from eastern Uttar Pradesh employed in Punjab as permanent farm labour on an annual basis constitutes 5 per cent of total farm labour. See, his *Gains of Green Revolution (How they have been shared in Punjab)*, Punjab Agricultural University, Ludhiana.

[16]Chatterjee, op. cit.

[17]Johl, op. cit. Failure to take account of migrant labour for harvesting could yield unrealistic estimates of labour shortage. For instance, a recent study (*Demand for Harvest Combines*, NCAER, October 1972) estimates the shortage of harvest labour in Punjab and Haryana in 1970-71 to range between 10 to 15 per cent of the requirement and suggests that the minimum number of combines to fill this gap would be 3,072 as against the then existing stock of about 600.

from private sources such as wells have increased. However, the inter-state variation with regard to the proportion of area irrigated by public sources such as canals declined so that the variability in respect of total irrigation remained the same. The inter-state disparity in the consumption of fertilisers per hectare declined to some extent. In per capita terms, however, inter-state variability in respect of fertilisers increased.

Although, inter-state disparity in productivity per hectare of major food crops experiencing technological change increased, the variability in output of major crops did not increase owing to the compensatory changes in area allocated to these crops. Inter-state variation in the per capita output of foodgrains as a whole increased because crops like wheat and bajra which experienced a breakthrough in output showed higher variability than other crops. However, these disparities in per capita output might be exaggerated somewhat because the Census does not fully capture the number of seasonally migrant labour and Punjab accounts for a large number of inmigrant labourers for harvesting operations.

CHAPTER 9

Impact of Technological Change on Farm Employment*

OBJECTIVE

The objective of this chapter is to find out the absolute as well as the relative impact of tube-well irrigation, HYV, tractorisation and harvest combines on employment when these techniques are regarded as independent and when the complementary relation-ship between them is taken into account. Employment is measured as man-hours per annum and is studied at the farm level. That is, the indirect employment generated at the level of marketing and distribution of additional output as well as the employment genera-ted in the process of manufacturing, distribution and servicing of tractors, fertilisers, etc., are not considered.

Since irrigation as well as the area under the HYV can be expanded up to a point without the use of tractors, particularly among the small farms and the labour-abundant regions, these techniques can be regarded as alternatives for the expansion of em-ployment opportunities. It would, therefore, be interesting to know the relative employment potential or the units of labour required for producing an extra unit of output (labour coefficient) with each of these techniques.

HYPOTHESIS

No one seriously doubts that the Green Revolution or the use of High Yielding Varieties (HYV) *as such* results in a substantial

*An earlier version of this chapter was discussed at a seminar convened by the National Commission on Agriculture and at a staff seminar in the Institute of Economic Growth.

increase in output and employment in agriculture. What is not equally clear is the impact of farm mechanisation—particularly tractorisation—on output and employment. Since tractor power is employed for ploughing, threshing and transportation, etc.,—jobs hitherto performed by human and bullock labour—there would be some displacement of human labour along with bullock labour. However, it has been contended that the use of farm tractors would facilitate multiple cropping (cropping intensity) by ensuring timely operations, as well as raise yield per planted acre owing to the better quality of tractor-ploughing.

Some of the techniques such as tube-well irrigation and HYV may not be adopted beyond a point among large farms unless they can use tractors for overcoming the diseconomies of large size associated with labour-intensive techniques.[1] If such complementarity

[1]S.S. Johl holds a similar view: 'The tractor input goes in package with other inputs, serving essentially as an enabling factor, without which other inputs would not be used at that high level.' See his 'Mechanisation, Labour-Use and Productivity in Agriculture', (mimeo), Department of Agricultural Economics and Rural Sociology, The Ohio State University.

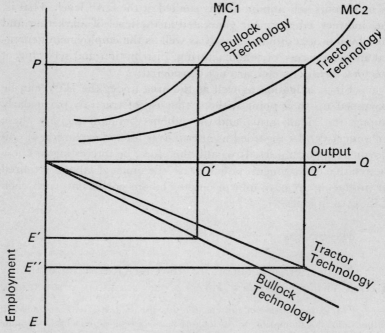

Figure 9.1

exists in reality,[2] then it would be more meaningful to consider the joint effect of such modern inputs on output and employment. Complementarity in this context does not mean either technical complementarity such as the one existing between human and bullock labour nor does it imply that the joint effect of these inputs is greater than the sum of the individual effects of inputs taken separately. Complementarity or the joint use of certain modern inputs along with tractor implies that owing to the diseconomies of large size, it may not be profitable to bring the extra land under tube-well irrigation and HYV without the use of tractors, or the use of tractors becomes more profitable owing to the possibility of bringing additional area under tube-well irrigation and HYV.[3]

Farmers with a better resource position may be able to exploit this complementarity by investing in tractors as well as tube-wells and in the extra inputs for HYV. However, a better resource position *as such* cannot explain this combination of investment which would not be undertaken unless it is profitable. Moreover, investment in current inputs like fertilisers among large farms need not be constrained by resource position in the same way as investment in a lumpy equipment like a tractor, and yet, if tractor farms are found to allocate more area to HYV than bullock farms of similar size and irrigation levels, this could be explained largely by the complementarity between these inputs.

Whereas the impact of tractor-use, in the first instance, is the technological displacement of part of the existing labour, some new employment could be generated for interculturing, harvesting, etc.,

[2]Figure 9.1 illustrates how output and employment could increase with tractorisation owing to the improved economies of large size. With tractorisation the cost function is shown to shift rightwards. As a result, the increase in output would be Q' Q'' and increase in employment would be E' E''. Even through labour input per unit of output would be lower under tractor technology when compared to bullock technology, the expansion in output is such as to yield higher employment. (The diagram implies a constancy in unit cost of labour but the argument need not be modified if unit cost of labour is assumed to vary with output).

[3]This hypothesis is strengthened by the fact that the investment in tractors would not have been profitable if human and bullock labour input per acre were to remain at the levels existing in the mid-fifties under traditional technology and that tractor-use has become profitable owing to the rise in the scale of operations among large holdings consequent on the widespread use of High Yielding Varieties. See, Ch. 5.

through its secondary effects. The latter effects could be significant in regions experiencing technological change in the developing countries, as there is a growing demand for agricultural commodities and hence an incentive for farmers to expand agricultural output in such regions. Thus, the impact of tractorisation on farm employment in such regions depends upon the extent to which its labour-substituting effect is compensated by its land-augmenting effect.[4]

DATA

The study is based upon two sets of data, one collected in the course of a study in the Economics of Farm Management in Ferozepur (Punjab)[5]—the seat of Green Revolution and mechanisation—for the years 1968-69 and 1969-70 and the other collected by the Programme Evaluation Organisation (PEO) of the Planning Commission for Punjab, Haryana, Andhra Pradesh and Tamilnadu for the year 1969-70.[6]

The Ferozepur (Farm Management) data pertains to 150 farms—10 each from 15 villages. Regarding tractorisation, we do not have the data on the input of tractor power (e.g., tractor hours) per farm. However, we have information on the ownership of tractors. We have classified the farms owning tractors (about one-fifth) as tractor farms and the remaining as non-tractor farms. However, many of these bullock or non-tractor farms may be using some tractor power by hiring tractor services from tractor owners. Similarly, tractor farms are found to own a few bullocks in order to supplement tractor power and presumably also to provide against contingencies arising from mechanical failures. The comparison, therefore, is not between the tractor and non-tractor farms but is rather between the predominantly bullock and predominantly tractor-using

[4]While analysing the impact of tractorisation on employment, some scholars have restricted themselves to the impact of tractor-use *per se* ignoring the impact of inputs which would not have been used without tractorisation. See, for instance, Raj Krishna, 'Measurement of the Direct and Indirect Employment Effects of Agricultural Growth with Technical Change', in *Externalities in the Transformation of Agriculture*, Iowa State University, Ames, Iowa, U.S.A.

[5]A.S. Kahlon, S.S. Miglani and S.K. Mehta, *Studies in the Economics of Farm Management*, Ferozepur District (Punjab), 1968-69 and 1969-70, Directorate of Economics and Statistics, Ministry of Agriculture, New Delhi.

[6]Programme Evaluation Organization, Planning Commission, 'Study of Financing of Capital and Current Inputs by Farmers Adopting High Yielding Varieties (HYV) 1969-70', (unpublished).

farms. Such a comparison will underestimate somewhat the impact of tractorisation on cropping intensity and output per acre. For example, if cropping intensity or multiple cropping increases with tractorisation, the observed cropping intensity among the non-tractor farms would be somewhat higher than would have been the case if they did not hire tractor services at all. On the other hand, the observed cropping intensity among tractor-owning farms would be lower than would be the case if they could completely dispense with bullocks. However, the element of overestimation among bullock farms does not seem to be significant because some studies for Haryana and Punjab show that only about 5 to 10 per cent of tractor power was hired out by tractor-owners to bullock farms.[7]

From the PEO data, it is possible to classify the farmers into two groups: those resorting to tractor-ploughing and those not using tractor services at all. The data on actual input of tractor power (e.g., standard tractor hours) is not available from the PEO study. Nor is it possible to know the extent of the area ploughed by tractors and the area ploughed by bullocks among the tractor-using farms. The tractor-using farms include, apart from tractor-owners, those hiring tractor services. Since many of these tractor-using farmers might be using bullock power also, our analysis will reveal the employment effects when tractorisation of farm operations is partial or incomplete.

We have selected two states namely, Punjab and Haryana from the north and two states, namely, Andhra Pradesh and Tamilnadu from the south. These states have been selected because in these areas the percentage of cultivators adopting tractor-ploughing is very high. For instance, according to another PEO study on the High Yielding Varieties programme during 1968-69, the percentage of participants resorting to tractor-ploughing was 44 in Punjab and 39 in Andhra Pradesh in the *kharif* season as against about 10 per cent in Uttar Pradesh and Kerala. In the *rabi* season such farmers accounted for 58 per cent in Andhra Pradesh, 34 per cent in Haryana and 22 per cent in Punjab, whereas they formed not more than 15 per cent in the states of Kerala, Rajasthan and Uttar

---

[7]R.K. Sharma, 'Economics of Tractor versus Bullock Cultivation (A Pilot-study of Haryana)' (mimeo), Agricultural Economics Research Centre, University of Delhi, 1972; and Baldev Singh, 'A Note on the Cost of Tractor-Use and Combine-Harvester-Use' (mimeo), Institute of Economic Growth, 1973.

Pradesh.[8]

SEPARATE IMPACT OF INDIVIDUAL TECHNIQUES

Since our purpose is to know cropping intensity, yield per cropped acre, output and employment associated with each of the techniques taken singly such as irrigation, quality of irrigation represented by tube-wells, tractorisation, HYV and fertilisers, the results have been obtained by using multiple regresion analysis. The results based on the Ferozepur data for 1968-69 and 1969-70 are given in Tables 2 and 3 in Appendix D. These can be summarised in the following manner.

Tube-well irrigation is the most important factor explaining cropping intensity. The High Yielding Varieties turn out to be the next important factor. Tractorisation by itself does not seem to be significant in explaining cropping intensity. Also, irrigation (all sources) is not significant in explaining cropping intensity, which should not be surprising because 80-90 per cent of operated area among sample farms is already irrigated so that further expansion of irrigation at this level may not be as important as the quality of irrigation (e.g., tube-wells) in influencing cropping intensity.

HYV is the most important factor explaining yield per planted acre. The impact of tractorisation on yield per planted acre seems to have been positive for the year 1968-69 but not so for 1969-70. The impact of tube-wells on yield per planted acre appears to have been negative in both the years. This does not mean that tube-well water reduces yield. The quantitative aspect of tube-well irrigation namely, the supply of water, is already reflected in the irrigation variable, the impact of which is positive. The negative effect of tube-wells does imply, however, that the impact of tube-well irrigation on yield per cropped (planted) acre would be smaller than that of irrigation in general. This may be attributed to the fact that cropping intensity is higher under tube-well irrigation and yield per cropped (planted) acre in this situation could be lower than when the same piece of land is cropped less number of times in a year.

Apart from operated area and HYV, tube-wells have a positive effect on farm employment. This is understandable in view of

[8]G.A. Sastry and P.K. Mukherjee 'Tractor Farming and Employment of Hired Labour: A Case Study in HYVP areas', *Problems of Farm Mechanisation*, Seminar Series IX, The Indian Society of Agricultural Economics, 1972.

the importance of tube-wells, observed earlier, in accounting for the variation in cropping intensity. Tractorisation is the only variable the impact of which is not significant in both the years.[9] It would appear that even if complementary effects are ignored, the technological displacement of labour consequent on the use of tractor is roughly compensated by the rise in employment as a result of the increase in yield associated with tractor-use. That is, if complementarity is ignored, labour coefficient or the employment generated for producing a unit of additional output is zero in the case of tractor technology.

The labour coefficient estimated for various techniques in 1968-69 suggests that the addition to operated area has the highest employment potential (0.33 hours of labour per rupee of output produced) followed by HYV (0.24 hours) and irrigation (0.19 hours). Tube-wells would rank above irrigation for reasons mentioned earlier and tractors would rank the lowest. Labour coefficient expressed as the ratio of employment elasticity to output elasticity is highest in the case of operated area (0.83) followed by HYV (0.60) and irrigation (0.48).

IMPACT WHEN TRACTORISATION IS COMPLETE

We have examined above the impact of tractor-use on output and employment by comparing bullock and tractor farms when tractorisation is partial on tractor-owning farms and when bullock farms also use some tractor power. As noted earlier, such a procedure cannot reveal the full impact of tractor-use, i.e., the impact when tractorisation is complete. It would, therefore, be interesting to know the increase in output required, as a result of tractorisation, if the technological displacement of labour is to be compensated by new employment generated. The tractor displaces human and bullock labour mainly for ploughing and transportation. In the mid-fifties, when tractor-use was not popular in Ferozepur, tillage operations accounted for about 19 per cent of total human labour-days used on the farm (excluding transport) in a year (see Table 9.1). With the

[9]Using the same data for 1968-69 and employing the analysis of variance and covariance, Prem Vashishtha has shown that tractorisation by itself does not increase cropping intensity, output and employment per acre. See his 'An Econometric Study of the Effect of Tractorization on Farm Output and Employment', (mimeo), Institute of Economic Growth, Delhi.

introduction of High Yielding Varieties, the requirements of human and bullock labour per cropped acre would increase, especially for transportation. It would, therefore, be reasonable to assume that tractorisation would displace between 20 to 30 per cent of total human labour-days per cropped acre on account of tillage and transportation.[10]

If the proportion of labour thus displaced is denoted as L, then the proportion actually employed would be $1—L$ and the required rate of increase in employment for compensating this decline

TABLE 9.1: OPERATION-WISE EMPLOYMENT OF HUMAN AND
BULLOCK LABOUR PER ACRE

Operation	Desi (local) Wheat (irrigated) : Ferozepur (1954-55)				Mexican Wheat: Ferozepur (1968-69)			
	Human Labour Days	Per cent to Total	Bullock Labour Days	Per cent to Total	Human Labour Days	Per cent to Total	Bullock Labour Days*	Per cent to Total
	(1)	(2)	(3)	(4)	(5)	(6)	(7)	(8)
Preparatory tillage	5.7	19.0	10.9	40.5	4.9	19.5	7.12	67.4
Sowing and bunding	1.6	5.3	2.4	8.9	1.1	4.4	1.94	18.2
Manuring	1.1	3.7	1.1	4.1	0.5	1.7	0.08	1.1
Interculture	2.3	7.7	—	—	2.4	9.5	0.24	1.9
Irrigation	3.8	12.7	3.7	13.8	5.0	19.7	0.16	1.6
Harvesting	6.1	20.3	0.5	1.9	5.3	21.0	—	—
Threshing and winnowing	9.4	31.3	8.3	30.8	5.3	21.0	0.56	5.6
Others	—	—	—	—	0.8	3.2	0.40	4.2
Total	30.0	100.0	26.9	100.0	25.3	100.0	10.50	100.0

Sources : Government of India, Directorate of Economics and Statistics, Ministry of Food and Agriculture: (a) *Studies in the Economics of Farm Management* in Punjab, 1954-55, pp. 88-9; (b) *Studies in the Economics of Farm Management*, (Punjab), 1968-69, pp. 122-4.

*Bullock labour *pair days* given in the Report have been converted into bullock labour *days* (1 pair day=2 days).

[10]An analysis of some studies on this subject shows that in India, tractorisation resulted in a reduction in the labour requirement within the range of 12-27 per cent of man-days per hectare. See Montague Yudelman, Gavan Butler, and Ranadev Banerji, *Technological Change in Agriculture and Employment in Developing Countries*, OECD, Paris, 1971, p. 100.

would be $L/(1—L)$. Thus, if the technical displacement of labour with the introduction of a tractor is 20 per cent, then the required rate of rise in employment to offset this displacement is $0.20/(1—0.20)$ or 25 per cent. Alternatively, if the technical displacement of labour is 30 per cent, then the required rate of rise in employment would be about 43 per cent. If we assume a labour coefficient of 0.75, i.e., a 1 per cent increase in output would be associated with 0.75 per cent rise in employment, then output would have to rise by about 33 per cent $(0.25/0.75)$ and 57 per cent $(0.43/0.75)$ respectively. The increase in output would have to be higher if the labour coefficient assumed above is on the high side. Thus, if complementarity between tractor-use and other inputs is ignored and the effect of a tractor *per se* is considered, then it is unlikely that the increase in output as a result of tractorisation through increase in cropping intensity and yield per cropped acre would be such as to compensate for the technological displacement of labour.

However, whereas the net employment effect of tractorisation *per se* is likely to be negative, the net land-augmenting or output effect would be positive. This is because even if we ignore the impact of tractor-use on cropping intensity and yield per cropped acre, there would be a saving on bullock cost leading to the diversion of some agricultural resources for producing output for human consumption instead of animal feed. Table 9.1 shows that in Ferozepur whereas human labour input per acre for wheat declined from 30 man-days in 1954-55 to 25 man-days in 1968-69 or by about 17 per cent, the bullock labour input declined from 27 bullock-days to 10.5 bullock-days or by about 61 per cent, the decline being mainly in threshing operation in the case of human as well as bullock labour.

IMPACT OF MECHANICAL THRESHERS AND
HARVEST COMBINES

Harvest combines displace human labour employed for harvesting and threshing and winnowing. According to Table 9.1, about 20 per cent of total labour-days per acre for wheat were used for harvesting and another 31 per cent for threshing and winnowing in 1954-55. However, where mechanical threshing is already in vogue—and it is now widespread in Punjab, which according to figures in Table 9.1, seems to have displaced about 13 per cent of labour used per acre in 1954-55—harvest combines would displace labour essentially for harvesting, apart from displacing some labour for threshing and winnowing because harvest combines are more capital-intensive than mechanical threshers. Therefore, it would be reasonable to assume that when harvest combines are used in place of mechanical threshers, at least another 25 per cent of labour employed under traditional techniques would be displaced. If a harvest combine is used on farms already using tractors and mechanical threshers—as is most likely to be the case—then the amount of labour displaced as a proportion to that actually employed would be much greater. If a tractor displaces 20 per cent of labour, a mechanical thresher another 15 per cent and a harvest combine at least 25 per cent in addition to that displaced by mechanical threshers, then the proportion of labour displaced by harvest combines on farms already using tractors and mechanical threshers would be about 40 per cent [(25)/(100-20-15)].

The rise in employment on the farm needed to compensate for this decline would be 0.40/(1—0.40) or 66.6 per cent. If we assume a labour coefficient of 0.5 (which may well be on the high side), then the rise in output needed to absorb the required labour would be about 133 per cent (66.6/0.5) on farms already using tractors and mechanical threshers. Unlike the tractor, which displaces human as well as bullock labour, a harvest combine displaces human labour only, as bullock labour for threshing would have already been displaced by mechanical threshers. In this case, therefore, there would be no land-augmenting effect either on account of saving on bullock-cost or rise in yield per cropped acre. There may, of course, be some saving of output on account of greater efficiency (including timeliness) of harvesting and threshing. It is highly unlikely, therefore, that the use of harvest combines on farms already using tractors and mechanical threshers would enable a rise in output of over 133 per cent through the rise in cropping intensity consequent on the use of harvest combine. Harvest combines would thus result in a net displacement of labour on a large scale.

Since wage rates for harvest labour are much higher than the rates for the rest of operations, harvest labour may account for more than 40 per cent of the total wage-bill on farms already using tractors and mechanical threshers. In Punjab, Haryana and west Uttar Pradesh, harvesting is done at present mainly by unskilled labour which is known to migrate on a significant scale from the overpopulated and depressed regions like east Uttar Pradesh and

Rajasthan. Mechanised harvesting would thus hit the rural labour, particulary those migrating from the depressed regions by significantly reducing their employment and income.

IMPACT OF COMPLEMENTARY INPUTS

The combined impact of the extra investment in tube-wells, HYV and fertilisers (on tractor farms in comparison to bullock farms of similar size and irrigation levels) and the use of tractors on cropping intensity, yield and employment has been investigated in Appendix D (Tables 4, 5 and 6) by using the Farm Management data for Ferozepur as well as the PEO data for four states mentioned earlier. The results obtained from this analysis are summarised below.

The results pertaining to Ferozepur for 1968-69 as well as for 1969-70 show that cropping intensity and employment per acre decline with the increase in the size of holding. A similar position was revealed by the Farm Management Studies conducted in mid-fifties in this district as elsewhere in the country. However, unlike in the mid-fifties, output per acre does not seem to decline with the increase in the size of holding, which is explained by the greater use of modern inputs among large farms.

It appears that the combined (net) impact of tractor-use together with complementary inputs like tube-wells, HYV and fertilisers on cropping intensity, output and employment is positive and substantial (see Table 9.2).

TABLE 9.2: IMPACT OF COMPLEMENTARY INPUTS, FEROZEPUR, 1968-69
(Estimated at tractor farm size and mean irrigation levels)

	Non-Tractor Farm (53 acres)	Tractor Farm (53 acres)	Per cent Difference
	(1)	(2)	(3)
1. Cropping Intensity	109.5	138.9	+26.8
2. Output per acre held (Rs)	583.5	805.0	+38.0
3. Human labour hours per acre held	192.0	254.3	+32.5
4. Bullock Cost per acre held (Rs)	67.0	42.5	−36.7

Source : Estimated from equations in Table 4, Appendix D.

Increase in cropping intensity turns out to be the predominant source of increase in output and employment. Tractor farms are able to dispense with only about 37 per cent of bullock costs incurred on the comparable bullock farms. We found in another study[10] that if complementarity between tractors and other inputs is ignored, private investment in tractors would be profitable only when tractors replace bullocks totally so that bullock and associated human labour costs are entirely saved. Since tractor farms are able to dispense with bullocks only to a limited extent and since, as mentioned earlier, hiring out of tractors is not significant, the observed investment in tractors can be explained only in terms of their complementarity with other inputs.

The results from the PEO data show that farm size has a negative effect on cropping intensity whereas irrigation has a positive effect in all the four states, e.g., Punjab, Haryana, Andhra Pradesh and Tamilnadu. The superiority of tractor farms over bullock farms with regard to cropping intensity increases with the rise in farm size in Punjab, Andhra Pradesh and Tamilnadu (see Fig. 9.2). The results for Andhra Pradesh indicate that as the percentage of area irrigated increases, the impact of irrigation on cropping intensity would be greater among tractor farms than among bullock

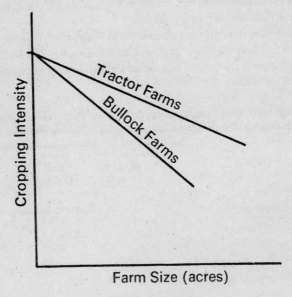

Figure 9.2

[10]See Ch. 5.

farms of comparable irrigated area (see Fig. 9.3). Tractor-use is associated with an increase in cropping intensity to the extent of about 6 per cent in Punjab and 36 per cent in Andhra Pradesh (see Table 9.3).

Since the proportion of area allocated to HYV as well as cropping intensity are higher among tractor farms, the latter can be expected to use more labour than bullock farms. The PEO data on employment relate to hired labour only.

The estimated levels of employment at average farm size and irrigation levels show that tractor-use along with complementary inputs is associated with a significant increase in the employment of hired labour (see Table 9.3). The estimated wage-bill indicates that the differences in wages paid between bullock and tractor farms are, in general, more pronounced than the differences in labour days. This suggests that the skills and the operation-wise composition of hired labour among tractor farms may be biased towards high-wage labour such as tractor drivers and harvest-labour.

The net impact of technological change (i.e., farm mechanisation and HYV) and the expansion of traditional resources, e.g., irrigation, has been a rise in total employment. Ferozepur, for instance, is one of the few districts in the country where the rate of technological change—especially farm mechanisation—has been the fastest and where despite such a rapid rate of technological change, farm employment—total as well as per acre—has been increasing. The employment of labour among the sample farms in this district increased from 20.8 man-days per cropped (planted) acre in 1954-55 to 24.5 man-days in 1969-70 or by about 18 per cent, despite a decline in labour input per acre for wheat owing mainly to the widespread use of mechanical threshers (see Table 9.1). The rate of rise in total farm employment has been much higher owing, among other things, to the rise in cropping intensity from 117 in 1954-55 to 130 in 1969-70. The rise in employment per cropped (planted) acre despite a high rate of mechanisation may be attributable to the rise in the proportion of sown area irrigated from 68 per cent in 1954-55 to 88.5 per cent in 1969-70 and the widespread use of fertilisers and HYV.[11]

[11]The data on employment, irrigation and cropping intensity relate to the samples of Ferozepur farms in 1954-55 and 1968-69 and are contained in the *Studies in the Economics of Farm Management* in Punjab conducted by the Directorate of Economics and Statistics, Ministry of Food and Agriculture.

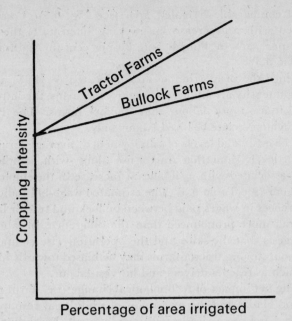

Figure 9.3

TABLE 9.3: IMPACT OF COMPLEMENTARY INPUTS, PEO DATA, 1969-70
(Estimated at mean farm size and irrigation levels)

	Punjab	Haryana	Andhra Pradesh	Tamilnadu
	(1)	(2)	(3)	(4)
1. *Cropping Intensity:*				
Bullock farm	1.6	1.4	1.4	1.7
Tractor farm	1.7	1.4	1.9	1.6
Per cent Difference	6.3	—	35.7	−5.9
2. *Employment of Hired Labour-days:*				
Bullock farm	181.0	164.1	987.1	484.1
Tractor farm	244.0	217.6	1602.4	670.4
Per cent Difference	34.8	32.6	62.3	33.5
3. *Wage-Bill (Rs):*				
Bullock farm	1035.1	765.3	2845.9	1161.0
Tractor farm	1357.4	1114.9	5618.8	1339.3
Per cent Difference	31.1	45.7	97.4	15.4

Source : Estimated from the equations in Tables 5 and 6, Appendix D; from Table 6, the equations with tractor dummy (size slope) have been used.

SEASONAL DISTRIBUTION OF EMPLOYMENT

Technological changes, in so far as they facilitate an increase in cropping intensity or multiple cropping, may lead to a more intensive utilisation of the services of a family farm worker or permanent farm servant and hence, to a more even distribution of work put in by them during the year. Among Ferozepur farms, the number of days put in by a farm worker in a year for crop pro-

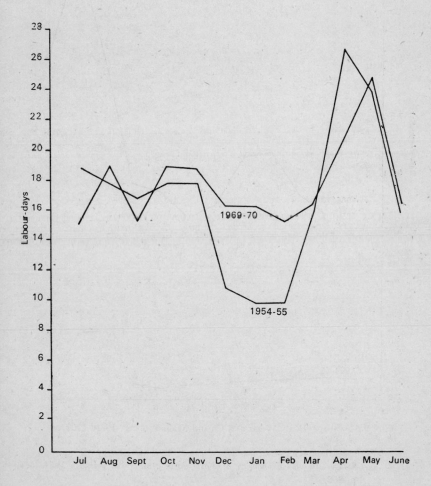

Figure 9.4 : Monthly Distribution of Labour-days put in by a Farm Worker for Crop Production (Ferozepur Distric

duction increased from 204 in 1954-55 to 217 in 1969-70 and the coefficient of variation in monthly input of labour declined significantly from 29 per cent to 15.5 per cent (see Fig. 9.4).[12]

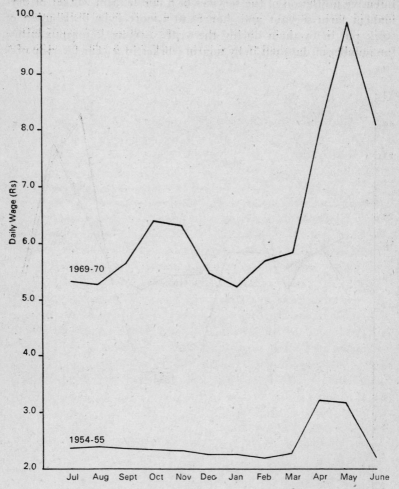

Figure 9.5 Average Daily Wage of a Casual Male Worker (Field Labour)

[12]For the data see :
  (i) *Studies in the Economics of Farm Management* in Punjab, 1954-55, p. 202.
  (ii) *Studies in Economics of Farm Management*, Ferozepur district (Punjab), 1969-70, p. 66.

Although the employment of casual labour increased significantly over this period, the position is less clear with regard to its monthly distribution. The data in Table 9.1 suggest a similar tendency of a more even distribution of labour input for wheat owing to a significant reduction in labour-use for threshing and winnowing. However, in view of the increase in the proportion of area planted with HYV wheat, the seasonal distribution of casual labour for farm business as a whole needs to be considered.[13] The data on monthly wage rates for casual labour reveal an increase in the coefficient of variation from 13 per cent to 21 per cent over this period owing to a greater rise in the peak demand for casual labour during the quarter April-June (see Fig. 9.5).[14]

SUMMARY

If the Green Revolution is regarded as a package consisting of HYV and fertilisers, its contribution to employment has been substantial. Also, tube-wells seem to have contributed significantly to the employment of labour. The technological displacement of labour associated with tractor-use seems to have been roughly compensated by the employment of labour consequent on the increase in yield as a result of tractor-use among farms characterised by partial tractorisation. However, among different techniques, the labour coefficient or the incremental labour-output ratio appears to be the lowest for tractors. The highest labour coefficient relates to operated area followed by HYV and irrigation.

The net employment effect of tractor-use may turn out to be negative when tractorisation of farm operations is complete. A harvest combine would displace farm labour on a large scale while its land-augmenting effect would be negligible. The overall impact of

[13]A Study of Udaipur and Chittorgarh farms (Rajasthan) reveals lower coefficient of variation in the seasonal use of labour among farms participating in the Green Revolution when compared to non-participants. As can be expected, this study also shows the rising importance of casual (hired) labour among participants, particularly among tractor operated farms. See S.S. Acharya, 'Green Revolution and Farm Employment', *Indian Journal of Agricultural Economics*, July, September 1973.

[14]For the data see:
   (i) *Studies in Economics of Farm Management* in Punjab, 1954-55, p. 19.
   (ii) *Studies in Economics of Farm Management*, Ferozepur District (Punjab) 1969-70, p. 19.

tractorisation on employment would be positive if its complementarity with other techniques is taken into account. The increase in the wage-bill is even more significant owing to the greater use of high-skill and high-wage labour among tractor farms.

Technological changes have led to a more even use of services of permanent farm workers during the year. However, the variability in the wages of casual hired labour has increased owing presumably to the rise in peak-season demand for such labour.

CHAPTER 10

Changes in Factor Shares

FACTOR SHARES AND INCOME DISTRIBUTION

Changes in factor shares or in factorial distribution of income by themselves cannot provide a complete picture of the distribution of gains between different groups of people unless the owners of different productive factors constitute distinct classes, which is hardly the case in reality. Large landowner farmers depend on hired labour but invest their own savings to a considerable extent so that their gain from technological change would consist of the net change in the shares for land, capital and entrepreneurship-management. Small family farmers provide practically all the productive services— land, labour, a substantial proportion of capital and entrepreneurship-management. Changes in net(factor) income would thus provide a reasonable measure of their gains from technological change. The tenants who supply their own labour and capital would gain or lose depending upon the net changes in shares of labour and capital.

There are at least three classes of people in whose case movements in individual factor shares by themselves can indicate the changes in their income. For example, changes in rent-share would indicate the gains or losses for those land owners who derive their incomes exclusively as rentiers by leasing out their land. Similarly, capitalist farmers who hire labour and lease land would derive their income as manager-entrepreneurs and suppliers of capital resources. Changes in shares attributable to labour would give the income position of landless labourers. Of the six groups mentioned above, large landowner farmers, family farmers and landless labourers happen to be important in India, in numerical terms. Pure rentiers as well as tenants constitute a small group while the group of pure capitalist farmers is negligible.

HYPOTHESIS

Land-augmenting technological change, in so far as it raises yield per unit of land area, would mean an increase in the effective supply of land relative to other factors. Therefore, other things remaining equal, land-augmenting technological change should result in a decline in the relative as well as absolute share of land (rent) in output. In reality, however, the behaviour of rent-share would depend upon the growth in the demand for agricultural output, the growth in the supply of various input resources including land and the rate of technological advance. As far as the industrially advanced countries are concerned, there has been a secular decline in the relative share of output accruing to land as a productive factor.[1] For a developing economy like India, with its rapid growth of population and the slow expansion of complementary resources, the observed rate of technological advance may not be sufficient, as yet, to cause a decline in the relative share of output accruing to land. However, for areas experiencing the Green Revolution or land-augmenting technological change, there could be this decline. Rent per acre and the absolute share of land could, nevertheless, rise, owing to the increased demand for land consequent to the increased profitability of investment in modern inputs complementary to it.

With the application of land-augmenting or yield-increasing technology, the requirements of labour input per acre or the demand for labour may increase, though proportionately less than the rise in yield per acre. In view of the biological character of agriculture, innovations which raise output per acre invariably raise the bargaining power of labour owing to the increased demand for critical short-duration operations such as harvesting, so long as these operations are not mechanised. Also, the rise in per capita income as a result of the Green Revolution may lead to the withdrawal of some family labour from manual work which may raise the demand for hired labour as well as the supply price of such labour belonging to the small farm-households. All these factors may lead to the rise in wage rates. Employment, wage rates and the absolute share of labour in output may thus rise as a consequence of land-augmenting technological change. However, the relative share of labour or the ratio of wage-income to output may decline because the rise in wage

[1] T.W. Schultz, *The Economic Organization of Agriculture*, McGraw-Hill, 1953, pp. 125-45.

rates may not compensate for the considerably reduced requirements of labour per unit of output owing to the complementarity
between land and labour. Thus, land-augmenting technical change,
(i.e., seed-fertiliser revolution or a Green Revolution) may also represent a labour-saving (non-neutral) technical change and assuming two factors of production, say, capital and labour, the marginal
product of the former would be raised more than that of the latter.[2]
Since with land-augmenting technological change, land becomes
much less critical or limitational than labour, one should expect the
relative share of land in output to decline more than that of labour.

Labour-substituting technological change or farm mechanisation would, other things remaining equal, result in the reduction of
the share of labour in absolute as well as relative terms. In reality,
however, the impact of farm mechanisation on employment, wage
rates and the share of labour would depend on the rate of mechanisation in relation to the growth in the demand for output. Under
the existing Indian conditions where the (derived) demand for farm
labour for the agricultural sector as a whole might well be lagging
behind the growth in the supply of farm labour, labour-substituting
technological change would result in lower than attainable employment and in a reduction in the relative share of labour (wage-income)
in output. Even in areas where output has been growing at a significantly high rate, the relative share of labour can decline as a result
of mechanisation despite an increase in employment and wage rates.

In India, since land-augmenting technological changes are so
far more widespread than labour-substituting technological changes,
we should expect the relative share of land to decline more than
that of labour in areas experiencing technological change. Within
the large farm sector, however, the relative share of labour could
decline more than that of land owing to greater mechanisation of
farm operations.

In addition to the non-neutral character or factor-saving
(using) bias of the innovations mentioned above, received theory on
the distribution of income brings out the importance of at least two
other forces which influence the changes in factor shares: the changes
in the relative prices of factors (associated with the changes in the
relative factor supplies) in conjunction with the elasticity of factor
substitution and the changes in the elasticity of substitution itself. In
a two-factor case, if the elasticity of substitution is more than unity,

[2] J.R. Hicks, *The Theory of Wages*, Macmillan, 1963, pp. 121-2.

then the relative share of the factor whose relative price is falling would go up, but if the elasticity of substitution is less than unity, its relative share would decline.[3] The elasticity of substitution itself may change owing to the non-neutral technological change as well as to the change in factor intensity as one factor is substituted for another along the same isoquant. A rise in the elasticity of substitution would favour the factor whose relative price is falling, as the use of the more expensive factor can now be economised.[4] Conversely, a decline in the elasticity of substitution would favour the more expensive factor.

LAND-AUGMENTING TECHNOLOGICAL CHANGE AND FACTOR SHARES

PROCEDURE

Much of the theoretical as well as empirical work on the distribution of income in relation to technological change has been done in the context of two factors, i.e., capital and labour. However, land is an important productive factor in the agricultural sector, especially in the developing economies. Although it is more difficult to handle the three-factor situation, the two-factor model, say, when land is clubbed with capital, cannot yield satisfactory results because the elasticity of substitution between land and capital is neither zero (e.g., the case of fixed proportions) nor infinite and land-augmenting technological changes alter the elasticity of substitution between capital and land. Besides, the elasticity of substitution between labour and capital is markedly different from that between labour and land and these elasticities change significantly in varying degrees with non-neutral technological change.

Instead of attempting to draw inferences on the distribution of income from the character of technological change identified independently, we shall try to draw the inferences on the character of technological change itself on the basis of the observed behaviour of the distributive shares. A direct appeal to the data on technique-wise differences in relative shares to factors would thus help to deter-

[3]Ibid., pp. 117-20.

[4]Murray Brown and John S. DeCani, 'Technological Change and the Distribution of Income', *International Economic Review*, Vol. 4, No. 3, September 1963.

mine simultaneously the character of technological change as well
as its impact on the distribution of income.

PRE-GREEN REVOLUTION DATA

It would be interesting to study the factor shares under different land-augmenting techniques in India prior to the current Green
Revolution because land-saving techniques have been introduced
in Indian agriculture in the past from time to time. The land-saving
nature of these techniques in this period is indicated essentially by
the differences with regard to irrigation and the type of crop grown.
Data on the value of labour input and output per acre relating to a
number of crops in different regions of the country (e.g., Uttar
Pradesh, Punjab, Madhya Pradesh, West Bengal, Maharashtra and
Tamilnadu) are available from the Farm Management Studies. We
have used the averages of 3 years, 1954-55, 1955-56 and 1956-57, in
order to correct for abnormal variations, if any, in yields due to
weather. These data and the elasticities of labour income (per acre)
with respect to output (per acre) estimated for each of these regions
are given in Appendix E.

These results show that in Madhya Pradesh, where the crops
studied are unirrigated, the elasticity of labour income per acre
with respect to output per acre is less than unity, indicating that as
output per acre increases, the absolute share of labour rises but its
relative share declines. In the rest of the regions, however, the elasticity of labour income (per acre) with respect to output (per acre) is
not different from unity. This evidence suggests that, by and large,
traditional land-saving technique such as irrigation is not characterised by a significant labour-saving bias.

POST-GREEN REVOLUTION DATA

A comparison of factor shares between the local and High
Yielding Variety of the same crop in any particular period would
reveal the impact of land-augmenting technological change because
the rate of mechanisation in any particular period can be expected
to be roughly the same for two varieties of the same crop grown in
any region.

Tables 10.1 and 10.2 based upon the Farm Management data
for Ferozepur (Punjab) give such information for wheat and rice.

These data are the averages for 1968-69 and 1969-70 and are collected through the cost accounting method. Shares for land and labour include the values of own resources imputed on the basis of the prevailing market rates. Interest on capital (working as well as fixed) has been calculated on a similar basis. Profit has been obtained as a residual after deducting all the fixed and variable costs including the interest cost and the shares for land and labour. Net output is defined to consist of factor income after deducting the material costs.

These figures show that the absolute shares of all the factors are higher for HYV wheat when compared to local wheat. The rise in the absolute share of labour is attributable to the rise in employment per acre as well as to the changed composition of labour which may be biased towards high-wage labour (see Chapter 9). The higher absolute share of land (rental value) in the case of HYV wheat is indicative of better quality of land and irrigation. It will be seen that the relative shares of both land and labour—whether as proportion to gross or net output—are lower for HYV when compared to the local variety of wheat[5] and the relative share of land

TABLE 10.1: FACTOR SHARES FOR WHEAT IN FEROZEPUR (PUNJAB) 1968-70

	Wheat (Mexican)			Wheat (Desi)		
	Absolute Share (Rs)	Relative Share (Per cent)		Absolute Share (Rs)	Relative Share (Per cent)	
	per Acre	R.G.O.	R.N.O.	per Acre	R.G.O.	R.N.O.
	(1)	(2)	(3)	(4)	(5)	(6)
Labour	161.1	20.8	30.7	117.1	23.7	36.5
Land	215.5	27.8	41.1	175.2	35.5	54.6
Interest	30.0	3.9	5.8	22.5	4.6	7.0
Profit	117.5	15.2	22.4	6.0	1.2	1.9

R.G.O.=Relative to Gross Output
R.N.O.=Relative to Net Output

[5]We should note here a contrary result in the case of HYV wheat in Bihar: Clive Bell in his study ('The Acquisition of Agricultural Technology: Its Determinants and Effects', *The Journal of Development Studies*, October, 1972) finds that the share of labour in value added shows a small increase pointing to a labour-using bias in the innovation. He, however, warns that 'in view of the sensitivity of labour's share to variations in output, this conclusion should be treated with due caution'.

declines more than that of labour. There is some decline in the relative share of interest income and a sharp rise in the relative share of profit. A similar position holds true in the case of rice (see Table 10.2) except that the absolute share of land is somewhat lower for

TABLE 10.2: FACTOR SHARES FOR RICE IN FEROZEPUR (PUNJAB), 1968-70

	Rice (Local)			Rice (IR-8)		
	Absolute Share (Rs)	Relative Share (per cent)		Absolute Share (Rs)	Relative Share (per cent)	
	per Acre	R.G.O.	R.N.O.	per Acre	R.G.O.	R.N.O.
	(1)	(2)	(3)	(4)	(5)	(6)
Labour	147.8	27.2	37.0	186.1	20.6	28.2
Land	160.8	29.6	40.2	153.1	17.0	23.2
Interest	30.0	5.6	7.6	35.1	4.0	5.4
Profit	60.7	11.3	15.2	284.5	31.6	43.2

R.G.O.=Relative to Gross Output
R.N.O.=Relative to Net Output

IR-8 when compared to local rice, which may be indicative of a possible difference in the quality of land (or irrigation).

Table 10.3 gives the share of hired labour for local and IR-8 rice in the East and West Godavari districts of Andhra Pradesh for the year 1968-69. The absolute share of hired labour per acre is higher for HYV rice when compared to local rice but its relative share in output is lower in the *kharif* as well as *rabi* seasons in both the districts.[6] It may be noted further, that the relative share of labour in output for HYV is significantly lower in the *rabi* season owing to the greater yield per acre (see column 1 of Table 10.3). Since HYV rice is grown more extensively in the *rabi* season, the decline in the relative share of labour as a result of land-augmenting technological change should be regarded as substantial.

[6]A Study of Andhra Pradesh farms in the late fifties showed that as between different methods of rice cultivation (broadcasting, transplantation and Japanese methods), a larger output per acre was associated with larger absolute share of both wages and profits, but with a lower share of the former relative to that of the latter. See C.H.Hanumantha Rao, 'Wage-Profit Relations in Agriculture: A Study in Andhra Pradesh', *The Economic Weekly*, 21 September 1963.

TABLE 10.3: Share of Hired Labour in the Output of
Rice (1968-69) in Andhra Pradesh

(Value in rupees per acre)

	Gross Value	Wages for Hired Labour	Per cent of Col. 2 to Col. 1
	(1)	(2)	(3)
East Godavari			
Kharif:			
Local	700	142	20.3
IR-8	878	170	19.4
Rabi:			
Local	634	129	20.3
IR-8	1,238	158	12.8
West Godavari			
Kharif:			
Local	739	193	26.1
IR-8	977	229	23.4
Rabi:			
Local	731	238	32.6
IR-8	1,191	267	22.4

Source: G. Parthasarathy and D.S. Prasad, 'Season-wise progress of High Yielding Varieties in Andhra Pradesh and the Role of Economic Variables', *Economic and Political Weekly*, Review of Agriculture, September 1971.

It will be noted from Tables 10.1 and 10.2 that despite a steep decline in the relative share of land, the combined share of rent, interest and profit income rises indicating that land-owner farmers operating with hired labour gain absolutely as well as relatively from land-augmenting technological change whereas landless labourers gain somewhat absolutely but lose in relative terms. Land-augmenting technological change may thus widen the income disparities between large land-owner farmers and landless labourers. The rentiers may lose relatively to the tenants even if absolute rent per acre rises, because the combined share of labour, interest and profit income per acre rises absolutely as well as relatively to output whereas the relative share of land declines steeply. Rise in profit income is the greatest, indicating the rising importance of entrepreneurship and management with technological change.

CHANGES IN FACTOR SHARES OVER TIME

Tables 10.4 and 10.5 give the changes in factor shares for the farm business as a whole (all crops) in Ferozepur (Punjab) between the pre-Green Revolution period, i.e., mid-fifties and the Green Revolution period. Table 10.4 gives the average figures for all farms whereas the figures in Table 10.5 relate to large farms (above 50 acres). The changes in factor shares between these two periods are the combined result of land-augmenting as well as labour-substituting technological changes, changes in product and factor prices and the possible changes in the elasticities of factor substitution.

TABLB 10.4: FACTOR SHARES AMONG FEROZEPUR (PUNJAB) FARMS (ALL FARMS)

	Absolute Share (Rs) per Acre		Relative to Gross Output (per cent)		Relative to Net Output (per cent)	
	1954-57	1968-70	1954-57	1968-70	1954-57	1968-70
	(1)	(2)	(3)	(4)	(5)	(6)
Labour	42.6	184.4	28.2	24.7	42.4	36.7
Land	52.7	219.7	34.8	29.4	55.0	43.8
Interest	1.8	34.8	1.2	4.6	1.9	6.9
Profit	0.7	63.6	0.5	8.5	0.7	12.6

The figures in Table 10.4 confirm the conclusions arrived at from Tables 10.1 and 10.2: the relative shares of both land and labour have declined, the share of the former declining more steeply. However, the relative share of interest income has risen over this period indicating a rise in capital intensity—a combined result of labour-substituting technological change, changes in the relative prices of labour and capital and the possible changes in the elasticity of substitution. The relative shares of land as well as labour are lower and those of interest and profit are higher on the large farm sector when compared to the farms as a whole in both the periods (see Table 10.5). The rise in the relative share of interest income is much greater in the case of large farms when compared to the farms as a whole. Further, the decline in the relative share of labour is much steeper than that of land among large farms owing to greater substitution of capital for labour.

The experience in areas where the Intensive Agricultural District Programme (IADP) has been in progress and where the Green Revolution has made a significant impact confirms the declin-

TABLE 10.5: FACTOR SHARES AMONG FEROZEPUR (PUNJAB) FARMS (LARGE FARMS OF ABOVE 50 ACRES)

	Absolute Share (Rs) per Acre		Relative to Gross Output (per cent)		Relative to Net Output (per cent)	
	1954-57	1968-70	1954-57	1968-70	1954-57	1968-70
	(1)	(2)	(3)	(4)	(5)	(6)
Labour	36.5	121.4	25.5	15.1	34.9	20.3
Land	49.2	237.0	34.5	29.5	48.5	39.7
Interest	0.8	37.0	0.5	4.6	0.8	6.2
Profit	16.0	201.5	11.2	25.0	15.8	33.8

ing relative share of labour in output. Table 10.6 based on the IADP data shows that the real income of labour (i.e., after deflating the money income with the price index of foodgrains) lagged behind the growth of foodgrain output between 1962-63 and 1967-68. However, there has been a significant rise in the absolute income of labour owing to the increased demand for labour generated by the Green Revolution as well as to the consequent rise in wage rates. For instance, in the leading districts of the Green Revolution, e.g., Ludhiana and West Godavari, the employment of labour per hectare

TABLE 10.6: RELATIVE GROWTH OF OUTPUT AND INCOME OF LABOUR PER HECTARE IN THE IADP DISTRICTS (IN 1967-68 WITH 1962-63 = 100)

	First Group of Districts	Second Group of Districts	All Districts
	(1)	(2)	(3)
All foodgrains (tons)	127.0	110.6	121.0
Real Income of Labour (adjusted with price index of foodgrains)	124.0	105.0	114.0

Source: Ministry of Food and Agriculture, Government of India, *Modernizing Indian Agriculture: Report on the Intensive Agricultural District Programme,* (1960-68), Vol. I, pp. 110, 114.

is reported to have increased by 49 per cent and 70 per cent respectively between 1962-63 and 1967-68 while the wage rate adjusted with price index increased by 16 per cent and 12 per cent respectively.[7]

PROBABLE CHANGES IN FACTOR SHARES IN THE AGRICULTURAL SECTOR AS A WHOLE

We have already noted how factor shares are likely to be altered by the non-neutral technological changes. It would be interesting to speculate on how the factor shares might have been influenced by the other two forces, namely, the possible changes in the relative prices of factors and in the elasticity of substitution. We found in Chapter 3 that the (private) cost of labour has been rising relative to that of capital in Indian agriculture, especially for large farmers. It would be reasonable to suppose, however, that the cost of labour may have been declining relative to the (implicit) cost of land, because the supply of land has virtually remained constant. It follows from the above reasoning that the price of capital has been declining relative to that of land. The available evidence suggests that in the pre-Green Revolution period, e.g., from 1954 through 1956-57, the elasticity of substitution between land-labour was significantly lower than unity and those between capital-land and capital-labour were not significantly different from unity.[8] We assume that the technological changes in Indian agriculture since the mid-sixties have reduced further the elasticity of substitution between land-labour and raised those between capital-land as well as capital-labour to more than unity.[9] Land-augmenting technological changes, in so far as they

[7]Ministry of Food and Agriculture, Government of India, *Modernizing Indian Agriculture: Report on the Intensive Agricultural District Programme* (1960-68), Vol. I, p. 114.

[8]Gian S. Sahota, 'Land-Labour-Capital Substitution in Traditional Agriculture', *The Journal of Economic Studies*, (UK), I, No. 2, 1966.

[9]A recent study by Uma K. Srivastava and Earl O. Heady based on the Farm Management data for Punjab and Uttar Pradesh shows that the elasticity of substitution between capital (including land) and labour is much higher, though still less than unity, in the post-Green Revolution period (late sixties) when compared to pre-Green Revolution period (mid-fifties). See their 'Technological Change and Relative Factor Shares in Indian Agriculture: An Empirical Analysis', *American Journal of Agicultural Economics*, August 1973. For reasons discussed earlier, the elasticity of substitution between capital (exclusive of land) and labour could be much higher than is indicated by this study. If Sahota's finding of unitary elasticity of substitution in the mid-fifties is accepted and if the

have considerably raised labour input per acre, may have reduced the scope for substitution between land and labour within the new technology.[10] Also, labour input per acre may have risen significantly over this period, regardless of technological change, owing to the growth of labour force in the agricultural sector. On the other hand, capital-land and capital-labour ratios are very low in Indian agriculture (e.g., when compared to other countries), so that technological changes might well have increased the possibilities of substituting capital for land as well as labour.

Let us now reflect on the probable impact of these changes in a two-factor framework considering land and labour, to begin with. Since cost of labour may have been declining relative to that of land and since the elasticity of substitution between them may be less than unity, the share of labour may have declined relative to that of land. If the elasticity of substitution between land and labour has been declining, the above tendency of the decline in the relative share of labour may have been reinforced because it may have become increasingly difficult to substitute (cheap) labour for (costly) land. Let us suppose now that capital and labour exhaust the list of factors. Since cost of labour has been rising relative to that of capital and since the elasticity of substitution between them is likely to have been more than unity, the relative share of labour in output may have declined. This tendency may have been reinforced by the rise in the elasticity of substitution.[11] On a similar reasoning, in a land-capital framework, where capital has become cheaper relative to land, the relative share of capital would rise if the elasticity of substitution is more than unity and has been rising. It is probable, therefore, that, on balance, the relative shares of labour as well as of land in output

rising trend in the elasticities of substitution brought out by Srivastava and Heady is considered reasonable, then the elasticities of substitution between capital-labour and capital-land are likely to be more than unity in the post-Green Revolution period.

[10]There is plenty of evidence to suggest that factor proportions between land and labour are relatively inflexible under irrigated conditions (which represent land-augmenting technological change) than for unirrigated farming. See for instance, C.H. Hanumantha Rao, 'Uncertainty, Entrepreneurship and Sharecropping in India', *Journal of Political Economy*, May/June 1971.

[11]This result is contrary to the general expectation for developing economies where labour is assumed to be cheaper than capital. See for instance, Brown and Cani, op. cit.

may have declined while that of capital may have risen.

SUMMARY

While the absolute share of hired labour has risen, its relative share in output has declined in areas experiencing the Green Revolution. The same may be true for the agricultural sector as a whole. Although, land-augmenting technological change by itself seems to reduce the relative share of land more than that of labour, the relative share of hired labour in the large farm sector has declined more than that of land owing to mechanisation, indicating the widening income disparities between large land-owner farmers and landless labourers.

CHAPTER 11

Farm Size and the Distribution of Gains

HYPOTHESIS

Since technological changes currently underway in Indian agriculture can be expected to raise the share of capital as well as of entrepreneurship-management in output, and since all modern inputs including non-material ones such as education and skills have to be acquired by investing in them, the distribution of gains from technological change among farms of different sizes would be determined by the latter's relative access to capital resources. The relative growth of different firms depends essentially on their initial wealth position,[1] because, among other things, the ability of a firm to borrow on reasonable terms in the market depends on its 'credit-worthiness'. Also, since large farmers save a greater proportion of the increment in their income than do the small farmers, they can augment their investable resources at a higher rate than the small farmers.

In many parts of the country, small farmers have been found to irrigate a larger proportion of their cultivated area than the large farmers.[2] Also, owing to the greater availability of family labour, whose cost is lower, these farmers use more labour per acre than large farmers who have to hire labour.[3] Besides, the intensity of land-use can be expected to be lower among large farms owing to the prob-

[1]M. Kalecki, 'The Principle of Increasing Risk', *Economica*, New Series, IV, No. 16, 1937.

[2]C.H. Hanumantha Rao, *Agricultural Production Functions, Costs and Returns in India*, Asia Publishing House, 1965; see also B. Sen, 'Opportunities in the Green Revolution', *Economic and Political Weekly*, Review of Agriculture, 28 March 1970.

[3]A.K. Sen, 'An Aspect of Indian Agriculture', *The Economic Weekly*, Annual Number, February 1962.

lems of supervision and management under labour-intensive techniques.[4] So far as improved seeds and fertilisers are concerned, small farmers do have an advantage in the sense that owing to greater availability of labour and irrigation, they can use more fertilisers per acre than the large farmers. But this prospect need not materialise because large farmers, owing to their better access to credit and modern inputs, may in fact use more of these inputs per acre.[5] For the same reason they can bring more area under irrigation through pumpsets and can manage with a smaller amount of labour per acre by using tractors. Further, mechanisation contributes to overcoming the traditional aversion to manual labour, thus increasing the effective supply of labour among the large farmers. Thus whereas the new technology is size-neutral in the sense that improved seeds, fertilisers and even tractors can be used on all farms independent of their size, it is not resource-neutral. That is to say, only those farmers who have a greater command over resources can buy and use these inputs while small farmers cannot benefit unless drastic changes are brought about in the working of credit institutions and administrative procedures. It is, therefore, highly probable that technological changes are contributing to wiping out the inverse relationship between farm size and output per acre found under the traditional labour-intensive technology which was favourable to the small farmers.

Small farmers can, therefore, be expected to become the effective participants in the Green Revolution only with considerable lag. The late-comers invariably benefit less than the earlier adopters of new technology because the output growth achieved in the earlier

[4]C.H. Hanumantha Rao, 'Alternative Explanations of the Inverse Relationship Between Farm Size and Output per Acre', *Indian Economic Review*, October 1966.

[5]Assuming that (a) *absolute* risk aversion does not increase; and (b) *relative* risk aversion does not decrease, as income increases, T.N. Srinivasan has shown that in view of yield-uncertainty due to vagaries of weather, small farmers can be expected to use more labour input per acre than large farmers even if there is no difference between them regarding the percentage of area irrigated and the access to labour market at a constant wage rate (see his 'Farm Size and Productivity: Implications of Choice Under Uncertainty', *Sankhya: The Indian Journal of Statistics*, December 1972). However, since the use of current inputs like fertilisers per acre *in fact* rises with the increase in the size of holding, it appears that, in reality, factor market imperfections exert a significant influence. As to the larger labour input per acre among small farms, it is difficult to test Srinivasan's proposition because, on the basis of the available evidence, the hypothesis of 'cheap' family labour among small farms cannot be rejected.

stages brings down the relative prices of crops concerned.

Whereas technological changes in a situation of unequal access to capital resources or imperfections in capital market would result in widening the disparities in income between small and large farms, other factors such as the imposition of legal ceilings on the ownership of land-holding, sale of land by large landowners and the sub-division of larger holdings owing to population growth could reduce the levels as well as the share of higher incomes in the agricultural sector. It should not be surprising, therefore, if the skewness in the size distribution of income within the agricultural sector becomes smaller despite technological changes.

DISTRIBUTION OF AGRICULTURAL CREDIT

Since marginal propensity to save rises with the increase in the level of income,[6] large farmers have greater capacity to invest own resources in modern inputs than small farmers. The distribution of institutional credit has been heavily biased towards large farmers which strengthens further their ability to adopt innovations at a faster rate. Their greater capacity to take risk, better access to information, and improved capabilities in terms of education and skills are positive contributory factors and are determined, in a substantial measure, by their better wealth position.

According to the All India Rural Debt and Investment Survey (1961-62), the distribution of credit from the cooperatives was inequitous as among different asset groups(see Table 11.1). Although productive assets (e.g., irrigation and cattle) per acre decline with increase in size of holding,[7] credit per acre extended by the cooperatives is found to increase significantly with increase in operated area (see column 6 of Table 11.1). Among the various states, wherever concentration of assets is higher, concentration of cooperative credit

[6]The marginal propensity to save of rural income classes above Rs. 1200 per annum works out to 0.18 whereas it is not significantly different from zero (0.03) for those below Rs. 1200. These estimates have been derived from the data contained in *All India Rural Household Survey, Volume II, Income, Investment and Saving*, conducted by the National Council of Applied Economic Research.

[7]For the data on irrigation see 'Agricultural Production Functions, Costs and Returns', op. cit. For the data on the distribution of cattle see C.H. Hanumantha Rao, 'India's "Surplus" Cattle: Some Empirical Results', *Economic and Political Weekly*, Review of Agriculture, December 1969.

TABLE 11.1: RELATIVE IMPORTANCE OF COOPERATIVES IN THE TOTAL BORROWINGS OF
CULTIVATORS AMONG DIFFERENT ASSET GROUPS, 1961-62

Asset Group (Rs.)	Percentage of Families Borrowing from Co-operatives	Percentage of Borrowers from Co-operatives to all Borrowers	Percentage Distribu- tion of Borrowing from Co- operatives	Percentage of Amount Borrowed from Co- operatives to Total Borrowing	Average Area per Cultivator Household (Acres)	Average Borrowing per Acre (Rs.)
	(1)	(2)	(3)	(4)	(5)	(6)
Less than 500	2.6	5.7	0.5	5.1	1.27	1.81
500 - 1000	3.9	8.2	1.5	7.3	2.14	2.38
1000 - 2500	6.2	12.7	7.4	9.6	3.35	2.81
2500 - 5000	9.4	17.6	14.3	12.6	5.35	3.66
5000 - 10000	12.3	22.0	20.7	14.2	8.06	4.42
10000 - 20000	15.4	27.6	21.4	16.5	11.86	5.36
20000 and above	19.0	34.9	34.2	23.1	23.26	7.33
All asset groups	9.4	18.1	100.0	15.5	6.63	4.81

Source : Reserve Bank of India, *Report of the All India Rural Credit Review Committee,* 1969, pp. 127-8.

TABLE 11.2: COEFFICIENTS OF CONCENTRATION

	Assets	Cooperative Credit
	(1)	(2)
Punjab	0.775	0.782
Jammu and Kashmir	0.811	0.802
Assam	0.825	0.751
Orissa	0.830	0.786
Rajasthan	0.830	0.818
Gujarat	0.838	0.831
Madhya Pradesh	0.843	0.822
Uttar Pradesh	0.857	0.838
Maharashtra	0.859	0.862
Karnataka	0.863	0.874
All India	0.870	0.864
West Bengal	0.871	0.856
Tamilnadu	0.878	0.872
Andhra Pradesh	0.882	0.885
Bihar	0.884	0.878
Kerala	0.895	0.858

Note : Rank correlation between the coefficient of concentration of assets and the coefficient of concentration of cooperative credit is 0.9.
Source : Reserve Bank of India, *Report of the All India Rural Credit Review Committee*, 1969, p. 130.

is also higher[8] (see Table 11.2), indicating that the political power of the large farmers, which derives largely from the disparities in wealth is an important factor determining the distribution of cooperative credit. It is interesting to note that the concentration of assets in Punjab—the seat of technological change—is the lowest among all states, and consequently, the concentration of cooperative credit is also among the lowest. It is also noteworthy that in southern and eastern rice states, the concentration of assets as well as of cooperative credit is higher than the national average whereas Gujarat and Maharashtra, where the progress of cooperative movement has been impressive, show lower coefficients of concentration than the national average.

[8]About 70 per cent of the inter-state variation in the concentration of credit is explained by the concentration of assets. An increase in the coefficient of concentration of assets by 0.10000 is associated with an increase in the coefficient of concentration of credit to the extent of 0.10450 (significant at 1 per cent level).

TABLE 11·3: Credit Availed by Farmers of Different Holding Size
Classes in the Intensive Agricultural District Programme Area
(Loan per hectare of cultivated area taken from Cooperatives or Government)
(In Rupees)

	First Group of Districts	Second Group of Districts
	(1)	(2)
Small Farmers		
1962-63	28	19
1967-68	43	30
Percentage increase	54	58
Medium Farmers		
1962-63	28	13
1967-68	47	35
Percentage increase	68	169
Large Farmers		
1962-63	20	13
1967-68	40	33
Percentage increase	100	154

Source: Ministry of Food and Agriculture, *Modernising Indian Agriculture, Report of the Intensive Agricultural District Programme*, Vol. 1, p. 100.

The experience in the IADP districts is that the disparity in the distribution of credit was further accentuated in the last decade. Table 11.3 shows that, between 1962-63 and 1967-68, loan per hectare, taken from cooperatives by the large farmers, increased by 100 per cent to 154 per cent—as against the increase of 54 to 58 per cent in the case of loan taken by the small farmers. It may be noted, however, that the average loan per hectare taken by the small farmers was higher in 1962-63 when compared to the loan taken by the large and medium farmers and these differences have been very much reduced in 1967-68.

The distribution of short-term credit advanced by the public sector banks appears to be less iniquitous. Holdings operating above 10 acres accounted for 34.4 per cent of advances as short-term loans to agriculture as at the end of March 1973,[9] which is significantly less than their share in total land.[10] Medium and long-term loans

[9]'Agricultural Advances of Public Sector Banks: An Analysis', *Reserve Bank of India Bulletin*, April 1964, p. 644.

[10]According to the 17th Round of the National Sample Survey, such holdings accounted for about 60 per cent of total operated area in 1961-62. However, the share of such holdings must have declined significantly by 1971.

constituted about 60 per cent of total advances to agriculture by the public sector banks, such credit being used mainly for the development of minor irrigation and acquisition of tractors, etc.[11] As much as 62 per cent of such credit (term loans) was availed of by holdings operating above 10 acres,[12] which could be well above their share in total land.

Farm Size and Output Per Acre

Despite better access to resources, output per acre among large farms under the traditional labour-intensive technology was lower than among small farms, as the cost of (hired) labour was higher for them than for small family farms. Also, managerial and supervisory diseconomies of large size under labour-intensive methods accounted for lower labour input per acre among large farms. Technological changes created new production possibilities for large farms who could now increasingly substitute capital for labour by adopting biological as well as mechanical techniques and produce output at a faster rate than small farms. The latest evidence shows that the inverse relationship between farm size and output per acre found under traditional technology no longer holds true with the adoption of new technology.

Table 11.4 shows the relationship between farm size and output per acre[13] under traditional technology in the fifties as well as

[11]*Reserve Bank of India Bulletin*, April 1964, pp. 643, 646.

[12]Ibid., p. 648.

[13]The results for Muzaffarnagar and Ferozepur are borrowed from the work by N. Bhattacharya and G.R. Saini who fitted long-linear equations ($Y=a+bX$, where $Y=$output per acre and $X=$size of holding) to the individual (disaggregated) farm data. We have obtained the results for West Godavari by fitting a similar equation to the farm data aggregated into eight groups according to the size of holding. In the case of late fifties, the West Godavari data for three years were averaged before they were grouped into size classes. The consequences of using aggregate data have been explored sufficiently by the research workers interested in size-productivity relationships. The general outcome of these exercises is that the size-productivity relationships are broadly the same whether single-year, single-village individual farm data are used or when the data are aggregated across the years, villages and groups of farms. See for instance, the work by N. Bhattacharya and G.R. Saini, 'Farm Size and Productivity: A Fresh Look', *Economic and Political Weekly*, Review of Agriculture, 24 June 1972. See also C.H. Hanumantha Rao, 'Alternative Explanations of the Inverse Relationship between Farm Size and Output per Acre in India', *Indian Economic Review*, October 1966.

with the adoption of new techniques in the late sixties in Muzaffarnagar (Uttar Pradesh), Ferozepur (Punjab) and West Godavari
(Andhra Pradesh)—areas of fastest change in regard to wheat and
rice.

TABLE 11·4: Relationship Between the Gross Value of Output
Per Acre and Farm Size

	Muzaffarnagar (Uttar Pradesh)	
Year	*Slope (b)*	*Coefficient of Correlation*
1955-56	—0.25*	—0.46
1956-57	—0.17*	—0.33
1966-67	—0.14*	—0.25
1967-68	—0.09**	—0.25
1968-69	—0.04***	—0.17
	Ferozepur (Punjab)	
1955-56	—0.06	—0.09
1956-57	—0.17**	—0.28
1967-68	—0.03	—0.05
1968-69	—0.03	—0.04
	West Godavari (Andhra Pradesh)	
1957-60		
Output	—0.11***	—0.62
Labour	—0.13**	—0.82
Fertiliser	—0.05	—0.21
1969-70 Output	0.02	0.15
Labour	—0.16**	—0.86
Fertiliser	0.10***	0.77

*Significant at 0.1% level; ** Significant at 1% level; ***Significant at 5% level;
the remaing coefficients are not significant at 5% level.

Sources: (1) The results pertaining to Muzaffarnagar and Ferozepur are taken
from N. Bhattacharya and G.R. Saini, 'Farm Size and Productivity:
A Fresh Look', *Economic and Political Weekly*, Review of Agriculture,
24 June 1972.

(2) The results relating to West Godavari for the period 1957-60 are ob-
tained by using the data contained in Directorate of Economics and
Statistics, Ministry of Food and Agriculture. *Studies in Economics of
Farm Management, West Godavari.*

(3) The results relating to West Godavari for the year 1969-70 are obtained on the basis of the data contained in Waheeduddin Khan and
R. N. Tripathy, *Intensive Agriculture and Modern Inputs: Prospects of
Small Farmers—A Study in West Godavari District*, National Institute
of Community Development, Hyderabad, 1972, pp. 13, 64 and 76.

The inverse correlation between farm size and output per

acre was statistically significant in the fifties in Muzaffarnagar and West Godavari. For Ferozepur, the inverse correlation was statistically significant in 1955-56. In the sixties, with the adoption of new inputs, the inverse relationship between farm size and output per acre was weakened very much in Muzaffarnagar (Uttar Pradesh), the regression coefficient having been progressively reduced from —0.25 in 1955-56 to —0.04 in 1968-69.[14] In the case of Ferozepur (Punjab) as well as West Godavari (Andhra Pradesh), the correlation was not statistically significant.

The weakening or disappearance of the inverse relationship between farm size and output per acre implies a higher rate of growth of output among large farms when compared to small farms. This has been achieved by large farms not through greater application of labour inputs per acre but through the greater use of capital inputs or the increasing substitution of capital for labour. The figures in Table 11.5 indicate a steeper decline of labour input per acre with the increase in the size of holding in Ferozepur in the late sixties when compared to the position in the fifties. Fertiliser input per acre, however, rises significantly with the increase in the size of holding as against a mild inverse relationship in the fifties.[15] In West Godavari too, fertiliser input per acre shows a significant positive correlation with farm size in 1969-70 whereas it was non-significant in 1957-60.[16] The inverse relationship between farm size and labour input per acre, on the other hand, has become

[14]A recent study for Meerut District of Uttar Pradesh (Rajvir Singh and R.K. Patel, 'Returns to Scale, Farm Size and Productivity in Meerut District', *Indian Journal of Agricultural Economics*, April-June 1973) pertaining to 120 farms in 1969-70 concludes that in the context of new technology there is no indication of decrease in output per hectare with an increase in farm size. The equation fitted is log $Y = a + 1.081$ log X_1 $(R^2 = 0.82)$ where $Y =$ output of the farm and $X_1 =$ size of holding. Since the regression coefficient is significantly different from zero but not from unity, a constancy in output per hectare with the increase in the size of holding is indicated.

[15]A Study by the Programme Evaluation Organization of the Planning Commission (*Evaluation Study of the High Yielding Varieties Programme: Report for the Rabi 1968-69—Wheat, Paddy and Jowar*) shows that 'the average dose applied was broadly found to be increasing with increased operational holding of the participants' (p. 24).

[16]The higher rate of adoption of new technology by large farms is responsible for the 'increasing returns to scale' revealed by some recent studies (e.g., Singh and Patel, op. cit., and Khan and Tripathy, op. cit.). Since technology is not the same at different levels of farm size, these findings do not reflect economies of scale *as such.*

pronounced, the regression coefficient with respect to labour (on farm size) having changed from -0.13 in 1957-60 to -0.16 in 1969-70 (see Table 11.4).

TABLE 11.5: VALUE (Rs.) OF LABOUR INPUTS (FAMILY AND HIRED) AND FERTILISER INPUT PER ACRE IN PUNJAB

1954-57 (Ferozepur & Amritsar)			1968-70 (Ferozepur)		
Size of Holding (Acres)	Labour Input	Fertiliser & Manure	Size of Holding (Acres)	Labour Input	Fertiliser & Manure
(1)	(2)	(3)	(4)	(5)	(6)
Less than 5	56.20	4.71	Less than 15	236.26	40.93
5–10	49.94	4.00	15–22	179.25	45.73
10–20	45.87	3.57	22–35	189.35	48.24
20–50	39.98	3.86	35–59	165.92	49.61
50 and above	35.49	3.86	Above 59	121.44	58.98

Note : Values are not corrected for changes in prices between the two periods.
Source : Directorate of Economics and Statistics, Ministry of Agriculture, *Studies in Economics of Farm Management in Punjab, 1954-57 and 1968-70.*

A higher rate of growth of output among large farms indicates that income disparities between small and large farms have grown as a result of technological change.[17] In so far as technological

[17]S.S. Johol's study indicates that in Ludhiana district (Punjab) the (proportionate) difference between the per capita income of small and large farmers was higher in 1969-70 when compared to 1967-68. See his, *Gains of Green Revolution (How they have been shared in Punjab)* (mimeo).

S.L. Bapna in his study for Kota district of Rajasthan concludes that between 1968-69 and 1971-72, the income of the small farmers increased by 9.3 per cent, while that of the large farmers by 50 per cent and that of the medium farmers by 12 per cent. Inequality in relative income of the farmers as measured by concentration ratio has also increased despite a mild reduction in the concentration of land ownership. See his, *Economic and Social Implications of Green Revolution: A Case Study of the Kota District* (mimeo), Agro Economic Research Centre, Sardar Patel University, Vallabh Vidyanagar, 1973.

A study for Haryana (*Changing Structure of Agriculture in Haryana: A Study of Impact of Green Revolution, 1969-70*, Department of Economics, Punjab University and the Economic and Statistical Organisation, Government of Haryana) shows that income disparities between the poorest non-progressive and the richest progressive cultivators have widened as a result of the Green Revolution but there is less income disparity within the class of progressive cultivators compared with the disparity within non-progressive cultivators. However, from this, the conclusion that the 'Green Revolution has tended to reduce income inequalities amongst those who have adopted the new technology' would not follow

changes are cost-reducing, the growth of net income must have been even faster among large farms.

Whereas technological change *as such* may have contributed to the widening of income disparities according to farm size, two qualifications have to be kept in view before drawing inferences as to the emergence and the degree of income disparities. First, the rate of technological change has been faster in regions like Punjab where the physical and institutional infrastructure has been favourable for wider participation of farmers in the Green Revolution. Table 11.2 indicates, for instance, that between different states, concentration of assets as well as of credit is the lowest in Punjab. Second, there seems to have been a decline in the concentration of operated area in the recent period which by itself should lead to a decline in income disparities. It would, therefore, be necessary to consider the net impact of all these factors on income disparities.

DISTRIBUTION OF LAND HOLDINGS AND THE DISTRIBUTION OF INCOME

The data on the size distribution of ownership and operational holdings and on the distribution of area owned and operated are not yet available for the period subsequent to the adoption of HYV. However, a comparison of such data between 1953-54 and 1961-62 shows that the inequality in the distribution of owned land remained unchanged whereas the inequality in the distribution of operated area declined.[18] This may have been the combined result of several

straightway if the distribution of land and irrigation, about which there is no information in the Report, is less unequal within the class of progressive cultivators compared to non-progressive cultivators.

[18]The concentration ratios pertaining to the distribution of total owned area by size groups of ownership holdings were 0.67 and 0.68 for 1953-54 and 1961-62 respectively, whereas those pertaining to the distribution of total operated area by size groups of operational holdings declined from 0.62 to 0.58 over the corresponding period. See Dharm Narain, 'The Changing Agricultural Structure Over the Years—Some Aspects', *Yojana*, Independence Silver Jubilee Issue, No. XV, 15 August 1972.

N.V.A. Narasimham in his study 'Inequalities in the Distribution of Holdings and Incomes of Farmers in India in 1961-62' (*Agricultural Situation in India*, September 1969) found a decline in inequality in respect of ownership holdings between 1953-54 and 1961-62. However, his data on the number of households in 1961-62 pertain to the number of sample households and not to the estimated number of households.

factors including (a) land reform measures such as the transfer of land to the tenants as well as the imposition of legal ceilings on the ownership of agricultural land and the distribution of 'surplus' land in the fifties; (b) the sale of land by large landowners as well as the sale of marginal holdings to the small and medium landowners; (c) a higher rate of subdivision among large landowners than among small owners with a view to keeping the size of holding below the ceiling level; and (d) *benami* (spurious) transfers of land to relatives and friends with a view to evading ceiling legislation.

It is not possible to measure the relative contribution of each of these factors to the observed tendency in inequality in the distribution of land especially because no evidence is available on the latter two factors. In so far as landless labourers and tenants are given land through redistributive land reform measures, the skewness in the distribution of land need not necessarily decline. The skewness may even increase if, as a result of land reform, the number of small holdings increases such that the proportion of land held by households in the bottom deciles declines. However, available evidence indicates that land transferred through land reform measures has been negligible and bulk of the land so transferred may have gone to the medium and small owners already owning land.[19] Thus, transfer of land through market sales seems to have been more important than through redistributive land reform.[20] Further, several marginal

[19]For instance, of the land distributed by the Government of Maharashtra since 1954, only about half was distributed to the landless. See, G.R. Mulla, 'Government Lands for Cultivation: A Case Study of Maharashtra', *Economic and Political Weekly*, Review of Agriculture, 29 September 1973.

[20]V.M. Rao in a detailed analysis of land transfers in Gujarat and Maharashtra concludes that in the period prior to 1956, landownership tended to get concentrated in the hands of larger cultivators; during the period 1956-65, on the other hand, the land market worked to lessen the concentration of landownership. See his 'Land Transfers in Rural Communities: Some Findings in a Ryotwari Region', *Economic and Political Weekly*, Review of Agriculture, 30 September 1972.

A study for Punjab (M.S. Randhawa, *Green Revolution*, Vikas, Delhi, 1974, p. 168) suggests that as a result of purchase and sale transactions over the three year period 1967-68 through 1969-70, the farmers in the smallest size group (below 9.5 acres) registered 0.95 per cent net increase in area owned as against a decline of 2.5 per cent in the case of the largest size group (above 29 acres).

Ashok Rudra, A. Majid and B.D. Talib in their study, *Big Farmers of Punjab* (Agro-Economic Research Centre, University of Delhi) observe that although the number of large farms operating above 20 acres may have gone down in 1967-68 when compared to 1961 owing to sub-divisions, a section of large holdings seem to drop out every year from the list of ownership holdings owing to the sale of such holdings,[21] which by itself could contribute to a decline in inequality in the ownership of land as measured by the concentration ratio.

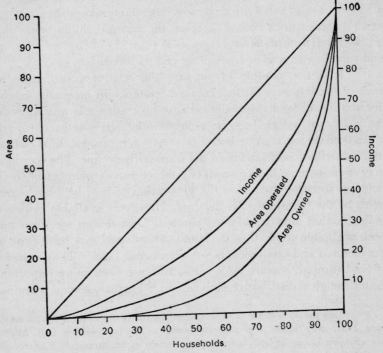

Figure 11.1

Note: Distribution of Income relates to Rural Households (All India) in 1962. Distribution of Area relates to Ownership as well as Operational Holdings (Rural-All India) in 1961-62.

Sources: 1.   N.S.S., Seventeenth Round, Report Number 144.
2.   N.C.A.E.R., *Report on All India Rural Household Survey*, Vol. III.

farms has become bigger between 1955-56 and 1967-68 principally through purchase of land. However, in the absence of data on the purchase of land by farms below 20 acres, it is not possible to draw any inference as to the changes in the concentration of landownership, especially because absentee landowners could account for a large proportion of land sold.

[21]In Bihar, for instance, about 67,000 ownership holdings (with an average size of less than one acre) or about 1.2 per cent of the total ownership holding were being sold off annually by their owners during the period 1959-62. See, S.R. Bose, 'Land Sales and Land Values in Bihar', *Indian Journal of Agricultural Economics*, April-June 1970.

The inequality in the distribution of rural income (consumption) is significantly lower than that in the distribution of ownership or operational holdings (see the Lorenz Curves in Fig. 11.1), because output per acre is generally higher among smaller holdings (which, however, may not hold true for areas experiencing the Green Revolution) and because small income groups account for a predominant share in income from non-crop enterprises and derive a significant part of their income as wage-bill from the large farmers.[22] Although the degree of income (consumption) inequality would be less than that in land holdings, the former is directly related to the latter.[23] Therefore, the declining trend in inequality in respect of area operated *per se* might have had the effect of reducing the income disparities in the rural sector. The analysis of consumer expenditure data shows that the inequality in consumer expenditure in the rural sector—which is clearly less than that in the urban sector—declined between the early fifties and the early sixties, although this may not hold true at constant prices, because the prices of essential commodities like food, on which small expenditure groups spend proportionately more, have risen at a faster rate.[24]

To sum up, it appears that technological changes *as such*, have the effect of widening the income inequality in the rural sector even though technological changes have been widespread in areas like Punjab where the distribution of assets and institutional credit is less unequal than in the rest of the country. Income distribution in real terms might be worsening owing to the greater rise in the price of essential commodities. However, the decline in disparities in regard to area operated might be exerting an opposite influence. On the basis of the available data, it is not possible to gauge the net impact of each of these factors on income distribution. However, if changes in prices are ignored and change in the distribution of nominal income alone is considered, the available evidence suggests that for the country as a whole, the net impact of technological changes and the changes in the distribution of area

[22]A. Vaidyanathan, 'Some Aspects of Inequalities in Living Standards in Rural India', *Sankhya*, The Indian Journal of Statistics, Series C, Vol. 36, Parts 2 & 4, June and December, 1974. See also, Narasimham, 'Inequalities in the Distribution of Holdings and Incomes of Farmers in India in 1961-62', op. cit.

[23]Vaidyanathan, op. cit.

[24]G.S. Chatterjee and N. Bhattacharya, 'On Disparities in Per Capita Household Consumption in India', *Sankhya*, The Indian Journal of Statistics, Series C, Vol. 36, Parts 2 and 4, June and Dec. 1974.

operated is a decline in the relative share of large incomes and in income disparities in the rural sector.[25]

SUMMARY

Technological changes in Indian agriculture are being introduced within an institutional framework characterised by marked disparities in investable resources per acre (from own soures as well as borrowings) between large and small farmers. Consequently, the growth of output among large farms is much faster than on small farms. This higher growth among large farms is achieved mainly through the use of capital inputs and the substitution of capital for labour. As a consequence, the inverse relationship between farm size and output per acre found under the traditional labour-intensive technology, which was favourable to small farms, does not seem to hold good in areas undergoing technological changes. Although technological changes *as such* have contributed to the widening of income disparities, the declining trend in the inequality in the area operated exerts an opposite influence and it is likely that, on balance, the distribution of income in the rural sector in the country as a whole has become less unequal during the last decade.

[25]Additional Rural Income Survey (ARIS) conducted by the National Council of Applied Economic Research (NCAER) covering a sample of about 5,000 rural households in the country revealed that the Gini Concentration ratio declined from 0.43 in 1968-69 to 0.39 in 1969-70 and 0.38 in 1970-71 (the earlier NCAER Survey of rural household incomes for 1962 showed this ratio to be 0.406). The proportion of rural households with incomes of 10,000 and above per annum declined from 2.02 per cent in 1968-69 to 1.81 per cent in 1969-70 and 1.75 per cent in 1970-71. Their share in income declined from 12.32 per cent to 10.39 per cent and 9.93 per cent over the corresponding period. See, 'A Note On the Additional Rural Income Survey' (unpublished), prepared by M.T.R. Sarma, NCAER.

Another interesting study, 'The Impact of New Agricultural Technology on Farm Income Distribution in the Aligarh District of Uttar Pradesh' (*Indian Journal of Agricultural Economics*, April-June 1973), by Katar Singh shows that farm income inequality in 1968-69 was significantly less than in 1963-64 and that this was due mainly to a decline in the relative variance of per farm expenditure on new technology over the period. However, the decline in the relative variance of cropped area per farm (from 0.999 in 1963-64 to 0.699 in 1968-69) is greater than that in farm expenditure on new technology (from 1.022 to 0.847). It is thus possible that per acre expenditure on new technology is higher for large farms so that new technology could have led to an increase in income inequality if there was no reduction in the variance of cropped area.

CHAPTER 12

Tenancy and the
Distribution of Gains

HYPOTHESIS

Technological change would affect the distribution of gains between landowners and tenants by altering, in general, (a) rent per acre and its relative share in output per acre; (b) the extent of area under tenancy; and (c) the terms or tenancy such as mode of rent payment (i.e., whether fixed or share rent) and cost-sharing in the case of crop-sharing tenancy. The distribution of gains would depend on the character of technological change (i.e., whether it is land-augmenting or labour-substituting etc.) and the relative capacities of landowners and tenants to invest in modern inputs as well as their relative bargaining power.

Land-augmenting technological changes may be classified broadly into two types. Irrigation can be regarded as a land-augmenting technological change because more output can be produced on the same piece of land with irrigation owing to the possibility of multiple cropping (i.e., same area being cropped more than once in a year) as well as to the rise in yield per cropped (harvested) acre. Irrigation represents technological change essentially embodied in land so that the capital value (and hence rental value) of land is raised substantially. Traditional irrigated farming is carried on mainly with human labour as current input with very little commitment of working capital for modern (current) inputs. On the other hand, land-augmenting technological change such as the introduction of High Yielding Varieties involves a sizeable commitment of working capital for the purchase of current (modern) inputs, for example, fertilisers, pesticides, etc. These two types of technological changes may have differing impact on tenurial relations because in the case of the second type, the relative capacities of landowners and tenants to invest in current modern inputs becomes an important variable.

Irrigation, in so far as it increases the effective supply of land, may, other things remaining equal, lead to a reduction in economic rent (i.e., exclusive of rent for the irrigation factor) per acre and an increase in the area leased out. But, insofar as irrigation increases yield and reduces its variability over time, the tenants' demand function for such land may also shift upwards particularly because irrigated farming can be carried on with labour-intensive methods involving very little extra investment in current (modern) material inputs, and the landless poor place a high value on stable (assured) income flows. This explains the historically observed migration of labour on a large scale to the irrigated areas which are eventually characterised by high population density. Similarly, the increase in the effective supply of land for lease after irrigation may be significant, especially because landowners' own demand (for land) for self-cultivation may decline owing to the managerial and supervisory diseconomies associated with labour-intensive irrigated farming.[1] Because of the relative yield certainty for irrigated paddy, rent per acre does not seem to differ significantly from net income when land is self-cultivated with traditional methods.[2] Thus, area under tenancy may rise significantly owing to both supply and demand factors. The impact on economic rent per acre would depend upon the relative strength of supply and demand factors.

Technological change such as the introduction of High Yielding Varieties, in so far as it is land-augmenting and increases the effective supply of land, may, other things remaining equal, reduce rent per acre and increase the area under tenancy. But the landowners' own demand (for self-cultivation) may increase owing to the rise in the profitability of investment in current modern inputs,

[1] This seems to be especially true for predominantly paddy areas in India where there is evidence of decreasing returns to scale among owner-operated farms and constant returns under sharecropping. See C. H. Hanumantha Rao, 'Uncertainty, Entrepreneurship and Sharecropping in India', *Journal of Political Economy*, May-June 1971. See also, Pranab K. Bardhan, 'Size, Productivity and Returns to Scale: An Analysis of Farm-Level Data in Indian Agriculture', *Journal of Political Economy*, November-December 1973. The finding of diminishing returns to scale in this study relates to the overall samples predominated by owner-farmers.

[2] C. H. Hanumantha Rao, *Taxation of Agricultural Land in Andhra Pradesh*, Asia Publishing House, 1966, pp. 86, 88.

especially because landowners have a better access to capital resources and cultivation with hired labour enables them to capture the returns on investment in modern inputs.[3] The substitution of capital for labour made profitable by the new technology enables them to overcome the diseconomies of scale associated with labour-intensive farming. This may lead to a rise in rent per acre and a decline in the area leased out.[4]

However, where tenants happen to be large farmers with better access to capital resources, their demand for land may increase resulting in a rise in rent per acre as well as the area under tenancy.

[3] A necessary condition for this to happen is that the rate of return on investment in technologically new inputs is high enough to match the high rates of interest that the landowners are able to realise through money-lending. The ruling high rates of interest might thus be one of the factors responsible for the lower intensity of land-use among large farms. See C. H. Hanumantha Rao, 'Alternative Explanations of the Inverse Relationship Between Farm Size and Output Per Acre in India', *Indian Economic Review*, October 1966.

Amit Bhaduri ('A Study in Agricultural Backwardness Under Semi-Feudalism', *The Economic Journal*, March 1973) has argued that in eastern India, where landowners frequently combine share cropping with usury, it may not be in the interest of landowners to adopt new technology if their gain from technical progress is not sufficient to compensate for the decline in income from usury consequent to the increase in the productivity of the sharecropper. His point seems valid in its generalised form namely, in regions like eastern India, new agricultural technology may not be adopted unless its profitability is high enough to match the high rate of return from usury. But he comes out with pessimistic conclusions regarding the prospect for technical progress because of his implicit assumption that technological change would not affect either the area under sharecropping or the rental share and that the tenant would be permitted to gain from technological change. However, as we have argued, landowners may resume land for their own cultivation with hired labour in which case the tenants are deprived of the gains from technological change, and the gain to the landowner would be higher than implied in Bhaduri's analysis. If a legal ban on resumption of land and a ceiling on rental share *can* be implemented, then landowners can *also* be forced to adopt new technology by sharing cost with tenants.

[4] P. K. Bardhan and T. N. Srinivasan in their analysis of cropsharing tenancy arrive at an opposite result: '...the rental share is a declining function of the land-augmenting technical progress parameter....With land-augmenting technical progress the equilibrium amount (and the percentage) of land leased out under cropsharing goes *up*.' Evidently, they have not taken into account the possible rise in the landowners' own demand for land for self-cultivation (owing to their better access to capital resources for investing in current modern inputs) induced by the profitability of land-augmenting technical change such as the introduction of HYV. See their 'Cropsharing Tenancy in Agriculture: A Theoretical and Empirical Analysis', *The American Economic Review*, March 1971.

Although in certain regions large farmers happen to be net leasers-in as a group rather than the small farmers, bulk of the tenanted area in the country is owned by the large landowner-farmers who have greater access to capital resources than small farmers. Even in cases where small landowners lease out area, some of them may have access to capital resources and may resume land for own cultivation with new techniques. One should, therefore, expect the land-augmenting technological changes involving greater use of current modern inputs to result in a rise in rent per acre and a reduction in the area under tenancy.

For reasons mentioned earlier, the share of land (economic rent) in output per acre could decline despite an absolute rise in rent per acre. Further, owing to the decline in the area under tenancy, the share of rental income in output can be expected to decline significantly. Land-augmenting technological change would thus raise the landowners' income *vis-à-vis* the erstwhile tenants (who now probably become wage-labourers) via the resumption of land for self-cultivation with hired labour.

Where landowners are absentees or lack investable resources, they may not be in a position to resume land from the tenants for self-cultivation. In such a situation it would be beneficial for landowners to convert fixed rents (whether fixed in cash or kind) into cropsharing rentals, as this would enable them to gain from the investments made either (exclusively) by the tenants, or (exclusively) by the landowners themselves or through cost-sharing by both the parties.[5] This tendency for sharecropping to increase mainly through the conversion of the fixed-rent system may not outweigh the other tendency on the part of the landowners to resume land from the sharecroppers, because bulk of the land leased out belongs to the resident landowners who have the capacity to invest in modern inputs. On balance,therefore, one should expect the area under share-cropping to decline with the progress of land-augmenting technological change involving the use of current inputs. Even for the remaining area under sharecropping, the landowners' role as

[5]Hanumantha Rao, 'Uncertainty, Entrepreneurship, and Sharecropping in India', op. cit. This paper also suggests that 'the incentives for increased investment as well as for capturing the returns on such investment may lead to the preference for fixed-cash rents and own cultivation of land with hired labour'. Conversion of cropsharing rentals into fixed-cash rents may be possible only in those situations where tenants have a greater bargaining power.

investor-entrepreneurs can be expected to be greater than before.

Since, survival of tenancy (whether sharecropping or fixed rent system) despite technological change in certain situations (e.g., when landowners are absentees) indicates the greater bargaining power of tenants, the latter may gain in varying degrees from technological change. Except where landowners do not share the costs on modern inputs used under sharecropping with the given rent-share, the tenants may be expected to gain at least in proportion to the gains accruing to the landowners. Under the fixed rent system as also when landowners bear the entire costs on modern (variable) inputs applied under sharecropping with the given rent-share, tenants may benefit proportionately more than landowners. Under sharecropping, when both the parties share the costs on modern (variable) inputs in the same proportion in which they share output, the gains would also be shared in a similar proportion.

Labour-substituting technological change such as tractorisation implies an increase in the effective supply of draft power at the disposal of farmers using such equipment. Where landowners lease out land owing to the managerial and supervisory diseconomies of large size under labour-intensive techniques, labour-substituting technological change may improve the landowners' capacity for self-cultivation (with hired labour) leading to a decline in the area under tenancy as well as a rise in rent per acre. But where tenants happen to be large farmers using such equipment, rent as well as the area under tenancy may increase. However, in view of the fact that bulk of the tenanted area in India is owned by large landowner farmers, we should expect the labour-substituting technological change to lead, on balance, to a decline in the area under tenancy and to a rise in rent per acre.

Labour-substituting technological change is complementary to land-augmenting technological change inasmuch as the former enables the landowners to benefit from the latter by resuming land from tenants for self-cultivation. Even where net income from self-cultivation with tractorisation is not higher than the rental income from leasing out, landowners may, nevertheless, find tractorisation beneficial if it helps them to evict tenants who might claim a legal right to posses land or pay lower rents. In every case, therefore, labour-substituting technical change may raise the bargaining power of landowners and may thus reduce the incomes of the tenants, many of whom are forced to become wage labourers.

CHANGES IN AREA UNDER TENANCY AND IN RENT-SHARE

The data on the area under tenancy for the country as a whole in the post-Green Revolution period are not available. However, the evidence available from village studies is suggestive of a decline in the area under tenancy, particularly sharecropping, as a result of technological change. Several village surveys carried out by the Agro-Economic Research Centres in different parts of the country indicated that, between the mid-fifties and early sixties, i.e., much before the High Yielding Varieties programme was introduced, there was a decline in area leased-in owing to the resumption of land for self-cultivation induced, among other things, by improved prospects for cultivation resulting from the rise in agricultural prices as well as the provision of an infrastructure supporting and promoting improved technology.[6] A recent study for the Kota district of Rajasthan shows that between 1968-69 and 1971-72, the proportion of leased-out area to owned area declined from 7.2 per cent to 2.5 per cent and the proportion of leased-in area to operated area declined from 18.4 per cent to 14.8 per cent over this period.[7] As a consequence of resumption of land for self-cultivation, the concentration ratio of operated area increased from 0.46 to 0.49, although it was still less than that of owned area which declined from 0.55 to 0.52.[8] In the Ferozepur district of Punjab, where there has been a rapid rate of tractorisation, the proportion of tenanted area to the area under cultivation declined steeply from 37 per cent in 1954-55 to 11.6 per cent in 1969-70, and whereas the area under sharecropping declined from 33 per cent to 6.6 per cent, the area under the cash rent system showed a marginal increase from 4 per cent to 5 per cent over the corresponding period.[9] Another study[10] for the same

[6]Dharm Narain and P. C. Joshi, 'Magnitude of Agricultural Tenancy', *Economic and Political Weekly*, Review of Agriculture, 27 September, 1969.

[7]Bapna, op. cit.

[8]Ibid.

[9]Randhawa, op. cit., p. 165. The observed decline in area under tenancy may be attributed, in part, to the landlords' attempts to bypass the protective tenancy laws. However, this factor may have been less important in the sixties than in the fifties. In any case, such resumptions are very much facilitated by technological change, particularly tractorisation.

[10]A. S. Kahlon and Gurbachan Singh, *Social and Economic Implications of Large Scale Introduction of High Yielding Varieties of Wheat in Punjab with Special Reference to the Ferozepur District*, (U.N.D.P. Global Project), Department of Economics and Sociology, Punjab Agricultural University, Ludhiana, 1973.

district shows that the area under cash rent increased from 32 per cent of total tenanted area in 1967-68 to 74 per cent in 1971-72.

Where rents are fixed—either in kind or cash—there has been a rise in rent per acre. In regard to sharecropping rentals, either the share has remained constant or increased but in no case is there any decline in rent-share.[11] In Kota district (Rajasthan), for instance, the increase in rent took the form of interest-free loans to the landowners leasing out land over and above the traditional rent-share, the alternative being to pay two-third of output as rent.[12] In Karnal district (Haryana), share-rents were raised in quite a few cases from one-third to half the share in gross produce.[13] Similarly, according to a case study of a village in West Godavari (Andhra Pradesh), whereas rent payment to the extent of two-third share of produce is not common for local varieties, landlords insist on two-third share if the tenant chooses to grow HYV and majority of tenants growing HYV in *rabi* season paid two-thirds of gross produce as rent.[14] However, according to another study in the same district, the most common form of rent in the *rabi* season was 50 per cent of gross output before as well as after the introduction of HYV.[15]

RESOURCE-USE, COST-SHARING AND
THE DISTRIBUTION OF GAINS

In areas experiencing technological change, landowners and

[11]Bardhan and Srinivasan show how the equilibrium rental share would go up with increased cost-sharing by landlords (regardless of technological change). See their 'Cropsharing Tenancy in Agriculture: A Theoretical and Empirical Analysis,' op. cit. However, the studies we are dealing with focus on the Green Revolution period and hence abstract largely from the secular increase in the practice of cost-sharing.

[12]Bapna, op. cit.

[13]H. Laxminarayan, *The Social and Economic Implications of the Large-Scale Introduction of High Yielding Varieties of Wheat in Haryana* (mimeo), The U.N.D.P. Project, Agricultural Economic Research Centre, University of Delhi, 1973.

[14]G. Parthasarathy and D.S. Prasad, 'Responses to, and Impact of, H.Y.V. Rice According to Land Size and Tenure in a Delta Village, Andhra Pradesh, India', *The Developing Economies*, Vol XII, No. 2, June 1974 (Institute of Developing Economies, Tokyo).

[15]Waheeduddin Khan and V.B.R.S. Somasekhara Rao, 'On Tenancy, Rent-Systems and Improved Technology—An Investigation in West Godavari District', *Community Development and Panchayati Raj Digest*, April 1973.

tenants have generally been found to share costs on modern inputs such as fertilisers in the same proportion in which output is shared between them.[16] A study of the package (IADP) districts before the introduction of HYV showed that in Ludhiana district (Punjab), 'the landlords get 50 per cent of gross produce' as rent and, in regard to the rate of utilisation of fertilisers, sharecroppers 'do not seem to make much distinction between owned land and tenancy land. Where rent is paid as a share of produce, the cost of fertiliser is shared half and half between the owner and the tenant.'[17] A recent study for Ferozepur (Punjab), shows that in all the three years ending with 1969-70, the costs on seeds and fertilisers were shared equally between the landowner and the tenant and those on irrigation were shared in the 40:60 ratio by the respective parties.[18] A study of progressive villages in Gujarat adopting HYV shows that 'the most common form of tenancy agreement, namely, that involving half-share, postulates that the tenant supplies family labour, bullocks, implements, seeds, and seedlings. The landlord and the tenant share expenses on the remaining inputs in equal measure.'[19] In villages of Haryana adopting new technology, where rent constitutes 50 per cent of output, the landlord and the tenant share the costs on modern inputs equally.[20] The case study of the West Godavari village mentioned earlier brings out that when rent is paid as a share of gross produce, whether one-half or two-third, 'costs on fertiliser and pesticides are borne by the landowner proportionate to his share in the gross produce'.[21] Another study for West Godavari mentioned earlier, points out that in all instances of sharecropping arrangements for HYV paddy, landlords provided modern inputs, for example, HYV paddy, seed, fertiliser and pesticides, during the season and deducted the tenant's share of the costs (which is in proportion to his share in gross produce) from his

[16]It can be shown that the allocation of resources would be optimal under such situations, that is, when costs on variable inputs are shared by the landowner and the tenant in the same proportion as output is shared.

[17]W. Ladejinsky, *A study on Tenurial Conditions in Package Districts*, Planning Commission, New Delhi, 1965.

[18]Randhawa, op. cit.

[19]V. S. Vyas, 'Tenancy in a Dynamic Setting', *Economic and Political Weekly, Review of Agriculture*, 27 June 1970.

[20]Laxminarayan, op. cit.

[21]Parthasarathy and Prasad, op. cit.

share in the output after the harvest.[22]

Much of the received theory on the allocation of resources under sharecropping emphasises the inefficiency of this system arising from the restriction of inputs because the sharecropper may not have the incentive to apply inputs beyond a point when the landowners do not share the costs,[23] and that under certain situations it may not be profitable for the landowner to share the costs on variable inputs.[24] These theories tend to overlook that sharecroppers lack investable capacity and that under certain circumstances, landowners may have the incentive to share the costs and may indeed encourage cost-sharing by the tenants.[25] Thus, these theories ignore, in the first place, the possibility that resource-use may be restricted even under the fixed rent-system[26] because of the tenant's weaker resource position and that the level of resource-use could in fact be

[22]Khan and Rao, op. cit.

[23]'When the cultivator has to give to his landlord half of the returns to each dose of capital and labour that he applied to his land, it will not be to his interest to apply any doses the total return to which is less than twice enough to reward him.' See Alfred Marshall, *Principles of Economics*, Macmillan, London, 1956.

[24]A. K. Sen and T. C. Varghese, 'Tenancy and Resource Allocation', *Seminar* (India), No. 81, May 1966. See also D. W. Adams, and N. Rask, 'Economics of {Cost-Share Leases in Less-developed Countries', *American Journal of Agricultural Economics*, Vol, 50, Number 4, November 1968.

Their argument assumes that sharecroppers will use the inputs upto the point where the marginal product net of rent share is equal to the price of input. But in view of the greater investable capacity of landowners, their argument can be employed to yield the opposite and more plausible result that, in the case of variable inputs like fertilisers, cost-sharing may not be profitable for the sharecroppers when they know that the landowners would pay for these inputs upto the point where the marginal product net of tenants' share is equal to the price of input.

[25]It can even be argued, as Jagdish N. Bhagwati and Sukhamoy Chakravarty have done (see their 'Contributions to Indian Economic Analysis: A Survey', *The American Economic Review*, Supplement, September 1969), that since landlords have control over the public credit institutions, higher rental shares for the landlords may lead to greater fertiliser absorption, if the investment decisions are made by the landlords.

[26]A Study by N.D.A. Hameed relating to Thanjavur district ('Prospects for Increasing Agricultural Production through Intensive Cultivation—A Case Study of the Rice Economy of Thanjavur district, India', Ph. D. dissertation, University of Delhi) reveals that the tenants paying fixed-kind rents were found to invest less in fertilisers compared with owner-operators of similar size. This evidence suggests that the lower investment by sharecroppers can not be attributed to the sharecropping system *as such*, but to lower investable surplus and capital rationing by credit institutions.

higher under sharecropping than under the fixed rent system or owner-farming owing to the possibility of cost-sharing which spreads the risk of investment to both the parties.[27] Second, these theories do not take into account bargaining situations where cost-sharing could prove profitable to both parties, for example, when each party is confronted with the possibility that the other party will not pay for inputs like fertilisers at all unless the costs are shared.[28] Such situations may be common because, unlike the fixed rent-system, sharecropping permits landowners to benefit by promoting the use of fertilisers through cost-sharing where the sharecroppers may not otherwise apply such inputs owing to lack of knowledge, shortage of capital, risk aversion, etc. In fact, the evidence cited above is consistent with bargaining situations favourable to cost-sharing under sharecropping.

As mentioned earlier, survival of sharecropping with cost-sharing in certain situations may indicate a weaker bargaining position of landowners (in comparison to those who can undertake self-cultivation), and consequently, a better bargaining position of sharecroppers when compared to landless labourers.[29] The bar-

[27]The P. E. O. Study, (op. cit.), states that tenants had applied higher doses of fertilisers than owners. C. H. Shah's Study, 'Impact of Tenancy Reform on Level of Technology (Gujarat and Maharashtra),' *Artha-Vikas*, July 1972, reveals a similar position.

Vyas in his study points to the higher use of modern inputs on the small sharecropper holdings when compared to the pure owner farms of similar size, owing to the practice of cost-sharing between the landowner and the tenant. See his 'Tenancy in a Dynamic Setting', op. cit.

The Study by Khan and Rao ('On Tenancy, Rent-Systems and Improved Technology', op. cit.) reveals a paradoxical situation where input and output per acre is higher under sharecropping (with cost-sharing) than under fixed rent-system but the tenant's net income per acre as well as the rate of return is higher under the latter because he captures the entire returns on whatever investment he makes. However, owing to cost-sharing, the sharecropper's contribution to expenditure is less than that incurred by the tenant under the fixed rent-system.

[28]New technology may typically give rise to such a bargaining situation because, owing to steeper marginal product curves for fertilisers under new technology, the difference betewen the individual optimum (without cost-sharing) and the market optimum (when marginal product is equal to price of input) is considerably reduced so that the rate of return for the party undertaking investment is almost doubled when half the cost is shared by the other party under the half-share lease. For the evidence on the response curves, see Ch. 7.

[29]Differences in the personal circumstances of landowners, such as, the inability to resume land or the inability to supervise the allocation of inputs by

gaining position of tenants who pay fixed rents while adopting new technology could be even greater.[30] The evidence cited above indicates that in a large number of cases, landowners as well as share-croppers gained proportionately from technological change because rent-share remained unaltered and the costs on modern inputs were shared by both the parties in proportion to their share in output. Compared to this, in cases where rent-share is raised with the adoption of new technology,[31] although sharecroppers like wage labourers may have gained in absolute terms, their gain may have been proportionately less than that of landowners.[32]

The practice of cost-sharing under sharecropping seems to be common in the erstwhile *ryotwari* areas where the ownership holdings of those leasing out are not very large and where, as mentioned earlier, the social structure in general is conducive to technological

tenants or the inability even to share costs constitute imperfections in the lease market. These imperfections give rise to varying bargaining positions between landowners and tenants resulting in differential gains to the parties concerned with technological change. It is, therefore, an oversimplification to believe that 'the terms in a share contract mutually agreed upon by the landowner and the tenant will include the rental percentage and the ratio of non-land to land input that are consistent with equilibrium'. Steven N.S. Cheung, *The Theory of Share Tenancy*, University of Chicago Press, 1969, p.19.

[30]Hameed's study mentioned earlier brings out that the fixed rent-system is common in cases where landowners happen to be absentees and cannot ascertain the yields on the field let alone supervise the allocation of inputs by the tenants. Therefore, the expectation that 'under fixed rent, the land size per farm and the rental annuity received by the landowner will be exactly the same as under share tenancy' (Cheung, op. cit., pp. 27-28) is unrealistic.

[31]These cases virtually amount to the resumption of land for self-cultivation, and sharecropping increasingly partakes the character of a piece wage system for ensuring efficient management. According to Parthasarathy and Prasad under this situation the 'tenant becomes indistinguishable from a permanent farm servant and tenancy system is nothing but a convenient arrangement under which a big owner who leases out in part relieves himself from the burdens of labour management while performing the major entrepreneurial functions', See their, 'Responses to, and Impact of, *HYV* Rice According to Land Size and Tenure......', op. cit.

[32]Parthasarathy and Prasad show for instance, that even after raising the rents from one-half to two-third of produce, the net share (after deducting costs) of the tenant increased by 35 per cent, though that of the landowner increased by 170 per cent (Ibid.). This rise in the net share of the tenant is significantly higher than the rise in the share of hired labour with the adoption of new technology on owner farms (See Table 3 in Chapter 10), indicating the greater bargaining power of tenants *vis-a-vis* landowners when compared to that of landless labourers *vis-a-vis* cultivating landowners.

change. However, the practice of sharing costs seems to be very much restricted, in cases where those leasing out are big landowners. For instance, in the Kosi project area of the Purnea district (North Bihar), there are several landowners who own, and effectively control, at least 1,000 acres each, a few of them owning as many as 5,000 acres. They are resuming lands from sharecroppers and are resorting to self-cultivation by using tractors. But land records show them to be owing not more than 15 acres—the upper limit according to the proposed ceiling laws—the rest of the land being transferred mostly to *benamis* (fake owners).[33] There is a gross under-utilisation of land, as large areas are left fallow in the *rabi* season despite the availability of water.[34]

The restriction of inputs and the absence of cost-sharing under this situation may be attributable not to the sharecropping system *as such* but to the concentration of landownership and the prevalance of poverty on a wide scale. Tenants are not left with an investable surplus and landowners may find usury more attractive than investment in the available 'modern' inputs. The use of inputs could thus be restricted in such a situation even with a fixed rent system and the tenants themselves may prefer sharecropping because it ensures a more stable consumption stream. Also, the level of input and output per acre among the large owner-farms need not be higher at the margin when compared to that on share-rented farms.[35] A more equitable distribution of landownership and the adequate provision of institutional credit would seem to be necessary under such a situation for promoting technological change itself irrespective of the system of cultivation.

[33]For an account of land relations in this area based on field visits see Wolf Ladejinsky, 'Green Revolution in Bihar—The Kosi Area: A Field Trip', *Economic and Political Weekly*, Review of Agriculture, 27 September 1969; and C.H. Hanumantha Rao, 'Land Reforms in Eastern Zone: Lack of Political Will', *The Times of India*, 12 March 1973.

[34]Pradhan H. Prasad, *Economic Benefits in the Kosi Command Area* (mimeo), A.N.S. Institute of Social Studies, Patna, 1972.

An adequate explanation of why land is left fallow in the *rabi* season would require investigation of the relevant economic as well as cultural aspects. It appears, however, that this phenomenon is associated with concentration of landownership, widespread poverty and the semi-feudal social structure.

[35]This was found to be true even in a progressive *ryotwari* region like West Godavari. See Hanumantha Rao, 'Uncertainty, Entrepreneurship, and Sharecropping in India', op. cit.

PATTERN OF TENANCY AND INCOME DISTRIBUTION

The picture regarding the distribution of income in relation to farm tenure would be incomplete without an idea as to who leases out and who leases in. Much of the literature on tenancy implicitly assumes that those who lease out are big landowners or landlords and those who lease in are small tenants or subsistence farmers. Tenancy reforms such as security of tenure and reduction of rents would have intended effects on income distribution only under the above assumptions. However, available data suggests that a good part of the area leased out belongs to the small landowners —presumably widows, orphans and absentee owners—and large farmers account for a substantial part of the area leased in. In such cases, tenurial reforms like the above can have adverse effects on income distribution.

Table 12.1 gives the percentage distributions of area leased

TABLE 12·1 DISTRIBUTION OF AREA LEASED OUT AND AREA LEASED IN ACCORDING TO THE SIZE OF HOLDING, 1961-62

Size Class of Holding (Acres)	All India	Andhra Pradesh	Tamil-nadu	Punjab	West Bengal
	(1)	(2)	(3)	(4)	(5)
(a) Percentage Distribution of Area Leased out according to the Size of Ownership Holdings :					
Upto 4.99	21.6	22.4	32.3	13.4	51.0
5.00 – 9.99	19.9	24.6	15.6	20.2	16.6
10.00 – 19.99	22.0	16.2	32.1	29.2	17.3
20.00 and above	36.5	36.8	20.0	37.2	15.1
(b) Percentage Distribution of Operational Holdings Reporting Area Leased in according to the Size of Operational Holdings :					
Upto 4.99	64.2	48.0	75.8	25.2	72·5
5.00 – 9.99	19.9	25.5	17.2	29.6	22.5
10.00 – 19.99	10.3	17.4	5.9	29.6	4.6
20.00 and above	5.6	9.1	1.1	15.6	0.4
(c) Percentage Distribution of Area Leased in According to the Size of Operational Holdings :					
Upto 4.99	26·8	18.5	47.6	7.1	58.3
5.00 – 9.99	22.7	25.5	32.7	22.1	29.2
10.00 – 19.99	22.2	28.1	15.2	37.2	10.2
20.00 and above	28.3	27.9	4.5	33.6	2.3

Sources : Indian Statistical Institute, *The National Sample Survey, Land Holdings Enquiry, Seventeenth Round*, Nos. 140, 141 and 146.

out according to the size of ownership holding and of the number of holdings leased in as well as the area leased in according to the size of operational holding. According to these data, at least 40 per cent of area leased out belongs to small landowners owning land below 10 acres and farmers operating 10 acres and above account for as much as 50 per cent of area leased in. In West Bengal, small landowners owning below 5 acres account for as much as 51 per cent of area leased out. In all probability, these figures exaggerate the share of small landowners in the area leased out as well as the share of the large farmers in the area leased in. This is because large land-owners may have under-reported the area leased out for fear of land reform measures whereas small landowners may not have been in-hibited to the same extent. Similarly, small farmers leasing in from the large landowners could be compelled not to report such leases whereas such a compulsion may not exist in the case of large far-mers leasing in area. Even so, these figures serve to illustrate that consideration as to who leases out and who leases in is important for influencing income distribution in the desired direction through tenancy reforms.

SUMMARY

The area under tenancy, particularly sharecropping, has been declining under the impact of technological change. Rents per acre have risen and in certain cases rental shares have been raised under sharecropping, although, in quite a few cases, rent-share after the introduction of new technology remained the same as before. The practice of sharing costs between landowners and sharecroppers seems to be widespread in the former *ryotwari* regions where the social structure is conducive to growth. Costs on modern inputs in such areas are generally shared by the tenants and landowners in proportion to their respective shares in output. As a result, input and output per acre under sharecropping seem to be higher than under fixed rent system or on big owner farms. In a large number of cases, landowners and sharecroppers seem to have gained proportionately from technological changes. Even in cases where rent-share has been raised following technological change, sharecroppers seem to have gained more than landless labourers, although proportionately much less than landowners.

In the Eastern Zone, on the other hand, there does not seem

to be enough incentive for the adoption of innovations. Tenants are too poor to be in a position to invest in modern inputs. Landowners too may have very little incentive to invest in modern inputs because of greater return from usury. The concentration of landownership and the widespread incidence of poverty may be responsible for the relative stagnation of agriculture in such areas.

A good part of the area leased out belongs to small landowners and large farmers account for a significant share in the area leased in. Therefore, consideration as to who leases out and who leases in becomes important for influencing income distribution in the desired direction through tenancy reforms.

CHAPTER 13

Distribution of Gains in Real Terms

HYPOTHESIS

Gains from technological change may accrue both as increased incomes to certain productive factors and as increased real incomes to the consumers because of a decline in the (relative) prices of crops as a result of the reduction in unit costs.[1] Agriculture is a highly competitive industry and the reduction in unit costs resulting from technological changes can be expected to lower the relative prices of the commodities concerned. In fact, in view of the low income and price elasticities of demand for food products and the competitive character of agriculture, technological change has, in general, given rise to the need to support farm prices in order to prevent a steep fall in farm incomes. Nevertheless, it is possible that owing to the imperfections in the distribution system, lower farm prices may not be passed on fully to the consumers. However, such imperfections cannot be attributed to technological change, which, by itself, should lead to a reduction in prices paid by the consumers, unless the price support policy is such as to maintain prices at unduly higher levels.

The proportion of income spent on food is quite high—in some cases as high as 80 per cent—for the poorer sections in India.[2] This proportion declines as income increases and is significantly

[1] T.W. Schultz has repeatedly emphasised the need to take into account the 'consumer surplus' while assessing the distributive consequences of new agricultural technology. See, for instance, his paper, 'Knowledge, Agriculture and Welfare,' (mimeo), presented at Pugwash 21st Conference meeting at Sinaia, Rumania, 25-31 August 1971.

[2] See, for instance, Government of India, *The National Sample Survey, Tables with Notes on Consumption Expenditure*, Number 179, Nineteenth Round, July 1964-June 1965.

lower for the higher income groups. Therefore, lower income groups would benefit proportionately more than higher income groups from the reduction in the relative prices of foodgrains. Technological change could thus improve the distribution of real income both in the urban and the rural sectors. This improvement in real income distribution could be greater in the rural sector, partly because the decline in foodgrain prices can be expected to be greater in the rural sector than for consumers in the urban sector who depend on the distribution systems, and also because rural income groups—particularly the poorer sections—spend a much larger proportion of their income on foodgrains than their urban counterparts.[3] The largest (proportionate) benefit in real incomes can thus accrue to the rural poor as a result of technological change in the production of foodgrains.

It is important to see to what extent the income disparities created in the production process with the adoption of new technology are likely to be corrected by the improvement in real incomes. If the regional disparities in agricultural development increase as a result of technological change, then the costs on account of transfer (distribution) of foodgrains from the surplus to the (distant) deficit regions would also increase. Also, greater withholding capacity of the prosperous regions may lead to an added rise in the prices of foodgrains in situations of scarcity. Thus, because of the regional concentration of surpluses and the deficiencies in the distribution system, the consumer prices in the deficit regions can rise despite a fall in the prices of foodgrains in the surplus zones. In a country as large as India, the costs of transfer from the surplus to the distant deficit regions could be greater than the reduction in production costs, especially in the initial stages of technological change. Sharp

[3]This is attributable mainly to the higher physiological requirements of food arising from heavy manual labour in agriculture (associated with labour-intensive techniques) in a harder physical environment. See C.H. Hanumantha Rao, 'Resource Prospects from the Rural Sector: The Case of Indirect Taxes', *Economic and Political Weekly*, Review of Agriculture, 29 March 1969.

The favourable impact of lower relative prices of cereals on the welfare of the rural poor could thus be significant even if part of the increase in cereal output is achieved at the expense of pulses, because in the case of the poor engaged in manual labour in a low income country like India, energy deficiency in nutrition may be more serious than the protein deficiency. See P.V. Sukhatme, 'Protein Strategy and Agricultural Development', Presidential address at the 31st Annual Conference of the Indian Society of Agricultural Economics, *Indian Journal of Agricultural Economics*, January-March 1972.

regional unevenness in the rate of technological change may, therefore, confer much greater benefits to the consumers in the surplus zones than to those in the deficit regions. The regional disparities in income gains from technological change may thus be reinforced by the regional disparities in real income gains so long as there is an overall scarcity in foodgrains.

Cost-reduction may have been relatively greater so far on account of land-augmenting technological change than from labour-substituting technological change. Also, the decline in the share of wage-income in output would be comparatively less in the case of land-augmenting technological change. It is, therefore, probable that in the case of land-augmenting technological change, the relative real income gains for the wage earners and erstwhile tenants compensate substantially for the relative decline in the share of wage income in output. At any rate, the compensating impact of real income gains seems greater in the case of wage earners and tenants affected by land-augmenting technological change whereas this impact may be the least in the case of labour-substituting technological change as it reduces sharply the relative share of wage-income.

The widening income disparities between small and large farmers as a result of technological change may also be corrected to some extent by the comparatively greater incidence of adverse terms of trade on large farmers. With the fall in the prices of agricultural commodities resulting from technological changes, urban consumption goods become costlier in terms of agricultural commodities. And since large farmers spend a much larger proportion of their income on urban goods of consumption than small farmers, the decline in real income would be proportionately greater in the case of large farmers.

It appears that technological change may, on balance (taking into account nominal as well as real income gains), worsen the relative income position between the better-endowed and the lagging regions in a large country like India, whereas the widening disparities in nominal incomes between the small and large income groups within the regions experiencing mainly the land-augmenting technological change may be corrected to a significant extent by the proportionately greater real income gains for the small farmers and wage earners.

EVIDENCE

None of the expectations outlined above has come true because the supply gap in respect of foodgrains has persisted and the prices of foodgrains have been rising relative to those of manufactures. It is thus likely that despite the technological changes witnessed in Indian agriculture since the mid-sixties, the expenditure on food accounts for a larger proportion of consumer's budget now than it did a decade ago.[4] Even the relative price of wheat did not decline despite a breakthrough in its output. Table 13.1 shows that the wholesale prices of wheat have risen relative to those of foodgrains and of agricultural commodities as a whole in the post-Green

TABLE 13.1 : INDEX NUMBERS OF WHOLESALE PRICES (BASE: 1961-62=100)

Year	Wheat	Foodgrains	Agricultural Commodities	Percentage of Wheat to Foodgrains	Percentage of Wheat to Agricultural Commodities
	(1)	(2)	(3)	(4)	(5)
1962-63	98	105.4	102.3	93.0	95.8
1963-64	106	115.2	108.4	92.0	97.8
1964-65	138	145.5	130.9	94.8	105.4
1965-66	149	154.3	141.7	96.6	105.2
1966-67	178	182.9	166.6	97.3	106.8
1067-68	214	228.4	188.2	93.7	113.7
1968-69	204	201.0	179.4	101.5	113.7
1969-70	215	208.2	194.8	103.3	110.4
1970-71	209	206.8	201.0	101.1	104.0
1971-72	208	214.9	199.6	96.8	104.2

Source : Reserve Bank of India, *Reserve Bank of India Bulletin*, January 1970, September 1972.

Revolution period. Apart from the favourable demand for this cereal

[4]This can be expected because the elasticity of demand for foodgrains is less than unity and the change in per capita income is not significant during this period. For instance, between 1960-61 and 1965-66 when the prices of foodgrains relative to manufactures rose significantly, the percentage of expenditure on food to total consumer expenditure recorded a rise: Between the sixteenth (1960-61) and the twentieth (1965-66) round of the National Sample Survey, the proportion of expenditure on food to the total expenditure for all classes rose from 67.9 per cent to 74.0 per cent in the rural sector and from 60.9 per cent to 64.0 per cent in the urban sector. The indications are that in 1967-68, these proportions increased further.

reflected in the higher expenditure and price elasticities of demand, the favourable price for wheat is attributable to (a) the domestic supply gap reflected in sizeable imports of this commodity prior to the technological breakthrough; and (b) the influence of producer interests on the price policy for wheat (e.g., fixation of procurement prices and the regulation of inter-zonal movement of foodgrains).[5]

To the extent the increase in the domestic output of wheat displaced imports and contributed to self-sufficiency, there was a social gain, including the expansion of farm employment and income, within the country. To the extent procurement prices have been pegged at artificially higher levels, producers—especially the large farmers with greater marketable surplus—have gained at the expense of consumers in general including the rural poor in regions experiencing technological breakthrough.

Insofar as the price elasticity of supply is positive, higher producer prices would lead to higher output resulting in greater gains to the large farmers. Although this would mean more employment and income to the rural poor, they may, on balance, lose on account of higher prices. This is because, a rise in the price of foodgrains would mean a significant fall in the real income of such groups, as foodgrains account for a substantial proportion of their total expenditure. On the other hand, the increase in employment (income) consequent on price rise would be proportionately much less. This is because the price elasticity of supply for wheat is small, and the price elasticity of supply for agricultural commodities as a whole—which is more relevant for considering the net impact on employment—would be much lower. Since the labour coefficient is significantly less than unity, the derived demand for labour would be still less. For example, even if it is assumed that a 10 per cent rise in the price of wheat leads to a 5 per cent rise in its output,[6] employment in wheat production may rise by not more than 2.5 per cent if the labour coefficient is 0.5. The net increase in employment in the agricultural sector as a whole would be much

[5]See Ch. 7.

[6]Raj Krishna's Study for Punjab shows that the short-run acreage elasticity of wheat with respect to its expected relative price is as low as 0.08. See his 'Acreage Response Functions for Some Punjab Crops', *Economic Journal*, September 1963.

However, technological changes in the recent period may have raised the yield response to the changes in the relative price of wheat via the use of purchased inputs.

less because part of the increase in wheat output would be at the expense of other commodities.

The figures in Table 13.2 show that despite the technological breakthrough and increased concentration of wheat output in Punjab, farm harvest as well as wholesale prices of wheat have increased relative to those in the deficit states in the post-Green Revolution

TABLE 13.2 : FARM HARVEST AND WHOLESALE PRICES OF WHEAT
(RUPEES PER QUINTAL)

Year	Bihar	Gujarat	Maharashtra	Punjab
	(1)	(2)	(3)	(4)
(a) Farm Harvest Prices				
1964-65	80.3	78.7	96.9	56.9
1965-66	90.5	77.2	112.0	66.6
1970-71	83.1	82.2	100.8	76.8
1971-72	81.5	91.2	101.8	76.2
(b) Farm Harvest Prices in Punjab as percentage to Prices in other States				
1964-65	70.9	72.3	58.7	
1965-66	73.6	86.3	59.5	
1970-71	92.5	93.5	76.2	
1971-72	93.5	83.5	74.8	
(c) Wholesale Prices (Indigenous White Wheat)				
1964	79.3	71.4	94.8	52.7
1965	99.6	85.6	110.4	56.5
1971	101.9	94.5	109.2	79.7
1972	100.1	99.8	113.7	83.9
(d) Wholesale Prices in Punjab as percentage to Prices in other States				
1964	66.4	73.8	55.6	
1965	56.7	66.0	51.2	
1971	78.2	84.3	72.9	
1972	83.8	84.1	73.8	

Note : Wholesale prices for 1971 and 72 in the case of Bihar, Gujarat and Maharashtra relate to one market only in each state.

Sources : (1) Directorate of Economics and Statistics, Ministry of Food and Agriculture, *Agricultural Situation in India*, August 1967 and August 1973.

(2) Ministry of Food and Agriculture, *Report of the Agricultural Prices Commission on Price Policy for Kharif Cereals for 1967-68 Season*, September 1967.

(3) Ministry of Food and Agriculture, *Report of the Agricultural Prices Commission on the Price Policy for Wheat for 1972-73 and 1974-75.*

period when compared to the pre-Green Revolution year. These data are suggestive of the role of producer interests in fixing higher

procurement prices (which influence the farm harvest and wholesale prices) and in relaxing restrictions on the inter-zonal movement
of foodgrains. However, the entire burden of higher procurement
prices and of increased transportation and distribution costs associated with regional concentration of output has not been passed
on to the consumers of the deficit regions in the form of higher
prices. This has been absorbed in the form of increased subsidies
on the public distribution of foodgrains,[7] the burden of which would
ultimately fall on the community as a whole.

SUMMARY

The technological breakthrough in respect of wheat has not
led to the expected results in regard to income distribution in real
terms because of persisting high prices of wheat. However, to the
extent the domestic gains in wheat output have substituted imports,
there has been a social gain—especially in the expansion of farm
employment and income within the country. The influence of producer interests in the fixation of higher procurement prices and in
relaxing zonal restrictions on the movement of foodgrains is indicated by the fact that despite the technological breakthrough, farm
harvest as well as the wholesale prices of wheat in Punjab increased relative to those in the deficit states in the post-Green Revolution period. However, these costs have been absorbed in the form
of public subsidies on the distribution of foodgrains.

[7]The Report of the Agricultural Prices Commission on Price Policy for
Rabi Foodgrains for the 1972-73 season observes that 'the loss on the indigenous
wheat procured and distributed out of the public distribution system works out
to Rs. 24 per quintal' and that 'the total subsidy involved could rise to Rs. 132
crores'.

Part III

Summary of Experience and Expected Trends

Technological Change, Agricultural Growth and Distribution of Gains: Summary of Experience

Despite technological changes, the growth of the agricultural output in India slowed down in the 1960s as compared to the 1950s, so that it barely kept pace with the growth of population. The technological changes seem to explain only about 27 to 40 per cent of the growth achieved since the mid-sixties.

Technological changes, in general, and mechanisation, in particular, have been taking place mainly among the large farms in the high-income and high-growth pockets. Apart from the high profitability of these innovations, a major incentive for their adoption among these segments has been the rise in the cost of the biological sources of energy (e.g., human and bullock labour) relative to the mechanical sources. This is attributable, in turn, to the rise in the prices of the agricultural commodities following the growth of demand (as a result of the population growth and the rise, albeit slow, in the per capita income) unaccompanied by adequate public investments in irrigation and the public policy to increase the agricultural output in the backward regions and among the small farms, which have sizeable underutilised labour.

The steep rise in the prices of agricultural commodities has been a cause as well as the consequence of a capital-intensive or high-cost agricultural growth through private investment concentrated among the developed pockets and the large farms. Growth would have been less costly from the social point of view and the prices would have been lower if public investments (e.g., in the major and medium irrigation projects and public tube-wells, which account for lower unit costs for the services rendered because of economies of scale) were stepped up and technological changes were wide-spread in the labour-abundant sectors, such as the backward regions and the small farms. The regional concentration of output has raised the cost of distribution on account of the transfer of food-grains from the surplus to the distant deficit regions. The greater withholding capacity of the prosperous regions and the big farmers has accentuated the rise in prices of foodgrains in situations of scarcity. Although, technological change in wheat has contributed to stabilising output over time, because the gains in this case have been concentrated in the irrigated pockets, the annual fluctuations in the output of foodgrains in the country, as a whole, have in-creased because of the yield per acre becoming a predominant component of growth, as fluctuations in the yield are greater than those in the cropped area and have increased in the recent period.

The rise in the prices of foodgrains and the uncertainty of their supplies have led to unrest and tensions in the urban areas, particularly in the food-deficit regions. The inequality in the distri-bution of income in the urban sector, which is decidedly greater than in the rural sector, has been increasing,[1] especially in real terms. A part of the growing urban poverty is the spill-over of the rural poverty, created by the migration of the landless labourers and the marginal farmers.[2] This migration may have increased recently, because of the slow (insufficient) pace of land-augmenting (labour-absorbing) technological change and the slow rate of agricul-tural growth. Further, the slow rate of agricultural growth in the lagging regions may have increased the demand for higher education and for non-farm jobs by the rural youth. Thus, the urban sector may have served, to a considerable extent, as a 'safety valve' for the lagging rural sector, giving rise to unrest and tensions in the urban areas, owing to a greater awareness and better organisation of those involved.

[1]V.M. Dandekar and Nilakantha Rath, *Poverty in India,* Indian School of Political Economy, 1971, pp. 30 and 31. According to them, the inequalities have been increasing in the rural sector as well, but to a smaller extent than in the urban sector.

[2]Dandekar and Rath, op. cit., p. 32.

Although inequalities in income and wealth are smaller in the rural sector (when compared to urban sector), the social inequalities are greater, so that the rate of outmigration among the 'lower castes' or the socially oppressed groups can be expected to be greater, when the opportunities for non-farm employment become available.

New agricultural technology has induced a high rate of growth of output among the already developed regions and large farms owing to their better resource position. In many of these pockets, the supply of labour has been lagging behind the demand for farm labour. Despite the migration of labour from the labour-surplus regions to these high growth pockets for operations such as harvesting, there has been a significant rise in real wages owing to the supply of labour falling short of demand.

It should not be surprising, therefore, that tractorisation in these areas has been associated with an increase in output and employment. However, for a large country like India, the real question is not whether tractorisation in specific areas has led to an increase in output and employment. The right question to ask is whether output and employment would not have been greater for a similar investment in alternative techniques such as irrigation and the spread of HYV among the small farms as well as the lagging regions.

Technological change in the agricultural sector must have created additional employment through the increased demand for inputs especially those produced in the non-farm sector as well as through an increased demand for rural and urban goods of consumption following the increase in farm incomes.[3] Also, additional employment must have been generated for the marketing and distribution of increased agricultural output.

The additional employment created for marketing the increased output as well as for the production and distribution of additional consumption goods can be expected to be roughly the same irrespective of the type of technology adopted for producing a given volume of additional agricultural output.[4] Therefore, the relevant question to examine would be the relative employment potential of alternative technologies such as pump-sets, fertilisers, tractors

[3]John W. Mellor and Uma Lele, 'Growth Linkages of the New Foodgrain Technologies', *Indian Journal of Agricultural Economics*, January-March 1973.

Raj Krishna has done an illustrative exercise by using an input-output model to estimate indirect employment created in the non-farm sector. See his 'Measurement of the Direct and Indirect Employment Effects of Agricultural Growth with Technical Change', op. cit.

[4]A more labour-intensive technology for producing a given volume of agricultural output may result in a reduction of marketed surplus thereby reducing the employment potential in the process of marketing as well as in the production and distribution of non-farm consumption goods. However, the study by

and harvest combines from their use in the farm sector as well as from their production and distribution in the non-farm sector.

It is quite likely that the difference in non-farm employment potential between a given investment in pump-sets and fertilisers on the one hand and in tractors and harvesters on the other, has been such as to yield lower aggregate (farm as well as non-farm) employment for the latter, because on-the-farm employment potential of pump-sets and fertilisers is much greater than that of tractors and harvesters.[5]

Technological changes have contributed to widening the disparities in income between different regions, between small and large farms and between landowners on the one hand and landless labourers and tenants on the other. In absolute terms, however, the gains from technological change have been shared by all sections. This is indicated by the rise in real wages and employment and in incomes of small farmers in regions experiencing technological change. The favourable terms of trade for agriculture have also contributed to a rise in the real incomes of even small and medium farmers, though proportionately less than for big farmers. Also, owing to the widespread practice of cost-sharing between landowners and tenants in such regions, tenants have been able to improve their income position relative to that of landless labourers. Sale of land by the large landowners and sub-division of their holdings induced by population growth (increase in family size) have had an opposite tendency of lowering their incomes from agriculture contributing to a decline in the relative share of large incomes.

Regional (horizontal) disparities in income seem to have increased more than (vertical) disparities between different income groups within regions experiencing technological change. Apart from the differences in factor endowments—natural as well as manmade—inherited from the pre-independence period, public investments in major and medium irrigation projects which have a greater

---

Mellor and Lele (op. cit.) indicates that the non-farm consumption basket of the rural poor is characterised by greater labour-intensity in its production than that of the rural rich, although the latter's consumption basket has a greater employment potential than that of their urban counterparts.

[5]The evidence presented by Bruce F. Johnston and Peter Kilby in their *Agriculture and Structural Transformation: Economic Strategies in Late Developing Countries* (forthcoming), shows that the indirect employment created in the manufacture and distribution of tractors is trivial when compared to the direct displacement of labour on the farm.

potential for reducing regional disparities have lagged behind private investments in well-irrigation which have a potential for widening the regional disparities. Besides, in a large and diversified country like India, factors determining the adoption of innovations differ more between different regions than between different holding size groups. Nature of technology (e.g., its crop-specificity), availability of irrigation, development of credit institutions, human attitudes and motivation for change seem to differ more between different regions than with respect to different individuals within any region. Moreover, participation in the modernisation process is usually greater in regions which have shed the feudal and semi-feudal structures and attitudes and where the inequalities in wealth and status are not conspicuous, so that the transformation lag between different sections within a region experiencing change would be smaller than between different regions.

This may explain why in areas of fastest change, namely, Punjab, Haryana and west Uttar Pradesh, there is little evidence of growth in tensions between different classes in the rural sector. Such tensions cannot be expected because real wages have risen in these regions despite immigration of labour, and employment has increased despite tractorisation. In the labour-abundant rice regions such as Thanjavur, on the other hand, the rise in the demand for labour resulting from technological change was not sufficient to cause an appreciable rise in wages through a competitive process of market mechanism. The landowners tried to counter the landless workers' demand for higher wages by bringing in labour from outside. However, these tensions could not last long because workers demanded a share in *increased* productivity and landowners were better off as a result of technological change even after agreeing to share a part of the gains with landless workers. It is interesting to note that, even in Thanjavur, technological changes led to tensions between classes, not so much in the New Delta where the change was rapid as in the lagging Old Delta where the inequalities in land-ownership and status are conspicuous.[6]

Tensions between classes would have been sharp and perpetual if technological changes led to a decline in the incomes of tenants or landless labourers in absolute terms through the eviction of tenants and the retrenchment of workers, as, for instance, in the

[6]Andre Beteille, *Studies in Agrarian Social Structure*, Oxford University Press, Delhi, 1974, p. 169.

case of labour-displacing mechanisation which has little impact on productivity per acre.[7] This process is very much limited in India and seems to be restricted to certain pockets like the Kosi area of north Bihar where there is a large concentration of landownership.

[7]According to Hamza Alavi, such a process has been very much in evidence in Pakistan. See his 'Elite Farmer Strategy and Regional Disparities in Pakistan', *Economic and Political Weekly*, Review of Agriculture, March 1973.

CHAPTER 15

Socio-Political Factors and Agricultural Policies*

FEATURES OF THE PREVAILING AGRICULTURAL STRATEGY

The agricultural output has been growing at about 2.5 per cent per annum in the post-independence period as against a decline in the foodgrains output in the 15 years preceding independence.[1] However, the performance in the post-independence period should be judged in relation to the requirements as well as the social goals set.[2] Besides, a good part of the agricultural growth in the post-independence period is traceable to autonomous factors, which are not attributable to conscious public policies. Rather, the latter were very much influenced by the forces generated by the former.

The two major factors accounting for such spontaneity in

*This chapter draws considerably upon the author's earlier work, especially his, 'Agricultural Policy Under the Three Plans', in N. Srinivasan (ed.), *Agricultural Administration in India*, Indian Institute of Public Administration, New Delhi, March 1969.

[1]Because of this, M. L. Dantwala disagrees with the proposition that agriculture has not received adequate attention by the planners in India. See his, 'From Stagnation to Growth', Presidential address to the 53rd Annual Conference of the Indian Economic Association, *The Indian Economic Journal*, October-December 1970,

[2]It is clear from the findings of this study summarised in the previous chapter that the achievements, in regard to agricultural growth, are significant in the post-independence period, especially when viewed against the background of the experience in the colonial period. It is equally clear, however, that the achievements, with regard to the growth, fall considerably short of the expectations as well as the goals and targets set by the planners. The analysis in this chapter is prompted by the conviction that a forward-looking approach needs to pay greater attention, than has been done so far, to the identification of the socio-political constraints accounting for these shortfalls.

agricultural performance are the growth of the population and the rise of the agricultural classes to political power. The population growth has meant an increasing agricultural labour force that is younger and healthier. This contributed to a better exploitation of land through the intensive cultivation, involving the greater use of labour for augmenting irrigation and for multiple cropping etc.[3] The political power wielded by the rural rich at the district and the state levels has meant an increasing use of the state machinery and the resources for agricultural betterment. This was reflected, for instance, in a significant expansion of the credit facilities, though big farmers benefited proportionately more, in this process, than the small ones. The extension of the traditional techniques of farming as well as the adoption of new techniques was very much induced and sustained by the growing demand for agricultural commodities, as a result of the population growth and urbanisation. This was reflected in the favourable terms of trade that agriculture has enjoyed over a greater part of the plan period.

A deficiency of public investment in the agricultural infrastructure,[4] especially in irrigation and land reclamation, is a glaring feature of the prevailing strategy. This deficiency is indicated by the realised growth falling very much short of the targets set, with regard to the output and the steep rise in the relative prices of the agricultural commodities.[5]

[3] This implies that the marginal productivity of labour was positive and significant, at least for a sizeable segment in Indian agriculture. That this was indeed so has been indicated by several empirical studies on production functions in the recent period. For an incisive analysis of how, historically, the population growth has induced the adoption of labour-intensive techniques contributing to an intensive use of land, see Ester Boserup, *The Conditions of Agricultural Growth—The Economics of Agrarian Change Under Population Pressure*, George Allen & Unwin, London, 1965.

[4] Michael Lipton, among others, has been focussing on this deficiency in Indian planning. See his 'India's Agricultural Performance : Achievements, Distortions and Ideologies', in *Society and Development in Asia*, Martin Rudner (ed.), *Asian and African Studies*, Vol. 6, Jerusalem: The Israel Oriental Society, 1970. This is reproduced in, *Agricultural Development in Developing Countries: Comparative Experience*, The Indian Society of Agricultural Economics, Bombay, 1972.

[5] A measure of the optimal rate of public investment for agriculture should take into account the demand for the agricultural commodities, productivity of investment and the social goals regarding income distribution, etc. Therefore, the observed trend in the ratio of investment allocations for agriculture to the overall investment serves, at best, as a rough indicator of the importance given to agriculture.

The big farmers, who are unable to make intensive use of their available land through labour-intensive techniques, are interested not so much in public investment for reclaiming new land,[6] as in making intensive use of their available land through greater investment in private wells, fertilisers and farm machinery by using public resources, for example, from credit institutions. Although the big farmers from the dry regions have actively worked in the past for major and medium irrigation projects, such efforts seem to have slowed down very much, in the recent period. This is because, in the first place, the groups wielding power in quite a few states belong to the prosperous, irrigated regions and are not immediately interested in expanding the public irrigation to new areas. Second, even where dry regions predominate, those in power—who come mainly from the rich farmer class—seem to be reconciled to the paucity of the investable resources, because the expansion of resources would necessitate, among other measures, taxing the rural rich. Third, even the available resources tend to get allocated to projects which yield greater benefits for the elite, especially because the new technology and the rising prices provide profitable alternatives for the big farmers, such as, investment in private wells, fertilisers, etc., by using institutional credit.[7]

This strategy suits the urban elite as well, because they spend a small proportion of their income on food and the loss in their real income, as a result of the rise in the prices of the agricultural commodities could be more than compensated by the availability of the non-agricultural goods and services, made possible through a greater priority assigned to them in relation to agriculture. The losers in the process are the urban as well as the rural poor, because they spend the bulk of their income on food. So far as the investment for any

[6]According to Gunnar Myrdal, landowners, having an interest in high rents and low wages and in preventing soil erosion, display little enthusiasm for an expansion of the cultivated area, even though there is considerable scope for reclaiming new land. See his, *Asian Drama*, Vol. II, Part Five, p. 1266.

[7]When irrigation water comes to a region through the public canals, all the classes of farmers are benefited in proportion to the area held by them and the 'big farmers', who are the effective decision-makers in regard to the public investment at the state level, may not account for more than 20 per cent of the area held in a region benefiting from public irrigation. There are, however, some exceptions, such as, the Kosi area in north Bihar.

A lack of a sense of urgency, on the part of the ruling groups in regard to the public irrigation, is also reflected in the prolonged disputes between different states on sharing the waters of the common rivers.

particular sector such as agriculture is concerned, the problem is not so much the paucity of the total investable resources as the allocation of the available resources. However, the 'paucity' of resources as well as insufficient allocation to agriculture from the available resources are traceable, in a large measure, to the increase in non-essential consumption by the elite.[8]

The urban elite is, nevertheless, interested in the assured supplies of the marketed surpluses of foodgrains and agricultural raw material at 'reasonable' prices. It seeks to solve the problem of the shortage of foodgrains arising from an insufficient investment in agriculture, partly through imports for the public distribution system involving compulsory levies and administered prices—which its rural counterpart has been able to undermine to a large extent[9]—and partly through the concentration of resources, e.g., fertilisers in the developed irrigated pockets and the large farms where the results are quick, substantial and assured. This is how the slow growth of agriculture and the unevenness of gains are interrelated. The two facets of this strategy, namely the deficiency of public investment in broadening the agricultural base and the concentration on prosperous segments, reinforce each other.

THE ROLE OF ECONOMISTS

Although, the socio-political factors outlined above are mainly responsible for the relative neglect of agriculture, the prevailing thinking, among a large body of economists, has not been favourable to adequate public investments in agriculture. These economists have naturally been impressed by the experience of the countries showing a very high rate of growth during the 'comparable' period, e.g., Japan, Soviet Union and China. They systematise, with a considerable degree of sophistication, the relationships between the key economic variables in these high-growth economies and then use

[8]Such an inference seems reasonable, if one judges the performance by the concrete results achieved, and not by the avowed 'intentions' of the elite or the 'design' of many of the development programmes.

[9]While joining issue with Michael Lipton, M.L. Dantwala concedes the big farmer-bias in the agricultural policy but denies an urban bias. He is right when he says that the agricultural prices are unduly high which undermine the objective of the removal of poverty. But it is difficult to reconcile this with his assertion that the investment allocation for agriculture is all right. See his Preface to *Agricultural Development in Developing Countries—Comparative Experience,* op. cit.

these models—overlooking the institutional and the political framework within which such a high rate of growth was achieved—to prescribe economic policies for the developing countries, like India. They easily ignored that, unlike these countries, India was embarking upon planned economic development with a much poorer agricultural base, a rapidly growing population and a socio-political framework which ruled out compulsion and the concentration of the decision-making.

For such economists, agriculture provides interest mainly as a source of cheap labour, marketed surpluses and tax revenues.[10] Their accent is more on *mobilising* such resources from agriculture, through the appropriate institutional devices, than on *generating* surpluses through significant increases in the agricultural productivity,[11] as the latter would involve the diversion of the scarce investable resources from the 'priority' sectors, such as, heavy industry.[12] They

[10]These economists have largely been responsible for the view, which has persisted throughout the planning period in India, that there are significant revenue prospects from the taxation of agriculture. Recently, however, the Committee headed by K.N. Raj on Taxation of Agricultural Wealth and Income found that additional revenues through the progressive taxation of holdings with rateable value of Rs. 5,000 and above would amount to only about Rs. 150 crores per annum. The net addition would be much less if land revenue on holdings with rateable value below Rs. 5,000 per annum is abolished. Thus, instead of focussing on the 'equity' aspect of agricultural tax reform, these economists have been emphasising the 'revenue' prospects from taxing the agricultural sector as a whole. Incidentally, the big business in the country, in its attempt to divert attention, has always pointed to the 'revenue prospects' from agriculture. Our study, *Taxation of Agricultural Land in Andhra Pradesh* (Asia, 1966) showed that whereas the tax incidence was regressive, a restructuring of the tax system may not result in a significant net addition to the revenues.

[11]When it comes to public investment in agriculture, these economists overlook the usual and well accepted criteria of investment and regard the net resource flow into or from agriculture (i.e., the public investment in agriculture minus the tax revenues from agriculture) as a basis for the investment decision. Bruce F. Johnston, who was a strong exponent of this approach, has recently been emphasising the complementarity between agriculture and the non-farm sectors. See Bruce F. Johnston and Peter Kilby, *Agriculture and Structural Transformation: Economic Strategies in Late Developing Countries* (forthcoming).

[12]Those still committed to the 'heavy strategy' within the prevailing social structure, overlook the fact that the output from the heavy industry, e.g., steel and cement, is not ploughed back into the 'heavy sector', as visualised by them but is instead used essentially for supporting elitist consumption, e.g., luxurious residential construction in preference, for example, to irrigation projects which produce foodgrains for mass consumption.

seldom regard the growth of the agricultural sector, *as such*, as a major source of the national income growth or of general welfare.

REDISTRIBUTIVE REFORMS

Policies on land reform, taxation, credit and prices have been heavily biased towards big farmers who wield considerable political power at the state level and who influence the formulation as well as implementation of such policies. Unlike the zamindars and the jagirdars, these rich farmers are rooted in the villages and display considerable drive for modern farming. They wield considerable influence over the peasantry and constitute the social base and 'vote banks' for the ruling party as well as for many of the opposition parties. They neither have the political courage nor feel the need to openly oppose the Central leadership on several schemes of agrarian reform. They, in fact, 'support' some of these radical measures but see to it that they become infructuous in implementation. Agriculture being a state subject, they have been in a position to undermine, if not reject, measures which go against their interests and to mobilise state power and resources to subserve their interests.

Owing to the growth of population and to the resulting subdivision of holdings, the amount of land potentially available for redistribution after the imposition of ceilings is not substantial, even if the ceilings are not evaded, and the requirements of uneconomic holdings and the landless are too great to permit adjustment with any reasonable level of ceilings.[13] The contribution of legislation on ceilings on land-holdings so far consists not so much in the 'surplus' land that is made available for redistribution as in arresting or slowing down the growth of large-scale (capitalist) farming in agriculture.[14] A substantial contribution of the drive for ceilings is to be found in the sale of land by the big landowners and in their reluctance to acquire more land in future. In such a situation, the land market could have been tilted in favour of the landless and the marginal holders by extending to them long-term, interest-free loans

[13]The estimates of 'surplus' land for different states arrived at by V.M. Dandekar and N. Rath in their *Poverty in India*, (op. cit. 1971, pp. 30, 31) support this proposition.

[14]However, despite a ceiling on ownership holdings, a capitalist farmer can enlarge his operational holding to some extent by leasing in land.

from the public financial institutions, e.g., nationalised banks for the purchase of land. The elite being avowedly committed to the 'free distribution' of land could not take to such a course, nor was it necessary for them to do so because land could be sold at remunerative prices to those who already owned some land.

Likewise, tenancy reforms, for example, security of tenure and the regulation of rents have been, by and large, ineffective. In the absence of effective implementation and because of the scarcity of land in relation to demand, such legislation has contributed mainly to driving tenancy underground. Attempts to regulate rents without the effective regulation of wages have proved to be self-defeating, because, when the wages are not raised, it is more profitable for landowners to resume land for self-cultivation through hired labour instead of accepting lower rents. Also, they could resume land in many cases by resorting to tractorisation. However, regulation of rents and wages has been difficult in the absence of effective ceilings and redistribution of land. Performance has been dismal on all these counts because of the common socio-political factor, namely, the dominance of big farmers.[15] Given the structure of land holdings, however, the practice of tenancy has contributed to efficiency in resource-use and consequently to higher output and employment, because output and employment per acre on tenanted farms is greater than on large owner farms. At any rate, this practice has not been inequitous in every case because a good part of the land leased-out belongs to the small landowners who cannot undertake self-cultivation.

Whereas the rural rich have been arguing against ceiling on landholdings on the plea that there is no similar ceiling on urban property or income, they have not been prepared to accept tax burden on par with their urban counterparts. Despite the ceiling on the ownership of agricultural land, there is a large number of farmers, especially in the irrigated pockets where technological changes have made an impact, whose incomes exceed Rs. 5,000 per annum. Whereas the corresponding income groups in the non-agricultural sector are required to pay income tax, the rural income groups pay direct taxes at present in the form of land revenue

---

[15]Dandekar and Rath (op. cit.), recommend the 'abolition of tenancy altogether rather than regulation' (p. 64). It is not possible to abolish tenancy altogether, assuming that it is proper to do so, when even the regulation of rents has proved to be politically infeasible.

which constitutes only about one per cent of their farm business income.

Big farmers appropriate institutional credit more than proportionate to their share in land. Small farmers depend essentially on moneylenders, including agricultural moneylenders (big farmers), who re-lend institutional credit to small farmers at high rates of interest and whose advances increased very much during the plan period. Contrary to the general belief, big farmers have been greater defaulters in respect of repayment of loans than small farmers. In the case of small credit societies, where big farmers wield considerable influence and power, the percentage of overdues to loans outstanding has been significantly higher among large farmers as compared to small farmers.[16]

The real need of small farmers has been an adequate availability of institutional credit rather than lower interest rates, as the rates charged by these institutions are already much lower than those at which small farmers have to borrow from moneylenders. Yet, instead of rationing the institutional credit for ensuring equitable distribution, attention has been focused recently more on lowering lending rates for small farmers through a scheme of differential interest rates. Another issue which has been recently greatly debated on is that small farmers might use the money so borrowed for re-lending at high rates of interest. Institutional credit constitutes a small fraction of the total borrowings of small farmers and the rates of interest on borrowings from private sources exceed the 'higher' interest rates to be charged to the richer sections by the institutional sources, so that poorer sections stand to gain by substituting institutional credit for credit from private sources instead of re-lending to the richer sections. In any case, the scheme of differential interest rates cannot be expected to succeed in the absence of credit rationing, because so long as large farmers are able to corner a substantial proportion of credit and small farmers are denied their due share from institutional sources, it would be possible for the agricultural moneylenders (large farmers) to shift the burden of high interest rates (at which they borrow under the scheme of differential interest rates) to the small farmers by raising market rates of interest because the demand for such loans is relatively inelastic.

[16]C.H. Hanumantha Rao, 'Farm Size and Credit Policy', *Economic and Political Weekly*, Review of Agriculture, 26 December 1970.

PRICE POLICY

In view of the shortage of agricultural commodities and the rising prices, it was expected that the agricultural price policy would be directed to ensure adequate supplies of foodgrains to the consumers at reasonable prices and to prevent unduly favourable terms of trade for prosperous agricultural regions and big farmers. However, big farmers have always succeeded in getting higher procurement prices than those recommended by the Agricultural Prices Commission and have evaded the producer levies.[17] Whenever some compulsion became inevitable for the sake of procurement, they often opted for the zonal system—whereby surplus zones are cordoned off for purposes of procurement—as, unlike the levy on large producers, this system spreads the incidence of 'lower' procurement prices on all classes of farmers even when there is a levy on traders and millers. The grain so procured has been used by certain surplus states to contain consumer unrest in their own deficit pockets, even when it means greater hardships for the consumers in the deficit states, and as a bargaining counter with the Central Government and the deficit states. Despite the existence of significant interregional differences in free market prices approximating to costs of transportation and distribution from the surplus to the deficit states, the practice has been to fix uniform procurement price for wheat all over the country, which, in any case, has to cover the cost of production in the high-cost regions. Such a policy could result in added gains to the producers in the surplus states, misallocation of resources in such regions,[18] and heavy subsidies on public distribution,[19] the burden of which would ultimately fall

[17]K. Subbarao, 'Market Structure in Agriculture (A Study of the Economic Efficiency of Paddy/Rice Marketing System in West Godavari District, Andhra Pradesh)', Ph. D. dissertation, University of Delhi, 1973.

[18]The procurement prices of wheat have been pegged at levels higher than free market prices in Punjab for a few years which may have resulted in the diversion of resources from other crops.

Alternatively, uniform procurement prices approximating to the cost of production in the low-cost surplus regions would cause misallocation of resources in the deficit regions by moving resources away from the crop concerned, because free market prices in such regions can be expected to approximate to the cost of production in the surplus regions plus the cost of transportation and distribution.

[19]This is because, consumer prices in the deficit states can not be raised so as to cover the cost of distribution including transportation from the surplus

on the community as a whole.

DISTRIBUTION OF INPUTS

The concept of 'trade-off' between growth and improved distribution[20] is used sometimes not only to rationalise the prevailing unequal distribution of agricultural land but also to justify the intensive use (per acre) of scarce inputs like fertilisers and water on large farms and in the developed regions when it is clear that the social product would be greater by spreading such inputs relatively thinly over a large number of farms in a wider area.[21] Considerations of private profitability dictate that such inputs be applied up to the point where the marginal value product is equal to the price of input whereas maximisation of social product from such scarce inputs requires that they be spread among different farms in such a way that the average product is maximum. In view of their greater capacity to invest and bear risk, large farmers and the deve-

state—which would be quite high in a large country like India—as this would raise the retail prices far out of proportion to the local procurement prices which are the same as in the surplus region.

[20]According to this concept, even though redistribution of land from the large to the small farmers or the landless may increase output and employment in the short-run, the growth of output and employment may slow down in the long-run owing to the reduction in savings and investment as the small farmers consume a larger proportion of their income than do the large farmers.

For a presentation of 'the possibility of a conflict, in densely populated agrarian economies, between the long-term objectives of an overall employment strategy on the one hand, and on the other the limited though immediate benefits derived from redistributing land so as to constitute small farms', see J.N. Sinha, 'Agrarian Reforms and Employment in Densely Populated Agrarian Economies: A Dissenting View', *International Labour Review*, November 1973.

For a critical examination of the concept of 'trade-off' between growth and improved distribution, see Appendix 'F'.

[21]B.S. Minhas and T.N. Srinivasan had shown that even with the use of High Yielding Varieties, it owuld be socially profitable to spread the use of fertilisers relatively thinly over a larger area for old as well as new varieties instead of concentrating them in limited pockets. See their 'New Agricultural Strategy Analysed', *Yojana*, 26 January 1966.

In view of the impending shortage of fertilisers resulting from the oil crisis, V.K.R.V. Rao recommends that countries in Asia should try to maximise the returns from the available quantity of fertilisers by spreading them relatively thinly over larger areas. See his *Growth and Social Justice in Asian Agriculture: An Exercise in Policy Formulation*, United Nations Research Institute for Social Development, Geneva, 1974.

loped regions intensify the use of such inputs producing less than the socially—optimum output.[22] With the introduction of High Yielding Varieties, the divergence between the private and the social optimum is likely to have increased because it is now privately profitable to apply fertilisers in much higher doses than before.[23]

A similar argument may apply to the use of irrigation water. The concept of 'productive irrigation' which has become popular after the introduction of HYV can be used for rationalising the appropriation of water by the influential sections in water-scarce regions even when it is socially more profitable to spread the use of water relatively thinly. This suspicion arises because in certain cases, 'protective irrigation' practised under traditional irrigation systems has been found to be socially productive as it yields greater total output than when applied in larger quantities per acre.[24]

Even in regard to the allocation of resources as between different sections among the poor, preference is sought to be given to the relatively better-off among them. One of the arguments advanced in justification is that productivity of inputs as well as surplus generation for the given investment would be higher among such sections. The Small Farmers Development Agency (SFDA) is one such scheme [25]under which small farmers who are not presently viable in terms of a certain income norm but who can be made viable

[22]Incidentally, small farms using less quantity of fertilisers per acre may be nearer the social optimum so long as the average product (for fertilisers) among them is higher than that among large farms.

[23]Taxing fertilisers so as to raise their price relative to those of products may contribute to a restricted use among the prosperous segments, apart from appropriating to the exchequer the black market margins, but such a policy may discourage their use among the weaker segments also. Equitable distribution of such inputs through rationing would, therefore, be a better alternative. However, an increase in the divergence between the private and the social optimum owing to the scarcity of inputs or to technical change or to the rise in the relative prices of output would render rationing more difficult and has a potential for misallocation. The recent rise of about 90 per cent in the price of fertilisers may, however, be excessive for the weaker segments as, essentially, it restores the product-fertiliser price ratio obtained a few years ago.

[24]Deepak Lal, *Wells and Welfare: An Exploratory Cost-Benefit Study of the Economics of Small-Scale Irrigation in Maharashtra*, OECD, Paris, 1972, p. 135.

[25]The evidence so far suggests that the progress with this programme has been very slow in many parts of the country and much of the benefits are appropriated by those who are already viable. See, for instance, D.P. Gupta, 'Small Farmers' Development Programme—An Evaluation of Progress and Problems,' (mimeo), Agricultural Economics Research Centre, University of Delhi, 1973.

with the application of new technology are to be provided necessary credit and inputs. Those owning below this holding are to be taken care of by other programmes such as the one for Marginal Farmers and Agricultural Labourers (MFAL) designed to provide employment mainly through non-crop enterprises. However, it is unlikely that, for a long time to come, alternative non-crop avenues can be provided for raising the incomes of these potentially non-viable farms so as to bring them on par with the viable farms. Considerations of productivity[26] as well as of equity require that the scarce inputs be allocated to the small and marginal farms at least in proportion to the cultivated area held by them.

PROGRAMMES FOR RURAL EMPLOYMENT

The failure of the current strategy to bring about the pro-

[26]Owing to the greater availability of labour and other complementary inputs such as irrigation among small and marginal farms, a rupee spent on current inputs. say, fertilisers, brings forth higher returns than on big farms. According to G.R. Saini's study for Uttar Pradesh and Punjab covering two years (1955-56 and 1956-57), the marginal productivity of a rupee invested in fertilisers ranged between Rs. 2.04 to Rs. 2.44 among small farms as against Rs. 0.99 to Rs. 1.84 among large farms. See his 'Resource-Use Efficiency in Agriculture', The *Indian Journal of Agricultural Economics*, April-June 1969. It may be noted, however, that the marginal productivity of working capital is likely to be lower among small farms owing to the inclusion of the imputed value of family labour as part of working capital. Even in regard to fertilisers, the position may be reversed if the rate of adoption of new (HYV) technology is higher among large farms owing to their better resource position which, however, can not be attributed to farm size *as such*.

The fact of lower fertiliser-use per acre and its higher marginal product among small and marginal farms with the given technology, suggests the inapplicability of Dharma Kumar's conclusion (based on the assumption of perfect capital market) that 'since labour-land ratio is lower in the commercial sector, more fertiliser per acre will be applied in the family sector... this unequal distribution of both labour and fertilisers must yield an output less than the maximum possible'. See her 'Technical Change and Dualism Within Agriculture in India', The *Journal of Development Studies*, October 1970. Thus, her recommendation that 'the correct policy would, therefore, be to encourage the use of fertiliser in the commercial sector whether by subsidy or by direct distribution' may produce opposite results in regard to output and employment for the additional reason that cheaper fertilisers for large farms may induce the adoption of techniques which economise on labour rather than induce more employment in this sector, as visualised by her on the assumption of complementarity between labour and fertilisers.

mised agricultural growth and employment through the necessary public investments and the redistribution of resources within the agricultural sector has accentuated the problem of unemployment and underemployment in rural areas, particularly because the growth of output and employment in the non-agricultural sector has also been slow. Instead of stepping up public investment for increasing agricultural output several *ad hoc* crash programmes such as the Crash Schemes for Rural Employment (CSRE) as part of the Rural Works Programme[27] have been undertaken to provide employment opportunities. Such programmes usually fritter away the scarce investable resources and thus widen the resource-gap for developmental programmes.[28]

If agricultural output did in fact grow at the rate of about 4 per cent per annum—the minimum envisaged in the Five Year Plans—employment in the production of agricultural commodities alone would have grown by about 3 per cent per annum, as the labour coefficient (i.e., percentage increase in labour input as a result of a 1 per cent increase in output) is likely to be around 0.75 for all the techniques (e.g., irrigation, multiple cropping and HYV, etc.) taken together.[29] This is in addition to the employment that would have been generated in marketing and distribution of additional output, in the production and distribution of additional inputs and consumption goods and in the service sector. This growth in employment would have been sufficient to absorb not only the growing labour force in agriculture but would have also helped to clear much of the backlog of rural unemployment and underemployment. This is because, the growth of labour force in the rural sector would be significantly less than the growth of population owing, among other factors, to the migration to the urban sector and to the fact that in the initial phases of development in the low

[27]Amartya Sen in his book, *Employment, Technology and Development* (Oxford University Press, London 1975) has made a critical evaluation of these schemes and has expressed serious doubts about the productive contribution as well as the egalitarian impact of these programmes.

[28]For instance, the Rural Works Programme envisaged by Dandekar and Rath (See *Poverty in India*, op. cit., p. 134) is estimated to cost between Rs. 800 to Rs. 1,000 crores annually, constituting between 20 and 25 per cent of public revenues to be employed in the Fourth Plan. Since many of the developmental programmes such as irrigation projects are held up owing to the shortage of resources, a cost-benefit analysis of the Rural Works Programme versus the proposed irrigation projects is very much in order.

[29]See Ch. 9.

income countries, as the income level increases, the participation rate of the unskilled labour, particularly females, decliness ignificantly.[30]

A Rural Works Programme designed to strengthen the land base of agriculture, e.g., soil conservation and minor irrigation through consolidation of holdings as part of the plan for achieving the targeted growth of agricultural output would be non-inflationary in character and would provide the basis for the sustained growth of output and employment as and when such works are completed[31] But the Rural Works Programme envisaged essentially as a means of providing employment because growth of output has been slow and is likely to be slow would have an inflationary potential.[32] Indeed, the Programme as it has been actually operating, may have been inflationary.[33] It is difficult to conceive how adequate employment can be generated and poverty mitigated despite the slow growth of the wage goods sector like agriculture and when the bulk of even these small gains in output are appropriated by the richer sections.

Apart from the growing concern with the problem of unemployment, the proliferation of such crash programmes owes very much to their political suitability for the elite. Unlike the lumpy investments in projects like major and medium irrigation which are

[30]See Ch. 3.

[31]The Rural Works Programme envisaged by B.S. Minhas (see his 'Rural Poverty, Land Redistribution and Development', *Indian Economic Review*, April 1970) was essentially of this type, although its demands on organisation (administrative preparedness as well as public response) are too onerous to make the programme immediately practicable in areas like the Eastern Zone where poverty is most wide-spread and where such works appear to be most needed.

[32]The Rural Works Programme advocated by Dandekar and Rath is clearly of this type, as, according to them, it would be difficult to make a dent on unemployment and poverty through the process of economic development 'firstly because, judging by the experience of the last decade, the rate of growth attainable in the coming decade is likely to be small and inadequate for the purpose, and secondly because, again judging by the experience of the last decade, the small gains of development will most likely accrue, in large measures, to the upper middle and the richer sections of the society'. See *Poverty in India*, op. cit., p.137. They recommend taxation of the rich for financing this programme, but experience has shown that politicians are reluctant to tax the rich and push through these programmes by resorting to deficit financing.

[33]This programme needs to be distinguished from the famine relief programmes undertaken in specific areas for specific periods. Such programmes are necessary, although public investment in irrigation would induce migration from drought-prone areas thus reducing the incidence of famines.

location-bound and which have a long gestation period, the Rural Works Programmes offer the promise of an immediate gain to a large number of people in wide areas.[34] Second, these programmes help those in power to distribute patronage to a large number of middle-men who have to be rewarded and whose services need to be ensured for the future.

SUMMARY

Although agricultural growth has been significant in the post-independence period, the achievements fall considerably short of the basic requirements and the goals set. A good part of the growth, in this period, is traceable to autonomous factors such as the population growth and the rise of the agricultural classes to political power.

Deficiency in public investment in the agricultural infrastructure, especially in irrigation, is a glaring feature of the prevailing strategy. This strategy suits the rural as well as the urban elite. Paucity of resources as well as the insufficient allocation to agriculture from the available resources, are attributable to the inessential consumption by the elite.

Policies on land reform, taxation, credit and prices have been heavily biased towards big farmers who wield considerable political power at the state level. Also, there has been a tendency for the concentration of scarce inputs like fertilisers on large farms and in the developed regions when it is clear that social product would be greater, and its distribution more even, by spreading such inputs relatively thinly over a wider area.

The failure of the present strategy to step up public investments for agricultural development has accentuated the problem of unemployment in rural areas. Several *ad hoc* Crash Programmes have been undertaken to solve this problem. Such Crash Programmes help those in power to distribute patronage to a large number of middlemen and fritter away the scarce investable resources thus widening the resource-gap for development programmes. These programmes tend to be unproductive and as such add to the inflationary pressures in the economy.

[34]Given the diffused character of such programmes, it is difficult to make them productive, partly because productive works are not usually available in many areas to which the programme has to be extended and, even when such works are available, funds are not sufficient to execute them efficiently.

CHAPTER 16

Technological Change, Agricultural Growth and Income Distribution: Expected Trends

Technological Change

The prospective sources of agricultural growth, which are by no means mutually exclusive, are: (a) the exploitation of the known technological possibilities, e.g., HYV technology for wheat and rice and dry farming technology, etc., as well as investment in the research for the evolution of new techniques; (b) the intensification of inputs like fertilisers in the existing irrigated areas and by exploiting the ground-water potential, largely through private investment; and (c) public investment in major, medium and minor irrigation projects including the exploitation of ground-water, e.g., through tubewells.[1]

So far, the HYV technology has proved most impressive in areas served with controlled irrigation and sufficiently exposed to solar radiation.[2] Monsoon clouds in heavy rainfall areas and the lack of moisture in the dry areas seem to be the most challenging bottlenecks faced by the scientists engaged in research for evolving suitable technologies.

[1]Whatever the technical possibilities for land reclamation, we rule this out as a policy alternative for quite some time, for reasons mentioned earlier, except insofar as irrigation projects contribute to the reclamation of new land. However, public investment in irrigation benefits, essentially, the farmers already cultivating the land, small as well as big. This should be distinguished from the possible increase in the net sown area through a reduction in the land left fallow among the large holdings.

[2]Ingrid Palmer, *Science and Agricultural Production*, United Nations Research Institute for Social Development, Geneva, 1972, pp. 47-61.

Experience shows that conscious and planned research may produce results in the intended direction in the long-run.[3] Technological change in the case of wheat has proved particularly beneficial for the prosperous northern wheat belt because, apart from wheat being a *rabi* crop, the income and price elasticities of demand are quite high for this commodity. For the same reason, the prospects for wheat may still be significant if irrigation is expanded in the western dry region, where this crop might replace millets. Millets like jowar and bajra, which are grown mainly in the low-income dry region may not have good prospects, unless low-cost technologies are evolved and the market for them is widened, because their production cost is high and the income and price elasticities of demand are quite low.[4] Therefore, if the research effort is directed towards commodities like cotton and oilseeds, which have a favourable demand, and are grown extensively in the dry region, then the terms of trade may not turn significantly against such regions, in the wake of a technological change in respect of millets.[5]

Monsoon rice is the most important crop in the wet (high rainfall) region. As noted in Chapter 7, unlike wheat, the land-augmenting potential of HYV rice cannot be fully realised because the bulk of the resources for rice production are now committed in the *kharif* season.

From the technological angle, therefore, a major breakthrough in the rice output seems possible, only if HYV capable of

[3]This is evident from the results obtained in the case of the commercial crops, such as, sugarcane, coffee, cotton, tea and jute, on which the research was focused in the pre-independence period. The increasing attention given to research in cereals in the post-independence period, especially in the sixties, has had a favourable impact, particularly in respect of wheat and bajra. Further, among different states in India, there seems to be some positive relationship between the investment in agricultural research and the performance in respect of agricultural output. See Rakesh Mohan, D. Jha and Robert Evenson, 'The Indian Agricultural Research System', *Economic and Political Weekly*, Review of Agriculture, 31 March 1973.

[4]Dharm Narain, 'Growth and Imbalances in Indian Agriculture', *Economic and Political Weekly*, Review of Agriculture, 25 March 1972. (This paper constitutes the Technical Address at the Silver Jubilee Session of the Indian Society of Agricultural Statistics, March 1972). See also N.S. Jodha, 'Prospects for Coarse Cereals: Permanent Constraints of Jowar and Bajra', *Economic and Political Weekly*, Review of Agriculture, 29 December 1973.

[5]Martin E. Abel, Delane E. Welsch, and Robert W. Jolly, 'Technology and Agricultural Diversification' (mimeo), Department of Agricultural and Applied Economics, University of Minnesota, January 1973.

withstanding the vagaries of monsoon are evolved. In any case, the profitability of the new technology has to be quite high for making it acceptable to the farmers in the eastern region because of the high ruling rates of interest and the low investable surplus.

Where irrigation water can be made available economically, irrigated farming with HYV technology would be more profitable than the dry farming technology. This is because traditional irrigated farming is more profitable than traditional dry farming and the available evidence indicates that the profitability of HYV technology relative to traditional irrigated farming is much higher than the profitability of the available dry farming technology relative to traditional dry farming.

For instance, the experiments conducted on the farmers' fields under the All India Co-ordinated Agronomic Experiments Scheme of the Indian Council of Agricultural Research during 1969-70, 1970-71 and 1971-72 indicate that the crops grown under dry conditions responded to fertilisers profitably up to 50 kg of nitrogen per hectare, the increase in the yield ranging from 20 to 70 per cent and the net return per rupee of fertilisers ranging from Rs. 0.37 to Rs. 2.50.[6] As against this, HYV wheat under irrigation responds to nitrogen profitably up to about 120 kg per hectare, the rise in yield ranging from 100 per cent to 150 per cent and the net return per rupee of fertiliser invested being as high as Rs. 7. Even at 50 kg of nitrogen per hectare, the wheat yield is almost doubled and the net return per rupee of fertiliser invested rises to Rs. 12.[7]

The dry farming methods require considerably increased input of energy,[8] greater receptivity to information, particularly to predictions on the weather, the capacity and the willingness to bear risk (which may be more important than the capacity to invest) and the readiness for group endeavour, on the part of the farmers. The

[6]I.C. Mahapatra, Rajendra Prasad and S.R. Bapat 'Fertilisers Pay Well Even Under Dry Land Conditions', *Indian Farming*, June 1973.

[7]I.J. Singh and K. C. Sharma, *Production Functions and Economic Optima in Fertilizer Use for Some Dwarf and Tall Varieties of Wheat*, U.P. Agricultural University, Pantnagar.

[8]For instance, at Kovilpatti (Tamilnadu) the data relating to demonstration farms—50 each for bajra and cotton in 1971-72—show that, of the additional costs per hectare under dry land technology (as compared to control plots), costs on human and bullock labour alone constituted 50 per cent in the case of bajra and 40 per cent in the case of cotton. This result is borrowed from P. Rangaswamy's Ph. D. work, *Economics of Dry Farming in Selected Areas*, in preparation at the University of Delhi.

cost of extending knowledge to the farmers would also be quite high. Therefore, for the dry farming technology to be acceptable to these poorer regions, the response of yield to the new practices has to be quite high and its variability low.

IRRIGATION

According to the latest estimates, about 60 per cent of the potential arable area can be ultimately irrigated from different sources and only about 42 per cent of this irrigation potential is likely to have been realised by the end of the Fourth Plan.[9] It will be seen from Table 2 in Appendix 'G' that, of the remaining irrigation potential, the major and medium projects account for as much as 65 per cent and the ground-water sources for only about 22 per cent. The ground-water potential seems to be much less important in the states constituting the western dry region, whereas it is relatively more important in the wet (high irrigation) region. It will also be seen that the inter-state disparities in the ultimate irrigation potential (i.e., the potential irrigated area as a percentage of the net sown area in 1969-70) are significantly lower, when compared to the actual position in 1969-70. However, the inter-state variability in the ground-water potential is greater than from the major and medium projects.[10]

Cost-benefit analyses of the potential projects can, alone, reveal the extent of the irrigation potential that can be profitably tapped. The area irrigated has doubled in 23 years from 22.6 million hectares in 1950-51 to 44.9 million hectares in 1973-74.[11] During the same period, the agricultural output has almost doubled. By 2000, A.D. i.e., in another two and a half decades, the demand for the agricultural output can be expected to increase by nearly 100 per cent, because of the growth in the population (of about 60 per cent)

[9]Government of India, Planning Commission, *Draft Fifth Five Year Plan, 1974-79*, Part II, p. 105.

[10]Besides, much of the ground-water potential is located in the states, which are already served adequately with major and medium irrigation sources: The correlation coefficient (r) between the percentage of the net sown area served with the major and medium irrigation projects in 1969-70, and the percentage of the net sown area potentially irrigable from ground-water sources, is 0.76. However, the correlation, of the former with the percentage of area actually irrigated by wells, is not significant.

[11]*Draft Fifth Five Year Plan*, op. cit., p. 105.

as well as the increase in the per capita income. On the basis of past experience, if this requires the doubling of the acreage under irrigation, another 45 million hectares will have to be brought under irrigation, bringing the total irrigated area to 90 million hectares or about 84 per cent of the potentially irrigable area.

The irrigated area may have to be increased at this rate despite technological change and increased use of fertilisers, because the area under controlled irrigation, which is conducive to modern intensive cultivation, constitutes only about 10 per cent of the sown area, at present, and it may be neither in the interest of efficiency, nor of equity to promote a greater concentration of inputs in these limited pockets, which, in any case, may not be capable of meeting the increasing demand for the agricultural output, despite a rise in prices. Similarly, given a perspective of about two and a half to three decades, there does not appear to be much scope for a choice between different sources of irrigation or between projects located in different regions, so long as they stand the test of social profitability.

Modernisation of the old irrigation projects (which cover about 21 million hectares, situated largely in the wet region with assured irrigation) is estimated to require an investment of about Rs. 900 crores,[12] which constitutes less than 10 per cent of the investment required for the new projects.[13] The modernisation of old projects may have a high pay-off because of the supplementary nature of such investments and because of the greater response of these areas to new technology. The paucity of investable resources with the Government as well as considerations of social justice require that these prosperous areas are made to share a major portion of this investment, especially in view of their better resource position and because of the high private benefits from modernisation.

The eastern Gangetic belt accounts for much of the untapped ground-water potential. Its exploitation has been slow, especially on private account, partly because, as a result of high rainfall in this region, irrigation is needed mainly for the second crop, which might render such irrigation systems relatively costly[14] and also because of

[12]According to B. Sivaraman, an additional coverage of about 6 million hectares can be achieved with this investment. See his, *Scientific Agriculture is Neutral to Scale—the Fallacy and the Remedy*, Dr. Rajendra Prasad Memorial Lecture, Indian Society of Agricultural Statistics, December 1972.

[13]A rough estimate places this figure at Rs. 10,000 crores. See, Government of India, *Report of the Irrigation Commission*, 1972, Vol. I, p. 243.

[14]B. D. Dhawan found the normal rainfall to be the most important

the fragmentation of holdings and the semi-feudal social structure characterised by widespread poverty, a low investable surplus, high interest rates and administrative inefficiency. All this is reflected, for instance, in the very slow growth of co-operative credit institutions in this region. Also, since rice is essentially a monsoon crop, in respect of which the new technology has not made an appreciable impact, there may not be enough economic incentive, as yet, for a profitable exploitation of the ground-water potential. Therefore, public tubewells may continue to be the major source for the exploitation of the ground-water potential in this region as the social profitability is likely to be greater than the private profitability.

The underground water potential as well as other minor irrigation schemes in the dry areas, especially in the western region where the credit institutions are relatively well developed, are likely to be exploited with greater success in the next decade or so.[15] However, such sources being costly,[16] private investment in them can be undertaken only within a framework of high product prices, as the sub-

variable explaining the level of utilisation of public tubewells in Uttar Pradesh, the partial correlation coefficient being -0.96. See his, 'Demand for Irrigation: A Case Study of Government Tube-Wells in Uttar Pradesh', *Indian Journal of Agricultural Economics*, April-June 1973.

[15]Of the total advances by the public sector banks for minor irrigation purposes (Rs. 867.44 million) at the end of March 1973, Maharashtra alone accounted for 26.1 per cent followed by Gujarat (17.6 per cent) and Tamilnadu (8.7 per cent), whereas the three eastern states—Bihar, Orissa and West Bengal—together accounted for only about 10.8 per cent. See, 'Agricultural Advances of Public Sector Banks', *Reserve Bank of India Bulletin*, April 1974, pp. 647, 659.

S.K. Rao's study ('Inter-Regional Variations in Agricultural Growth, 1952-53 to 1964-65: A Tentative Analysis in Relation to Irrigation', *Economic and Political Weekly*, 3 July 1971) confirms that the private investment in well irrigation is explained mainly by the inducement to invest provided by low (and uncertain) rainfall, scarcity of available irrigation, e.g., from the public canals and the public subsidies and loans. He doubts whether the private saving *per se* has been an important factor. However, the greater importance of private investment in irrigation, albeit by using public resources, may mean higher costs and prices of farm products as well as more unequal distribution of income.

[16]The cost per unit of water provided, seems to be much higher in the case of minor works and their potential for mobilising private resources seems also to be limited: The actual expenditure in the Fourth Plan on major and medium schemes benefiting 3.3 million hectares amounted to Rs. 1170 crores. A similar achievement (3.2 million hectares) in respect of the minor irrigation schemes has cost almost twice this investment (Rs. 2195 crores), out of which only about 20 per cent (450 crores) was financed by the cultivators from their own resources. See, *Draft Fifth Five Year Plan*, op. cit., p. 106.

202 Technological Change in Indian Agriculture

jective rates of discount would be high. Besides, in the dry regions, where minor irrigation potential is much scarcer than the potential from major and medium irrigation sources, the large farmers may appropriate such water, despite the possible attempts to pre-empt such sources for the small farmers. As latecomers, small farmers may have to incur higher cost for digging (boring) the wells because of the adverse externalities imposed, e.g., lowering the water table, by the early exploiters.[17] Indeed, in view of the possible adverse externalities (lowering the water table as well as the quantity of water), there are already moves for imposing a ceiling on the number of wells for each area, in which case the small farmers stand to lose on both counts—the denial of water for some, as well as high cost of water for those getting it.

REDISTRIBUTION OF RESOURCES

Owing to the population pressure in the rural sector as well as to the growing awareness among the poor, the demand for limiting landholding is likely to continue for a long time.[18] As in the past, this may contribute to the transfer of land from the big to the medium and small holders mainly through sales and purchases in the market.[19] Such a transfer, by itself, may reduce capital-intensity

[17]In principle, the early exploiters can be held as much responsible for the 'adverse externalities' as the late exploiters, although usually this is attributed to the latecomers. For an analysis of adverse externalities imposed because of private decision-making, see, Juan Antonio Zapata, *The Economics of Pump Irrigation: The Case af Mendoza, Argentina*, Ph. D. dissertation, University of Chicago, 1969.

[18]However, given the prevailing socio-political framework, the prospect of a major redistributive land reform through the organisation of the rural poor does not seem to be bright in India. The Social structure in rural India is characterised by the competitive co-existence of highly stratified but non-polarised class and caste groups and interests which considerably overlap each other and whose initiative for productive effort has been released, though in a differing measure, owing to political independence and a democratic framework. It may be noted in this connection that land reforms in Japan, Taiwan and South Korea were introduced, following the Second World War, by the occupation forces and not by the local dictatorships.

[19]Dandekar and Rath think that, as a result of technological change, large capitalist farms may grow by absorbing small and medium holdings through the competitive process. (*Poverty in India*, op. cit., pp. 67, 88). This is an unlikely possibility so long as alternative avenues of employment are not available to the small and marginal holdings. Because of the lower dependence

in agriculture, and contribute to an increase in output and employment.[20]

Owing to the secular increase in awareness and the bargaining power of the peasantry, especially in a democratic framework, one should expect an improvement, albeit, gradual, in the share of the small farmers in public resources, e.g., institutional credit. Therefore, the proportion of large incomes may decline in the rural sector for some period, even if the income inequality in terms of concentration ratio increases—which, however, is unlikely in the light of the recent experience. Further, it may no longer be possible for big farmers to resist the demand that they be taxed on par with their

of small family farms on the market for inputs as well as for selling output, historically, they have survived the severest depressions whereas capitalist farms are hit hard even by mild depressions. Since the demand for agricultural commodities will be elastic for quite some time in India, both types of farms can co-exist, although output among large farms may grow faster than among small ones.

It is interesting to note V.I. Lenin's observations in a similar context: '...to prove the inevitability of small farms being ousted by large ones, it is not enough to demonstrate the greater advantage of the latter (i.e., the lower price of the product), the predominance of money (more precisely commodity) economy over natural economy must also be established; under natural economy, when the product is consumed by the producer himself and is not sent to the market, the cheap product does not encounter the more costly product in the market, and is therefore unable to oust it.' V.I. Lenin, *Collected Works*, Vol. I, Foreign Languages Publishing House, Moscow, p. 37.

[20]Dandekar and Rath regard the growth of capitalist farming, through a process of squeezing out the small farms, not only inevitable but also socially desirable (Ibid., p.88). This arises from their belief in the 'trade-off' between growth and improved distribution as well as in the scale-bias (as against scale-neutrality) of new technology (Ibid., pp. 67, 88).

A. M. Khusro (*Economics of Land Reform and Farm Size in India*, Macmillan, Delhi, 1973) feels that ceilings on land holdings may not be inimical to efficiency because output per acre among large farms is still not higher than on small farms despite technological change. However, large farms are stepping up output per acre in the wake of technological change not by using more labour per acre but through the substitution of capital for labour. Therefore, in the context of capitalist farming, efficiency of farm size should be judged not by output per acre but by the factor proportions, e.g., land-labour and capital-labour ratios. Where there is widespread unemployment and underemployment, farms using more capital in relation to labour can not be regarded as efficient from the social point of view even if they produce more output per acre, because a redistribution of land *and* capital from the large to the small and marginal farms adopting new technology may raise total output and employment.

urban counterparts,[21] although, owing to the difficulties inherent in taxing agriculture as well as to the influence of big farmers, the effective incidence on them may continue to be lower than on their urban counterparts.[22] Similarly, it would be difficult to resist the demand for the abolition of land revenue on holdings below the rateable value of Rs.5,000 per annum, as their urban counterparts are exempt from direct taxes.[23]

MIGRATION

Experience in India shows that regions which have progressed most are those with low and medium rainfall but served with assured sources of irrigation and endowed with necessary human motivation for growth reflected, as for example, in the development of cooperative credit institutions. (Appendix G). Thus irrigation undertaken in the Western Dry Region are likely to have the greatest potential for growth of output as well as for improvement in the distribution of income. This is particularly so, because, as the experience in this country and elsewhere shows, such ventures are likely to induce migrations of labour from the depressed regions[24] as

---

[21]Considering the difficulties of assessing agricultural incomes objectively, a steeply graded surcharge on land revenue would be a better alternative for many parts of the country. For areas where land revenue ratings are quite out of line with the relative productivities of land, as is the case in the ex-*zamindari* areas, Agricultural Holding Tax, broadly on the lines recommended by the Raj Committee on Taxation of Agricultural Wealth and Income, would be better suited. See in this connection, C.H. Hanumantha Rao, 'Agricultural Taxation: Raj Committee's Report,' *Economic and Political Weekly*, 25 November, 1972.

[22]It may be noted, however, that the real incomes of the rural rich would be lower than those of their urban counterparts on account of the prices of urban goods of consumption—which account for a large proportion of the budget of the rich—being higher in the rural sector. See Hanumantha Rao, 'Resource Prospects from the Rural Sector—the case of Indirect Taxes', op. cit.

[23]There may be a case for a property tax on agricultural land holdings. But this has to be considered on its own merits, for all classes of farmers, quite independent of land revenue which is admittedly an outmoded tax.

[24]The arid and semi-arid northern Mexico, where major public irrigation works were undertaken was receptive to large-scale migration of labour from the backward and high rainfall regions during 1940-60. See Luciano Barraza Allande, 'Regional Agricultural Growth and Economic Development', in Nurul Islam (ed.), *Agricultural Policy in Developing Countries, Proceedings of a Conference held by the International Economic Association at Bad Godesberg, West Germany*, Macmillan, London, 1974.

well as of capital and skills from the developed regions. Indeed, such out-migration from the depressed regions may raise the prospects for growth in the latter areas by relieving the demographic pressure.[25] Such projects, insofar as they provide productive outlets for the surpluses and skills from the developed pockets, would contribute to restricting unessential consumption in such areas. Indeed, the indirect employment created in the developed areas following technological change seems to be largely of this nature and has a potential for increasing regional disparities.

Experience suggests that resistance to migrant labour is unlikely when there is a shortage of local labour and when wage rates are rising.[26] In such a situation, there would be little danger that unionisation of labour would lead to bargaining situations which would prevent an expansion in employment. So far, migration of unskilled labour to the project areas has been effected mainly through the institution of private contractors. This system is inefficient in bringing about relative equalisation of wages between regions through the desired transfer of labour owing to the high private costs of movement, and is also exploitative.[27]

Public investment in migration by way of providing information about irrigation works, free or subsidised transportation, construction of houses for labour and training in skills as a part of the command area development programme for irrigation projects may have a high pay-off from the social point of view in a large country like India where there are significant interregional differ-

[25]The evaluation of the social profitability of public investment in irrigation should include such prospects of large-scale employment through migration of labour from labour-surplus regions. Also, since such projects would lead to some saving in expenditure currently incurred on drought relief, these expected savings should also be taken into account while evaluating the benefits from such irrigation projects. For example, at the All India level, during the four-year period, i.e., from 1969-70 to 1972-73, the expenditure on drought relief amounted to Rs. 800 crores. See, Government of India, Planning Commission, *Draft Fifth Five Year Plan 1974-79*, Part II, p.91.

[26]The resistance to the immigration of capital and skills is also likely to be insignificant, if such immigration is regulated, for example, by putting a ceiling on the proportion of land that such persons can hold. The 'sons of the soil' movements in India are directed against giving employment in the public sector, especially government jobs, to the 'outsiders' and not so much against private investors from outside, who in fact contribute to increasing employment opportunities for the local people.

[27]K.N. Raj, *Some Economic Aspects of the Bhakra Nangal Project*, Asia Publishing House, 1960, pp. 77-83.

ences in the marginal productivity of labour. Such investments may contribute to increasing the efficiency of labour and may thus reduce the private costs of labour-intensive methods. This may contribute to slowing down considerably the rate of farm mechanisation such as the use of tractors and harvesters.

SUMMARY AND CONCLUSION

Technological change, especially in respect of crops grown in the low income regions and the public investment in irrigation projects (including the exploitation of the ground-water potential),[28] are likely to be the major sources of growth in Indian agriculture.[29]

Although effort is likely to be directed simultaneously on all the three areas, namely, technological change, private investment in irrigation and public investment in irrigation, the prospects from which have been indicated above, the relative emphasis on each may differ and the sequence is bound to be from the softer or the easier one to the more difficult one, the impetus for shift being the pressures of shortages and rising prices.[30]

The prospects of further growth from technological change seem to be limited and uncertain in the short-run. There is some scope for extending the known techniques, e.g., HYV and for intensifying the use of inputs like fertilisers, by exploiting the ground-

[28]Yujiro Hayami brings out the crucial role of large-scale public investments in irrigation in the successful adoption of HYV technology for rice in several countries of Asia including Japan, Taiwan and Korea, and emphasises the need for massive public investments in irrigation and adaptive research in the countries of Southeast Asia where the land/man ratio has been declining. See his, 'Conditions for the Diffusion of Agricultural Technology: An Asian perspective', *The Journal of Economic History*, Vol. XXXIV, No. 1, March 1974.

[29]According to K. N. Raj, however, the scope for the development of irrigation and the extension of the new techniques is limited in India, so that a more efficient utilisation of the available resources, e.g., land, through their redistribution, needs to be given greater emphasis. See his, 'Some Questions Concerning Growth, Transformation and Planning of Agriculture in the Developing Countries', op. cit.

For a discussion of the prospects for agricultural growth through an improved distribution of the available resources, see Ch. 15, 16.

[30]However, experience suggests that the path is unlikely to be unidirectional. The impact of the weather on policy-making in India is so great that two to three good harvests in a succession in the recent period had set the officials of the Government of India seriously thinking in terms of finding markets for the export of foodgrains!

water potential through private investment, but the limits of even this may be reached soon because of the low potential, in relation to the requirements, as well as of its being a high-cost and uncertain source[31] in low rainfall (dry) areas. The largest prospect for increasing the output and employment with certainty in the next two to three decades (through a wider application of the known technology such as HYV) and for improving the distribution of income—horizontal as well as vertical—lies with the third source, namely, public investment in irrigation including the exploitation of ground-water potential, which is also the most difficult and the least attractive for the elite as it has a sizeable demand on public resources for investment that cuts into the elitist consumption; has a long gestation period; is devoid of an immediate popular appeal; carries, on the other hand, political risks associated with the recovery of costs through betterment levies and water rates; offers less scope for sustaining middlemen and yields, in any case, smaller benefits for the elite when the projects are completed. Therefore, the process of transformation is unlikely to be smooth: greater hardships for the poor leading to unrest and tensions, which may in turn induce the necessary changes in policies.[32]

[31]Unlike the traditional irrigated farming which reduces uncertainties of output growth because of its being familiar to the cultivators as well as its potential for reducing the yield variability, the present strategy has prematurely increased the dependence of agriculture on industry as well as the Government. To weather uncertainty are added the uncertainty of industrial performance (regarding, for example, fertilisers and power) and the uncertainty as to the policies and the response of the administration, which are greater in the initial stages of development.

[32]Foreign aid, insofar as it can help to strengthen the land base of agriculture. through irrigation, can reduce such tensions. However, foreign aid, irrespective of the ideologies of the aid-givers, has become increasingly favourable to inputs like tractors and fertilisers which suit the industrial structures of these countries as well as the large farm sector in India. The potential demand from the large farm sector in India even for machines (e.g., tractors) designed to suit western conditions, still remains largely unsatisfied (Ch. 1).

Appendices

Factors Affecting Farm Mechanisation

INTER-CORRELATIONS

The interrelationships between some of the important variables analysed in Chapter 3 are brought out by the correlation matrix given in Table 1. These correlations are based on the observations relating to 250 districts in the year 1961. The correlations relate to two types of mechanical equipment, namely, tractors and pump-sets. Two measures of the rate of mechanisation or the capital-intensity have been adopted—the number of tractors (pump-sets) per 1000 acres of the net area sown and per 100 agricultural workers. The composition of the tractors and pump-sets in regard to the horse power, make and age, etc., would obviously differ between different districts. The data on these attributes are not available. The measures, as to the rate of mechanisation, adopted are, therefore, crude and may provide only a rough approximation to the reality.

The rate of tractorisation (Y_1 and Y_2) bears a high positive correlation to the per capita income (output) of the agricultural population, the wage rate, the percentage of area irrigated and the percentage of males in the age group 15-59 among the agricultural workers. Whereas this is understandable, a high positive correlation with the young male agricultural workers may appear puzzling. One might expect this relationship to be negative because the mechanical power would be in greater demand where the proportion of male workers in the productive age group is lower and vice versa. However, it will be seen from the correlation matrix that there is a high inverse correlation ($-.91$) between the proportion of young male workers and the participation rate of the agricultural population in this age group. Further, as expected, the correlation between tractorisation and participation rate is negative and significant. These correlations imply,

TABLE 1: FACTORS ASSOCIATED WITH MECHANISATION IN INDIA, 1961: CORRELATION MATRIX

Variables	X_1	X_2	X_3	X_4	X_5	X_6	X_7	X_8	X_9	X_{10}	Y_1	Y_2	Y_3
Percentage of net area irrigated to net area sown* (X_1)													
Percentage of males among agricultural workers** (X_2)	0.32												
Percentage of urban population to total (X_3)	0.04	0.04											
Normal rainfall (X_4)	−0.10	−0.04	−0.06										
Percentage of area held by farmers above 30 acres (X_5)	−0.33	−0.39	0.25	−0.44									
Agricultural wage rate (plougher/field labour) (X_6)	0.27	0.38	0.30	−0.06	0.02								
Per capita crop output* for agricultural population (X_7)	0.22	0.17	0.29	0.08	0.20	0.43							
Participation rate of rural population** (X_8)	−0.43	−0.91	−0.04	−0.05	0.43	−0.44	−0.11						
Percentage of literates among rural population** (X_9)	0.19	0.12	0.28	0.46	−0.18	0.24	0.24	−0.31					
Percentage of villages electrified (X_{10})	0.33	0.03	0.27	0.26	−0.20	0.07	0.27	−0.16	0.56				
No. of tractors per 1000 acres of net area sown (Y_1)	0.38	0.42	0.27	−0.21	0.02	0.49	0.47	−0.43	0.02	0.10			
No. of tractors per 100 agricultural workers (Y_2)	0.30	0.37	0.28	−0.25	0.17	0.56	0.57	−0.37	−0.01	0.02	0.91		
No. of pump-sets per 1000 acres of net area sown (Y_3)	0.22	−0.13	0.24	−0.08	0.00	0.00	0.15	0.06	0.17	0.58	0.06	0.02	
No. of pump-sets per 100 agricultural workers (Y_4)	0.13	0.12	0.40	−0.22	0.26	0.20	0.28	0.04	0.19	0.43	0.14	0.17	0.84

Note : Correlations above 0.166 are significant at 1 per cent level.
*Average of 1959-60, 60-61, 61-62. **In the age group 15-59.

that where the participation rate is low—which can be expected to induce tractorisation—the proportion of young males is high among the agricultural workers. Thus, what seems to be relevant is the supply of labour as influenced by the participation rate and not the composition of labour, as such. The participation rate seems to vary mainly on account of the variation in the female participation rate, which is much lower than that of the male labour and which varies between 19 per cent and 55 per cent, as against about 91 and 94 per cent in the case of the males of the same age group (see Table 3.6). It is, therefore, reasonable to expect that where the participation rate of the rural population in the age group 15-59 is lower because of the females abstaining from work, the proportion of male labour should be higher.

There is a positive association between tractorisation and urbanisation and a negative association between tractorisation and the normal rainfall. Urbanisation can induce mechanisation through a complex of factors: a high wage rate because of reduced labour supply in the rural areas, a high per capita income, literacy and the general awareness and the existence of an infrastructure. In this connection, it is interesting to note a significant positive association between urbanisation on the one hand and the area held by the large farms, the wage rate, the per capita output, literacy and the proportion of the villages electrified, on the other. A negative association between tractorisation and rainfall can be expected because the areas of very high rainfall are not generally amenable to tractorisation, and in the semi-arid zones tractors would be in greater demand, in view of the need to plough immediately after the rains and for the purposes of deeper ploughing.[1] The proportion of the area held by large farms is greater in such areas, which by itself would be an important factor inducing tractorisation.

The correlations with respect to pump-sets (diesel as well as electric) are generally in the same direction as those pertaining to rate of tractorisation, although they are much smaller in magnitude. This is understandable because the investable surplus (income level) would not serve as a constraint to the same extent in the case of a pump-set as in the case of a lumpy equipment like a tractor. Further, pump-sets are essentially land-augmenting in character, and

[1]N.S. Jodha's finding for the dry areas of Rajasthan confirms this proposition. See his, 'A Case of the Process of Tractorisation', *Economic and Political Weekly*, Review of Agriculture, 28 December 1974.

large as well as small family farmers may go in for them, even where
the wage rates are lower. The high positive correlation of the pump-
sets with the percentage of villages electrified is to be expected, by
definition, because the electric pump-sets constituted about 47 per
cent of the total number of pump-sets in 1966. This correlation,
therefore, does not have any explanatory value. Again, a high
positive association with the percentage of the net area irrigated is
also not of much explanatory value because of the fact that much of
the irrigated area is accounted for by minor irrigation sources employing pump-sets. However, the high positive correlation with
urbanisation is important and is to be interpreted in the same
manner as in the case of tractors.

REGRESSION AND PARTIAL CORRELATION COEFFICIENTS

Multiple regression equations, with rate of tractorisation as
the dependent variable, have been fitted by using the method of least
squares, to the data on some of the variables mentioned above. The
regression coefficients estimated by these equations are presented in
Table 2. The squares of the partial correlation coefficients are given
in brackets.

Judging by the square of the partial correlation coefficient,
the per capita income of the agricultural population turns out to be
the most important variable in the equations, regardless of the definition of the rate of tractorisation. The wage rate and rainfall
seem to be the next important variables, when tractorisation is
measured as a ratio of the number of tractors to the agricultural
workers.[2] When tractorisation is measured as a ratio of the tractors
to acreage, rainfall seems to be more important than the wage
rate. This is understandable, in view of the impact of the rainfall
on the soil characteristics. Perhaps for similar reasons, the regression coefficient for irrigation turns out to be significant when tractorisation is measured in terms of tractor-acreage ratio, whereas

[2]It is interesting that a similar relationship has been observed in a
developed country like Japan. Multiple regression for the period 1957-69 shows
that the farm household income relative to the price of power tillers was the most
important factor followed by the wage rate, in explaining the ownership of power
tillers by the Japanese farmers. See Sung-Ho Kim, 'A Socio-Economic Analysis
of Farm Mechanisation in Asiatic Paddy-Farming Societies with Special Reference to Korean and Japanese Cases', in Herman Southworth (ed.), *Farm Mechanisation in East Asia*, Agricultural Development Council, New York, 1972.

TABLE 2: FACTORS AFFECTING TRACTORISATION IN INDIAN AGRICULTURE, 1961
(Regression Coefficients)

Independent Variables		Dependent Variables	
		Tractors per 1000 acres of Net Area Sown	Tractors per 100 Agricultural Workers
		(1)	(2)
1. Percentage of net area irrigated to net area sown	RC SPC	0.000831** (0.01)	0.000106† (neg)
2. Percentage of males in the age group 15-59 among agricultural workers	RC SPC	0.000317† (neg)	—0.000195† (neg)
3. Percentage of urban population to total population	RC SPC	0.001460** (0.02)	0.000193† (neg)
4. Normal rainfall	RC SPC	—0.000047* (0.04)	—0.000022* (0.07)
5. Percentage of area held by farmers above 30 acres	RC SPC	—0.000131† (neg)	0.000383† (0.01)
6. Wage rate for male agricultural labour: plougher/field labour	RC SPC	0.044282* (0.03)	0.028673* (0.07)
7. Per capita crop (output) income of agricultural population (1959-60, 1960-61 & 1961-62)	RC SPC	0.000653* (0.11)	0.000364* (0.20)
8. Participation rate of rural population in the age group 15-59	RC SPC	—0.002689** (0.01)	—0.001382* (0.02)
Constant		0.090345	0.035951
R²		0.47	0.57
Number of observations (Districts)		235	235

RC	Regression Coefficient.	SPC	Square of Partial Correlation Coefficient.
Neg	Negligible.		
†	Not significant at 10% level.		
*	Significant at 5% level.		
**	Significont at 10% level		

the coefficient is not significant when tractorisation is measured
as the tractor-worker ratio. As expected, the regression coefficient
for participation rate is negative and significant in both the equations. The regression coefficient for urbanisation is positive, and
significant when the rate of tractorisation is measured as a tractor-
acreage ratio. The coefficient for the proportion of the young male
labour is not statistically significant, which may be due to the very
high correlation between the participation rate of the rural population and the proportion of the young male workers. Further, the
coefficient with respect to the area held by the large farms is not
significant. However, the inter-correlation between rainfall and the
area held by the large farmers is quite high (—0.46) indicating
that the area under the 'large' farms is, generally, higher in the low
rainfall areas.

APPENDIX B

Factors Affecting the Area under High Yielding Varieties of Seeds

An attempt is made here, through a multiple regression analysis, to know the impact of tractor-use on the percentage of the area allocated to HYV. The following equation has been fitted to the PEO sample data (bullock and tractor farms combined) for each of the four regions mentioned in Chapter 4.

$$Y = a + b_1 X_1 + b_2 X_2 + b_3 (Z) + E$$

where:

Y = percentage of the total cropped or the harvested area allocated to HYV of wheat, rice, jowar, bajra and maize; X_1 = the operational holding (farm size); X_2 = percentage of the irrigated area to operational holding; Z = dummy variable : 0 for bullock farms, and 1 for tractor farms; E = the disturbance term.

The results given in Table 1 show that the independent variables explain a small percentage of the variation in the dependent variable. This correlation seems to be spuriously low. The dependent variable—the percentage of the holding allocated to HYV—is in a ratio form and is obtained by deflating the area under HYV by the size of the holding, which itself is one of the independent variables in the equation.[1] The correlation between the area (undeflated) allocated to HYV and the size of the holding can be expected to be high for a cross-section of observations. If there is a

[1]For an analysis of a related problem, namely, the consequences of dividing the two series by a common deflator, see John R. Meyer & Edwin Kuh, 'C rrelation and Regression Estimates when the Data are Ratios', *Econometrica*, XXIII, October 1955; An abridged version of this article is also contained in their, *The Investment Decision: An Empirical Study*, Harvard University Press, 1959, pp. 258-67.

TABLE 1: FACTORS AFFECTING THE AREA UNDER HIGH YIELDING VARIETIES
(Regression Coefficients)

(The dependent variable: Per cent of the gross cropped or harvested area allocated to the High Yielding Varieties of wheat, rice, bajra, jowar and maize)

	Punjab	Haryana	Andhra Pradesh	Tamilnadu
	(1)	(2)	(3)	(4)
Constant	19.47	4.61	8.25	2.57
Independent Variables:				
1. Farm Size	0.16	−0.06†	−0.06**	−0.22†
	(0.05)	(0.07)	(0.04)	(0.23)
2. Percentage of	0.20	0.21	−0.01†	0.52
operated area irrigated	(0.05)	(0.07)	(0.13)	(0.06)
3. Tractor dummy	7.10	11.85	17.93	−4.79†
(intercept)	(1.22)	(2.67)	(2.63)	(9.08)
R^2	0.22	0.14	0.15	0.21
Number of observations:	365	193	280	289
Value of the Dependent Variable at Mean Farm Size and Irrigation:				
(a) Bullock farm	40.95	22.02	6.14	46.72
(b) Tractor farm	48.06	33.87	24.07	41.93
Percent difference	17.34	53.79	292.11	−10.26
Mean Levels:				
(a) Farm size (acres)	16.36	24.31	18.62	5.42
(b) Percentage of operated area irrigated	95.92	88.59	97.31	86.52

Note : Figures in brackets are standard errors.

†Not significant at the 10% level.

**Significant at the 10 % level.

The remaining coefficients are significant at the 1% level.

high positive correlation between the two series, deflation of one by the other would amount to a correction for this relationship, so that the correlation between the deflated and the deflator series would be low.

Irrigation has a positive impact on the use of HYV. Except in Punjab, the farm size, by itself, does not seem to be a significant variable, influencing the percentage of the area allocated to HYV. However, this result may be attributable to a high positive correlation between the farm size and tractorisation, which turns out to be important as a variable accounting for the area under HYV. The intercept dummy with respect to the size for the tractor farms is positive and significant. This result is illustrated in Figure 1, where the horizontal axis depicts the farm size in acres and the vertical axis represents the percentage of the area allocated to HYV. The regression line for the tractor farms shifts bodily upwards because of its higher intercept and is parallel to that for the bullock farms.

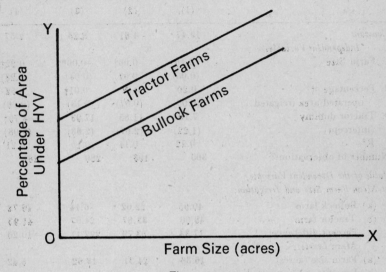

Figure 1

APPENDIX C

Costs and Benefits of Investment in Farm Tractors

TABLE 1: Purchase Price of an Imported Tractor (Rs): International B 276 (U.K.)

c & f	15,296.00
Insurance	184.56
c.i.f.	15,480.56
Plus:	
Handling and Misc. Charges	458.91
Margin	2,524.00
Other Charges	150.00
Customs Duty (30% of c.i.f.) and Excise Duty (10% of landed cost)	6,656.64
Ex-Godown price	25,270.11
	OR
	25,300.00
Complementary Equipment:	
Disc Harrow	2,350.00
Tyres	2,000.00
Trollies	3,000.00
Total Capital Cost	32,650.00

TABLE 2: PRIVATE COSTS AND BENEFITS OF INVESTMENT IN FARM TRACTORS
(Values in rupees per farm)

	Small Farm (10 acres)		Large Farm (50 acres)	
Labour Coefficient (Increase in the input requirement):	25%	50%	25%	50%
	(1)	(2)	(3)	(4)
Bullock labour costs saved:	917	1100	6113	7336
Human labour costs saved:	—	—	3341	4009
Total costs saved:	917	1100	9454	11345
Annual Costs:				
Tractor Fuel	500	500	2500	2500
Tractor Repairs	120	120	600	600
Tractor Driver	144	144	720	720
Total Annual Costs	764	764	3820 (3100)	3820 (3100)
Net Returns (A)	153	336	5634 (6354)	7525 (8245)
Present Value at :				
9% Discount Rate	982	2156	36157 (40777)	48292 (52913)
12% Discount Rate	865	1899	31833 (35901)	42518 (46586)
Net Output Added	928	928	4640	4640
Net Returns (B)	1081	1264	10274 (10994)	12165 (12885)
Present Value at :				
9% Discount Rate	6938	8112	65934 (70555)	78070 (82691)
12% Discount Rate	6108	7142	58050 (62118)	68735 (72803)
Capital Cost	6530	6530	32650	32650

Note : The figures in brackets exclude the wages of the tractor driver.
The present Value of the Scrap Value:

Discount Rate	Large Farm	Small Farm
9%	2110	422
12%	1610	322

TABLE 3: SOCIAL COSTS AND BENEFITS OF INVESTMENT IN FARM TRACTORS
(50 acre farms; Values in rupees per farm)

Labour Coefficient (Increase in the input requirement):	25%			50%		
Shadow Price of labour (ratio to market wage)	0.25	0.50	0.75	0.25	0.50	0.75
	(1)	(2)	(3)	(4)	(5)	(6)
Bullock labour costs saved	4967	5348	5729	5962	6423	6884
Human labour costs saved	836	1672	2508	1000	2000	3000
Total Costs Saved	5803	7020	8237	6962	8423	9884
Annual Costs:						
Tractor Fuel	1250	1250	1250	1250	1250	1250
Tractor Repairs	600	600	600	600	600	600
Tractor Driver	180	360	540	180	360	540
Total Annual Costs	2030	2210	2390	2030	2210	2390
Net Returns (A)	3773	4810	5847	4932	6213	7494
Present Value at:						
9% Discount Rate	24214	30869	37524	31652	39873	48094
12% Discount Rate	21318	27178	33037	27867	35105	42343
Net Output Added	4640	4640	4640	4640	4640	4640
Labour Costs saved on Output Added	435	290	145	435	290	145
Net Returns (B)	8848	9740	10632	10007	11143	12279
Present Value at :						
9% Discount Rate	56783	62507	68232	64221	71511	78802
12% Discount Rate	49993	55033	60073	56542	62960	69379
Capital Cost	32650	32650	32650	32650	32650	32650

Impact of Technological Change on Farm Employment

SEPARATE IMPACT OF INDIVIDUAL TECHNIQUES

METHOD

Each dependent variable of this study, namely, multiple cropping, yield, output and employment is made a function of the following independent variables: (a) operated area of the farm; (b) percentage of operated area irrigated; (c) tube-wells; (d) tractorisation, (e) HYV; and (f) fertilisers. Since our purpose is to know, through the output and employment equations, the amount of labour used per unit of output under each of these techniques, we are not including labour input as an independent variable. Moreover, since our purpose is to know the impact of tractor-use on output and employment, the inclusion of human and bullock labour as independent variables would not be meaningful as there is a technical substitutability between a tractor on the one hand and human and bullock labour (which are technically complementary), on the other. It may be further noted that the independent variables used in our equations represent technologies or practices and *not* input levels. The purpose of including a tractor technology (dummy) variable in the output equation is to know the net impact of using tractors *instead of bullocks* on output. As an input in the production function, however, tractor power must have a positive output effect regardless of whether the net impact of tractor-use in place of bullocks is positive or not.

The following equation has been fitted to the Ferozepur (Farm Management) data pertaining to the sample of 150 farms including 29 tractor farms separately for the years 1968-69 and 1969-70.

$$Y_1 = a + b_1 X_1 + b_2 X_2 + b_3 X_3 + b_4 X_4 + b_5 X_5 + b_6(Z) + b_7 (ZX_1)$$
$$+ b_8(Z_1 X_1) + E$$

where

Y_1 = ith dependent variable; X_{1a} = planted or gross cropped area; X_{1b} = operated area; X_2 = percentage of net irrigated area to operated area from all sources; X_3 = percentage of cropped area planted to HYV; X_4 = expenses on tube-well irrigation; X_5 = expenses on fertilisers; Z = (dummy variable): 1 for tractor farms; 0 for others; Z_1 = (dummy variable): 1 for thresher farms, and 0 for others; and E = disturbance term.

The equations are linear, all except dummy variables being in logarithms, and have been estimated through the method of least squares. The use of an intercept dummy (Z) alone for the tractor would imply that the proportionate effect of tractorisation on output and employment is the same regardless of the variation in the size of the farm. Since this is an unrealistic assumption, a slope dummy for the tractor with respect to the operated area or farm size (ZX_1) was also tried. However, when both the dummies were tried they turned out to be non-significant because of high inter-correlation between them. The coefficients of determination (R^2) were higher for equations with slope dummies than for those with intercept dummies. As stated above, this is what one should expect if the assumption implicit in the use of an intercept dummy is unrealistic. It was decided, therefore, to use the equations with slope dummies only.

Owing to the high inter-correlation $(r = .70;$ see Table 1) between HYV (X_3) and expenses on fertilisers (X_5), the coefficient with respect to HYV turned out to be non-significant but was significant when the variable X_5 (expenses on fertilisers) was excluded from the equation. We have, therefore, presented equations with HYV only.

Harvesting is not mechanised and is still done with human labour among farms studied. However, mechanical threshing, about which information on the quantity of produce threshed is not available, is reported to be common both among tractor and non-tractor farms. As in the case of tractorisation, the only information available is on the ownership of threshers. About 62 per cent of tractor farms in 1968-69 were reported to own mechanical threshers as against 12 per cent among non-tractor farms, the correlation coefficient (r) between the ownership of tractors and threshers being .45

TABLE 1: CORRELATION MATRIX (1968-69)

Variables :	X_{1a}	X_{1b}	X_2	X_3	X_4	X_5	ZX_{1a}	ZX_{1b}	Z_1X_{1b}
	(1)	(2)	(3)	(4)	(5)	(6)	(7)	(8)	(9)
1. Gross Cropped Area (X_{1a})									
2. Operated Area (X_{1b})	0.92								
3. Percentage of Net Irrigated Area to Operated Area (X_2)	−0.04†	−0.16*							
4. Percentage of Cropped Area Planted to HYV (X_3)	0.32	0.17*	0.30						
5. Expenses on Tube-wells (X_4)	0.11†	−0.10†	0.34	0.46					
6. Expenses on Fertilisers (X_5)	0.49	0.60	0.36	0.70	0.22				
7. Tractor Dummy (ZX_{1a})	0.56	0.50	0.07†	0.34	0.21	0.39			
8. Tractor Dummy (ZX_{1b})	0.57	0.52	0.06†	0.33	0.20*	0.39	1.00		
9. Thresher Dummy (Z_1X_{1b})	0.35	0.22	0.22	0.33	0.45	—	0.45	0.45	
10. Output	0.86	0.81	0.13**	0.51	0.13**	0.75	0.58	0.59	0.33
11. Employment	0.88	0.76	0.14**	0.52	0.33	0.71	0.52	0.52	0.35

Note: †Not significant at the 10 per cent level.
*Significant at the 5 per cent level.
**Significant at the 10 per cent level; the remaining coefficients are significant at the 1 per cent level.

(see Table 1). A dummy variable for a thresher tried on the same lines as for the tractor turned out to be non-significant in all the equations. Since mechanical threshing can be expected to displace some human labour, and since such threshing seems to be more common among tractor than among non-tractor farms, it is possible that our equations underestimate somewhat the employment attributable to tractorisation.

RESULTS[1]

The difference between the actual area planted (gross cropped area) and the operated area is a measure of cropping intensity or multiple cropping. The residual variation in gross cropped area after accounting for the variation in operated area can be attributed to the factors contributing to cropping intensity, as for example, irrigation, type or quality of irrigation, HYV and tractorisation. Equations 1 and 2 show that tube-well irrigation is the most important factor explaining this residual variation (see Table 2). This is indicated by the values of partial r^2 (.14 and .18 respectively) which are much higher than those for HYV (.03 and .14). Tractorisation by itself does not seem to be significant in explaining cropping intensity. The irrigation variable is not significant which is not surprising as 80 to 90 per cent of operated area among sample farms is already irrigated so that further expansion of irrigation at this margin may not be as important as the quality of irrigation in influencing cropping intensity.

The residual variation in output after accounting for the variation in area planted or gross cropped area can be attributed to the factors affecting yield per planted acre. Equations 3 and 4 reveal HYV to be the most important factor (partial r^2 being .23 and .24) explaining this component of output. The coefficient for tractor dummy was positive and significant for the year 1968-69 but not so for 1969-70. The regression coefficient with respect to the expenses on tube-wells is negative and significant in both the years (Table 3). This does not mean that tube-well water reduces yield. The quantitative aspect of tube-well irrigation, namely, the supply

---

[1]The results pertaining to the year 1968-69 discussed in this appendix were reported by the author earlier. See his 'Employment Implications of the Green Revolution and Mechanization: A Case Study of the Punjab', in Nurul Islam (ed.), *Agricultural Policy in Developing Countries*, op. cit.

TABLE 2: IMPACT OF TRACTORISATION AND HYV ON OUTPUT AND EMPLOYMENT (FEROZEPUR, PUNJAB, 1968-69 and 1969-70): Coefficients of Partial Determination

	Dependent Variables:							
	Cropped Area		Output		Output		Employment	
Equation Number	1968-69	1969-70	1968-69	1969-70	1968-69	1969-70	1968-69	1969-70
	(1)	(2)	(3)	(4)	(5)	(6)	(7)	(8)
Independent Variables:								
1. Gross Cropped Area (X_{1a})	—	—	0.67	0.76	—	—	—	—
2. Operated Area (X_{1b})	0.84	0.91	—	—	0.67	0.75	0.66	0.61
3. Percentage of Net Irrigated Area to Operated Area (X_2)	0.01†	neg.	0.07	0.08	0.11	0.08	0.04*	neg.
4. Percentage of Cropped Area Planted to HYV (X_3)	0.03*	0.14	0.23	0.24	0.28	0.36	0.17	0.14
5. Expenses on Tube-wells (X_4)	0.14	0.18	0.08	0.19	neg.	0.04*	0.20	0.05
6. Tractor Dummy (ζX_1)	0.01†	0.01†	0.03*	0.01†	0.04*	0.01†	neg.	neg.
R^2	0.89	0.95	0.83	0.86	0.83	0.85	0.80	0.75

Note: † Not significant at the 10 per cent level.

* Significant at the 5 per cent level; the remaining coefficients are significant at the 1 per cent level.

neg. Negligible.

TABLE 3: IMPACT OF TRACTORISATION AND HYV ON OUTPUT AND EMPLOYMENT
(FEROZEPUR, PUNJAB : 1968-69 and 1969-70) : Regression Coefficients

	Dependent Variables							
	Cropped Area		Output		Output		Employment	
Equation Number	1968-1969	1969-70	1968-69	1969-70	1968-69	1969-70	1968-69	1969-70
	(1)	(2)	(3)	(4)	(5)	(6)	(7)	(8)
Constant	0.06†	0.10†	1.83	1.74	1.73	1.79	2.04	2.77
	(0.15)	(0.12)	(0.24)	(0.23)	(0.24)	(0.24)	(0.21)	(0.22)
Independent Variables:								
1. Gross Cropped Area (X_{1a})	—	—	0.95	1.04	—	—	—	—
			(0.06)	(0.05)				
2. Operated Area (X_{1b})	0.85	0.90			0.88	0.97	0.73	0.68
	(0.03)	(0.02)			(0.05)	(0.05)	(0.04)	(0.05)
3. Percentage of Net Irrigated Area to Operated Area (X_2)	0.09†	0.01†	0.38	0.40	0.50	0.42	0.24*	−0.06†
	(0.07)	(0.06)	(0.12)	(0.11)	(0.12)	(0.12)	(0.10)	(0.11)
4. Percentage of Cropped Area planted to HYV (X_3)	0.03*	0.06	0.18	0.17	0.20	0.24	0.12	0.13
	(0.02)	(0.01)	(0.03)	(0.03)	(0.03)	(0.03)	(0.02)	(0.03)
5. Expenses on Tube-wells (X_4)	0.05	0.04	−0.06	−0.08	−0.01†	−0.04*	0.09	0.04
	(0.01)	(0.01)	(0.02)	(0.02)	(0.02)	(0.02)	(0.02)	(0.02)
6. Tractor Dummy (ZX_1)	0.02†	0.01†	0.05*	0.02†	0.05*	0.02†	−0.01†	0.01†
	(0.01)	(0.01)	(0.02)	(0.02)	(0.02)	(0.02)	(0.02)	(0.02)
R^2	0.89	0.95	0.83	0.86	0.83	0.85	0.80	0.75

Note: Figures in brackets are standard errors.

† Not significant at the 10 per cent level.

* Significant at the 5 per cent level; the remaining coefficients are significant at the 1 per cent level.

of water, is already reflected in the irrigation variable *(X₂)*, the coefficient for which is positive and significant. The negative coefficient for tube-wells does imply, however, that the impact of tube-well irrigation on yield per cropped acre would be smaller than that of irrigation in general.

The variation in output after accounting for the variation in operated area is attributable to the variation in yield per acre of operated area. The yield per acre of operated area is a function of both cropping intensity and yield per planted acre. Equations 5 and 6 reflect this combined effect. HYV turns out to be the most important explanatory variable (partial $r^2=.28$ and .36) in these equations followed by irrigation (partial $r^2=.11$ and .08). Tractorisation was significant in 1968-69 (partial $r^2=0.04$), whereas the regression coefficient for tube-wells was significant in 1969-70 (partial $r^2=.04$).

Apart from operated area and HYV, tube-wells seem to be important in explaining the variations in farm employment. Tractorisation is the only variable the coefficient for which is not significant in both the years.

The estimated levels of output and employment at the geometric mean levels of all variables including that of HYV (19 per cent of 25 acre holdings) came to Rs. 14,200 and 5,819 hours respectively in 1968-69. This represents an increase of 80 per cent in output and 43 per cent in employment as compared to the estimated levels when only 1 per cent of holding is allocated to HYV while every other variable is held at its geometric mean. From equation 5 the contribution of tractorisation to output at the tractor farm mean size (50 acres) comes to Rs. 5,800 which is about 22 per cent higher when compared to the output on a non-tractor farm of a similar size.[2]

IMPACT OF COMPLEMENTARY INPUTS

We shall examine the combined impact of the extra investment in tube-wells, HYV and fertilisers (on tractor farms in

[2] A Study for Gujarat State reveals that output on tractor farms was much higher than on bullock farms at the same levels of inputs, indicating better output-mix and better management in tractor technology. See D.K. Desai and C. Gopinath, *Impact of Farm Tractorization on Productivity and Employment (Gujarat State)*, (mimeo), Centre for Management in Agriculture, Indian Institute of Management, Ahmedabad, 1973.

comparison to bullock farms of similar size and irrigation levels) and the use of tractors on cropping intensity, yield and employment. We shall use the Farm Management data for Ferozepur as well as the P.E.O. data for four states.

FARM MANAGEMENT DATA FOR FEROZEPUR

The following equation has been fitted to the data pertaining to the sample of 150 farms in 1968-69 as well as in 1969-70:

$$Y_1 = a + bX_1 + CX_2 + a(Z) + E$$

where

Y_1=ith dependent variable; X_{1a}=Gross cropped or planted area; X_{1b}=operated area; X_2=per cent of net irrigated area to net operational holding; Z=(dummy variable: 0 for nontractor farms, and 1 for tractor farms); E=disturbance term.

The dependent variables in the equation for 1968-69 are expressed in per acre terms (i.e., as ratio to the size of holding) whereas those for 1969-70 are in absolute terms. Further, the equation for 1968-69 is linear where a sthat for 1969-70 is linear in logarithms. The coefficients of determination in the equations relating to 1968-69 are lower than those relating to 1969-70 (Table 4). These can be expected to be lower when the dependent variable is expressed in the form of a ratio. (See Appendix B, P. 216).

The results for both the years presented in Table 4 show that cropping intensity and employment per acre decline with the increase in the size of holding. This is indicated by the negative sign of the respective coefficients in 1968-69. This conclusion holds true for 1969-70 as well—the equations are log-linear in this case and the dependent variables are in absolute terms—because the corresponding elasticity coefficients are positive and less than unity, indicating that cropped area and employment increase less than proportionately to farm size. After accounting for the variation in farm size and irrigation, tractor farms show significantly higher cropping intensity, output and employment when compared to non-tractor farms in both the years.

TABLE 4: IMPACT OF TRACTOR USE AND COMPLEMENTARY INPUTS (PUMPSETS AND HYV) ON OUTPUT AND EMPLOYMENT FEROZEPUR, PUNJAB, 1968-69 and 1969-70 : Regression Coefficients

	Dependent Variables:							
	1968-69				1969-70			
	Cropping Intensity (Ratio of Cropped Area to Net Sown Area)	Output per Acre Held (Rs)	Bullock Cost per Acre Held (Rs)	Employment per Acre Held (hrs)	Cropped Area	Output	Output	Employment
Equation Number	(1)	(2)	(3)	(4)	(5)	(6)	(7)	(8)
Constant	112.6	132.5	89.7	152.0	0.13† (0.14)	2.19 (0.29)	2.10 (0.27)	2.89 (0.24)
Independent Variables:								
1. Gross Cropped Area (X_{1a})	—	—	—	—	—	—	1.07 (0.06)	—
2. Operated Area (X_{1b})	—0.77	—1.41†	—0.89	—2.45	0.86 (0.03)	0.94 (0.06)	—	0.62 (0.05)
3. Percentage of Net Irrigated Area to Operated Area (X_2)	0.43*	6.00	0.28†	1.94	0.09† (0.07)	0.38 (0.14)	0.28* (0.13)	0.02† (0.12)
4. Tractor Dummy (Z)	29.36	221.42	—24.59*	62.36*	0.08 (0.02)	0.13 (0.04)	0.05† (0.04)	0.11 (0.03)
R²	0.27	0.25	0.26	0.26	0.92	0.77	0.80	0.68

Note: Figures in brackets are standard errors.

†Not significant at the 10 per cent level.

* Significant at the 5 per cent level; the remaining coefficients are significant at the 1 per cent level.

P.E.O. DATA

Cropping Intensity

The factors affecting cropping intensity are studied by fitting the following regression equation to the sample data:

$$Y = a + b_1 X_1 + b_2 X_2 + b_3 (Z) + b_4 (Z X_1) + b_5 (Z X_2) + E$$

where

$Y =$ cropping intensity (ratio of gross cropped or harvested area to operated area); $X_1 =$ farm size (operated area); $X_2 =$ Percent of irrigated area to operated area; $Z =$ (dummy variable: 0 for bullock farms, and 1 for tractor farms); $E =$ disturbance term.

The equations are linear in logarithms and have been esti-

TABLE 5: FACTORS AFFECTING CROPPING INTENSITY: REGRESSION COEFFICIENTS

(Dependent Variable: Cropping Intensity)

	Punjab	Haryana	Andhra Pradesh	Tamil nadu
	(1)	(2)	(3)	(4)
Constant	1.152	0.852	1.125	1.130
Independent Variables				
(a) Farm Size	—0.012	—0.005**	—0.013	—0.029
(Operated Area)	(0.002)	(0.003)	(0.003)	(0.006)
(b) Percent of Operated	0.007	0.007	0.005**	0.008
Area Irrigated	(0.001)	(0.002)	(0.003)	(0.001)
(c) Tractor Dummy	—0.020†	0.174†	—0.670†	0.410†
(Intercept)	(0.271)	(0.205)	(0.510)	(0.472)
(d) Tractor Dummy	0.009	0.002†	0.011	0.027
(Size slope)	(0.002)	(0.003)	(0.003)	(0.009)
(e) Tractor Dummy	0.001†	0.002†	0.009**	—0.007†
(Irrigation slope)	(0.003)	(0.002)	(0.005)	(0.006)
R^2	0.26	0.23	0.27	0.21
Number of Observations:	365	193	280	289

Note: Figures in brackets are standard errors.

† Not significant at the 10 per cent level.

** Significant at the 10 per cent level; the remaining coefficients are significant at the 1 per cent level.

mated through the method of least squares. The results given in
Table 5 show that the independent variables account for only about
21 to 27 pent of the variance in cropping intensity. Such lower
values of R^2 are not uncommon when the dependent variable is
expressed in the form of a ratio. We find from Tables 3 and 4 (see
the Ferozepur equations for 1968-69) that the values of R^2 are
raised considerably when instead of ratios, the absolute values of
the dependent variables are used.

As can be expected, the regression coefficient with respect
to farm size is negative and significant in all the four states, whereas the regression coefficient with respect to irrigation is positive and
significant. The intercept dummy for the tractor with respect to
size is not significant, while its slope dummy is positive and significant for Punjab, Andhra Pradesh and Tamilnadu. This means
that the superiority of tractor farms over bullock farms in regard
to cropping intensity increases with the rise in farm size. For Andhra Pradesh, tractor slope dummy with respect to irrigation (ZX_2)
is positive and significant which implies that as the percentage of
area irrigated increases, the impact of irrigation on cropping intensity would be greater among tractor farms than among bullock
farms of comparable irrigated area.

Employment of Hired-labour and Wage-bill

The following equation, linear in logarithms, has been fitted
to the data:

$$Y = a + b_1 X_1 + b_2 X_2 + b_3(Z) + b_4(ZX_1) + b_5(ZX_2)$$

where

Y=employment of hired labour (days) per farm; X_1=farm
size (operated area); X_2=per cent of irrigated area to
operated area; Z=(dummy variable: 0 for bullock farms,
and 1 for tractor farms); E=disturbance term.

When the intercept (Z) as well as the slope dummy (ZX_1)
for tractor were tried in the same equation they turned out to be
non-significant owing to a high inter-correlation between them. We
have, therefore, estimated two equations with each of these dummies separately. When the farm size and the percentage of area
irrigated are held constant, the tractor dummy (intercept) turned

TABLE 6: FACTORS AFFECTING FARM EMPLOYMENT OF HIRED LABOUR: REGRESSION COEFFICIENTS
(Dependent Variable: Hired-Labour per Farm)

	Punjab		Haryana		Andhra Pradesh		Tamilnadu	
Equation Number	(1)	(2)	(3)	(4)	(5)	(6)	(7)	(8)
Constant	−279.23	−176.33	−250.66	−227.31	−270.88	−342.49	−422.71	−352.27
Independent Variables:								
1. Farm Size	16.20	10.00	8.17	8.96	33.81	44.67	88.35	81.36
(Operated area)	(0.63)	(1.37)	(0.65)	(1.66)	(2.62)	(12.29)	(2.06)	(2.80)
2. Percentage of Oper-	2.34	2.02	2.38	1.96	5.58†	5.12†	4.99	4.57
ated Area Irrigated	(0.61)	(0.59)	(0.65)	(0.68)	(8.63)	(9.04)	(0.55)	(0.55)
3. Tractor Dummy	38.14*	—	57.86*	—	714.45	—	302.47	—
(Intercept)	(16.49)		(25.50)		(181.56)		(81.04)	
4. Tractor Dummy	—	7.66	—	−0.90†	—	−11.38†	—	14.26
(Size slope)		(1.52)		(1.71)		(12.55)		(4.27)
5. Tractor Dummy	—	−0.65*	—	0.85*	—	8.50	—	1.26†
(Irrigation slope)		(0.26)		(0.43)		(2.29)		(1.21)
R^2	0.70	0.72	0.52	0.52	0.43	0.43	0.90	0.90
Number of Observations	365	365	193	193	280	280	289	289

Note: Figures in brackets are standard errors.
† Not significant at the 10 per cent level.
* Significant at the 5 per cent level; the remaining coefficients are significant at the 1 per cent level.

out to be positive and significant (see Column 1 in Table 6). The slope dummy for the tractor with respect to farm size is positive and significant for Punjab and Tamilnadu and non-significant for Haryana and Andhra Pradesh. However, the tractor slope dummy with respect to irrigation is positive and significant for Haryana and Andhra Pradesh.

The estimated levels of employment at mean farm size and irrigation show that tractor-use along with complementary inputs is associated with a significant increase in the employment of hired labour. The estimated wage-bill from the comparable equation (with wage-bill as the dependent variable) indicates that the differences in wages paid between bullock and tractor farms are, in general, more pronounced than the differences in labour days.

Labour's Share in the Output of Crops

(Average for the years 1954-55, 1955-56 and 1956-57)

DATA

	Value of Gross Output per Acre (Rs)	Value of Labour Input per Acre (Rs)
	(1)	(2)
Uttar Pradesh		
Wheat (Irrigated)	205.3	35.6
Wheat (Unirrigated)	114.0	27.3
Gram	72.0	14.0
Maize	126.0	45.0
Paddy	153.0	38.9
Cotton	121.0	42.8
Punjab		
Wheat (Irrigated)	173·0	42.0
Wheat (Unirrigated)	79.0	21.0
Wheat-Gram (Irrigated)	120.0	32.0
Wheat-Gram (Unirrigated)	88.0	23.0
American Cotton	182.0	50.0
Desi Cotton	136.0	46.0
Madhya Pradesh		
Cotton (Mixed)	90.5	21.6
Cotton (Unmixed)	40.2	17.2
Jowar (Mixed)	71.7	19.6

Jowar (Unmixed)		35.4	8.0
Groundnut (Mixed)		88.6	25.6
Groundnut (Unmixed)		55.6	21.3
Wheat (Unmixed)		114.3	15.6
Wheat-Gram		121.5	21.1

West Bengal

Paddy (Aman)		242.0	91.0
Paddy (Aus)		134.0	84.0
Jute		235.0	146.0
Potato		851.0	272.0
Pulses		58.0	28.0

Maharashtra

(a) *Ahmednagar*

Jowar	(Irrigated)	110.4	31.9
Wheat	(Irrigated)	110.3	40.9
Gram	(Irrigated)	57.0	22.2
Jowar	(Unirrigated)	35.4	9.9
Bajra	(Unirrigated)	30.0	12.3
Wheat	(Unirrigated)	53.2	16.0
Gram	(Unirrigated)	34.4	10.2

(b) *Nasik*

Wheat	(Irrigated)	115.9	46.2
Gram	(Irrigated)	53.5	24.0
Bajra	(Unirrigated)	40.8	15.0
Wheat	(Unirrigated)	46.6	13.4
Gram	(Unirrigated)	37.9	14.9

Tamilnadu

Rice I	(Irrigated)	361.0	67.0
II	(Irrigated)	343.0	58.0
III	(Irrigated)	340.0	73.0
Cholam	(Irrigated)	210.0	27.0
Cotton	(Irrigated)	200.0	53.0
Cumbu	(Irrigated)	108.0	31.0
Ragi	(Irrigated)	185.0	58.0
Cholam	(Unirrigated)	97.0	10.0
Cotton	(Unirrigated)	97.0	13.0
Cumbu	(Unirrigated)	43.0	9.0
Ragi	(Unirrigated)	102.0	18.0
Groundnut	(Unirrigated)	113.0	24.0

Source: C.H. Hanumantha Rao, *Agricultural Production Functions, Costs and Returns India*, Asia Publishing House, 1965, pp. 75-89.

REGRESSION EQUATIONS

Uttar Pradesh	Log $Y = -0.443 + 0.926$ Log X
	(0.429)
	$N=6$ $R^2=0.54$
Punjab	Log $Y = -0.602 + 1.018$ Log X
	(0.163)
	$N=6$ $R^2=0.91$
Madhya Pradesh	Log $Y = 0.397 + 0.462^*$ Log X
	(0.254)
	$N=8$ $R^2=0.36$
West Bengal	Log $Y = 0.094 + 0.817$ Log X
	(0.142)
	$N=5$ $R^2=0.92$
Maharashtra	
(a) *Ahmednagar*	Log $Y = -0.470 + 0.994$ Log X
	(0.132)
	$N=7$ $R^2=0.92$
(b) *Nasik*	Log $Y = -0.582 + 1.090$ Log X
	(0.205)
	$N=5$ $R^2=0.90$
Tamilnadu	Log $Y = -0.820 + 1.046$ Log X
	(0.163)
	$N=12$ $R^2=0.81$

Note: Figures in brackets are standard errors.

*Significantly different from unity at the 5 per cent level.

The remaining coefficients are not significantly different from unity at the 5 per cent level.

$Y =$ Value of labour input per acre.

$X =$ Value of gross output per acre.

APPENDIX F

On the 'Trade-Off' between Growth and Improved Distribution

The concept of 'trade-off' between growth and improved distribution by itself has little to do with the prevailing strategy of agricultural development in India but is, nevertheless, used to rationalise this strategy.[1] According to this concept, even though redistribution of land from the large to the small farmers or the landless may increase output and employment in the short-run, the growth of output and employment may slow down in the long-run as a result of the reduction in savings and investment as the small farmers consume a larger proportion of their income than do the large farmers.

Even if it is assumed that such a 'trade-off' does exist, this proposition is uninteresting on two counts. In the first place, the decision on a question like this is seldom made through a process of 'choice' between alternatives after weighing the relative costs and benefits to the society, because processes of decision-making are not immune to, and in fact are actively influenced by, the efforts of the dominant groups to promote their own interests. Second, 'growth rate' is an aggregate magnitude which abstracts entirely from the distribution of gains. For, it is quite possible that as a result of improved distribution, even if the overall growth of output is slowed down, the share of the poorer classes may remain higher in the long-run when compared to what they would have obtained in the absence of redistribution and with a higher growth rate. In such a case, slower growth implies a cut into the share of the richer classes because higher growth would have served largely to support elitist

[1]Gunnar Myrdal in his *The Challenge of World Poverty*, (Allen Lane, the Penguin Press, London, 1970, p. 4), describes how ideologies and theories are influenced by the interests of dominant groups.

consumption. Thus, the concept of 'trade-off' has little meaning when certain sections gain at the expense of others. It is not like a trade-off, say, between income and leisure, when an individual sacrifices some leisure, in return for additional income or *vice-versa*.

However, the proposition that improved distribution must slow down the overall rate of growth is itself open to serious doubts. If better distribution reduces investable surplus because it increases the consumption by the poor, it may, for the same reason, raise their efficiency.[2] A rise in the efficiency of labour and in labour-intensity would mean an improvement in the output-capital ratio. Besides, much of capital formation in a labour-intensive agriculture is of a non-monetary type, done through the use of labour, especially during the off-season. It is conceivable, therefore, that the decline in savings, if any, as a result of improved distribution could be more than compensated by the improvement in the output-capital ratio and non-monetary capital formation, so that output could grow faster with improved distribution.[3] Further, such a growth process ensures that gains of development accrue to the poorer sections.

A more fundamental objection to the 'trade-off' proposition is that it assumes that the institutional and behavioural patterns would remain unaffected by so radical a reform as redistribution of land. A community which *can* bring about a radical redistribution of income and wealth *can also* bring about the required changes in institutions and behavioural patterns for mobilising more savings by cutting down unessential consumption. Further, such a community can introduce and absorb technical changes which would not otherwise be possible. The experience of several countries suggests that the phases of radical redistribution have been dynamic in respect of other innovations as well, so that growth has in fact been higher in periods following redistribution.

[2]Harvey Leibenstein shows that in poor economies there may exist, upto a point, a more than proportionate relationship between increase in calorie intake and increase in productivity. See his *Economic Backwardness and Economic Growth*, John Wiley, New York,1957, pp. 64-65.

In view of widespread under-nutrition in South Asia, Gunnar Myrdal thinks that, contrary to general belief, 'work practices in agriculture are not labour-intensive but, instead, labour-extensive. The labour input per worker is generally low in terms of man hours and is of low efficiency.' See his *The Challenge of World Poverty*, op. cit., p. 86.

[3]Implied in this argument is the possibility of substituting profitably human (working) capital for material capital as well as of augmenting material capital itself through the investment in human capital.

Agricultural Development Regions

Several attempts have been made to identify homogeneous agricultural zones in the country, on the basis of the soil-climatic conditions.[1] The number of such zones depends upon the degree of homogeneity or the level of disaggregation sought. Our purpose is to get a broad picture in regard to the levels of the regional agricultural development in India in relation to the climatic factor as indicated by the rainfall. The classification of the country into homogeneous agricultural zones has been attempted at a fairly aggregated level. However, a more disaggregated classification would be necessary for formulating concrete programmes of development.

For a tropical and sub-tropical country like India where agriculture is dependent mainly on erratic monsoons, and where the uncertainty of rainfall diminishes with the rise in the level of rainfall,[2] the availability of water through precipitation and artificial irrigation serves as a reasonable basis for a broad demarcation of agricultural development regions. The states where the bulk of the area accounts for low and medium rainfall (i.e., upto 1150 mm per annum) and where the proportion of the net sown area irrigated

[1]See, for instance, A. Krishnan and Mukhtar Singh, 'Soil-Climatic Zones in Relation to Cropping Patterns', in *Proceedings of the Symposium on Cropping Patterns in India*, Indian Council of Agricultural Research, New Delhi, 1972.

This paper demarcates 8 climatic zones by superimposing the moisture and temperature indices on the soil map of India. However, availability of artificial irrigation—left out in this attempt—needs to be taken into account for demarcating agricultural development regions.

[2]The (inter-state) correlation coefficient between the normal rainfall and the coefficient of variation in the actual rainfall (during 1952-62) comes to -0.56 which is significant at 5 per cent level. For the data see, C.H. Hanumantha Rao, 'Fluctuations in Agricultural Growth: An Analysis of Unstable Increase in Productivity', *Economic and Political Weekly*, Annual Number, January 1968,

TABLE 1: PERCENTAGE DISTRIBUTION OF NET SOWN AREA IN 1967-68 IN
DIFFERENT NORMAL RAINFALL REGIONS

State	High Rainfall Region (1150 mm and above)	Medium Rainfall Region (750 to 1150 mm)	Low Rainfall Region (upto 750mm)	Per cent of Net Sown Area Irrigated in 1969-70
	(1)	(2)	(3)	(4)
Dry (Low Irrigation-Low Rainfall) Region:				
1. Karnataka	9.2	24.0	66.8	11.2
2. Maharashtra	21.4	42.3	36.3	7.8
3. Gujarat	8.1	24.9	67.0	12.0
4. Rajasthan	—	11.6	88.4	15.7
Wet (High Rainfall) Region:				
5. West Bengal	100.0	—	—	26.5
6. Bihar	80.0	20.0	—	27.2
7. Orissa	100.0	—	—	16.9
8. Kerala	100.0	—	—	19.5
9. Others (including Assam and H.P.)	76.0	20.0	4.0	26.1
Wet (High Irrigation) Region:				
10. Punjab and Haryana	—	11.3	88.7	56.0
11. Tamilnadu	16.8	83.2	—	41.3
Mixed Region:				
12. Andhra Pradesh	—	64.1	35.9	27.7
13. Madhya Pradesh	55.7	39.6	4.7	7.8
14. Uttar Pradesh	10.9	74.9	14.2	39.0
ALL INDIA	30.2	35.9	33.9	21.8

Source : Directorate of Economics and Statistics, Ministry of Agriculture, *Indian Agriculture in Brief*, 12th Edition.

is significantly below the all-India average are classified as dry regions. The states with high rainfall (1150 mm and above) are classified as wet regions, regardless of the proportion of the sown area irrigated. The states having medium and low rainfall but where the proportion of the sown area irrigated is significantly higher than the all-India average are also regarded as wet areas.

Table 1 gives such a threefold classification of the states on the basis of the relevant data. It may be noted, however, that there would be areas within many of these states which could fall into categories different from the one in which the state concerned is placed. Further, there are states like Andhra Pradesh, Madhya Pradesh and Uttar Pradesh which cannot be placed clearly in any

TABLE 2: IRRIGATED AREA (ACTUAL AND POTENTIAL) FROM DIFFERENT
SOURCES AS PER CENT OF NET SOWN AREA IN 1969-70

State	Actual			Potential			Difference		
	Major and Medium	Ground Water	Total	Major and Medium	Ground Water	Total	Major and Medium	Ground Water	Total
	(1)	(2)	(3)	(4)	(5)	(6)	(7)	(8)	(9)
Dry (*Low Irrigation-Low Rainfall*) Region									
1. Karnataka	3.9	2.5	11.2	17.7	7.8	33.3	13.8	5.3	22.1
2. Maharashtra	1.7	4.5	7.8	12.5	7.6	24.4	10.8	3.1	16.6
3. Gujarat	2.0	9.6	12.0	21.9	12.5	39.6	19.9	2.9	27.6
4. Rajasthan	5.8	8.3	15.7	24.4	10.7	38.2	18.6	2.4	22.5
Wet (*High Rainfall*) Region									
5. West Bengal	16.9	0.3	26.5	41·3	14.4	77.2	24.4	14.1	50.7
6. Bihar	9.7	5.8	27.2	52.4	21.4	95.3	42.7	15.6	68.1
7. Orissa	3.9	0.7	16.9	39.4	6.6	65.6	35.5	5.9	48.7
8. Kerala	9.4	0.2	19.5	27.7	4.6	69.3	18.3	4.4	49.8
9. Others (including Assam and H.P.)	13.5	2.1	26.1	24.7	9.0	73.0	11.2	6.9	46.9
Wet (*High Irrigation*) Region									
10. Punjab and Haryana	29.8	25.9	56.0	54.1	35.6	91.8	24.3	9.7	35.8
11. Tamilnadu	14.9	11.4	41.3	24.7	21.4	59.3	9.8	10.0	18.0
Mixed Region									
12. Andhra Pradesh	12.9	4.4	27.7	56.5	15.6	89.5	43.6	11.2	61.8
13. Madhya Pradesh	3.6	2.8	7.8	30.5	8.7	43.5	26.9	5.9	35.7
14. Uttar Pradesh	13.9	21.7	39.0	43.5	37.2	86.4	29.6	15.5	47.4
ALL INDIA	8.8	8.0	21.8	32.7	16.0	58.7	23.9	8.0	36.9
Coefficient of (inter-state) Variation	77.0	102.8	59.1	40.6	64.8	37.9	—	—	—

Sources : 1. Directorate of Economics and Statistics, Ministry of Agriculture, *Indian Agriculture in Brief*, 12th Edition.

2. Government of India, Ministry of Irrigation and Power, *Report of the Irrigation Commission*, 1972, Vol. I.

one of the three broad categories mentioned above and have, there-fore, been classified as mixed regions. The Telengana and Rayala-seema regions of Andhra Pradesh and the western parts of Madhya Pradesh belong to the dry region. The eastern parts of Madhya Pradesh and east Uttar Pradesh fall in the wet region with high rainfall, whereas west Uttar Pradesh, and deltaic Andhra Pradesh can be included in the wet region with assured irrigation.

The dry region covers, by and large, western India and the wet region with high rainfall is located mainly in the eastern zone of the country. It is not an accident that both of these regions, which are essentially dependent on rainfall have remained relatively back-ward and Punjab, Haryana and Tamilnadu, accounting for low and medium rainfall, but adequately served with assured irrigation, have shown rapid progress. The state-wise data on the actual and potential irrigation are given in Table 2.

Index

DATE DUE